For Brian

Thanks for
all your help
and support &
so glad you're

enjoying it
Brant

New York
23/5/18

# THE FABRICATIONS
## *by* BARET MAGARIAN

"*The Fabrications* is a brilliant achievement. The novel is extremely original, ambitious and accomplished. What I liked most about it – what seemed to be the most audacious *coup* that it pulled off – was the way it has so much to say about contemporary life and culture, without at any point descending to the level of journalism. There's a delicious unreality about the narrative and the characters and yet, somehow along the way Magarian manages to skewer the British Turner prize and the broadsheets' letters pages and any number of other, bigger satirical targets. The tone is wonderfully deadpan, the comedy beautifully underplayed…

The novel is also at times reminiscent of the films of Federico Fellini: in the grand set-pieces, the exuberant party scenes, and the picaresque sense of an amoral hero adrift in a large city (Oscar Babel reminded me of Marcello Mastroianni in *La Dolce Vita*) … Ultimately, Magarian uses his fiction to pose some of the biggest, most complex questions about life. The themes which excite him are permanent and universal. How does one live with the passage of time, the transience of things? Can our desires ever be satisfied? How can one live a complete, meaningful life? Like all the best writers and thinkers, Magarian knows that you cannot paint an accurate portrait of the world without recognizing its essential, desperate absurdity… *The Fabrications* aims high, unblushingly seeking out the company of the modern European masters."

Jonathan Coe, author of *Number Eleven, The House of Sleep* and *The Winshaw Legacy*

# THE
# FABRICATIONS

*For Boghos, Ayko, and for Margarete*

"You're a writer?" the poet asked with interest.

The guest's face darkened and he threatened Ivan with his fist, then said:

"I am a master." He grew stern and took from the pocket of his dressing-gown a completely greasy black cap with the letter 'M' embroidered on it in yellow silk. He put this cap on and showed himself to Ivan both in profile and full face, to prove that he was a master. "She sewed it for me with her own hands," he added mysteriously.

"And what is your name?"

"I no longer have a name," the strange guest answered with gloomy disdain. "I renounced it, as I generally did everything in life. Let's forget it."

from *The Master and Margarita* by Mikhail Bulgakov

# I

# THE GURU IDEA

# 1

Day was breaking, giving rise to the rumor of purity. For a few seconds the light might have been that of creation. Then, in that blinking which separates the final moments of night from day, the faint outline of the moon was hidden and the sky became a universal infusion of blue. High up from his study window a man stood watching, waiting for the city to wake. Indistinct sounds of life were reaching him and flooding his mind with memories. Particles of dust twirled lazily in the shafts of sunlight. He thought that London resembled the mind, and that its streets, avenues, sewers, and tunnels suggested parts of the brain, that London's grid-like complexity corresponded to the complexity of memory and thought. Having glimpsed the dawn, he sat at his desk and typed some words out hastily.

*21 May. Still no new ideas. Will Barny start hounding me?*

The centerpiece of the study was a magnificent mahogany desk. The only thing on it was an old Underwood typewriter. He hated computers and he sought to avoid contact with technology as far as possible and considered himself appealingly old-fashioned. The wooden floor was littered with pens, books, sheets of paper. Below, he could see a small boy delivering papers, and a lady walking her poodle. Further down a man was struggling with the padlock of a fish market. He studied them for a few more moments.

*No more popular junk. Time for something else. Barny can hound me but I shall not dance. I danced too long for Natalie. And five years ago I threw my dad off the dance floor when he joined her there. Old lech.*

\*

Eggs. He had a sudden longing for eggs. He passed through to the kitchen, found some, cracked them with a chef's precision and watched as they gurgled and popped in the oil of his battered frying pan. A teapot was unearthed from the wreckage of a cupboard and a plate and cutlery were laid out carefully. As the toast got under way the telephone started ringing. It was still far too early for a phone call.

'Did I wake you?'

'What's wrong?'

'I can't talk about it over the phone. I've been up all night. Can we meet? I need to see you. Really.'

'Well, when? Not now?'

'Say in a couple of hours? Can you come to the cinema? I'm here now. We could talk in the projection room. I have to see you.'

'At the cinema? Do you ever actually leave that place? All right. Around eight, then. Is there a bell or something? Do I knock? What do I do?'

'I'll leave the back door open. Just walk in.'

'Does this door have any distinguishing features?'

'No. It's just black and rusty.'

Daniel Bloch returned the phone to its cradle, and ate his breakfast. It already seemed as if the day's promise had been ruined.

*

Oscar Babel was the projectionist of the Eureka, a dilapidated Camden cinema, and one of the few left in London that still used an old style projector, linked up to giant, slowly revolving film reels. It sometimes felt to Daniel Bloch as though he were Oscar's surrogate father, offering him advice, buying him dinner, introducing him to influential people. They had met a decade ago, when Bloch had spotted him waddling out of a pub, decimated by alcohol. As he monitored this striking and yet shadowy figure Bloch thought of a pram that has somehow ended up on a race track, turning this way and that uncertainly, looking painfully vulnerable. He dispatched Oscar into a taxi, and gave the driver a twenty pound note. In the morning he received a call from Oscar, thanking him. But Bloch didn't remember giving him his number. When they eventually met for a drink, Oscar presented Bloch with a small gift – an ivory music box – perhaps the only thing Oscar owned which he actually valued. Bloch allowed Oscar to enter his life. He began to think he had met him for a reason, and so the matter was closed. Meanwhile, Oscar considered his new friend to be a source of sophistication and light in an otherwise atrophying life. Once a decidedly promising painter he now found himself earning his living by projecting films, the most invisible of professions he reflected, having dropped his painting, despite his obvious talent for it. Bloch sometimes imagined him as a big fish floating through the clouds of the sea, gazing at the giant vegetation, feeling the wonder of the beauty that ebbed past, but finally sinking, deeper and deeper into the seabed. An oblivion he did not seek would always find him.

After an artery-severing shave Bloch decided to walk to the cinema via Regent's Park.

*

The morning was shedding the shells of its birth and people were emerging from their homes, steeling themselves for the punishing journeys to work. Those in collars and ties were already looking flustered, foreheads coated in films of sweat.

He was surprised to find, after he had slipped through the gates of the park, that a few people were sun bathing. Despite the earliness of the hour people were already jabbering incongruously into their cellular phones. It was by now quite hot – and seemed as if it always would be. Walking incredibly rapidly it didn't take him long to reach the other end of the park. He gave himself a second to savor the abundant clusters of trees before emerging onto a road a few moments later. As he began to cross, an emission of sunlight struck dusty, dirty buildings of neglect like a laser. Reality seemed to be ablaze, a beautiful inferno. But then the sun was hidden and everything plunged back once more into urban decline.

The Eureka cinema stood battered and obsolete. He peered through the windows to see if anyone was inside. Not a soul. Cinemas don't have a life in the morning, he thought. He ambled round to the back and found the door open, as Oscar said it would be.

Inside it was very black. The change from light to dark made spots dance in front of him. He found himself in a small room, where an iron table and chair sat in respective states of decay. A newspaper had been carefully folded out on the table. An open slide door stood to its side. He walked through, calling out Oscar's name. Now he was in a little chamber full of tools and work tops, a dirty-looking table lamp shedding arthritic light. Oscar wasn't there. He could hear the heavy sound of the projector running, and the noise of this combined with the muted light and the black wall created an oppressive texture. He trotted down some steps, finally reaching what must have been the projection room. There, two large metal platters about a yard across were turning slowly. On them rested the reels of film, feeding into the projector. There was something relentless about the movement of the film as it spun round, sustaining the flickering image discernible through a small opening in the wall, playing to an empty auditorium. Bloch watched the film as it hovered in front of him, but with all sound severed. A woman with translucent blonde hair was framed in close-up, her lips moving. She looked stricken, pleading for some unknown cause. When he turned away colors and faces faded into a vague impression that nestled on his retina. As he was thinking he felt a hand touch him lightly on the shoulder. He jumped around, his face brushing against Oscar's.

'Oh God, you scared me,' Bloch mumbled.

'I'm sorry, I didn't mean to. Let's go through, it's less noisy.'

Bloch looked up at him, surprised as if for the first time by his height. He stood well over six feet. For an instant he envied his youthful, handsome face. It still bore the insignia of innocence, blue eyes widening in mute inquiry. They passed through into the outer room, and sat down. The sound of the projector persisted but at a lower level, the intervening door, which Oscar heaved to, creating a muffling effect.

'Why are you running a film at this hour?' Bloch asked.

'I find it comforting. Do you mind?'

Bloch shook his head slowly. Oscar looked sleepy and troubled. There was something about him that suggested an abnormal existence: he had a perpetually cauterized look.

'Do you want to tell me what the problem is now?' Bloch asked.

Oscar addressed the wall as he spoke in a soft voice.

'Well. Now that you've trudged all the way over here, I feel kind of shitty. It's nothing as concrete as a specific problem. That's to say, no doctor has diagnosed me with a rare disease. And I haven't just had my heart broken. I wish I had something … something juicy. Like, "I am being blackmailed" or, "I've been burgled, they smashed my Ming vase, nailed my priceless stamps to the toilet." But I have no Ming vase, you see, that's the problem. Not that I particularly want a Ming vase. What I mean is … the real problem is … I have no life. I'm no-one. I'm sick of watching the same film three times a day and not doing anything except changing reels and sitting in a dark room. And I can't paint anymore. But apart from that everything's rosy.'

'Why can't you paint anymore?'

Oscar turned to Bloch and made eye contact – an uneasy development.

'I'm sorry to have to do this to you, drag you out on this May morning …'

'Oscar, what's stopping you from painting?'

'What's the point, success seems so far away, I don't have the energy. I want a change but I haven't got the strength. I was hoping you could change things for me.'

'Me? How?'

'I don't know, perhaps you could introduce me to a big cheese.'

'I've done that in the past. I've introduced you to art dealers and you haven't exactly obliged them. You told Demian Small he was a charlatan. Maybe you need to think about another job; or perhaps you could go back into something educational, or charity work, or something that draws on your knowledge of art.' Bloch threw out these suggestions in the way in which a man offers sweets to a child to stop it from crying; he knew they were completely untenable.

'I don't want to draw on my knowledge of art, as I don't think I have any, and the prospect of an educational institution is nauseating.' He took a couple of deep breaths. 'I just don't want to be a blank space all my life. I want to be someone.'

'Well, be someone then. Do something. Take some action.'

'I can't. I'm crippled. I can't seem to ... actually ... make that first step. Last week I turned twenty-nine, but I already feel as if I've died. I mean, what's wrong with me? Do you think I'm aging prematurely?'

'No, I don't think you're aging prematurely. I should be the one who's moaning. I'm forty-eight, over the hill, divorced, childless, and regarded by the literary establishment as a joke. True, I've sold books in droves and never courted the critics but after awhile one longs to be read by people other than secretaries and accountants. Look, can we get out of this pit? I'm finding it hard to use my brain in here.'

'Just let me get the projector.'

There was a sound like that of a stalling car engine and then a very loud snap. Oscar dashed into the projection room. The print had coiled, and it was feeding out all over the floor uncontrollably, writhing around like a gathering of worms. He reached over and flicked a switch as Bloch joined him.

'I had a feeling this was going to happen,' he muttered, kneeling down to disentangle some of the ribbons.

'Can you do anything with it?'

'I don't know; I don't know. It'll take ages. Maybe you should go; I don't want you to sit here getting bored.'

As he stared into the still trembling film ribbons Bloch was struck by what he thought was a brilliant idea.

'I could write a story about you,' he said.

'What would you say? There's nothing interesting enough to write about.'

'I'll make it interesting.'

'Then it wouldn't be about me.'

'It would be about your potential.'

'I'm not sure I have any. Why?'

'I'd like to imagine a different life for you, a parallel reality. I could nail down a possible future in words.'

'How do you mean?'

'If I reinvented your life in fiction it might allow you to step to the side of your actual life, and see it from a different angle. Success needn't be as elusive as you think. Success is work. And a story with you as its subject might give you some self-respect, might help you to take action, to paint again, to be someone, as you say. It's just a thought.'

But as Bloch talked something created a block of foreboding, as if his words were committing him to the obligation of working miracles.

Oscar stopped what he was doing and stood up. He was touched by his friend's concern and ashamed of his own inertia. For a few seconds he caught a glimpse of a different kind of life rising up to snatch him from the empire of boredom. He had an impression – that shot through his mind like a lightning bolt, gone before it could be grasped – of great architecture, colossal trees, shimmering flowers. He could hear Bloch as he started speaking again but his words were far away, registering only as shapeless sound, and in the instants that made up this reverie he was surprised to find the future calling to him seductively.

Then he saw a face, a woman's face, with autumnal eyes. Her full mouth was raised in a smile. He turned to Bloch, to say something. But his mind was blank, he couldn't form words and he was tired.

Her name was Lilliana. She was standing in her flower shop in South Kensington, filled with pink hyacinths, and indigo-blue delphiniums, pink and red roses, red and white carnations. Pots of green, majestic calathea were gathered on shelves and hung from the ceiling, their sprawling leaves forming a fragmented canopy. The shop was popular, not only because of its slightly magical atmosphere, but also because of Lilliana's friendliness, as she single-handedly fussed over her customers, trimmed stalks, arranged their flowers, always attempting to capture the most beautiful combination, the most arresting image. The flowers provided her with both her livelihood and surroundings, in the shop and in her small house in Kentish Town.

She was rushing here and there, getting ready to open up the shop. She wore a broad, mustard-colored hat on her head and her strawberry hair, normally long and untamed, was tied beneath it. A few strands escaped the knot and shivered alongside milky white skin. She moved some giant earthenware pots into place beside candles as wide as tree trunks. They stood clustered together in front of a white spiral staircase, creating a theatrical effect.

She went to unlock the door. The first customer of the day, an agitated man with a moustache, had been waiting outside and he marched in after muttering his thanks brusquely.

'I'd like some white roses,' he declared.

As he did so a tanned young woman strode in, walked up to the counter and was on the point of asking Lilliana something when the man turned to the newcomer, and rumbled, 'Najette, don't ignore me.'

Najette looked around, visibly astonished. She gave herself a moment to regain her composure and said, 'Didn't we just say goodbye?'

'I can't help it if we're both after the same thing.'

'I doubt that very much.'

'I was talking about the flowers. Don't twist everything around.'

'Must we? Again? I wasn't ignoring you as I didn't see you.' And then, in the manner of an afterthought she added, 'Well, seeing as I can't get rid of you, do you want to go to Hyde Park? For the morning light. There's nothing like it, either for painting or sunbathing. Have you noticed how I'm making progress?'

'With what? Painting or skin cancer?'

In place of a verbal answer she rolled her face slowly, inviting him to examine her features, the elegant line of her tanned neck. Like some magnificent bird displaying its feathers, she was proud and imperturbable.

'Don't you think you might be overdoing it?' the man asked.

'Just an hour in the park, that's all, before the tourists and philistines descend,' she continued, 'and then to the shoebox to finish a canvas. Are you sure I can't persuade you to take anything? I know I'm doing something wrong, but I won't accept that my work's too grand for the Earl. Anyway, I look nice, don't I? By the way, I have a feeling that soon the sun will be something we'll all be paying for. It's depressing, isn't it?'

Lilliana felt it might be a good idea to join in and diffuse the tension between the two and said, 'I'm trying to imagine what a sun meter would look like.'

'It's a horrible idea,' said the as-yet-unidentified man.

'Believe me, it'll happen,' Najette declared merrily. 'Everything will happen sooner or later. Artificial love, wine recycled from lemonade, women begging to be relieved of their nipples. Just for fun.'

'What exactly is artificial love? Wait, don't tell me; you're an exponent,' said the stranger, then added emphatically, 'Are my roses ready yet?'

Lilliana handed them over nervously and he disdainfully pressed a twenty pound note into her palm. She had wrapped the flowers in delicate, transparent paper and tied them up with a beautiful copper colored bow but he didn't appear to notice any of this.

Najette said, 'Don't be so serious; we were only talking.'

'I have to go. These are for Georgia.'

Najette was about to say, 'I'll see you,' but he bolted out in a melo-dramatic whirl and she was left hanging.

'An obvious, botched attempt to make me jealous. Georgia indeed! He's a little touchy, isn't he?' she said in a low voice to Lilliana.

'Who is he? Who's Georgia?'

Najette was about to reply when three women streamed in and, speaking loudly, began to circulate, holding their overlapping conversations from different ends of the shop. All three wore multi-colored shawls and their faces were disconcertingly similar, so that Lilliana assumed they must be sisters. One of them, who had silvery blonde hair, moved towards the shelves, crowded with the large potted plants. Lilliana turned to Najette, anxious to resume their conversation, trying to ignore the confusing babble of voices.

'Your friend – though he didn't really seem to be much of one – you were going to tell me who he is,' Lilliana continued.

'Yes. The monster. Lately I've been referring to him as Oscar ... I think it suits him better.'

The largest pot of calathea came crashing down from its shelf, stalks and petals buried underneath the weight of the soil, as it landed the wrong way up. Its spreading, fibrous leaves were instantly ruined. The blonde woman uttered a small cry. Lilliana walked across and stared into the mangled plant. Her first reaction was one of disbelief, but it instantly gave way to sadness.

'I'm terribly sorry – I just touched it – I don't know what happened – it's like it wanted to fall – I'm really sorry,' the blonde woman was saying.

Lilliana's face changed imperceptibly. As Najette studied her she could discern the subtlest film of unshed tears in her eyes. The blonde woman instinctively reached inside her pocket. Her first thought was that money would make everything all right again. But she was mistaken. Najette watched them both attentively, already framing the scene in her mind as a painting; two women, one kneeling in melancholy and the other in consolation. To Najette, Lilliana suggested a madonna poised in a world of intense and incommunicable feeling. She had taken off her hat and more strands of her gossamer hair fell about her face. Najette watched as the blonde's hand found Lilliana's tentatively. The spilled soil was everywhere, firing out in random directions, forming brittle lines. In an instant Najette produced a digital camera – she carried one around with her to record moments like these, moments that might feed her painting – slipped a finger over the button, snapped a shot and tucked the camera away. Nobody noticed.

Lilliana got up slowly. The other woman followed and glanced at her companions, now huddled together in the corner. She turned back to Lilliana and said, feeling her way through the words, 'I work … down the road. Maybe I can buy you lunch sometime … to make up for the mess?' She handed over a card and Lilliana took it without a word. The ghost of a smile formed on her lips.

After a pause, the party of three shuffled out together in obvious relief.

'That was pretty weird. After that I need a drink. Do you have any booze?' said Najette.

'I think … I've got some white wine in the fridge upstairs. Shall I fetch it?'

'That would be glorious.'

As Lilliana climbed the spiral staircase Najette gathered up the cracked pieces of the pot and the disfigured plant and set everything down on the counter. She found a pan and brush and deftly swept up the soil. A minute later Lilliana returned with two filled glasses and said, 'That beautiful plant, the ruined one, was intended for a friend of mine, another Oscar. Oscar Babel.'

'Actually, my friend's name is Nicholas. But he's always fancied himself as a bit of a dandy, so sooner or later he had to be Oscar.'

'Nicholas is your ex-lover?'

'Well-spotted. That's why he was angry. Because of that little pre-fix: ex. As if the fact that he once had his penis up me gives him a divine right to be a shit because I no longer want it there. Imagine!' There was an infectious joviality about her as she conjured with the words, a defiance which registered in the glow of her eyes. She was feeling the rush of eloquence. Lilliana tried not to look shocked.

They pulled two stools towards the counter and sat down. Najette said, 'So tell me about Oscar. The real Oscar.'

'That plant was meant to be his birthday present.' She ran a finger along the gnarled, twisted stem.

'When's his birthday?'

'Last week. I was late. I usually am. He's a projectionist. Doesn't like it. Or says he doesn't.'

'Why doesn't he change jobs?'

'I'm not sure; fear of the unknown, perhaps. He likes things to be predictable, the same. He doesn't like experimentation.'

'Does he have any passions? Apart from the cinema?'

'The cinema isn't a passion, more of an addiction. I just think he likes being locked up in dark rooms.'

'Has he tried S&M? Photography? Confession boxes? Would he look good in a cassock?'

'Better in a hammock. He always looks … slightly out of place. Like he's just stepped off a flying saucer. But he's got a pretty face.'

Najette nodded and swept aside the ebony, twirling strands of hair that had been moving slowly across her face and the full glory of her sun tan was again revealed; this time, however, it quite took Lilliana by surprise. She also noticed her startlingly long eyelashes. When a customer came in a few moments later they were too preoccupied to notice him. They were also a little drunk.

*

Daniel Bloch returned to his flat at around ten in the evening. He had been to a drinks party, thrown by his publishing house, in the Serpentine Gallery, which was currently exhibiting the work of a celebrated installation artist called Tracy Pearn. Her work consisted of giant cauliflowers, immense leeks and gargantuan colanders with blades and knives emerging threateningly from the holes. Bloch had told his editor he was no longer happy writing books that sold but said nothing about life. He added that he wanted to try his hand at serious fiction. He wanted to offer something to the world, to be illuminating, no longer merely entertaining.

The sky was on the point of turning dark, though here and there some flecks of orange and burnished gold remained. As Bloch watched a feeling of infinite possibility came to him, flowing from the sky's rapidly changing, molten condition. The sun had turned into a slowly sinking dome of blood red. A few pink clouds nestled near it. One by one they vanished.

He was considering the story about Oscar. He sat at his desk and mused on this grand plan of his, which, in the end, Oscar had been extremely enthusiastic about. But, he reflected, Oscar's life didn't exactly provide fertile material for development. He decided his fictional Oscar would have to have a different profession, and considered some random choices. Usher. No – too passive, too much like a projectionist. Undertaker. Too morbid. Architect. Too scientific. A model. Maybe. A nude model. Yes, that had interesting possibilities and was related to painting. He would be a nude model who eventually realizes his ambition to paint. Then, rather more groundlessly, he decided that he would live with a cat and be an opera fan.

Oscar lived on his own, in a bedsit in Elephant and Castle, and didn't much care for opera. The landlord who owned, and also resided in, the half-ruined building that housed Oscar's bedsit was a rather unsavory character and unknowingly tormented Oscar by playing opera; in particular, works by Richard Wagner (which gave Bloch the idea of turning Oscar into an enthusiast), the music roaring through the floorboards. Bloch decided that the landlord would also appear in the story, but in a radically altered form, and that his odious traits would give way to generous ones.

He picked up a pen and paper. As he started to make notes he felt his skull grow heavy, as if his brain had doubled in size and weight. Yet his thoughts flowed quickly and connections followed fast. To his surprise, he found that the subject of Oscar was opening a door to unexplored and unfamiliar territory. He felt he was on the brink of finding a completely different voice to that of his previous work – analytical, with a hint of urbanity, and more than a little autobiographical. He wrote with frenzied ease, correcting and revising as he went. After a few hours he put the pen aside and read the scrawled pages back to himself.

*Oscar Babel. No doubt you're all familiar with his name. Reputation. Shoe size. Unsuspected ability to levitate amongst ethereal angels and plummet towards the despicable villains that inhabit the deepest pits of hell. Oscar Babel is arguably the finest life model of his generation. I'm joking. Life modeling has too often been pushed to the sides; it's my task to try and rectify this sorry state of affairs. Keeping as inert as a corpse, stark naked, for long periods of time can be tricky. Usually it's only those possessing inner peace and outer poise who are up to it. Thus, Mr. Babel: the great painter. He has them when he's transmogrifying a canvas. Though for the longest time, before, he was like a parasol caught in a gale. Before he became the great painter he is today he was something else entirely. He was filled with self-loathing; he squandered his talents. He was as ill-adapted to purpose as a surgeon who operates while wearing boxing gloves. I knew him then. I know him now. I have a fond memory of him watering plants. As he fooled around with the watering can he looked up and asked, 'Who will water* me?' *An enigmatic remark, but it lingered like an Irishman at closing time. At that period he was living in a hovel in South London, his love of opera driving his landlord – Mr.*

*Grindel – half-mad each morning as his tenant rose to the sounds of Wagner. Oscar's cat shared his musical tastes. This cat, a black, fat thing that purred when hungry and also when fed (a purring machine), would freeze as the first notes sounded, looking almost human. Mr. Grindel had a heart of gold, and he tolerated these intrusions. Oscar needed the music; it fed his shrinking soul, and reignited some of his lust for life.*

*I have many theories about Oscar's early unhappiness. Perhaps it was something to do with the fact that his most treasured companion departed from his life when he was six years old. His goldfish, Humphrey. Humphrey met its end one afternoon when Oscar's mother saw fit to wash the bowl, depositing the fish in the sink, and pulling the plug out by accident. Or so she claimed afterwards. It was the First Catastrophe. Afterwards, he felt a part of himself had also died with the pet he'd spent countless hours feeding and watching. No other fish, he realized, could replace Humphrey. It wouldn't be the same. The fragility of life. Yes, there were billions of fish floating in the sea, but this wasn't the point. He was already initiated into futility. A minor tragedy, perhaps. This, I hasten to add, is only one of many theories. At that time, the time of his early unhappiness, I had a sense of the man as emotionally crippled. How else can one explain his inability to grasp life and savor its juices? The huge melon had been offered, but Oscar suspected that inside it there was a rotten core that would ultimately taint the taste of the good bits. And so, he passed the melon on, for someone else to enjoy. The germ of imperfection sabotaged the moments of contentment when they came.*

*I went swimming with him. He advanced up and down dutifully, but his movements made me think of a punished schoolboy writing out lines. When he finished I asked if he'd enjoyed the swim. He turned to me with bloodshot eyes and muttered, 'I did it for the water.' Another of those cryptic remarks that I grew tired of decoding.*

*He lived, as I have said, in a hovel. Peeling wallpaper and a sagging bed made me long to slip him some mazuma. Would it, I thought, make any difference? Some nights I'd stay over at the hovel when it was too late to do anything else. His nervous movements as he undressed reminded me of a gazelle sensing it's being observed. (And yet he took his clothes off in public by way of a profession.) I looked away as he slipped on his pyjamas. Oscar didn't feel comfortable when there was another human being around. While I made a final cup of tea for him he tossed and turned, his body fusing with the mattress, his limbs entwined with the bedsheets, as if they were glued to him. When the kettle finally boiled, he was already asleep and I would drink the tea myself, resigning myself to his state of oblivion. The cat purred and arched its back. I would try and engage with it, in some form, as he lay snoring. But the cat had time only for its master. As I approached, it retreated.*

*In the morning he prepared for work. 'The good thing,' he said, 'about this job, is that you don't have to worry about what to wear.' Clutching a plastic bag he ventured out into the cold light of day. But all the time I knew all he needed was to be awakened. This self-destructiveness, this inability to seize various pregnant moments (moments which played tricks on time and existed outside it) would be discarded one day. His sinuous painting provided me with sufficient optimism. His was the problem of the introvert, the snail that cannot crawl out of its shell. He needed the light to come to him. But instead darkness fell, occasionally palliated by the prospect of love or bricks of chocolate. Of course, he had no real desire to go on life modeling. His vocation, truly, his calling, really, his purpose, utterly, was painting. He had once been approached by one of the most famous dealers in London, Barny Small, the latter having been stunned by two of his morbid canvases. Small gave Oscar his card and Oscar tossed it into a washing machine. Maybe he felt the card was unclean. Or perhaps it was the proximity of success that scared him. He also had that suspiciousness of the world – the sticky world of narcissists and self-promoters, marketing and the internet – that has always characterized the truly gifted. Deep down he had contempt for that dealer, because he did commerce with that world, felt at home in it, embraced the absurd injustices that being strong inevitably signaled. Oscar reasoned that if his work triumphed, someone else's was bound to fail as a result. And to constantly fuss over minutiae and errands and duties was not enough for Oscar. And if it became enough, it would be accompanied by the lingering fear that he was a charlatan. Whatever he accomplished wouldn't be enough. And he would remain unworthy in his own eyes, after the drinks had been dispensed and the journalists paid off with memorable insights and fished after glimpses of his life. He would retreat to his hovel, close the door on the world and mumble, 'I am a fake painter, I am a bogus manipulator of images, I am a voyeur.' And so he threw the dealer's card away and saved himself from all these dilemmas. After the machine's rinse cycle was completed the card was beautifully atomized among his clothes.*

*But there was another – more simple – reason for this reluctance to engage, to get off his arse. He was idle, bone idle. That idleness drew him to that other idle creation of nature's: the cat. So he retreated to his hovel and the consolations of his feline companion, as they both stirred with longing and the highest notes of* Tristan and Isolde *fulfilled some of their joint needs. But I always knew that Oscar was destined for great things, that he would someday triumph and see the light, and in doing so would have to rid himself of that inseparable cat of his. Only I knew this, however. He did not.*

He put the pages aside, feeling faintly uneasy. Had he been writing about himself or about Oscar? Had he been writing about his own motivations and preoccupations?

It was coming up to one-thirty in the morning. Almost at the same instant of putting his head on the pillow, he fell into a deep sleep.

At the same time Oscar was watching a film finishing in the Eureka cinema – the late show. He was thinking about the terrible prospect of going home. His little bedsit was the least enticing of places, he reflected. Its wallpaper was peeling, its bed sagged as much as a hammock, and the oven was encrusted in grime. He wondered when he had last changed his bedsheets and the thought appalled him. As he was thinking, his mind slowly being sucked into a mental quicksand, he heard a mournful wailing coming from outside. He walked up to the back door slowly, put his ear to it and listened. The sound stopped. He opened the door and saw a tiny cat perched on the steps. It began to whimper with heartbreaking pathos. It was about the size of his two hands laid end to end. He picked it up and murmured, 'Hello, were you looking for me?'

# 2

Two weeks passed. During this time Oscar decided to adopt the cat, as it seemed to have no owner. He named her Dove. She gave him a new lease of life, and he grew very fond of her in this short space of time. He bought her a wicker basket and loaded it with rugs and blankets, for the cat was quite emaciated and had to be taken care of. But he had to make sure that Mr. Grindel – his landlord – didn't find out about Dove, as the house rules stipulated that no pets could be kept in the tenants' rooms. Despite the fact that the house itself was falling into ruin Mr. Grindel didn't lift a finger to improve the living conditions, while at the same time threatening with eviction any who failed to comply with his rules. He was perpetually unshaven in the attempt to give the appearance of destitution – which he considered a useful posture, allowing him to appear to be on the same footing as his poverty-stricken tenants – and he always wore a thick overcoat, even in hot weather.

On the one occasion Oscar had been inside the maisonette where Grindel lived, in the same building, he had been astonished to find the place baking in unbearable warmth. Equally unbearable, to Oscar's ears, was the Wagner playing on Grindel's old record player. Sensing Oscar's surprise at the intensity of the heat Grindel had muttered some words about not being able to turn the heating off. When Oscar offered to open all the windows he barked a brief cry of 'Mind your own business', and added that the windows couldn't be opened because they were stuck. Oscar concluded that the man, like a baby who had been born prematurely, needed to exist in an incubator of heat, hermetically sealed from the outside world. And yet when dealing with his tenants he displayed all the callousness of the hardened businessman. He was convinced that ultimately they were all out to exploit him. So Oscar was very careful not to give Mr. Grindel an excuse to have him evicted.

That day he had the evening shift at the cinema, but had the afternoon free. He was getting ready to go out when there was a calamitous knocking at the door. He hurriedly stuffed Dove into a cupboard full of boxes of paint and dirty brushes, and, when he was ready, opened the door. His landlord had an annoying habit of dropping by whenever he felt like it. Oscar suspected it was because he hoped to catch him doing something wrong.

'Rent's due, Babel,' he barked, his eyes darting round dementedly.

'I know; I'll have it for you tomorrow.'

'You'd better have, weasel, or I'll have you.'

Oscar noticed that he was giving off a peculiar unpleasant odor. He shut the door in a hurry and released the cat. Then he put Dove in her basket and said, 'Sorry about that. Be good while I'm gone.' He put out some milk for her, within easy reach.

He walked quickly. He was late for an appointment with Lilliana in a bar near her shop.

*

Inside the bar vast drapes shivered, disturbed by currents of stale air. The place was lit with tangerine light and strange, bodiless music was playing. All around, the walls were painted in blood- red and the eye found relief from their intensity only in the surface of the wooden, scratched floorboards. The bar itself was a baroque construction and out of it hideous gargoyles rose, as if trying to come alive. A thousand and one bottles were arranged in rows at the back. Bottles of every size and appearance containing glossy green liqueurs, golden whiskeys and malts, transparent vodka and gin, rum as black as night, bottled brown beer of thundering potency. The vast mirror behind these begetters of oblivion reflected the feathered hats, the painted faces and the pallid splendor of the clientele, all lovingly recorded by London's ubiquitous and multiplying CCTV's. Giant candles were planted here and there, half-used, with intricate lines of wax encrusted around them like stalactites.

Oscar hunted for Lilliana for a little while, then found a chair, presuming she hadn't arrived yet, rather than that she had been and gone. A couple of identical twins were playing chess and sending text messages. A broker flicked and turned the billowing pages of the *Financial Times* with disturbing belligerence. Oscar turned around and was pleased to spot a woman seated on her own in a corner, beside a folding screen decorated with masked figures. She had abundant silvery blonde hair, tightly tied in a bun. As he watched her he wondered how Bloch's story was progressing and made a mental note to call him. A newspaper lay near to hand and he started to read it without much interest. When he glanced up again the woman wasn't there, though a luminous pink coat signaled her claim to the seat.

Upon her return she had been transformed by a generous layer of green lipstick. More crowds drifted in. The noise they made immediately repelled him. He sensed the woman in the corner also shared his distaste, and as he looked over to her again for some sign of solidarity her face was partially hidden behind her newly loosened locks, which she proceeded to adjust. For a moment he was stunned. Her appearance was so different it was as though her face had actually been reshaped.

She finally noticed his somnolent staring.

'You look confused,' she said sweetly.

'Yes, I am,' he replied.

'What's confusing you?'

Oscar caught some words from a conversation at the bar. A voice said, 'I can only eat salmon when I'm by the river, or better still when I'm in the river.' There was a brief lunatic burst of laughter.

'I have this feeling that something in my life is changing, something important.'

'Would you mind telling me what?'

'Everything. Nothing. I now own a cat. That's all, really,' he said.

'That's all?'

'Well ... not really.'

He wondered where Lilliana had got to. His face betrayed his agitation, despite his attempts at bullying it into composure.

'Is something wrong?'

'Oh, I was expecting someone. But I think she's slipped through my fingers. Everything, sooner or later, slips through my fingers, you know. Money, love, friends, painting.' He smiled, trying to deflate the seriousness of his remarks. He suddenly had a feeling he wouldn't be seeing Lilliana today. Resuming in a lighter tone, he asked, 'Do things slip through your fingers? Or do you manage to avoid that, and if so, how?'

'Sometimes: in answer to the first question, which means sometimes for the second as well. For the third: I put talcum powder on my fingers. Gives me a firmer grip with which to catch the customers when they fall. You see, I work in a hair salon but lately I've been feeling more like a therapist than a hairdresser.

'But to go back to the first question. Something did slip through my fingers the other day. I mean really slipped. A plant. The woman in the shop was gutted. I don't know what the hell happened. I'm not normally so clumsy. But ... the thing was ... her face, when she saw the damage ... for a moment, just for a second as I watched her ... I could have imagined falling in love with her ... I don't know if you can understand ... that vulnerability ... '

She stopped abruptly, and shrugged off the delicate demeanor these revelations had created. As if to cover up the cavity left by her honesty she started attending to physical matters, smoothing her skirt, folding her pink coat with care. Oscar averted his gaze, so as to give her room, and surveyed the others, who had become more and more animated. The search for pleasure was continuing, like some treasure hunt conducted in the night, in the capsizing chambers of the imagination, and on the dewy grass, wherein all pains and losses could be erased and the opiate of sensuality was at liberty to pursue its sweet, numbing agenda, the voices of human suffering barely reaching, and so dismissed as imagined and ghostly.

She stood up, a little self-consciously.

'I hope you find a net to catch the things that are slipping. Just don't get trapped in it.' Her face broke into a smile and he watched her go with a grace he envied. He decided to telephone Lilliana on his cellular phone. But then he remembered the phone had no credit. He stepped outside and found a red phone booth.

The booth was saturated in graffiti and the receiver was off the hook, swinging like a pendulum. He replaced it, picked it up and dialed. He heard the neutral pulse of ringing. A man answered, which was odd, as Lilliana lived alone.

'Hello ... Hello.'

Oscar realized he had just dialed Bloch's number.

'Daniel. It's Oscar.'

'Why didn't you say anything when I picked up?'

'How's the story going? Have you started it?'

'Yes, it's going. What's new?'

'I have a cat. That's about it.'

'What?'

'I said I have a cat. She's called Dove.'

There was a moment's silence. Then Bloch said, 'That's nice. Well, I better go. I'm late for a doctor's appointment.'

'What's wrong?'

'Nothing. I just need to pick up a prescription for some sleeping tablets. I'll see you.'

He stepped out of the booth. Bloch had sounded strange on the phone. Oscar was so distracted he forgot all about the phone call to Lilliana. He walked aimlessly for a while and then finally hopped on a passing bus.

A few minutes later Lilliana walked in to the bar, holding his birthday present. In the dim, tangerine light the white skin of her face appeared tawny.

As soon as Bloch returned the phone to its cradle he felt an odd twinge of discomfort. He stared out of his window, watching the traffic as it crawled along, at a snail's pace. Noxious fumes spluttered into the air, and taxis throbbed, threatening to melt. The crowds wrestled with their shopping and the heat.

Turning away, he switched the radio on. A wave of brass band music blew up. He reached for the dial and jiggled it about until he had found something which pleased him: a string quartet, full of grief, the lowest notes sounding from beyond the grave, stirring in a slow bass rumble. As he lost himself in the music a male voice began speaking.

'You know art can kill?'

Bloch's immediate thought was that the dial had just managed, by itself, to turn around and tune into another station. Dismissing this theory, he scrambled around for a paper to check the radio programs, wondering if he might be listening to some kind of play with background music. But the guide just said: '1pm: Beethoven: Quartet in A minor, Op. 132. Belcea Quartet.' It was then that he began to consider the possibility of an aural hallucination. He stared into thin air, stupefied. Had he imagined that voice? What's happening to me, he thought. He switched off the radio, plodded wearily to his bedroom and spread his soft body out on the big double bed. The walls and ceiling moved in closer; his bedroom metamorphosed into the cabin of a boat, lolling lazily in the tide. He closed his eyes and took a couple of deep breaths. He needed to work, to give his mind some ballast. He got up and walked unsteadily to his study.

The feel of his old typewriter's keyboard stopped him from floating away altogether, from turning into a speck of dust, pirouetting like a spinning top and rising above London and Hyde Park.

*Chapter Two*

Modeling. *This is the subject I have to tackle before I can do justice to the man's significance as a painter. Why for God's sake modeling? Perhaps it was the thought of exposing the external – the body – that attracted him, while keeping the internal – the soul – under wraps. When I spoke to him about it he would say he found the whole thing marvelously anonymous, even though he was so literally exposed. He was the center of attention but only in the way a patient is as he is scrutinized by acne-rich medical students in sanitized clinics. He never had to exchange words with anyone, never had to interact in any emotional sense. And that was the way he liked it, I'm afraid. He could observe. He also spoke about the cleansing quality of the process, spoke of how the cold and constant stillness offered wonderful openings for the mind. In that eternity of stasis the mind could dip its big toe into shores of the celestial, he claimed, then crawl back to shore as the break came. Then he could focus once more on the simple things, such as the cup of tea that would be his and his alone, a blanket draped over him, ignored by all the students, which was the way that he liked it, and there is nothing more delicious than the taste of reward that is deserved, and rest after labour is, in my opinion, only slightly less wondrous than warmth after cold.*

*'Well, Oscar,' I said one evening, after he'd returned from the art school (I had lingered on in his flat, sampling the mythical kindness of his landlord, Mr. Grindel – he made me some limpid soup), 'what happened today, did some young lady step over the fine line that separates artist from voyeur?'*

*He ignored my question and reached for his cat. The cat melted instantly in his embrace, sickeningly responsive to his caresses. He turned to me and intoned slowly, 'No, not today, but maybe tomorrow. Maybe in the oasis-mirage-stargate of tomorrow.'*

*The answer was stuffed with wisdom, somehow, as if he had found, in a phrase or two the distillation of clarity that normally only a lifetime can deliver. Perhaps that is what wisdom is, I reflected, the ability to see change and accept that it might not come today but tomorrow, the ability to transcend time with a little nonchalance. I imagine that mountaineers and explorers are able to visualize time more easily than I can. As they climb Mount Everest they must in some sense be stepping over and above the usual patter of time's motion, for how else could they do what they do? This seems obvious. I admire those fuckers. They manage to get the upper hand, all right. They manage to put time in its place. That tyrant, who never lets up, but forever taps at our shoulders, reminding us that life is finite, running after us with a whip and shouting, ever and again, 'I go on, see, but you don't.' But I digress. Oscar shared some of these apprehensions of mine. But he had a reluctance to talk about things. Such as happiness, misery, love. Small-fry stuff.*

*'Why are you reluctant?' I asked.*

*'Well, the way I see it, one shouldn't talk; one should do.'*

*'But that's silly.'*

*'It seems to me language butchers the delicate mysteries. Speaking of emotions renders them redundant.'*

*'OK then, I've tickets to see flamenco dancing tomorrow night. Care to join me?'*

*We went along and took our seats half an hour before the show was due to begin. A gaudy auditorium with plush red seats and an even plusher audience. He whispered, close, in my ear, 'Sometimes I'd like to leave all this, take off in a balloon.' I tried to ignore these melodramatic flourishes when they came. The supple dancers clicked and clapped. Throughout the performance Oscar's mind was elsewhere. He was incapable of surrendering to an experience, since he was constantly preoccupied with another problem. An obsessive need to keep a track on everything ripped the heart out of his pleasurable diversions. Since he was always monitoring how cramped a person, situation, or place made him feel, and since one part of his mind was always registering and computing and planning, he could never give in to life, even when alcohol was sabotaging his liver, its capacity for unleashing freedom sty-mied by Oscar's self-imposed strait jacket. As the flamenco dancing sped on with greater ferocity, one part of his mind admired the achievement while another registered the ephemeral component of all things, running underneath. Like London's underground system, buried dozens of feet beneath the concrete pavement, invisible but undeniably there. Myself, I have always considered London to be like the mind, and perhaps I'm losing my mind. London lost its long ago. I realize, of course, that art can kill, that metaphors and images are dangerous. By the way, I would not, for one second, dream of using Babel as a platform for my own story. Oh no. I grant you, I have been feeling strange lately and wonder if my skull is turning into a gaseous shell. I am a successful writer, or rather I have had a successful writing career, achieving fame in some form, enjoying the finer things, perusing art galleries, going to parties, sipping vintage wine. But who are all these people I have known, what are these light, watery words I've written? It all slips into the void, and I cannot now bear to look at a single fabrication of mine. What's the point of all this talk? If I have failed, I have failed with honor. This project about my friend is my last sustaining song. I wish it to be truthful. I wish it to have the clear mint of sincerity, ripping through the senses like a salty sea breeze. But perhaps it's too late for me; perhaps I've bitten off more than I can chew. Oscar has his life in front of him. He can still listen to music and pinch women's bottoms. What am I doing? I'll tell you. Float-ing along in middle-age. I only wanted to make a difference. But all I did was make money. Twenty years from now who will read my novels, my popular novels? That label 'popular' already seems to consign them to the rubbish tip. I grant you the search for immortality is an idle thing. But some achieve it. Do I envy them? I know I envy someone, but haven't worked out who that is yet. I should like to rattle humanity a bit, shake it up, hold forth on the eternal verities with weighted words, and make up some new verities of my own. Be a messianic martyr, the fool who tells the truth ... Inner peace. No, I certainly have none of that. Inner pieces, yes, clattering away inside me like loose change. And when it comes to love, who can say I have truly loved? I never gave enough of myself. A wife I no longer see, whom I think of rather like a broken trophy perched on my mantelpiece. By the way, before I start to get sentimental about Natalie's vagina, I must say the time for lust is over. (But perhaps it can be a gateway to the divine, to greater perception.) I will find something bigger and better. But I'm straying from the main point, Oscar. Who cares about him? Do I have to give him everything? Anyway, I'm not myself, things are a bit misty.*

Bloch blacked over the last three sentences with a fountain pen, put the manuscript aside, and – suddenly exhausted – dived into his bed. It was three o'clock in the afternoon.

\*

On the phone Lilliana apologized for having missed Oscar at the bar. She told him that a new friend of hers had invited them both for lunch the following week.

That following week as he walked, clutching a crumbling *A-Z*, checking street names, he wondered who this new friend of Lilliana's might be. As a rule she tended not to make many new friends, which was odd, as she was such an affable person. He had a suspicion that ultimately she preferred her flowers to people.

After taking a few wrong turns he finally found the right street – a broad avenue lined with oak trees, whose houses all shared magnificent bay windows. It was so quiet and deserted Oscar had the feeling he was the last man on earth. After establishing the direction in which the numbers ran, he found the right one and rang the bell, which was labelled MERIDIAN. He was standing in front of a grand but slightly dilapidated semi-detached house. After a short wait a woman he took to be in her late twenties emerged. She was wearing a bright yellow dress that fell to below her knees in one piece and sandals revealing bare feet, beautifully manicured toes, and skin as evenly-tanned as that of her face and arms. Her sinuous, silky black hair was tied up and set in place by five or six diamanté hair clips. Oscar instantly felt a wave of attraction pass through him like vertigo.

'You must be Oscar,' she said pleasantly.

'I think I am,' he replied.

She smiled, ignoring this rather cryptic remark. 'I'm Najette.'

'Is Lilliana here yet?'

'She couldn't make it. She's not feeling well.'

Oscar began to feel uneasy with the thought that he would have to spend the afternoon with a complete, albeit dazzling, stranger. She ushered him into a spacious front room, filled with china, flowers, various pairs of shoes and medium-sized perspex boxes full of immaculately clean sable brushes and palette knives. The sun streamed in brilliantly through the large bay window and gave the room a light, airy feel, as if it was housed within a hollow diamond. Propped up against the wall were a couple of canvasses of roughly the same size. A beautiful easel stood in the center and a giant sketch pad rested on it. Abstract, cylindrical shapes drawn in charcoal and graphite weaved in and out of each other, with some of the spaces shaded in. It was a delicate, highly refined composition.

'I'm afraid I didn't buy any wine,' he said.

'That's all right. I didn't buy any food.'

'Oh, but I thought we were going to have lunch.'

'So did I, but the light was so fantastic this morning I just had to take advantage of it; so I've been working all day and haven't had a chance to go shopping. I hope you understand, as a fellow painter.'

'Did Lilliana tell you I paint?'

'Yes.'

'Well, I used to.'

'I see. Why don't you still?'

'I'm not sure.'

He began to relax, warming to her, welcoming the chance to study the nuances of her face, solve the enigma of her aura of calm, so that even he might be able to adopt or imitate it.

Najette said, 'There must be a reason why you stopped.'

'Oh, yes, I'm sure there were many. You have a very nice house.'

'It's not mine. It's my uncle's. He's never here as he's always going round the world sampling different countries so he can write holiday junk for radio. So I can't complain.'

Najette smiled slightly mischievously, as if something – or perhaps everything – was amusing her. She lightened the atmosphere, offered a kind of antidote against anxiety.

Oscar, sensing that her work was as striking as she was, muttered tentatively, 'Could I take a look at those canvasses?'

'If you like. Just don't tell me what you think of them, unless it's positive. But then, that's stupid, isn't it, because your silence would reveal that you didn't like them as much as saying you didn't like them. Oh, fuck it, just say whatever you like.'

Oscar walked up and knelt down beside them. To Najette it looked like he was about to pray. He was vaguely aware of her silent, monitoring gaze.

Both were broadly expressionistic versions of the same subject. In the first a large woman was reclining on a chaise-longue. Her fluid, ripe hair was defined in a golden arch. In the background mask-like faces appeared to have escaped from the woman's mind, amorphous fixtures from her past or possibly future. The expression the woman wore was both ethereal and agonized, her cavernous eyes poised in diamond shapes, indian yellow and framed by glossy black eyebrows. She was naked and the arch of her sloping body conveyed an impression of indolence: perhaps she had just eaten a meal. In the second version the masks had disappeared and in their place there were blood-red outlines which subtly echoed the shape of the woman's body. Her tongue was lashed out insolently against the world, made of magenta, a vast and incredible gash, a tapestry of flesh.

Oscar was strongly drawn by the paintings, unable to break away. His own desire to paint was momentarily rekindled.

'You can take one, if you like,' said Najette, her face expressing perfect candor.

Oscar didn't hear her at first.

'Well, would you like one?'

Oscar turned to her and said, 'I don't deserve that.'

'Of course you do. Don't be so polite. It would make me happy. They obviously please you. Am I right?'

'Yes. They're … magnificent.'

As he said this her upturned lips and half-closed eyes somehow conveyed that she already knew this to be true, but at the same time communicated the sweetness of such an unequivocal confirmation.

'Well, have one then.'

Oscar was taken aback by her generosity. He was ashamed of his own inability to make similarly spontaneous gestures. Her insistence drew him towards her, and struck him either as evidence of incredible friendliness or – more flatteringly – of the ease she felt in his presence, as if they were actually old friends.

'I notice you haven't signed either of these.'

'So? Are you planning to sell one for pots of cash when I'm famous?'

'No, no, of course not.' Oscar was fumbling, panicking.

'I was only joking. I always sign on the back. I keep most of my stuff in my studio – which is actually a shoebox, off the Great Western Road, and which in fact I will probably have to say goodbye to as the savings are running out and waiting on tables isn't that lucrative. I was trained as an architect, but gave it all up to paint. God help me. So, have you decided which one you'd like?'

'Maybe … when I can give you something – something of mine – in return, except at the moment I have nothing …'

'You have to work again, Oscar!'

'Well, now that I've seen your stuff … I don't know … if I'm inspired or intimidated.  But … it's been so long since I've even held a brush.'

'I know what might get you started again.'

'What?'

'Modelling. Nude.'

Oscar lapsed into mystified silence, as if Najette had just suggested that dissecting a frog would help him to paint again.

'I don't understand.'

'No. I didn't think you would. But when you're on the other side of the canvas all you want to do is get back in front of it. Or at least that's what I discovered when I was blocked. A friend said I should do some nude modeling, and when I did I found the passivity, the sense of being a lynch-pin for other people's creativity made me anxious to get back to my own work. You see? It might do the same for you. And I think it would loosen you up. You're a little on the self-conscious side. Though you have a good physique. Your height helps. It would be good to expose yourself without getting ...'

Before she could get any further the doorbell rang. Najette floated out into the hallway and Oscar followed hesitantly. It was Nicholas, smiling with uncharacteristic enthusiasm. But when he saw Oscar his face changed.

'Can I come in?' he asked, eying Oscar suspiciously.

'Hello, Nicholas. Come in. This is Oscar,' said Najette.

'Ah, the *real* Oscar?' Nicholas demanded as he strode in with a proprietorial swagger.

'How do you mean?'

'Is Oscar your real name or have you been re-named Oscar, according to Najette's whims?'

'No, Oscar is my real name,' Oscar murmured.

'So you are the real Oscar, then,' said Nicholas.

'I suppose I must be,' Oscar said weakly, feeling more and more confused.

'Shall we sit down, instead of standing in the hall like this?' Najette asked.

'I won't stay; I just wanted to fetch my things before they end up in the charity shop.'

'You know I wouldn't do that ... I'll go and get them ... are you sure you don't want ...'

'No, I don't want to break up this cosy scene.'

For a split-second Najette's face was contorted with barely- suppressed rage, but she wouldn't rise to the bait and, after a pause, walked off with impressive restraint. Her absence added to Oscar's discomfort and he felt pinned down in Nicholas' scrutinizing eyes. As they both shuffled into the front room Oscar had hopes that the increased space might diffuse the tension.

'Have you known her very long?' Nicholas asked, in an effort to appear more friendly.

'Najette? We've only just met, this moment.'

'I'm not sure that means much. When it comes to Najette the normal rules of friendship don't apply. She achieves instant intimacy with people, you know. And then discards them. But don't think you're anything special. She's like that with everyone.'

These remarks triggered a pronounced distaste for Nicholas, which Oscar tried to communicate by maintaining an icy silence. Nicholas didn't notice and carried on regardless, twirling his moustache playfully.

'Tell me, do you paint as well?'

'I don't know.'

'I like that answer. Very much. Did you once paint?'

Oscar said nothing.

'If it's failure you're worried about, it's highly likely. But give me a call, I might be able to help you. I'm the director of the Earl Gallery, a small but loyally attended establishment. If you'd like to exhibit, I might be interested. I'm feeling generous and I know that real painters are hard to come by. Don't worry, you won't have to sleep with me. But before I go, how about a quick sketch? Of me? Otherwise I'll have nothing to go on. A quick portrait – in return for my offer?'

Oscar wasn't at all sure he wanted to reciprocate, and he felt an old dread of being revealed as talentless creep up on him.

'I haven't drawn anyone for a very long time; I'm not sure I could,' he said politely.

'Oscar, I'm instinctive. Impetuous. And I'm vain, and I don't like to be kept waiting. Think of it as a little gift you're sending my way, rather than transcendental art.'

Oscar took the time to study Nicholas' face, trying to fathom his real motives. There was nothing to go on, however. But as Oscar persisted Nicholas responded to his mute look of inquiry and something within Nicholas blurred and shifted. Oscar had the impression for a moment of tremendous emotion, a great release of feeling and then, it was gone, swallowed up once more in his regal bearing, his commanding voice, his expensive clothes. This unexpected moment of clarity, this revelation of Nicholas' pain magically nudged Oscar into acquiescence and, slowly, he made a few tentative strokes with the pencil, then began in earnest to draw him.

After quarter of an hour Oscar had something to show for his labors; and even he was pleasantly surprised by how good it was.

The portrait was slapdash, yet precise, with sinewy, throwaway lines. Nicholas was genuinely intrigued and impressed.

'Let me see something else, and I might be able to make the necessary arrangements.'

'But I don't really have anything I could show you. It's all unfinished.'

'Well, then, finish something. Work. You'll feel much better. But in the meantime, thanks. I look raw but refined … your little impromptu sketch is alchemical. I like that. Do you mind if I take a picture of it with my phone?' He did so. 'Say goodbye to Najette for me. Oh, by the way, I wouldn't mention this proposal of mine. Come and see me at the Earl. Bye bye.'

'But aren't you going to pick up your things?'

'Some other time.'

He left in a whirl.

Oscar waited for Najette. Eventually, after ten minutes, when she still hadn't materialized, he called out her name. Then he went upstairs. He searched in all the rooms. But he couldn't find her anywhere. In an undecorated bedroom on a small desk he saw a large teddy bear propped up. A note was taped to its hand:

*Dear Oscar,*

*If you find this please excuse my eccentricity – it's partly down to the presence of Nicholas. He makes me come out in spots. I've just gone for a breath of fresh air via the back door. I was on the point of coming in when I saw you sketching him. Not wishing to disturb you I withdrew. I can leave places without a sound, as I'm not very heavy. In fact I probably don't even exist. Or perhaps I was once a church mouse, burrowing through the organ loft, scurrying around as the heavy tread of humans went on around me. Anyway, I shall await our next meeting with bated breath. I wish you well in the meantime. The name of the place where you can be stark naked (and not be arrested) is the Mermaid Academy. It's in South Kensington. Najette.*

# 3

Bloch had invited Oscar to go to a new theater in Islington to see *The Voiceless Ones,* by a little-known German playwright, August Dinkl, whose works, Bloch speculated, were being re-discovered and championed a century after his death most probably by the same kind of people who had shunned and ridiculed him when he was alive.

The play was about a young shop assistant struggling to make ends meet in *fin-de-siecle* Paris. She has a love affair with a drifter who eventually murders her. In the second act her ghost returns to haunt the murderer, eventually driving him to suicide. In the end the coroner concludes that they had both killed themselves, and their grisly story becomes a romantic myth dissected by a group of intellectuals in the final act.

As they sat in the packed auditorium Oscar's mind wasn't really on the play. The intense dialogue, the murky lighting, the moments of desperate lust served only to create a transparent screen through which he discerned his life.

In the interval Bloch managed to buy them both a drink after a titanic struggle that required him to exercise all his skill and cunning in order to attract the attention of a single, frantic barman. They stood yelling in a corner, trying to be heard above the din generated by the crowd, which had miraculously managed to squeeze itself into the tiny bar.

'I'm going to leave the cinema. I know I've said that before but this time I'm serious.'

'What will you do?' Bloch yelled.

'Not sure – I've got plans.'

'Are you enjoying the play?'

'It's a bit morbid, don't you think? I'm not really in the mood. I'm more interested in that story about me. How's that coming along? Are you happy with it?'

For an infinitesimal time Oscar had the impression Bloch was no longer there with him. His body, his clothes remained, but the living, breathing entity contained within had been suspended. He might have been a waxwork model. Then the moment passed and the spark of life was restored.

'It's ... different,' he bawled. 'I've drawn on my own personality. Brought what I've got so far. Two chapters. Thought you might like to have a look.'

Bloch reached into an inner pocket and produced some neatly folded, typewritten sheets. A voice on the intercom stated that the second half of the performance would begin in five minutes. Oscar ignored it and began to read.

While Oscar read Bloch glanced around the bar. The throng was a well-groomed one. People were laughing and screeching and alcohol drove conversation with a merciless whip. After a climatic moment, in which voices collectively forced out an ear-splitting squeal bodies began to drift away, trying to forge a painless path back to the auditorium. At last only the hardened drinkers remained. Bloch turned back to watch Oscar reading. He seemed to have entered an impenetrable cocoon. As Bloch studied his face Oscar's features formed an unfamiliar pattern. At the same time Bloch felt his own face wilting as a flower does in an oppressive sun.

'We have to go or we'll miss the second half,' he muttered.

'You go,' said Oscar, without looking up. 'I'll join you later.'

As Bloch moved he felt his legs grow heavy. He stared at the floor; it was slowly separating into a double image. He found his seat in a cold sweat, seized with dizziness. He wiped his brow with a handkerchief. It was drenched in sweat. What's wrong with me? he thought.

Eventually the dizziness passed and he became distracted by the play. The ghost of the murdered woman was incredibly eerie; she was made of mist, hair flowing down her back like fleece drawn from snow.

At last Oscar returned, quietly took his seat and whispered in Bloch's ear.

'Your story is strangely fascinating. But the strangest thing is how it resembles what's been going on in my life recently. We'll have to talk about this later. I'm going to have to go; I'm too excited to sit through this. I'm going for a swim.'

'What – now?!'

'There were some flyers in the bar. An all night pool. Just opened, down the road. The Roman Leisure Centre.'

A man with a double chin asked them to be quiet.

'What about swimming trunks?' Bloch whispered, straining for an even lower volume.

'They're giving away free gym wear, according to the flyers, so I can use a pair of shorts. And there's a car in the pool.'

'What?'

This time the man demanded silence from them. Bloch apologized, produced a piece of paper and scribbled: WHY'S THERE A CAR IN THE POOL?

Oscar snatched the paper and wrote: THE CENTRE'S BEING SPONSORED BY SOME CAR COMPANY. IT'S AN ADVERTISING GIMMICK – PEOPLE CAN FRONT CRAWL THROUGH IT. SOUNDS INTERESTING. THEY'VE LAID ON OXYGEN CYLINDERS. WANT TO COME?

'No, I'm staying,' Bloch whispered.

'Fair enough. But if you change your mind, you know where to find me.'

'I'm staying,' said Bloch emphatically.

'Either go or stay, but for God's sake, shut up,' the disgruntled theater-goer growled, his double chin quivering like a jelly on a plate slammed down upon a floral table.

But eventually Bloch didn't stay either.

He found a deserted cafe on Upper Street with so many posters that they formed a second layer of wallpaper. He ordered a cup of strong black coffee which he knocked back so quickly he almost scalded himself. This story, he thought to himself, is turning into something strange. I have to tell him I'm not really happy with the idea of going on with it. It's too bad if he's invested lots of hope in it. After all, it was just an idea. As he was thinking about how best to erase it from his life he felt some fingers tapping lightly on his shoulder and turned round, half- expecting to find Oscar next to him.

'It's Mr. Bloch, isn't it?'

The owner of the fingers went by the name of Webster. Bloch had recently bought a silver tea pot from him at his antiques stall on Portobello Road. This had triggered a faltering but pleasant conversation which eventually morphed into a monologue by Bloch, fueled by five pints of beer guzzled in The Earl of Lonsdale pub. As Bloch's bladder swelled and ballooned he set out an intoxicated vision of utopia, which entailed marooning on a desert island all politicians, investment bankers, writers of memoirs and tabloid journalists who would eventually consume one another in a gigantic act of cannibalism or have their heads shrunken by voodoo priests.

Webster was clutching a bulging plastic bag and wore a badly-knotted cravat and waistcoat, a dozen colors wrapped within it in an unruly mix.

'Oh hello, Webster. How's the pottery?'

'*Porcelain*. Japanese Arita porcelain. Are you alone?'

'I've just walked out of a theater. The play was making me nervous.'

'Plays? What a royal bore. Can I join you? I'm whipped. I was on my way to Camden Passage – to take delivery of twelve Moroccan saucers.'

After this disconnected exchange Webster sat down, with much negotiation. His flabby face seemed to reflect his slumberous mind. During a conversation his remarks were always a little to the edge of things, never quite managing to embody the precision of relevance. This slightly displaced quality was reflected in the fact that when he spoke he always did so out of the corner of his mouth, his lips drooping at one end and making him mumble. This habit had been formed when he was a small boy and a female cousin had spied on him urinating – since he had left the door ajar – and announced her presence with hysterical squeals.

After the waitress had served Webster with a cappuccino he turned to her with a bashful smile, and, as if afraid the request would get him into trouble, asked for a piece of coffee cake. He beamed with the anticipation of pleasure.

'Webster,' Bloch began, 'can I ask you a question?'

'Of course.'

'What do you think of me?'

Webster wasn't expecting this and started squirming. He stared into his coffee for a moment, hoping the answer lay within it.

'Well, I don't know you that well … I mean … how do you mean? What do you mean when you say …. I mean?'

Bloch blurted out, suddenly desperate to reveal some buried part of himself, 'You know, sometimes I feel like a chef who travels the world, gathering the finest ingredients, the freshest vegetables, but never manages to start cooking, convinced as he is that something's always missing – a sprig of parsley, some anchovies, oregano.'

These comments might as well have been made in Japanese for all that Webster followed them. But help was at hand as Webster's coffee cake now arrived with some degree of ceremony. In an instant he was as breathless as a child presented with a new toy, and in his elation dropped his spoon with a loud clang. As he fished around for it (it seemed to have disappeared or at least sped across the floor so that it was beyond his reach) he struck his head under the table. Hollering in pain he emerged looking dazed. Bloch helped him.

'I'm in pain,' he spluttered, bulbous tears streaming down his cheeks.

Bloch said, 'Take it easy.'

The waitress noticed the commotion. She ran some water over a tea towel and walked over. As she did so her foot trod on the spoon, which had reappeared, disfiguring it forever. She applied the wet towel to Webster's head.

'Thank you,' he muttered, his face averted from hers.

The pain began to recede a little.

'All because of a cake,' he said. All his joy had fled and could never be recaptured.

While the waitress tended to him her lips rose in a beatific smile and her face at that moment seemed to be the embodiment of a mysterious, unconditional love. As though she had suddenly tapped into, or was now congruent with, an energy that had hitherto been separate from her. Bloch studied her – and this remarkable luminosity – for as long as he could without seeming intrusive.

She said, 'I'll just get you another spoon.'

Webster said, 'No, please. Don't bother. I don't want the cake anymore. It brought me bad luck.'

The waitress shrugged – and her transfiguration was at once over. Webster stared at the cake sadly as it floated away, back to where it had come from.

'That cake got me into trouble,' he muttered mournfully to himself. 'I should never have ordered it.'

'Will you forget that fucking cake!' Bloch yelled.

'Sorry, Bloch, it's just that my head's sore. In the morning I'll have a bloody great bump.'

'So what? Is that what constitutes pain for you? Are you telling me that knocking your head is pain for you? What do you know about pain anyway? The vicious lie they tell us, that life is sweet, that love is a well we can all draw from. That cow Natalie.'

'What's wrong with you?'

'I feel lonely. I'm detached from people. I have nothing. Nothing important.'

'That's not true Bloch; think of your marriage.'

'I'm divorced.'

'Oh yes. Right, it didn't work out but ...' – he floundered – 'at least you've tasted ... a bit of love. We're all alone. We're all alone,' he repeated stupidly.

'Are we? I'm not convinced. Perhaps I can help Oscar; perhaps I can offer a small contribution to humanity by helping him realize his ambitions. I could have been the love-filled host, offering the fatted calf. I would have been happy so long as I could have gone on speaking. A wind from a foreign clime which made others feel they weren't alone, but sincerity is so hard to find. Where do you begin? Perhaps by the light of the moon. Perhaps only at night. Or with a voice singing in a chapel. A taste of wine. The morning light of summer. But they fade. They fade and we fade with them.'

Webster took refuge in his coffee again, desperately wishing he were somewhere else. He racked his brains but couldn't think of a single response to Bloch's lofty remarks. Fortunately he was not required to give one, as Bloch now posed a reassuringly direct, though completely unexpected question.

'Fancy going for a swim?'

Apart from the attendant and instructor (who showed people how to use the breathing equipment) Oscar was the only other person at the pool. It was hard to discern him clearly in the low light of the candles mounted round the pool's rim – another unusual feature of the way in which the car manufacturers, Kazooi-Template, were choosing to present their sponsorship of the center – and his face was periodically submerged in the water as he chugged along mechanically so he didn't notice Webster's and Bloch's muted arrival. It was more or less impossible to distinguish his form from that of somebody else's. As Bloch regarded that moving supine figure Oscar's very anonymity made Bloch's mind flash back to the moments before their original meeting, when each of them had been strangers to one another, each locked into his separate trajectory until life or fate or nothing at all had pushed them together and their pathways had crossed, like train tracks that run parallel and then weave and converge as speed slackens and gathers. He thought of the billion souls he would never have time to coincide with, the billion encounters he would never know.

Clearly Kazooi-Template was going all out to promote its latest brainchild. The website promised that their latest model, the Tutor Saloon 101, was their greatest creation yet, a car that to all intents and purposes possessed autonomous intelligence. The male owners of this cross between a sentient being and a vehicle could look forward to transfigured social lives, job promotions, and god-like success with women who would surrender their deepest treasures in a somnambulist's trance.

The manufacturers had run into problems with the Islington Council. The breathing and diving equipment had been procured from DEFTOL, a highly-reputable German firm, then approved by the Health and Safety Executive, and checked by the council's own health advisers who knew nothing whatsoever about underwater breathing equipment. Then the car itself had been sealed with transparent plastic to ensure that no one would cut themselves on any jagged edges, and clamped down. The council stipulated that an instructor and doctor had to be on hand at all times. Kazooi-Template managed to persuade them that a doctor wasn't really necessary. A janitor was appointed for maintaining and supervising the candles.

The centre had been open now for two days and so far, including Oscar, two people had taken a swim there.

The candles continued to cast different clusters of weird shadows along the tiled walls. When the water was disturbed lines of yellow-blue light formed around the rim of the swimming pool, gigantic ripples of reflected light, which criss-crossed and hovered and flickered, creating a gossamer web of stunning beauty.

Bloch stared, strongly attracted by this dance of light and shadow.

Then he walked over to the edge and peered into the water, making out the blurred outlines of the car that – like a great metallic turtle – sat at the bottom.

Bloch was a very good swimmer, and he had no trouble in diving in and breaking free of the water's surface, not caring to be saddled with breathing equipment. As he pulsed downwards his languorous body experienced a brief revivification. On approaching the saloon he could see that it had no doors, so entry was possible from all sides. Light glowing from the bottom of the pool created a translucent effect. He drifted into the car from the back and stared at the leather seats and dashboard in bemusement.

Meanwhile, Webster had yet to take the plunge; he was sitting on the side of the pool, feet dangling in the shallow end. Oscar in the meantime had still been swimming up and down methodically, his head all the while concealed in the water. As he reached the end of a length he finally came up for air, spotting Bloch as the latter re-surfaced and began climbing up a metal ladder.

'Daniel, you're here! It's funny; I had a feeling you might change your mind ...'

'I was curious about that car.' Their voices were thin in the cavernous space.

Bloch didn't know what else to say, though Oscar's expectant eyes seemed to be waiting for some great illuminating remark from him. Bloch just stood there, shivering slightly. On getting his breath back, he felt the urge to go under once more. As he passed through the car a second time the glove compartment yawned open. He peered inside. A card was dislodged and floated dreamily towards the driver's seat. He reached out and grabbed it and came up for air sluggishly. When he held the card up in the light of the candles the three words that he saw there made his brain turn somersaults.

ART CAN KILL

'Oscar, got to get going,' he spluttered apocalyptically, globules of saliva flying from his lips. Oscar watched him in alarm. 'Got to get going … never should have come … in the first place.' The spittle that was being ejected out of his mouth abruptly reminded Bloch of all the liquids that stirred in tenebrous currents beneath the surface of bodily flesh; a disturbed recognition came that the physical form could revert back to amniotic non-existence, was not invulnerable, was not fixed. Bones and flesh and tendons could be smashed into a jelly, could themselves be liquefied.

Webster, still rooted on the far side of the pool, becoming, as it were, more and more of a permanent fixture there, peered up and asked, 'Do you have to get going now, Bloch?' as though seeking to clear up some elusive mystery.

'Daniel, wait a bit, I've got to talk to you,' said Oscar.

'Do they have hair dryers in this shit-hole?' Bloch demanded, not remotely interested in an answer, throwing out the question just to give himself something tangible to latch onto. Oscar caught up with him, took him by the hand and led him towards the changing rooms while Webster muttered, 'Where are you going? What's going on?' They ignored him, found a wooden bench and planted themselves on it, puddles of water widening around their feet. Oscar studied Bloch's body in fascination, as he had never previously set eyes on its mottled, pallid contours. Bloch seemed to collect himself and took some deep breaths.

'What the hell does it mean … Art can kill?'

Oscar said nothing. He had the impression Bloch was on the point of getting up to leave, so, in reverential tones, he declared, 'That story that you've dreamt up is absolutely great.'

'It wasn't very polite of you to leave the theater like that.'

'I'm sorry. I was feeling excited.'

'So you came for a dip … in this chamber of horrors.'

'The first time in a year I've taken exercise; it's a good sign. I'm so glad you came.'

'So you liked what I wrote?'

'I love it. It's so ... different, from your other stuff. But the resemblances are astonishing. Someone I just met suggested I take up nude modeling, as in the story. And you know about my cat, of course. I wonder how you managed to do that.'

'Do what?'

'Anticipate reality.'

'I wasn't aware of doing anything except making some things up. I thought life modeling would be an interesting idea to explore as it was related to painting. I liked the idea of a cat because I don't have one. And I put some of me into your personality. That's about it. Oscar, I have to tell you something. I don't really want to carry on with that story. It's pissing me off.'

'But – listen – ever since you've started it all these good things have been happening to me. It's true. This man offered me an exhibition.'

'That's ridiculous. What are you trying to say?'

'I don't know. But the fact is – I feel different. There it is. I know it doesn't make sense. But I just feel this story you've dreamt up is a good thing. And when I was reading it at the theater just now I felt plugged into something, like I'd finally come home. Can you see that?'

'There's something wrong with that thing. It's not mine. It's issuing from somewhere else. Some sewer. It's as dysfunctional as that car, water-logged and ruined.'

'It's beautiful.'

'These resemblances you talked about ... they're just coincidental. I wanted to give your life some exoticism, some flavor that was missing. I'm not a magician and I'm not a soothsayer and I can't work miracles.' He paused, and then, struck with a sudden realization, said, 'By the way, has your landlord suddenly turned nice?'

'No.'

'Do you like Wagner?'

'No, I don't.'

'Well, that's a relief.'

Webster finally found them. His eyes were bleary and bloodshot, his face puffed up and purple, and his body, which had the texture of a marshmallow, looked like it was on the verge of collapse. He looked less like someone who has swum one length of a swimming pool than the survivor of a natural catastrophe.

'Hello,' he wheezed. 'Finally had a dip ... water's a bit chilly. That car's freakish. Are you two pals then?'

'No, acquaintances. But we're very close,' Bloch replied cryptically.

# 4

During the next few days Oscar managed to get some modeling work at the Mermaid Academy. They paid fifteen pounds an hour, a figure he considered fantastically generous, considering he didn't really have to do anything. Speaking to Najette about modeling had piqued his interest but reading Bloch's story in the theater's bar had made the idea that much more intriguing. It was as if Bloch's words had lent the whole notion a secret allure, ignited a strange and mysterious flame that was proceeding to hypnotize him.

That morning, while Oscar slept, Bloch sat at his typewriter, staring into space. In the end he had agreed to Oscar's request to continue writing. While he realized that he shouldn't really try and write any more – he was increasingly unnerved by the way in which aspects of the story seemed to be coming true – at the same time he was loath to abandon any creative project. He was curious as to where his mind would lead him, and what further imaginative shards it might throw up.

*Chapter Three : the fabrication of wisdom*

*Oscar Babel, destined for greatness, destined to be admired from afar and from near. It is true that the man ultimately acquired a status which was mythic. In the end he transmuted into a philosopher who was popular, a thinker who was entertaining. His words became honed and weighted, sacred words. People were drawn to him. He spoke to future converts, dined at plush restaurants, enjoyed the attention of certain women. He became, in effect, a spiritual teacher, a guru, and the observations he made were received with an ardor which bordered on idolatry, as he held forth and horsewhipped society for its pursuit of the vacuous. The hotel room he finally embraced became his spiritual headquarters, the shimmering, flickering lectures like no others as the lackeys of the media elected to shut their mouths for once, as they journeyed along the road to enlightenment. Oscar proved fatally effective – he spoke words which made him the blessèd one, making mincemeat of our slumberous, constipated art worlds: corpses kept barely alive with heavy-duty drugs.*

*Inevitably I noticed a certain deterioration in him, of body and personality.*

*Oh, how the shining lights of the past, the noble grand dreams of men and women have been killed by hysterical consumerism and by the noxious oil spill of the ever-expanding, ever-lobotomizing, world-wide spider's web!*

*He was borne aloft on the wings of the mass turbating media, and certain figures that must remain nameless (and were already faceless) accompanied him and facilitated the journey, lubricated it so to speak. And yet*

He stopped, took some deep breaths. He yanked the sheet out of the typewriter and read the text back to himself slowly.

This final fragment was all he could manage. He noticed it was more tautly written than the earlier parts. Was this because the life he here imagined for Oscar was the life he wanted for himself, deep down? Didn't this final fragment reveal the cravings of a closet megalomaniac?

He folded the sheet up carefully, shoved it inside an envelope, sealed it and placed it in a drawer, where he wished it to stay. He got up, stripped and climbed in the shower. But while the water steamed his mind still spun. After drying himself off thoroughly he was back at his desk, still naked. He dispensed with the typewriter and took up a pen and paper.

*16 June*

*Something's happening to me.*

*I'll try and specify exactly what. I've been having hallucinations. In the first I heard a man utter a warning on the radio; in the second one the same warning appeared on a piece of paper which I found while swimming underwater. Is somebody trying to tell me something? I must dress and get ready for lunch. I'm meeting my agent: he wants me to squeeze out another shriveled fetus. He is Barny by name, barmy by nature. Got to pull myself together.*

Bloch drew a line through the words and began again.

*Was I always acting the goat? Or some other animal? Supermarkets and dinner parties and weddings and receptions. They allowed me to showcase my flair for discretion and civility, allowed me to practice the etiquette that shafts sincerity. All lies. Where have I been in my own performance? In the wings, never really daring to emerge with a voice clear and bright. The public me strutted about on stage, making noise, voicing opinions. That me was like a whale producing bloated sounds. But the whale was hiding a poor little salmon struggling to keep up, struggling against the strains in the water and the rhythms that stirred in the wake of the whale's fat fucking bulk.*

*Do some manage to dispense with these masquerades and deceptions? Do they embody constancy? Or does the heart of flux beat for them also, altering the contours and textures of their personalities, reshaping at every moment the essence? Poor humans. God's cocktail of divinity and bestiality hasn't been mixed very well. The earth cools. Time to bake a cake.*

Bloch crossed another line through the text and got up. He went into the kitchen and poured himself a whiskey. He wished the evening was upon London. What if life was an eternal dance? What if London was lit by a million candles at night-time?

*My mind's filled with hot air, so why don't I rise like a balloon? Into a place of light. Where clouds beckon. Am I dead or alive? How easily the paths of pleasure and pain entwine.*
*An almighty fart echoes throughout history.*
*Where am I?*

\*

In one of the large classrooms of the Mermaid Academy Oscar waited patiently. He heard the shuffling of the students as they walked in and took their places. There were seven men and two women, quiet and respectful.

He studied his pale flesh, studied its sinuous texture in silence. He watched himself with a new awareness; his limbs, white knuckles, and tender, sunken feet, struck him with their elegance and purity. Had he until now ever taken the time to study himself, to get to know the topography of his own body? It seemed so odd that he should regard as unfamiliar this frame that housed his consciousness, his mind.

A tall, slightly authoritarian woman touched him on the shoulder, signaling for him to take his place on a raised dais. He did so, surveying the students hurriedly, knowing this might be the only opportunity for awhile to study them. There were two women veering toward middle-age. One looked quite worldly, dressed in sleek black leather trousers and a loose lilac blouse, a thin silk scarf flung around her neck. The other was a nervous, fumbling creature, forever checking the pockets of her jacket, feeling for the hard metal of her car keys. The majority of the men wore beards and looked incurably earnest. A youngish man with orange-bleached hair seemed to stand apart.

Now Oscar tried to relinquish the normal trappings of consciousness and become motionless and soundless, a doll poised before dissecting eyes.

The scratching of pens, as the students began to draw him with nibs dipped in a mixture of black ink and water, seemed magnified. To his surprise he felt neither embarrassed nor uncomfortable. He had expected to find being watched would be arousing in some way; instead it was wholly neutral. He began to have the curious sensation that he was not really there, that reality was at some nameless remove and he was gravitating towards an external observation of himself, as he was himself observed by the artists, like mirrors reflecting mirrors into infinity....

He thought about his days and nights at the cinema, the sense in which he had been dying there, slipping further and further into twilight. His skin registered the subtle movements of air around him; he felt the breath created in the turning of the students' sketch pages. He felt at once anarchically alive. Taking off his clothes had also peeled away a layer of obfuscation from his mind.

Afterwards the tall woman told him he was welcome to come back – she was happy with his first session; he had kept sufficiently still, she said, and he had an interesting physique. For an instant he thought she might have been flirting with him.

As Oscar left the building a small man in blue overalls walked up and grabbed him by the arm. The man was clutching a folded miniature tripod screwed onto a digital recording microphone. Oscar's immediate thought was that he was being arrested.

'Excuse me,' the stranger said – his words broken by a hacking cough – 'are you one of the life models?'

'Only just,' said Oscar politely, disengaging himself.

'Oh good. I wonder, would you be at all interested in answering a few questions about modeling? I'm finishing a small documentary on the subject for Art Cable. You wouldn't have to do much. Just speak to the camera for a few minutes. The questions would be asked and then edited out. We would only see your answers' – he broke off to cough – 'to the questions, as it were. They would be interspersed with footage of students drawing and sketching. You'd get paid two hundred pounds. Please say yes; no one else seems terribly interested. They're a shy bunch these models. You wouldn't think so, would you? And I mean to say, it's good money.'

Oscar heard himself ask, 'How about making it two hundred and fifty pounds?'

'What? Two hundred and fifty? It's my own money making this happen, you know. Let me see. That's the lights and film stock. The make-up, the studio hire ... down in King's Cross, and the cameras. Payment for the crew. It was meant to be a modest little piece on a neglected subject. You see, I see possibilities in what others consider boring. I've made pieces on fun fairs, doll's houses, glass blowing, even the humble household bidet. But fifty pounds extra. That's an increase of twenty-five per-cent. Not that I'm a mathematician; no, I'm an artist myself, who cares about me though? They all get the grapes, and I get the pips. I've been making documentaries for twelve years; where's it got me? What I wanted was to design bicycles. God knows what the hell happened there. Still, mustn't grumble. Fifty pounds you say?'

Oscar nodded, exuding the serenity of indifference. This was all it took to unnerve the little man, who consequently agreed to the increased sum. And they shook hands.

'By the way, the name's Albert Lush. I knew I could count on you.'

Despite the fact that Oscar had agreed to be interviewed only in exchange for more cash Lush interpreted his assent as empirical evidence of another's belief in him as a documentary maker. Lush said, 'Can you come to the studios ... at 10 am on Monday 22 June? The whole thing shouldn't take more than an hour. Sasha will make you up and everything. Just sound informed when you speak. By the way, sorry about this cough of mine, but there's nothing I can do about it. This cough has made me a failure. I've had this cough for five years; it's ruined my lower spine. It's ruined my relationships with women; even dogs hate me. I've tried everything to get rid of it: sun, antibiotics, acupuncture, herbal medicine, saunas, syrups, eucalyptus oil, health farms, colonic irrigation, tranquilizers, homeopathy, osteopathy; nothing works. Oh well. See you soon.'

He hurried off with the nervous air of someone running for a bus. Oscar stared at him as he receded. It suddenly occurred to him that he didn't know where the television studios were. He was about to walk away when the little man rushed back breathlessly, placed a card in Oscar's hands without a word and bolted.

It was quite late when he got home. Dove was asleep in her basket, her small nose and mouth protruding from under crumpled blankets. From below the thunderous sound of the overture to *The Flying Dutchman* threatened to dislodge the floorboards. Oscar shifted the clothes and crumpled sketchpads that had piled up on the bed onto his desk. He switched on a bedside lamp; its light immediately made everything a little more palatable.

As he was preparing to boil some water there was a tentative knock at the door. He threw a tea-towel over the basket and the cat, and then Mr Grindel was upon him. He noticed that the additional epidermis of his overcoat was missing. This was the first time he had ever seen Grindel without it. The music continued blaring and swelling wildly.

'No coat, Mr. Grindel?'

By way of reply, Grindel raised his arm and started moving it this way and that, his mouth pulled up in a proud, noble arc as he imagined himself on the conductor's podium, heir to the musical colossi of the past.

'No, it's at the cleaners,' he said, still conducting. 'It needs mending, anyway. I daresay I'll have to think about getting it stitched up; there's a few pockets there where nature didn't intend, if you get my drift. By the way, thanks for the rent. Much obliged.'

This wasn't like Grindel – to express gratitude.

'I'm having a little soup, Mr. Babel. Do you want some? A few croutons thrown in to some vegetable stock and some bread as a humble side dish. Modest fare but made with love.'

This also wasn't like Grindel – to offer hospitality.

'Do you know much about Wagner, Mr Babel? He is ... what's the word? It'll come to me. I'm heating the soup now; there isn't much, but there's enough for two, if you know what I mean.'

But at that point, with fatal bad timing, the cat jumped out of her basket, scattering the tea-towel, and landed near Grindel's feet. For a moment Oscar stared helplessly, then seized with panic, shouted, 'What gives you the right to come in here whenever you like? It's outrageous.' Oscar didn't know what he was saying; he just wanted to generate enough noise to scare Grindel into leaving. 'And another thing, what about the peeling wallpaper, what about my mattress, I have to sleep on a piece of foam that wouldn't support a snail. Why are you so useless?'

As he went on Oscar picked the cat up and returned her to the basket, as if he could still salvage the situation. Throughout Oscar's tirade Grindel had smiled like an inebriated priest, his face swelling with absurd benevolence, discernible in blubbery, upturned lips and stupid, bovine eyes. When Oscar finished he waited a moment before setting out his case in a reasonable voice.

'Yes, yes, we must do something about this, Mr. Babel. It won't do at all. I have been lazy. This might have been connected with my cousin's recent visit. But may I say how much I love your kitten; it is so small. Just wait there a moment. I'll get her some chocolate. We'll have some with the soup.'

This wasn't like Grindel – to listen to criticism, express affection and choose to ignore his own house rule about pets. In fact this was so unlike Grindel that Oscar wondered whether it really was Grindel. He half-expected to find out that the man currently shuffling out of the room was an impostor, impersonating Grindel through some unfathomable sleight-of-hand, while his real landlord sat bound and gagged in his stifling maisonette. It was true then: another feature of Bloch's story had found its counterpart in reality – Grindel had turned into a nice human being ...

He re-appeared a few minutes later with a bowl, in which brick-like chunks of chocolate sat. He placed the bowl near the basket, then held it close to the cat.

'Go on, cat, try it,' he intoned, trying to sound inviting. Dove peered into the bowl, licked at a bar, nibbled at a corner reluctantly. Without warning, Grindel picked up a piece, growled, 'What's the matter, puss, not gourmet enough for you? This stuff's Swiss,' and thrust the chocolate violently into her mouth, pulling on her tail at the same time. She screeched in terror and vaulted off.

So Grindel's kindness proved to be short-lived.

But then as Oscar stroked and comforted her, the landlord emerged out of his shell of cruelty, looking faintly stunned, a stranger to himself and his own mind. The last few seconds were erased by virtue of some kind of amnesia, and he smiled once again, for all the world the spirit of saintly kindness. Was the old, shambling landlord teetering on a schizoid knife edge, manifesting opposing personalities, like an actor whose roles have usurped a continuous self?

'She'll have some later, Mr Grindel,' Oscar muttered, 'that's all right. Thanks for everything – really. Another time for the soup maybe, but right now I'm very tired. I know you understand.'

'I feel like I understand many, many things, Mr Babel. Many, many, many things.'

'Right. Actually, you don't seem quite yourself, Mr. Grindel.'

There was a meaningful, pregnant silence, broken at last by puppy-like gurglings; then his voice assumed an idiotically infantile pitch, 'I must confess – there is – this thing has happened ... with a cleaning lady. She is ... she reminds me so much of my armchair. The other day she trimmed my toenails for me. I felt like I was in heaven. Deep down, don't we all just want to be loved?'

'Yes, I suppose we do ... I do ...' Oscar said, his voice trailing off.

His landlord allotted himself a moment in which to look triumphant. Then, without another word, he walked out and shut the door with greatly exaggerated consideration.

Obviously, Oscar thought, Grindel's metamorphosis had taken place independently of Bloch's story, the transformation of his landlord couldn't have had anything to do with Bloch's imagination. Apparently Grindel was in love. And yet – Oscar couldn't help asking – would Grindel have changed if the story hadn't been written?

He closed his eyes, deeply bewildered, and the cat, deeply traumatized, slowly clambered into his lap. After some time it managed a muted purr.

*

Lunch with Barny Crane, his agent, had lasted for six-and-a-half hours so that it was evening by the time Bloch got back, fairly drunk. Between them they had demolished five bottles of Merlot. Barny was a short, corpulent man, a formidable connoisseur of wine, who had a habit in conversation of blowing his cheeks out after making a significant observation, in the manner of a visual exclamation mark.

Bloch struggled with the keys for a moment and then the front door yawned open. In the living room sheets of paper and postcards were swirling everywhere, spinning in a dance of fractured form. He had left the windows open and a strong wind was blowing, tearing sheets from tables, sending them shivering into space where momentarily they were held aloft in a vortex of motion. He shut the windows in a hurry and at once everything fell to the floor, thus revealing the extent of the room's disorder.

Opened bottles of wine were waiting to be consumed but they were destined for neglect. Piles of books sat in armchairs. Coffee cups nurtured liquids that were on the point of becoming solids.

Bloch made a basic attempt to order the chaos, picking up the sheets and cards, adjusting a bundle of papers here, wiping a surface there. But these half-hearted maneuvers only brought home how mammoth an undertaking it would be to really tidy the room. He went to the kitchen, drained three glasses of water in quick succession and made a pot of coffee to sober up with. He took a cup into the living room and slumped into one of the armchairs.

The shrill sound of his phone startled him. He staggered over to it, rehearsing speech with a few random words. He didn't sound too bad: he would be quite coherent.

'Yes, hello.'

'Hello, Daniel, it's Samuel.'

The voice was oddly familiar, yet Bloch wouldn't allow himself to realize who it was on the other end of the line.

'Samuel who?'

'Samuel. Your father.'

There was a pause. It was true then – joyous contractions scurried along the cranium of consciousness, but before he had a chance to savor them Bloch forced himself to quash his excitement as he remembered what his father had done to him.

'Where are you?' asked Bloch.

'What does it matter where I am? How are things?'

'Things? I don't know ... what ... how do I answer a question like that ... where do I start? Whose things?'

'Daniel, don't complicate everything. This is hard enough ... for both of us.'

'That's true. It's excruciating.'

The cigar-seasoned voice at the other end now started holding forth heartily, but there was a certain aftertaste of uncertainty in the voice, a hesitance which qualified his zeal.

'I have to tell you about this recurring dream. I'm asleep. A sound wakes me up. I get up and I hear it again. It's coming from the kitchen. Anyway, I go inside and instead of finding the uninvited guest, a burglar, I see two birds who've decided to pop in – a blackbird and a robin. One of them starts flapping about like a lunatic and makes his getaway, but the other takes it into its head to waddle into the bedroom – '

'Dad, where's this leading?'

'Just be patient, you'll see. So this robin wanders in and sits there, won't move. I try everything to shift it, but it won't budge. Then it starts to shit everywhere: on my floor, the bed, my jackets and ties. Pretty soon the whole room is covered in this bird's shit. The shit just seems to keep piling up. I have to leave the house and get some air. The next thing I know I'm dancing with this gorgeous belly dancer, having a great time. But then this bird shows up, and starts shitting everywhere again. Now, you tell me, what the hell does that mean?'

'Dad, why did you ring me?'

'I rang you ... I rang you ... because I want you to forgive me.'

There was silence, the vacuum of an unoccupied telephone line. Bloch tried his best to digest these details, to imprint the nature of the dream, as it had been told in all its oddity, on his mind, but everything was taking flight. His memory couldn't gain a foothold; unnamable vultures pecked at his awareness, made facts fade, made the essence of what had passed between them vague. He had been so unprepared, so unsuspecting of his caller's identity.

'Forgive you? You ... pop up after all this time. Let's talk about you. Are you well? Are you married? Have you found any more wives to seduce?'

'Listen, Danny. Natalie seduced me. I'm more sorry about that than you'll ever know, but it happened. I'm asking for forgiveness, humbly, as a man ...'

'Are you a man or a rat?'

Even in the middle of Bloch's effort to pull out melodramatic cards he realized some mechanism of defense had shut down, a pattern of resistance had resolved into one of acquiescence.

'Daniel. I'm a man – just about – not a rodent, but I'm scared I won't be around much longer. From where I crawl the sunset takes on worrying implications. As for Natalie, she's no longer a part of my life; she left me, and I'm here for you, if you'll have me back. Listen to me, I sound like I'm proposing. Danny, the thing is, in all this mess ... that affair ... Natalie ... spoke so fondly of you, did you know that? She kept saying no one else could touch you, was as interesting, as funny ...'

'Listen, Dad, I don't really want a character reference from my ex-wife relayed through my ex-father.'

'What does that mean?'

A note of grim anxiety had crept into the croaky voice on the other end.

'What does ex-father mean?'

'It means, old boy, that I don't really feel a phone call can change that much. You killed me. Both of you.'

'But I want to make it up to you, Daniel. I can make it up to you. I'm a better person now, I really am. Can't I see you? It's not right, father and son not talking like this.'

Bloch was aggressive once more, full of rage, his fury triggered by what he took to be a sanctimonious final remark.

'Whose fault is that? Did you ever take a look at yourself, once? Did you? Have you managed to acquire even a scrap of self-knowledge? Look at your life, and tell me what you see – no, I'll tell you: an adolescent chasing women a quarter of his age, diving into an ice pool every day to prove he should have been a bullfighter. People like you shouldn't be allowed to have children; you're too irresponsible. People like you should be made to take an offspring test and once you'd failed it, be sent packing to an island free of people since you just seem to bring disaster on everyone you come in contact with. I expect buildings to topple when you walk past them, dogs to go mad when you feed them, and children to cry when you play with them.'

During this Samuel Bloch felt pain shoot through him, but he bore it, determined to take the punishment his son was meting out, even if it stopped his heart from beating.

'Have you finished? Well, can I just say something? Can I? At the risk of boring you? I can't promise the same colorful images but – '

'You won't bore me; that's something you never do.'

'Well then ... listen, Danny, when you get to a certain age, as I have done, when you get to a certain age ... the personality hardens. It sets. That's where I am now. It's too late for me to change, too late ... I can't wipe out my faults, but I'm trying to make amends ... and afterwards, I might not be able to, if you know what I mean ... I just want to call on you ... I just want to see my son, the son I've thought about, who I've missed every day for the last five years.'

Bloch was suddenly crying – his father's words were unleashing whips which pelted his tear ducts.

There was another long silence. Through the glassy membrane speech came falteringly, painfully.

'Five years ... that's a long time, isn't it? Where did all it go? Sucked into a black hole, I suppose. All right, see me, if your heart's set on it. See me! .... But we'll talk about it later ... I can't talk now ... I just can't.'

He quietly, gently returned the phone to its cradle, walked over to the kitchen and poured himself more coffee. He took a big gulp and sat back shakily in his armchair.

Hours went by. Hours passed in meditation, in thinking about his father, recalling his strange character, the sense that he had never really known him, always perceived him as someone who may or may not have been his father, who had gradually to become his father all over again each time he rejoined the household – after one of his frequent periods of absence.

Then the phone interrupted him once more, inviting him to assume his life was further to have its shape changed.

'Daniel.'

'Oscar, what's up?'

'About ten minutes ago Mr. Grindel offered me soup and didn't mind Dove, though he did pull her tail ...'

'Who the fuck is Dove?'

'My cat. He offered her some chocolate. All right, it's kind of demented, but it's something wouldn't you say? What do you think?'

'What are you crapping on about now?'

'Oh, nothing, forget it,' Oscar said in a hurry, suddenly resolved not to mention the story, given the irritation in Bloch's voice. Rapidly coming up with another line, he continued, 'Can I tell you about this woman I've met? You'd like her. She's a brilliant painter. I saw these two nudes, in one the woman sat or rather melted into the sofa. The texture was so polished, she must have gone over the colors a hundred times, smoothing them down with a palette knife, so I didn't see the strokes. Beautiful. I feel my luck's changing. Suddenly this woman's crept into my life … the modeling, the prospect of painting again. It's fantastic. I wanted to talk about her before but didn't get round to it, and I thought talking about it might spoil it, make it too real in my mind or something, when it's still really just a day dream. But how should I go about things?'

Bloch was relieved Oscar wasn't still pressing him to go on with the story, and was determined not to mention the aborted third chapter he had started that morning.

'Are you there, Daniel?'

At last he said, 'Yes, I'm here. What was the question? Oh yes, women. I don't know; perhaps it's best to be subtle. Women are stronger than us. Since they're the life givers. The feminine spring of creativity gushes from them … so don't bung that spring up with words. Let her find the secret places naturally; don't feel you have to point out either hers or yours all the time. Don't offer it all on a plate. Anyway, that's my opinion. That's coming from someone who's made a mess of love, by the way. All right? Satisfied now? I've got some things to mull over.'

Oscar said nothing. Bloch's remarks seemed so important that he wished he'd recorded them but the fixity that he craved was unreachable, as words scuttled and hurried away into the dim caverns of memory.

# 5

Lilliana had to do some shopping off Tottenham Court Road on Saturday morning. She wanted to buy peat and plant food and camomile tea and almond oil. The particular shop she needed was tucked behind murky alleyways and side streets. She passed a Tapas bar, and then a barber's, and then a shop called "Lobgot", whose purpose was extremely difficult to ascertain. As she walked, on a pitifully inadequate pavement, unfriendly looking men pushed against her, repeatedly failing to apologize.

The side streets had the shape of jagged arcs and curves. A garage, its door opened, invited her to look in, which she did, catching a glimpse there of an old man in greasy overalls bending painfully as he spat on his shoes. As she watched him, an unfriendly eye leered at her. She moved on.

She started thinking about her life. The shop took up most of it, she reflected. It was all very well to think that she could brighten up people's living rooms by selling them roses, but she perceived now in all of this a fatal seed of the inconsequential that she had herself planted, now flourishing unstoppably. It seemed to her then that she had spent her whole life in being good, observing rules, (another man brushed against her; she looked at him pointedly, but he didn't see), and trying to lift others with her enthusiasm. The reason she had opened the flower shop was because she wanted to live among color. But among all those stems and petals where had her own happiness been? What had she really craved? To be well thought of? To be secure? To be loved? Perhaps ...

In the time it had taken her to get from the underground station to this street she had passed from contentment to mild despair.

She stopped suddenly, struck by a tattered poster that hung on a black door. She studied the words inscribed in a decaying Gothic script.

## MR. SOPSO: FORTUNE TELLING, TAROT READINGS, ETC.

Obeying some half-forgotten impulse, she gave the door a slight nudge, and to her surprise it yawned open easily. She could see some unlit steps leading to a basement. The last few steps vanished into a black cavity. All the signs suggested she should leave, but, resisting her fears, she began a careful descent, guided by the light of her cellular phone.

At the end of the stairs she came to another door, in green. She nudged at this and found it locked. She knocked, feebly and then more vigorously. From within sounds stirred. After what seemed like minutes a man with a foreign-looking face appeared and showed her in. She noticed her heart was beating very quickly.

She was in a large room. It was slightly surprising to find that its subterranean setting had not rendered it ugly and dangerous. In fact, in addition to being big the room was distinctly inviting.

The man smiled at her, informing her that Mr Sopso would be down shortly. He disappeared through a silk curtain which fluttered opposite the door by which she had entered. She found an armchair upholstered in rich red velvet and surveyed her surroundings, feeling a little less nervous.

Hardly an inch of the room wasn't taken up with clutter. Incense burned steadily and it was only now that Lilliana noticed the strange music playing: guttural chanting of some kind. She was intrigued by the innumerable objects scattered here and there: baskets of fruit, pairs of reading glasses and pince-nez, miniature bottles of vodka, broad-brimmed empty vases painted in serene colors, decanters and silver letter openers, wide, half- melted candles. There was too much information to assimilate; the curious chanting was ever-present in her consciousness, yet at the same time faint, as if it came from behind the walls.

A man dressed in a purple smoking jacket walked in through the silk curtain. It was hard to tell his age. He could have been anything between thirty and fifty. He was wearing an ill-fitting toupee that appeared to be held in place very uncertainly and his lips were raised in a half-smile which vanished as soon as it was scrutinized. He held a coffee cup and smoked a pipe, the aromatic smell of which joined that of the incense. The man found a large mat, slumped himself down on it and beckoned for Lilliana to do likewise. She joined him, cross-legged. He stared at her until she began to feel uncomfortable.

'Something to drink? I'm on Lebanese coffee. We have fruit teas, Indian teas, whatever you like.' He spoke in a very high-pitched, small voice.

Lilliana was unsure of what to say or do or even think. She suddenly felt a wild desire to laugh but bit her lip savagely to stop herself. She looked around once more, trying to adjust to the baroque atmosphere. Mr. Sopso produced a small fork and began to tinker with his pipe.

'Anything tickle your fancy? A drink?'

'Some tea, please.'

'Orange blossom, peppermint, ginger, darjeeling?'

'Orange blossom sounds nice. I don't think I've ever had that.'

Mr. Sopso called out a name and the servant appeared noiselessly. Mr. Sopso spoke some words in a foreign tongue with difficulty and turned back to Lilliana.

'Are you comfortable on the floor?'

'Yes.'

'Good.'

A minute passed. The chanting – a richly mournful male voice – was now held on one note for an endless time.

Mr. Sopso again tinkered with his pipe, and Lilliana's eye followed in turn the candles and vases, wondering what on earth she was doing here.

'How much do you charge, by the way?' Lilliana demanded in a slightly shrill voice.

'Fifteen pounds for half-an-hour's read; thirty for an hour.'

Mr Sopso tried to smile and look at her at the same time. As a result his face disintegrated into tiny triangles of flesh. His eyes became spots lost within creases. The cracked smile suggested that things were somehow not quite right, neither with himself nor with his establishment. Lilliana was trying to find the right moment in which to announce her departure. At last she spurted out, 'You know, I was thinking, perhaps I'd better ...'

But before she could finish the servant came in with the tea on a silver tray. The arrival of the tea made it harder for her to say she was going. The servant put the tray down and left after adjusting a picture frame. Mr. Sopso poured Lilliana her tea, but she had decided she wasn't going to drink it after all, in case it was drugged.

'Now... what's your name, by the way?'

'Lilliana.'

'Lilliana. Charming.'

He produced some tarot cards from his jacket's inner pocket. They promptly fell all over the floor, and as he picked them up he muttered, 'As above, so below.' He handed her the reassembled pack, walked over to a stereo unit and the chanting suddenly stopped. Lilliana instantly felt better, as if the music's cessation had relieved her of a physical pain.

'I want you to shuffle the cards, and while you're doing that I want you to think about the problems of your life, and what it is you'd like to learn about the future or the present. When you're ready I'll take the cards and lay them out in a spread.'

She began the shuffle, long and drawn out since she hoped to regain her composure during it. He watched her for a moment and then turned his attention to the tapestries, focusing on one in particular. In it a woman knelt by a stream, the curves of her hair blending with the water's waves. When he looked back to Lilliana some barrier which had been obscuring his view of her lifted. He had been too distracted earlier to notice the texture of her strawberry-colored hair, her white, unblemished skin, and her youth.

She handed him the cards when she was ready. Ten were plucked from the top of the pack and laid out into an H-shape, remaining face down. Mr Sopso's hand moved towards the central card of the H and flipped it over. On the reverse side there was a picture of eight coins.

'Ah, I see that you're a banker, or are connected with finance in some way,' he began confidently.

'No, I'm afraid I'm not connected with finance. I own a flower shop.'

'I see. But money is exchanged, isn't it, when the flowers are sold? Let me see now, let me see; let's have a look at the next card, which will describe the influences around you.'

His hand moved towards the card to the immediate left of the one he had just picked. The picture on it was of the hanged man.

'Now ... this card tells me that it probably isn't the right time to make any changes in your life. I can see you're quite a cautious person. Am I right?'

'Yes, I suppose so.'

Mr Sopso beamed, immensely relieved.

'In addition I'd say that you are quite sensitive to beautiful things – witness your love of flowers.'

'Yes, I suppose. Do I have to confirm the accuracy of everything you say?'

'Only if I ask you to.'

The next card had a picture of a red devil.

'You feel trapped, but there might be a way out. Am I right?'

'But Mr Sopso, isn't this a bit vague; I mean, doesn't everyone feel trapped? I want something more ...'

In a hurry he came up with, 'Love is just around the corner. You will meet a man … a theatrical man …. with green eyes. He is adventurous, but he has a sad heart, and he has very little money. But I know that you don't care about things like that; you're not attracted to the external but to what's inside and you have made the heart your own special territory.  But you must be alert and watchful otherwise you'll miss this opportunity.'

'What kind of opportunity?'

'The cards don't tell me everything! Now wait a minute; did I see an Empress just now? Where's it gone? Isn't your best friend named Gilbert?'

'No.'

'Geoffrey, Peter, Bartholomew?'

'No.'

'Harold, Cameron, Ronald?'

'No.'

'Well, then, let's move on. Obviously that was a little off the beaten track. We have to find the motorway again, as it were. But there aren't many men with green eyes, and you have green fingers, haven't you; I mean ...'

He managed a short, pathetic chuckle.

Something clicked abruptly in Lilliana's mind. How was it she hadn't seen it before?

'You don't have a clue about what you're talking about, do you?'

'Wait, wait, the cards are clearing up. You're at a crossroads, and you have to make a decision. A new business opportunity presents itself, but you have to be assertive and take on forces ...'

'You're no more a fortune teller than I'm a brain surgeon.'

There was a lull and then, suddenly, he gave up the struggle, his shoulders slumped, his head hung, and he muttered in a dirge-like undertone, 'You're right.'

She was surprised by the speed with which the confession came.

There wasn't even the pretense of a denial. She stared into his sad eyes. He appeared completely vulnerable, a fact that touched her, despite his mendacity. He's lost, she thought. She glanced round at all the bric-a-brac. She wondered if it was all there to create an air of exotic authority he himself conspicuously lacked. But she wasn't going to stay to humiliate him. She stood up decisively.

'Can I just explain? Won't you stay for a minute longer so I can explain?'

She had to admit she was curious. What could have driven him to take up something for which he was so obviously unsuited?

'Please stay. I must explain.'

She felt herself beginning to weaken.

'Only for a minute.'

'Well, then, won't you sit down for a minute as well. Please?'

She moved some papers from one of the armchairs and perched on the arm, smoothing her skirt out.

'You're right, I'm not really a fortune teller. To cut a long story short, I used to be an art dealer. I got arrested when they found out I was selling fakes. I didn't know they were fakes; the paintings were supplied by my partner. He was buying them from small time artists and getting me to sell them to clients for vast sums. When it came out they weren't genuine there was a big hullabaloo. He ended up in Shanghai, and became a pimp. And I ended up in jail for three months. They thought I was selling these fakes knowingly. I couldn't get any work in the art world again after I got out. So I tried my hand at bookselling. That went nowhere. Then I became a gardener but discovered I had an allergy to soil. The skin on my hands would start peeling. So I ended up fortune telling when a gypsy on Water-loo Bridge told me I had a gift. I worked it all out from a book called *The Book of Light and Sight*. I've tried to make it cosy in here.'

'Why are you telling me all this?'

'Well, I felt I owed you an explanation.'

'Yes, I suppose you did. I'll be on my way then. Don't worry, I won't publicize the fact that you're a charlatan.'

Despite Lilliana's obvious reluctance to stay a moment longer something about her urged him to persist, to bare his soul. It was in her eyes – a serenity that spelled tolerance. He felt he could talk to her and she would listen, if only she would first stay.

'Wait! Please, just a moment more. I have to tell you something; actually I have to ask you something. I can see you're a good sport.'

'Yes, but I'm not mad as well.'

He winced like someone with toothache.

'Look, just listen to what I have to say and then I promise if you don't want to help me, I'll understand.'

'All right,' she said at last.

'The thing is, I'm, how shall I say, I ... enjoy the company of men. The man who let you in – Milo – he's my boyfriend. My parents – who've been living in Germany for the last ten years – don't know this, and they keep saying, when am I going to meet a nice girl? They want me to provide them with grandchildren. The onus is on me because my brother's a priest and he's not the marrying type. But neither am I. Incidentally, they see fortune telling in the same light as Satanism. They're both very religious, especially my dad.'

'Do they know you went to jail?'

'No, of course not; I told them I went to Ireland.'

'So, what are you getting at?'

'Well, because they keep banging on about my finding a wife, the other day, just to keep them off my back, I said I'd got engaged. I didn't think there was any problem as they're over in Germany and after some time had passed I could say the engagement fell through.'

'And you haven't got engaged?'

'No. You see, in a few weeks' time they're meant to be taking a trip to Toronto, and now they've decided to break the journey in London to meet my fiancée. I never imagined they'd do that. But I have no fiancée to present them with.'

'Don't tell me you want me to pretend to be your fiancée?'

'Yes. Just for one evening. That's all.'

She was about to say, 'No', but resisted, and, finding herself caught up in his strange history, pressed further into it by asking, 'Why don't you just ask a friend to pretend?'

'I only have one female friend and I told her my parents know all about my sexual persuasions, so to ask her to be my wife-to-be might prove difficult.'

'Why did you tell her your parents know all about your sexual persuasions?'

'So she didn't think I was a coward, because I hadn't confronted them with the truth.'

'Couldn't you tell your parents you broke off the engagement, now, rather than later?'

'I told them I was madly in love.'

Lilliana took a deep breath, her eyes widening in disbelief.

'As far as I can see your life's just a tissue of lies.'

'Yes, but it's my way of dealing with things. It's because I've always had to hide the truth from my parents, so I started hiding it from everyone else as well, even when it didn't need hiding. You don't know what they're like.'

'Who?'

'My parents. They're monsters, irrational, hysterical.'

'And you want me to spend an evening with them?'

'They're very sweet really.'

'But why do you have to lie to them? Just tell them the truth.'

'If I did that they wouldn't support me anymore. They give me money, you see.'

'Oh ... I'm really sorry about your problems, Mr Sopso, but I'm afraid the answer's no.'

'Really? But I mean to say, I'll pay you and everything.'

'I'm sorry, but I don't really want your money.'

'But I'm poor, I don't have any money.'

'Well, then, how are you going to give me any?'

'That's not what I mean; I mean this is a big deal for me. I'm making a sacrifice; can't you do the same?'

'This is ridiculous, Mr Sopso; I don't know you, and I don't owe you anything either.'

'But I'm not asking for an arm and a leg; I just want you to dress up and have fun.'

'I'm sorry but ....'

She hesitated.

'What is it?' he asked.

'Will this really help your relationship with your parents, will it really solve the problems you have with them? Somehow I don't think so. It's time to confront the problems head on. Goodbye. Good luck.'

She began to move towards the door. He scrambled to his feet and hurried after her, racking his brains, trying to come up with a convincing argument.

'Look ... don't I count for anything in your eyes ... I mean ... just because we've only just met, don't I have needs? What I mean is – yes, I've got it now – would it be different if I were your best friend? Yes, probably, but why's that? Can't you imagine we are friends? I mean friends are sometimes strangers, so what's the difference really? We just have to be strangers who are sometimes friends. I mean, you can see that I'm all right. And then we might even become friends, if you gave it a chance. In a year from now we might be best friends, laughing about the circumstances of how we met, of how you pretended to be my fiancée. Why should a stranger's need be any less important than someone you know? You see, if I tell them the truth my name will be mud, and that will be the end as far as my parents are concerned. Won't you help me?'

A pause and then, 'Please?'

Her mind drifted. Surprisingly, his words had touched her. Would it really be so bad after all? Might it not actually be quite amusing to pretend to be his fiancée? The extraordinary room was magnetizing, difficult to break away from. She realized it was fear that was stopping her, fear in the abstract, not fear of Mr Sopso, but the fear that attaches itself to an unfamiliar experience. Even though she didn't really trust Mr Sopso and knew he was a liar at the same time his pathetic request had triggered some need in her to abandon common sense, had awoken a long-forgotten desire to experience life as a carnival free of conformity.

'How much will you pay me?' she asked rather solemnly. She was not really interested in a figure; she only asked the question because at that moment it seemed like the thing to do. Mr. Sopso immediately recovered some of his energy and enthusiasm.

'Two hundred pounds.'

'Two hundred. That's quite a lot. Make it one-hundred-and- fifty, I don't want to rob you.'

'Are you sure? You'll really do this for me?' He couldn't refrain from dancing a little jig. But his toupee fell off. As he scrambled around for it, Lilliana exploded with laughter.

Ignoring her laughter, too happy to let it worry him, he babbled, 'This is great. You've saved my bacon.'

Suddenly, his head snapped up, as if some great thought had just been born.

'To show you how grateful I am – I want to give you something in addition to money. See, I don't want this to be just a transaction – I want this to be special, personal. I want you to see I'm really a good egg.'

He took her hand, and led her through the silk curtain; his happiness was infectious and she wished he would perform his dance again. They climbed a flight of stairs and, passing through another door, found themselves in a large room full of statues and rails of clothing and tailors' dummies. The room felt very different to the one downstairs; it might have sprung from another century. After rummaging around in a mass of fused- together junk Mr Sopso pulled out a dusty painting, with an intricate golden frame. He blew on it and dust fizzed into the air.

'Here it is; I want you to have this. This is so right for you.'

He wiped the canvas with a cloth and she made out a consoling image in the dim light of the room's oil lamps. Two saints were standing side by side, one clutching a lily in a pose of fragile resignation, and the other reading from a book of scriptures. The figure on the left was dressed in humble robes, while his companion wore a resplendent cope and vestments that obscured his feet. They seemed weightless, incorporeal.

'This is one of my favorites. It's an exact copy of a panel from an altarpiece by Fra Angelico. *St. Dominic and St. Nicholas of Bari.* I don't know who did it, but it's beautiful, isn't it? And very very old. I've had it for many years, as the dust suggests. It was given to me by an Armenian bishop in San Lazzaro, a little island off Venice, in return for saving his life by slapping him on the back after he'd swallowed a chicken bone. So now it's yours because you saved my life. You can see St. Dominic is holding a lily. I think it pleases you, doesn't it? I want you to have it.'

Lilliana suspected that this story was another of his fabrications but she was too drawn by the painting to say anything, so she just stared into it. The saints' exquisite poise, the shimmering, golden texture of the background, the beautiful lily that was sunken, yet illumined with life. For once at least his instincts had turned out to be uncannily accurate; the work was mysteriously enticing, and as she stared into it, contemplated it with quiet ardor, she seemed to see within those forms and lines and colors the unravelling of some unnamed enigma, and its resolution deposited her into a place of baffling peace.

'I want you to have it,' he repeated.

'But why?'

'There isn't always a why about these things.'

He found some paper, wrapped it carefully around the frame and canvas, secured it with string, and handed the painting to her. She raised both hands in a gesture of polite refusal. He mimicked the gesture with his one free hand.

She gave in. It was no good. She had fallen in love with it.

*

That morning Najette was sketching Oscar. She was using compressed charcoal, creating deep black shadows from which the white of the paper peered. The charcoal felt tender and cool in her fingers. Oscar sat in an armchair, his face turned in profile, staring out of Najette's bay window.

By now he had left the cinema, and didn't miss it in the slightest. It had been quite easy to hand in his notice. He wondered why the prospect had seemed so daunting back in May.

He had brought Dove with him; she was wandering among baskets full of dirty laundry. Every now and then he glanced over to her and then turned back to the window. He found his cat's presence comforting. She provided visible evidence that his life was improving – she was like his talisman.

Outside the day was overcast and the clouds were grey and diseased. But Oscar felt very comfortable, unmoving, scrutinized, silent. Though he couldn't see Najette's face as she worked he sensed that she had altered in some way as her hands made intermittent contact with the paper through the charcoal. In her embrace of art, her fluid movements, and finally her proximity Oscar found delicious arousal, golden provocation.

'Am I allowed to talk?' he asked quietly.

'Afraid not. That's the rule.'

She applied a new piece of charcoal briefly to her tongue and tested it on a separate piece of paper. Her hair fell in cascades that alternately hid and revealed her eyes, her long, flickering eyelashes. There was anger in her face when she worked, a defiance that made her eyes sparkle and whitened the sinews of her knuckles. At such moments she was indomitable and supreme.

'Will you talk then, if I'm not allowed to?' asked Oscar.

'What should I talk about?'

'Anything. I'd just like to hear the sound of your voice.'

She watched him, then resumed her sketch, unbroken arcs of black forming the line of his nose and lips, creating a semblance of delicacy, which became more august, as she went over the lines again, and a new part of him slipped into place, in the way in which the moon becomes more rounded and distinct as the sky tumbles into darkness.

'When I work,' she said, 'I tend to smoke. But with you I don't feel the need. The work's enough.'

'Isn't it distracting to smoke when you're working?'

'Oh no, the lines of smoke interest me, they give me ideas, they're beautiful. The patterns and shapes as they spin away. But the life the smoke delivers on a plate of ash – that's already there with you. With other sitters, it's different. Some of them object. I'm always polite. I tell them I need the smoke. I tell them it's an aesthetic tool. They nod; they don't really know what I mean, but they sense they mustn't show their ignorance. It's amazing where manners and big words can get you.'

He nodded. Outside a small boy was being taught to ride a bicycle in the middle of the deserted road. His father clutched the back of the cycle and, as he rode, lifted his hands away at intervals. Eventually his father broke away completely while his son cycled on. Oscar could see the boy's lips moving, as he assumed his father was right behind him, still anchoring his bicycle.

'I'm just going to get another piece of charcoal,' said Najette.

After she had left the room Oscar scrambled over to the sketch. He looked younger than he had expected, and the general effect was rich and pleasing; his face was formed of clouds, ethereal forms so fine they seemed in danger of dissolving. As he studied the portrait he noticed a small photograph resting on a desk, almost obscured by various clippings and papers. He dug it out and immediately recognized the stricken figure of Lilliana kneeling down, staring at the broken pieces of a potted plant and next to her another woman who looked oddly familiar. Didn't he know her? He went back to his chair.

'I love the drawing,' he said when she returned.

'You weren't supposed to see it.'

'Another rule?'

'Yes. I like rules.'

'Why?'

'Keeps the pieces flying away. But now we have to be silent. But, before the silence, tell me one thing; how's the modeling going?'

'It's fine; not much money, about as much as the cinema, and I haven't returned to painting as we planned. But it's ... cleansing, though sometimes I feel like an idiot.'

She nodded and resumed her work.

'You'll paint again, don't worry.'

'I'm not sure I share your confidence. By the way, why have you got a photograph of Lilliana looking at a broken flower pot?'

'Where did you see that? Have you been going through my things? I suppose it's my fault for leaving it there. That was taken the day I met her. A woman knocked over one of the potted plants. It seemed to bring them together in quite an interesting way. I thought I might do a study of it at some point. It could make a very good painting if I can capture the way they both opened up even when they grieved. The funny thing is the plant was meant for you. As a belated birthday present.'

'For me?'

'That's right.'

'I seem to have insinuated myself into your life *and* your art.'

'You have.'

She smiled at him so seductively and nonchalantly that it seemed to him then as though he were like some half-delirious hunter dying of thirst and she like some enchanted princess who had guided him towards a crystalline lake whose waters were so still and etched that they formed a magnificent mirror and in its compass life loomed up and arched towards the heavens, as if seeking to conjoin with a force that had hitherto eluded it and in the moment of her smile life's sweetness was ineffable and Oscar felt that just to be near Najette was to be blissfully happy. But then her eyes grew dark all of a sudden. A minute passed, then there was a whisper, a faint shard of sound. Her voice broke the silence once more, though her words hung in the air afterwards and wouldn't fade.

'It's love that kills us.'

Oscar was about to respond, but he stopped himself just in time with the realization that her words did not invite a response, but asked merely to be submitted to. He considered the person before him in a new light, sensing the sadness at the tail end of her exuberance, probably remaining invisible to most of those who came in contact with her, but insistently etched, deep down. Those five words had prized open some more of her personality, the richness of which he was only just beginning to suspect.

'Oscar, that's good, good that you said nothing. You see, you already know me so well. But soon you'll find you hardly know me at all, and when that happens, so will other things.'

'I don't understand,' he said.

'Understanding's overrated. I like riddles as well as rules. Riddles protect me from being caged. See?'

But the enigma had only deepened further. He made no reply, trying to digest the half revelations, the shrouded references she seemed to have a constant supply of. When he finally spoke he cleared his throat with each sentence.

'Najette, I'm not a very deep person, but sometimes I have my moments of insight. I'm not a philosopher, but I could learn a lot from you, if you'll allow me to. Nothing would please me more than to spend time with you.'

She stopped sketching.

'Oscar, you do say the strangest things sometimes! Haven't we been spending time together? Isn't it clear I enjoy being with you?'

'Well ... I suppose so.'

'Well then. Isn't it silly to ask for something you already have?'

And with that remark she became less inscrutable and resumed her work. The last few exchanges drifted into buried, secret realms, from where they were destined to emerge again.

# 6

Albert Lush was badly constipated. It was always the same on the days when he was filming: his bowels seemed to fill with lead. Monday mornings were the worst.

On that particular Monday morning he had Studio 3 booked between 10 and 3. He had arrived early, a small figure in blue overalls at the back, observing the maniacal activity of those currently running around the studio. Nobody seemed to mind about his cough, and at one point the director had approached him and asked if he would like to be filmed coughing, an image which would sit comfortably with the piece he was making, which was about childbirth. Lush had declined politely, repelled by the director's grotesque headphones and the oversize rings lodged onto his bacon-tanned fingers.

He turned his attention to the set, which consisted of a universally orange living room, and to the actors; a pregnant woman was being asked questions by a doctor.

Eventually a dozen female dancers walked in and were received ecstatically by the producer and director. When Lush discreetly asked an important-looking woman what their relevance to childbirth was she declared, 'Dancing is another aspect of female creativity.' After that Lush didn't press her.

Five minutes later he was astonished to find catering ladies rolling in with trolleys full of champagne which the girls quickly polished off, their reason being that normally they never danced before nine in the evening and had to be warmed up artificially. Once suitably prepared they rehearsed a silent dance routine a couple of times, and then agreed to be filmed. A sumptuous backdrop was positioned behind them: a single enormous opened iris, whose rounded and flared petals reached out and engulfed the girls as they danced, their long legs dressed in red-purple stockings that blended with the color of the iris. Lush watched the girls as they fluttered about, and was seized with longing. His stomach squirmed with convulsions reminding him of the need to void his bowels but he knew that he was as blocked as a drain rinsed with cement.

At last the girls finished their routine and walked off the set triumphantly. Some fished about for more champagne, but were unable to dig any up. One, whose hair nearly touched the ground, asked the assistant director for a smoked salmon sandwich. The props girl had to be sent out for one. Meanwhile, the set was re-dressed and became a hospital room, also in universal orange (orange was important to the director because it was more or less the color of the director). The pregnant woman was filmed lying on her bed, perspiring and panting, her belly now miraculously distended, while a doctor explained the meaning of an epidural injection.

By the time the director was happy with these shots Lush's own shambolic film crew had arrived, as had four very old men dressed in crumbling dinner jackets, clutching violin and 'cello cases, and one or two life models, including Oscar, who was very intrigued by everything, never having been inside a television studio before. He decided to stay close to Lush and not say anything unless specifically asked to. He walked over and waved to him in a friendly fashion. Lush appeared not to notice. Oscar was about to go up to him when one of the prettiest of the dancers approached Lush, put her arms round him playfully, and began to express her concern for his thundering cough. Oscar eavesdropped on their conversation from a safe distance.

'The doctors can't do anything for me,' Lush observed, cradling his stomach with his hands, donning a pathetic expression.

'Poor baby. It's probably all in the mind.'

'Yes, but so is schizophrenia.'

'Are you very rich?' the girl continued, ignoring this.

'No, very poor. I survive by borrowing and then make documentaries nobody wants to see. Are you still willing to speak to me?'

The girl considered the question for a moment, then stared at him, with something like longing in her eyes.

'You look like someone who's very different to me, like a chimpanzee with a top hat. Poor baby.'

Lush wasn't sure if this remark was intended as flattering or not. Thinking about it only muddied the issue. In the past he had been rejected by women so often and in so many forms he decided one more rejection could do no harm and so, in his most charming voice, asked, 'Can the monkey buy you supper?'

There was a pause.

'Sure. So long as I get to wear the top hat. And choose where we go.'

Did she really just accept? His mind was already forcing her answer into the realms of fiction, unused as he was to such a positive response. There must have been a catch. Was she really a man in drag? She probably had a bulldog boyfriend, whose meaty hands would soon be forming a circle round his neck.

'All right, you choose.'

'Do you know The Omcat? It's in Mayfair,' she asked.

'No, but I gather it's a little on the pricey side.' That was the catch, then.

'Let's go there. I think it would be fun to dress up and drink cognac, cocktails, eat a little, talk a little, have a couple of cigarillos. You poor, poor baby.'

Lush instantly began to regret his generosity, rapidly engaging in some mental arithmetic, considering what necessities he would now have to do without for the next three weeks in order to buy dinner for both of them. If he didn't eat for a week he might be all right. Besides, he said to himself – immediately transmuting the bleakness of the prospect into a happier scenario, with the incurable optimism that always accompanied him even in his worst moments – not to eat might be a blessing and might clear his system out, which he had been planning on doing for some time.

'All right. We'll do it. By the way, my name is Albert Lush. What's yours?'

'Do you want my stage name or my real name?'

'Both.'

'My stage name is Polly French. And my real name is Tracy Fudge.'

'I think I'll stick to Polly French.'

At this point a bedraggled janitor approached Lush, who had been so swept up in the conversation that he hadn't noticed the studio was gradually emptying, and barked, 'You got till 3.00.'

Lush turned to the girl and said hurriedly, 'This Saturday, eight o'clock suit you?'

'Sure, poor baby,' she said.

'I'll see you there then.'

Lush walked off, glowing like a solar panel. My luck's changing, he thought.

Oscar, trying to catch him up, noticed his grin and said inoffensively, 'Will you be needing me for very long, Mr. Lush?' To his surprise, Lush, buoyed by his recent triumph and oozing generosity of spirit, yelled, 'Oh yes, you're the staaaar!'

'I am?'

'Now, meet Sasha, the make-up girl,' he said, taking Oscar by the hand with adroit mastery, chaperoning him around the studio, avoiding the props, planks of wood and lights being positioned about them. Sasha shook his hand, said, *'Ciao,'* and immediately walked off to attend to important business elsewhere.

'What I will require from you, later on,' Lush continued, speaking rapidly, so much so that Oscar didn't really absorb anything, 'is some brilliance, a few penetrating remarks about your profession that go beyond the soporific observations of these' – he gestured to the other models – 'birdbrains and toads. Oscar, I feel that you and I are very much alike.' He broke off to cough. 'Life has denied us a voice, even though we have much to say. Now I'm offering you a chance to say it. I'll ask you a few questions. Just speak naturally. Start with modeling, but expand, experiment, if you like. We're working with a ratio of sixteen to one, for the first time in my life, I should add. Glorious film, that is, not phony digital crud. Now go and get made up.'

He waltzed off, leaving Oscar to find Sasha again. She was sewing buttons onto a taffeta jacket with miraculous speed. When she had finished she applied various cosmetics to his skin and he found himself luxuriating in a mixture of comfort and arousal. The lights were switched on, the camera was set up on its tripod and the set cleared of rubbish. Oscar was told to sit down by a backdrop of Michelangelo's *David*.

At this point Lush instructed the four disintegrating musicians to get ready to play. They found some chairs and music stands, and began to tune up, looking hot and agitated under the glare of the big lights. Without further ado they launched into something dark and dramatic until Lush implored them to wait a minute. He disappeared and returned a few moments later, his small figure dwarfed by that of an exotic-looking woman dressed in high heels and a buttoned-up white raincoat. Her bare legs were immaculately waxed. This mysterious person slid into a corner, undid some buttons and did nothing more except smoke listlessly.

Lush then explained to the musicians, who were all a little hard of hearing, that the woman in the corner was a professional actress used to displaying her body in public. Furthermore, she was now going to stand in the middle of them while they played. Furthermore, she wouldn't be wearing any clothes. They weren't to notice her and to behave and play as if she wasn't there. It was likely, he informed them, that they might be a little distracted at first but they would soon get used to it. When one of them asked why Lush wanted to film a naked woman and a string quartet simultaneously, Lush was obliged to explain something about the nature of his documentary.

He told them his film was about nude modeling and the context that made it permissible in a civilized society. In order to do this he had to examine contexts in which nudity was not permissible: viz., a naked woman standing next to a string quartet presents a bizarre sight, but when she is put into an art room she becomes commonplace. They nodded but didn't really understand. Lush explained that in certain places nudity can be perfectly normal – the sauna, for example, a public shower, or indeed the art class – but what if nudity somehow slipped into chamber music? They still didn't really see the point and Lush started getting impatient.

With a single, majestic movement, the exotic-looking woman removed her raincoat, revealing an already-naked and sensational body. She stepped effortlessly out of her high heels and planted herself in the space formed in the middle of the string quartet. Most of them hadn't seen a naked woman in over ten years. They found their brows were moist within seconds and that their eyeballs were straining to pop out and achieve a life separate from their bodies, a perspective that would allow for a more comprehensive view of her shapeliness, her frictionless chestnut skin, her shapely breasts. Their hearts pounded frantically. There came a spectral recollection of their youthful lust. Had it always been so oppressive – so confusing – this business of arousal? Had it always been entwined with nausea? After a few minutes they calmed down and the camera began to roll on Lush's instructions. Unfortunately the continuing proximity of her flesh, limbs, and hair caused the musicians' intonation to collapse and they produced a whining sound as painful as the first scratchings of beginners. Lush asked Sasha to get them all glasses of water and as they sat slurping the crew took in the sight of a terrifyingly beautiful human form. Oscar tried to look away but couldn't. Apparently, the woman was oblivious of all the attention she was receiving. It mattered little to her that every inch of her body was now being scrutinized by all the men, including Lush. It would have neither pleased nor displeased her if she had known the cameraman was zooming in on her nipples. And if she had realized the women considered her to be the shocking embodiment of all the dreams they had for their own bodies, she would have been neither gratified nor flattered.

After several trial runs the octogenarian musicians were at last able to play more than three bars without making an unspeakable sound and Lush made do with these few seconds of footage.

An easel and chair were set up, an artist sitting between them, and the naked woman repeated her performance on a raised dais, this time assuming a more expressive position, bending her supple body this way and that. The camera came in for a lingering close-up of the canvas, as the drawing began to take shape. Meanwhile, the old men sat in a corner, some hyperventilating and turning various shades of green, others munching on restorative biscuits and marveling. Oscar watched them, almost as equally mystified. Eventually the artist and the exotic woman retreated to the back of the studio where she got dressed again before the two went off together. The set was cleared. Lush went up to Oscar, still seated beside the backdrop of the *David* and said, 'This is it, Oscar. It's your turn now, my boy.'

Oscar blinked rapidly and was given a final polish by Sasha.

'Number one ready? Right, let's roll.'

'Oscar can you tell me a little about your calling, your vocation, as it were, and tell us something about why in the past nude modeling has all too often been overlooked?'

'Well,' began Oscar uncertainly, suddenly nervous in the glare of the camera's eye, 'I actually want to paint.'

'Cut. Oscar, what are you doing? It's about modeling, remember. Don't be a toad. Let's go again.'

The cameraman nodded to Lush.

'And ready. Let's try it as a close up.

'Go.'

There was silence.

'Cut,' said Lush. 'What are you doing, Oscar?'

'I'm sorry, was I meant to say something?'

'Yes, you were meant to answer the question.'

'What was it again?'

'Look, forget that. Just talk about why you nude model. OK, let's roll. Number one ready, and action.'

'I nude model,' Oscar began hesitantly, but growing more confident as he went on, 'because … I feel alive … when I'm on the dais, naked … It doesn't require me to speak … it saves me from that. Because speaking is hard, as you can see from these efforts of mine. Modeling makes no promises; it's neutral, like an unused bullet. I can watch, observe. Before, at the cinema, I was dying, shriveling up, but … on the dais, I'm peeled clean, and what I notice is my mind buzzing, and I feel what it means to be a body, to have a brain that commands, limbs which obey … but also … stillness … can be beautiful. I've learnt that the body is miraculous, a perfect engine … The only way I can put it is that when I first started it felt like I was being baptized without water in front of all those strangers, who ceased to be real people and became more like features of the landscape, if you know what I mean. Whatever they did, it didn't matter. Perhaps they saw me as a kind of puppet; that didn't matter either. Because I had mental freedom, in that stillness my mind could roam into shores of the celestial, then come back to earth. I was able to transcend the circumstances in which I found myself. Perhaps because at first I was so aware of them.

'Have I said too much?'

Lush yelled 'Cut', then shook Oscar by the hand with a vigorousness Oscar hardly thought him capable of.

'That was brilliant, Oscar. Brilliant. How the hell did you think up the bit about the unused bullet? I haven't a fucking clue what it means, but it sounded fantastic. A few false starts, but I knew I was right about you. I'd get the champagne, but unfortunately the girls drank it. Oh well. Five minutes, everyone. Oscar come with me.'

They made their way to the back of the studio and Oscar found himself wondering how much of his speech had been moulded by Bloch's story. As he was thinking about this, Lush's foot became entangled in some cables and he had to yank his leg back and forth to free himself. From afar it looked like he was performing some kind of strange tribal dance. A tall, malevolent looking man, dressed in a stylishly-cut suit, appeared to be waiting for them, seated, or rather reclining, on a deck chair. Lush immediately recognized him and at the same instant his stomach whined in protest, so that he had to clutch his middle protectively. A frantic impulse to go to the toilet asserted itself but he couldn't afford to leave at such a critical moment. The stranger stood up, summoning up an air of magnificent and limitless indulgence.

'Hello, Lush,' he snorted and then, to Oscar, oozing considerable charm, in an astonishingly different tone of voice, said, 'I am Donald Inn. I'm a talent scout for, associate and emissary of, the über-publicist Mr. Ryan Rees – his name is doubtless familiar to you.'

Oscar's eyes instantly dilated in surprise and puzzlement.

'Ace material up there in that noodle of yours, if a little confused. Care to forge an association with Mr Rees?'

'Back off, Inn; Oscar's mine,' Lush interjected.

'Oscar,' Inn continued, icily ignoring him, 'you may be just what we are looking for; an authentic voice, not marred by cliches or gimmicks, not pandering to the masses. What a stroke of luck, my running into you like this. Ryan Rees could easily turn you into a household name.'

Oscar stared at nothing in particular. He realized he was expected to speak.

'No, thank you, Mr. Inn, but I prefer to stay with Mr. Lush. Besides, this is a one off arrangement, and I doubt if I have any other insights to offer.'

'Listen, Oscar, people would readily pay money to hear someone like yourself speak. Have you heard of Ryan Rees? He could set you up as a state-of-the-art sage, showing people the way. Somehow I feel you can't know his reputation, otherwise you wouldn't be so cavalier about such a twenty-four carat gold opportunity. Ryan Rees is one of the most respected publicists in the world. As an agent he was famous for getting his clients astronomically high fees.'

He extracted a menacing black card from a slit in his jacket – where it had previously been secreted in readiness – and deposited it into Oscar's palm in one deft, skilled motion.

'Call us if you know what's good for you.'

Then he marched off into a synthetic and neon world, a world which had long ago eclipsed the actual one. Both he and his boss hovered on the fringes of it like birds dipped in mercury.

Lush muttered, his voice thick and indistinct, 'You're doing the right thing. Stick with me. Chuck that card away, it's evil. Excuse me, I need to have a bowel movement.' He scrambled to the men's room, the shadow of incontinence hanging over him like some dark, frightening animal.

Donald Inn speed walked through the corridors. He whipped out a cellular phone, pressed some buttons and spoke slick, carefully chosen words. Had he just chanced, by accident, on the perfect candidate?

*

Ryan Rees had kicked off his illustrious career by writing advertising copy for Bentley and Rolls Royce. After leaving advertising he had edited *Scandalous!*, a glossy magazine specializing in important facts about the famous: the number of times they went to the hairdresser; whether or not they had dandruff, halitosis or body odor; the prescription or recreational drugs they were currently addicted to; whether or not they were rumored to be pregnant, anorexic, homosexual, or autistic; the size of their penises, and so forth. During its lifetime the magazine attracted libel suits rivaling in number the amount of corpses floating down the Ganges.

After he had resigned his post Ryan Rees decided to set up shop as an agent, and eventually accumulated over two-hundred clients in the world of television and broadcasting. During this time he had lunch with most of the important players in journalism and the arts, always very careful to conclude their meetings by showering them with gifts: picnic hampers from Fortnum and Mason, bottles of Chateau Talbot, *eau de cologne* and silk handkerchiefs from Jermyn Street, tickets to La Scala, tins of Russian caviar and (occasionally) cocaine.

In the end he decided to act as the publicist for a cluster of very important clients, while also inventing sensational or scandalous stories for those after such items (by no means confined to editors of the tabloids). But he had grown bored with his own game and needed something new and anthropologically interesting to occupy him – something different; concocting far fetched stories just wasn't that exciting anymore. When Donald Inn had recently come up with the idea of manufacturing the myth of a contemporary messiah, a sage, a guru, Rees had found it tantalizing and for once a strategy didn't spring fully-formed into his mind. This presented a real challenge … any braindead imbecile could be turned into a celebrity, but to take a complete nobody and turn him into a *prophet* – that required exceptional levels of propaganda, cunning, and inventiveness, a miracle of spin that only he was up to. To manufacture another Jesus Christ, to conjure one out of thin air would mean than Ryan Rees could literally do anything, would mean that the loftiest goal of all sat within the palm of his freely roving and yet manacled hand.

At one time Rees had been intrigued by the possibilities of money counterfeiting. And during his second divorce, he had forged documents to the effect that his wife was mentally ill, all signed by Dr. Manfred Feltersnatch, a fictional psychiatrist. He had the soul of an anarchist-nihilist whose blood has exploded yet remains inert and whose main longing in life is to bring ridicule and ruin upon all those who cross him or his path, just for the scorched hell of it.

# 7

The small cloakroom was overflowing with people. The fat man
with the thick glasses, wearing a badly-fitting uniform marked "The
Earl Gallery" stood behind the counter, dishing out coats. He looked
terribly upset, because the coats he was producing were not the ones
people had asked for. Those he had taken down from the hangers began to accumulate on the counter, forming a tower which threatened
to topple at any moment. The air was crackling with impatience. In
a little while all the coats had journeyed from their hangers to the
counter. Precisely nothing had been achieved except this mass mi-
gration. The tower finally gave in and those who had been standing
by dumbly, hoping the situation would resolve itself despite their
complete failure to do anything, uttered little cries. Whereupon a
military looking man, perhaps an ex-colonel (who always wore a
monocle and a perpetually outraged expression – which in this in-
stance coincided with what he was actually feeling) started rifling
through the scattered pile. The others joined in and soon the small
cloakroom was gripped by primal instincts and threatened to cave in
as the bodies pressed against the walls. But one by one the coats were
returned to their rightful owners and the room began to clear. It was
quiet again. The fat man with the thick glasses was able to breathe.

He squinted through his glasses. The first thing he saw was a delicately embroidered handkerchief. The second, the hand that held it.
Only then did he notice the person attached to all this.

'Mr. Earl, sir, we don't see you here very often, sir.'

'Buzby,' said Nicholas, speaking very rapidly, 'put that in the safe
would you? I've just found it after a long search. It was given to me

by a woman I serviced in Heidelberg.' He strode up, deposited the handkerchief on the counter and darted back, as if Buzby was manifesting the symptoms of full-blown leprosy.

Buzby, in addition to being grotesquely myopic, was rather deaf. All he had really caught of the speech was the word 'serviced', and assumed Nicholas was talking about his Jaguar.

'You're having your car serviced, sir, are you, sir?'

'What? Was speaking of an old flame of mine.'

Here Buzby heard, 'What? Was making a cold flame all the time.'

'Why's that, sir? Better get it checked, sir.'

'I reckon I'd better have *you* checked.'

Here Buzby heard, 'I beckon bed wetter crab blue flecked,' but couldn't think of an appropriate response and wondered what this statement had to do with Mr Earl's car. Nicholas stomped off in frustration, said, 'Forget it,' still clutching the handkerchief. In the hallway he brushed against a woman dressed in flowing purple shawls who was rummaging around inside her handbag. He stared at her for a moment, considered a rude remark, decided against it, drifted into his office, and started gathering pamphlets about the current exhibition. His mind flashed with imperfect remembrances of the different canvasses, until finally an uninvited image erased them all: that of a very clean incision in flesh, the crimson cascade that came spilling out ravishing until he stopped to realize it was fresh blood.

A few minutes later Oscar walked in. The woman in the shawls had by now emptied the contents of her handbag all over the floor and was sifting through them. Oscar stood and watched her. She was fully engrossed in her search, on her hands and knees, lipstick, keys, mirrors spreading round her in a circle.

He had just come from the Mermaid Academy. It was a cold day, and his bones felt chilled from standing around in the nude. He wanted to tell this strangely un-self-conscious woman he felt as if he'd been freed from the cage his body was turning into, tell her modeling was becoming a bore and a burden, despite the ecstatic account he'd given of it in the television studio. But he said nothing and just kept watching. At last she found what she wanted, refilled her handbag and stood up. As she straightened her clothes and brushed her knees she noticed him watching her. Even at that point of contact she reacted unexpectedly. Neither taken aback by his gaze nor ruffled by it she gaped back at him. The smile she left him with tantalizingly acknowledged the comedy of what had just happened. Then she was gone.

After a pause he followed her, not knowing why, or what he hoped to achieve. Outside she appeared to be lost in the throngs, but then he made her out, her shawls trailing behind her, gathering dust. He watched her figure shrinking, watched that little dot of purple until she finally vanished. It was as if by eking out the moments in which she remained visible the blow of her eventual loss would be softened. He stood there, watching the afternoon traffic, so locked into immobility that the accumulated cars seemed like one massive engine humming and buzzing with life. He counted twelve double-decker buses laid end to end like a gigantic red centipede.

He had to face the fact that she wasn't going to return, not going to hurry back through the crowds. Their moment of intersection was over.

He shook off his melancholy.

As he finally passed through the hallway Oscar felt like he was entering someone's house, not a gallery, given the emblems of domesticity all around: an armchair, a small, cracked flower pot full of white roses, shaded lamps perched on small tables. But the arrestingly large words on the red, fluttering drape left no doubt as to the space's purpose.

# THE ART OF NICK NAIDIREM:
## ILLUMINATING SHADOWS AND MASKS

Who's he? he thought.

He walked through a narrow corridor and entered a large, deserted central room painted in dazzling white. Only two or three canvasses hung on each wall. Oscar welcomed this uncluttered feeling, the sense that he could consider each painting at a leisurely pace.

But then out of nowhere dozens of people stomped in and he was caught up in the crowd's motion as a piece of driftwood is in a whirlpool. It took a while for people to disperse, creating sufficient room to study the paintings. Oscar planted himself near the doorway in case he needed to bail out. As he did so his eye was struck by the nearest painting and he was immediately drawn by it.

It was called "The Eleventh Hour." In it an abstract face and skull were superimposed, like a double-exposure. The androgynous face was boldly realized and had large eyes of Prussian blue, with unblemished, pale-ochre skin. By contrast, the skull was faint and spectral and appeared to dissolve, the lines less assured, charcoal grey teeth still visible, decaying. While the face embodied the essence of youth, the presence of the skull continually undermined this and so the painting pulled in two directions.

Two other paintings particularly impressed him. The first was entitled "Damaged Lake" – less ambiguous, more figurative. A small island in olive green formed the lower left quarter of the frame and a ruined, primitive church of wood and stone sat in its centre. The two were surrounded by a circular lake and in the distance spectral mountains loomed. The eye was led naturally to link the cerulean blue of the lake with the cobalt blue sky. But while the lake seemed to stir and move, the sky was an inert, etched field. On viewing the painting as a whole, an atmosphere of Mediterranean balminess leapt out. The artist had refined color to a point of extraordinary purity, while at the same time managing to create a living, visceral, landscape.

But the third piece was his favorite, technically adept and perfectly composed. "Butterfly" was a work of sheer exuberance. The frame was filled with the boldest, brightest colors as the wings of a butterfly hovered in a crystalline conception. Fresh yellow and light sienna blobs of color contrasted with long, unbroken reaches of gold, vermilion and copper. The painting was aglow, its subject on the point of taking life, its colors threatening to ignite the canvas.

As he stared into the painting, trying to discover its secret, the deadening blanket of habit slipped away and Oscar's consciousness came to rest on a plane where impressions pulsed and danced. The paint that had dripped and dried was speaking to him from the past with a voice only for him, as it seemed. And slowly, as this paint worked its magic, the anonymous figures milling around him began to resolve into symbols of an ineffable love.

There was a sharp metallic clang. Oscar looked around to see what it was. A wizened woman was kneeling to retrieve her keys. It was taking forever. The spell was shattered. He forced himself to move on.

He stopped in front of a simple portrait, trying to recapture that fecund state of mind, but it was gone. As he stood there a hand touched his arm.

'Oscar,' someone said quietly.

He turned to see Nicholas standing next to him.

'Nicholas. I'd forgotten all about you. I was going to pop in and see you. But Mr Naidirem's paintings seduced me.'

'Yes, they are good, aren't they? The artist is a great love of mine, even now, after all this time. The richness of the colors, the bleeding light. I wish I had a quarter of that talent. Very gifted, don't you find? And how's your own work going? Progress report?'

'I've nothing ... to show you. I haven't done a stroke since that sketch I made of you.'

Nicholas turned away. When he next spoke, after a pause, he appeared to be addressing the wall.

'Well. We all make mistakes, don't we?'

'I don't really think I deserve success. I'd rather just taste pleasure for a bit.'

Nicholas turned back to him, no longer happy with the wall. 'Are you serious? But you're changing the subject. I won't say I'm disappointed in you, because people no longer disappoint me. I just expect them to let me down at some point.

'Let's take Najette for a minute. I'd like to, I'd like to take her, but she was too much to take. She saw through me. I had to admire her for that. Her honesty, she couldn't abide pretension. I was too impure. Oh yes, she was feisty; yes, she had spirit; she had talent, no doubt. But in the end she couldn't laugh at herself, she took herself too seriously; in the end she was just that little bit lethal. I realized that our affair had been about her, all along, her precious art, her visions. I thought I'd have some say, but she was the one making the decisions, setting the agenda. Do you know how impotent that made me feel, how useless and voiceless?'

'I'm sure she had her reasons. In any case, those things you say aren't exactly kind,' said Oscar. 'You see, I happen to be very fond of Najette and I'd rather you didn't speak about her like that. Perhaps we can resolve this problem.'

'What makes you think I want this problem to be resolved, or that you're in a position to resolve it for me? You're just a child playing in the bathtub with your rubber ducks.'

'Najette is the most fascinating woman I've ever met. Just when you think she's coming into focus ... something else appears. It sounds like you can't have understood her. She's ... radiant, she seizes life with every fibre; and she makes me seize life. You can't treat Najette like you can other women; she's ... she's like vapor, so light ... so vaporous ...'

'Well done, Oscar, that was very poetic.'

'Maybe. But just because you've had a bad experience with her – and I'm not sure you really have – don't dress your grievances up so grandly.'

This silenced Nicholas and for once he recognized there was something in what Oscar had said. Nicholas had experienced a wonderful closeness to Najette, then seen it gradually slip away; the intimacy that had once been so natural had become a breeding ground for recrimination. On the other hand, Nicholas thought, perhaps Oscar was right; perhaps he hadn't really appreciated or understood her. Perhaps a stranger could grasp more about someone within the first moments of meeting them than a lover who had tasted everything, agony and ecstasy?

'Can I buy you a coffee?' Nicholas asked, slightly sheepishly.

Oscar looked around at the turning tide of people, standing, walking, sitting, sketching. He felt strangely apart, held at arm's length from any sense of participation. Nicholas too was apart, apart from the community; but he wanted to be different and made a point of it, wanting to stand out.

'If you like.'

They made for the exit. Once outside Nicholas lit a Turkish cigarette, and at intervals smoke seeped from his nostrils like two tiny tornadoes turned on their heads.

At the corner of the street a violinist was playing Bach and a small crowd had gathered round her, in spite of the unusually cold day. Nicholas tugged Oscar's arm, instructing him to stop. The music glowed brilliantly, arpeggios exploding in cascades of sound. As they stood there, fragments of Nicholas's earlier observations about Najette circulated in Oscar's mind. Oscar suspected that for Nicholas these remarks left no trace after they were made; whereas for him they became obstacles blocking his view of the present, as he intermittently considered and reconsidered their truthfulness. As a result he didn't really hear the music. And then, in turn, words from Bloch's story suddenly surfaced: *He was incapable of surrendering to*

*an experience, since he was constantly preoccupied with another prob-
lem.* Have I always been like that? he wondered.

'Are you busy tonight?' Nicholas asked.

'Not really.'

'Do you want to go to the pleasure cooker with me?'

'What kind of place is that?'

'It's a place for people like me.'

'And what are people like you like?'

Nicholas paused.

'Damned, if you really want to know.'

The music reached its final angry, defiant chord and the crowd started to disperse. The evening was gathering now and in the atomization of the sky, in the membrane of nebulous sounds stretching out all around them, Oscar was surprised to find a still point enclosing him. But then, with that purposefulness he could summon at will, Nicholas marched off and Oscar followed him, into a decadent and wine-splattered world.

# 8

A fortnight later Oscar had an appointment with the über-publicist Ryan Rees.

Albert Lush's documentary ("Naked Art") had been screened. Ryan Rees, after studying Oscar's contribution, had concurred with his associate Donald Inn that, potentially at least, Oscar seemed an ideal candidate for the role of a messiah. He had phoned him at his bedsit and Oscar had agreed at last to meet with him just to get him off the phone.

Their rendezvous was to take place in the unlikeliest of places – a small library hidden in the cloisters behind Westminster Abbey. Ryan Rees was there amassing information on the architecture of the small square that lay adjacent to the cloisters.

Having a few minutes to spare Oscar decided to wander around the square – Dean's Yard – beforehand. It was the middle of July and London was experiencing sub-tropical heat and scorching sunlight. When Oscar closed his eyes he could see a field of dancing colors, moving shapes and patterns. On opening them again everything was cast in a purplish haze that made existence unreal, and stripped life of its problems. But then they slowly returned to him; chiefly, his financial situation which had deteriorated dramatically – he no longer had even the small income from modeling. This was because he had given it up.

Lush's documentary had attracted negligible interest, though Oscar's contributions were singled out as mildly interesting. Because of the way Oscar's speech was edited – portions of it were slotted throughout the program at key moments – it appeared his was the dominant voice of the work, lending it an authoritative, authentic pulse that held it together, and provided much-needed continuity. The documentary consisted of interviews with models, footage of art classes in progress, (and the images of the flustered string quartet), shots of Michelangelo's sculptures, and nudes by Picasso. It was a competent, though somewhat plodding piece, obsessed with the body, questioning whether nudity in the art room was truly free of an arousing factor, examining the difference between the aesthetic and the erotic. The positioning of the footage of the naked model early on had amounted to a stroke of genius – since she made people stay with the program in the hope of seeing more of her later on. But they were disappointed to find she didn't return.

He began making his way towards the cloisters. In the central square a fountain gurgled agreeably; it was framed on all sides by an immaculate lawn, and surrounded by the venerable stone of the abbey. Oscar listened to the fountain. As he closed his eyes and focused on the sound he imagined he was in another country, in a strange land, lost in an abstract landscape. At last he started to make his way around the cloisters until he found a sign marked 'The Lowe Library.' He pressed an intercom.

'I'm here to see Mr. Rees.'

A metallic voice said, 'Up the wooden staircase. On. The. Left.'

The door snapped open. He walked through a passageway and entered the small, deserted library, carefully sealed from the world. It felt pleasingly cool after the heat of the courtyard. Huge books with red, cracked spines lined the shelves, dropping into the light pearls of their wisdom, but there were none to retrieve them. Crudely-shaped pipes ran along the circumference of the room, behind the shelves, sucked into walls. A withdrawn, etched silence enveloped everything, only occasionally disturbed by the creaking floorboards. Higher up, there was a small ledge crowded with endless piles of books and wads of what Oscar imagined were legal documents, tied in red ribbons. A ladder led up to this ledge, though it was hard to see how anyone who wasn't either a child or a midget could climb it. There was a portrait of a bishop hanging on the wall and his sinister eye followed Oscar as he made his way up the staircase. He reached the top and found himself in a windowless study, illuminated by a single table lamp. A small, middle-aged woman, with an obviously earnest manner, and a man he took to be Rees (he couldn't see his face as his back was turned to him) were deep in conversation. The woman's yellowing skin looked as if it might have been grafted out of the parchments lying on the desk. Neither of them was in any particular hurry to acknowledge him.

'Late Georgian and fourteenth-century for the school, a most excellent building,' she was saying, 'and the church house – a model if ever there was one – dates from the late nineteen- hundred-and-thirties, with a stone front and flint-faced ground floor.'

The man looked round and Oscar glimpsed his face for about three seconds. When he turned back again Oscar found he had instantly forgotten the shape of that face. The woman was still speaking. Her voice was low, as if by speaking softly she could better preserve the precious, crumbling parchments.

When she had finished the man said, in smooth tones, 'I'm very much obliged. I shan't take up any more of your time. I think I have all I need. Would you mind if this gentleman,' – he gestured to Oscar without turning – 'and I sat downstairs to discuss some business of our own?'

The librarian stared uneasily. 'It will not take too long?'

'No, no, we'll be gone before you can say Christopher Wren.'

The man turned round again and Oscar had a chance to study him. He was dressed in a light summer blazer, and immaculately creased trousers. While his clothes suggested the epitome of refinement his face and skin created an altogether different impression. His nose was slightly pressed in, and his eyes had receded into their sockets; he had a set of runner bean lips. It was even possible to imagine this was not a real face but an incredibly sophisticated mask since his features were bereft of the faintest suggestion of expressiveness. He seemed to have sprung intact from another planet. And about him there hung the possibility that he might at any moment transmogrify into an iguana or giant lizard.

He ushered Oscar downstairs and they found a couple of chairs. Now this uncanny figure took a moment to examine Oscar. What he saw pleased him: youth, height, a certain innocence and physical beauty. He did not see anyone obviously exceptional or brilliant or charismatic. He saw someone he could manipulate easily, without much fuss. He saw a blank space waiting to be filled. At last he managed something like a smile and declared, in that smooth, almost fabricated voice, 'Ryan Rees, at your service.'

'Oscar Babel at yours.'

'It's a pleasure to meet you at last. I must apologize if I might have been a tad exasperating when we spoke on the phone, but persistence is one of my chief character traits. Now then. People liked the documentary, but, to be honest, apart from your contributions I thought it was a piece of shit. The direction was appalling and I don't know what went wrong with the sound. The scene with the string quartet was plain ridiculous. But never mind. The reason why I called you was that I might just be able to get you a spot on BBC 2's new late night discussion forum – "After Meditation." They want to do a discussion on sexual love for the first edition. Each week they plan to rope in a member of the general public to join a panel of critics, intellectuals and other cunts. I think I can squeeze a grand out of them. Rather handsome, wouldn't you say? This is just what you need. Things will grow from there. You have to start to build a name for yourself and I'm in an optimum position to come up with the cement and bricks, if you follow. I can represent you Oscar. Open doors.'

'But build myself up as what?'

'An original voice. You have what it takes. To be the scourge of society.'

'But I always wanted to be a painter.'

'Well, you would have been one by now, if that was your destiny. It's obvious you have certain, shall we say, political, talents, and I'm here to push them, to set you up.'

'But in what capacity?'

'A vast one, with any luck. Think of it, Oscar. A philosopher who is popular, a thinker who is entertaining. Forget actors and writers and the rest. You'll be a one-off. There are a thousand writers, a thousand performers. I see you as a spiritual teacher, a visionary who has access to a microphone, not oblivion. Think of Christ. Christ was a philosopher; he also happened to work miracles. Leave the miracles to me, Oscar. You just get up there and speak; it's what you're good at. Whenever you open your mouth, something profound seems to seep out. We can call you the prophet of London. We'll get you a website, start rolling a few balls, turning a few heads. What's your e-mail?'

'Don't have one.'

Oscar thought about what Rees had just said. The prospect of being paid £1000 had obvious appeal, especially in his present circumstances. As he was considering his response he felt waves of palpable energy emanating round Rees's orbit. A distinct component of this energy seemed dangerous, as if he were standing uncomfortably close to a source of radioactivity or a vat of sulphuric acid. Rees' words appeared so well-chosen, flattering and judicious that Oscar realized he had none to offer in response. He glanced round at the massive monographs and encyclopedias, falling into ruin, the glutinous pipes that ran behind the shelves. They were gurgling and making ominous sounds, having chosen this moment to come to grotesque life.

'This thing is fixed for a week's time. I'll speak to my people,' Rees declared magisterially, sensing that he had wrung unstated acquiescence from him.

Then the librarian climbed down the stairs.

'Sirs, it pains me but I am obliged to ask you to take your leave. I overhear your worldly words. The library is not made for this. It is a place of learning.'

Oscar was irritated by the bizarre way in which she spoke.

'I have extended the hand of friendship, gilded with fine sentiments, and the best intentions. To do the work of kindness was welcome to me, but now my own work calls like a divine bugle; I must apply silence if I am to be productive. Besides, the Dean is due in the instant and he may be forlorn to find strangers here.'

'You need peace and quiet,' Oscar began seriously, 'but the world is noisy.'

'Sir?'

'Oscar, not now,' Rees growled. The pipes' gurgling was growing more defiant and disquieting by the minute.

Undeterred, Oscar continued, 'Don't shy away from life and love; don't do what I used to do, don't shut yourself up in a dark room, retreating from life! There's a whole world out there! Leave all this dust. You are a woman, bursting with the feminine springs of creativity; don't bung it up with books. Spread your legs – sorry, I mean wings …'

The librarian squealed dementedly, 'Not-another-word!' After this her face went into a kind of spasm. Her eyes blazed but did not move; her teeth locked and her face turned blood red. Then – her body clenched, her movements robotic – she picked up a sharp letter opener from a nearby table and held it aloft. For a horrible moment Oscar thought she was going to stab herself, but the instrument fell from her lifeless hands, clattering coldly, and at the same time she slumped into a chair.

Then she began to cry, long, broken sobs and her body heaved violently back and forth, like a rocking horse. 'It's no use … no use,' she kept saying. By now the pipes seemed like living creatures, hissing, groaning, unleashing a truly freakish set of sounds.

Rees grabbed Oscar by the collar and pulled him away while there was still time.

'Save all that shit for later, when there's a fucking camera present,' he screamed noiselessly.

On their way out they encountered the Dean who asked them what they were doing coming out of a private area. Rees was only able to mollify him by babbling something about research, speaking knowledgeably about the front of the church house and by offering him a large cigar, which the Dean eyed suspiciously before accepting.

Moments later the Dean discovered the librarian, dumbstruck, but humming a tune he hadn't heard in thirteen years.

\*

Later on Oscar had an appointment with Najette at the Lumiere Cinema in Covent Garden. He was late by twenty-five minutes. Najette had told him she wouldn't wait if he was late as she couldn't bear to miss the beginning of a film. After looking around outside he assumed she had gone inside.

There were about twenty people scattered round the auditorium. Oscar looked about; his attention was caught by the narrow beam of light issuing from the projection room, a brilliant thin essence, particles of dust dancing in its pathway. He studied it almost reverentially, then turned once more to the silhouetted heads, and took up his search, peering at each one, trying his best not to seem obtrusive. In the dark people were anonymous and characterless, mere shapes, oval structures of shadow. Any of those shapes might have been Najette, and the fact that he had to sift through them all stripped her of her distinctiveness. But as he was turning to begin the search again, he glimpsed a circle stirring in the front row, and saw the circle light up as it protruded into the bright image running at that moment. It was Najette. He crept up, and very gently sat down beside her. A series of whispers began.

'Did you meet him?'

'Yes.'

'And?'

'He promised me fame and money.'

'And do you want fame and money?'

'Doesn't everyone?'

They watched the film.

Oscar found he couldn't really enter into it. This was not only be-cause he had missed the opening but also because he was constantly on the lookout for a little black spot to appear in the top right hand corner of the frame, a spot that signaled the moment at which the reels of the film had to be changed, as he knew from his days as a projectionist. Even though this cinema – like almost all – projected films digitally, he found he couldn't quite shake off his old training.

Oscar felt a longing for Najette rise up and wash over him like a gathering tide, until he was helpless in its incoming rush and could only sit there, pinned down, incapable of moving his head, of turning to watch her. He badly wanted to touch her, to feel her ebony hair in his palms and fingers, to feel the hair curl and uncurl and release. Just her hair, Oscar thought, just let me touch that and I'll be happy. I have no right to taste her body. Within a moment he could stretch out a hand and connect with her. Within a moment it could be done, but he could not bridge the space between them. There might as well have been a valley separating them. When she crossed her legs Oscar stole a glance at the skirt tightly pressed along the slender line of her thighs, hugging her. He envied that simple material because it was close to her, moved with her, and never left her.

As the film drew to its end Oscar's thoughts led him away from Najette and he began to consider all that had happened in the last few weeks. Events appeared vague and indistinct and he couldn't properly recall the order in which they had happened. At last every-thing boiled down to one fear, one realization.

What the hell was he going to say on television?


On their way to a cafe he told her about the meeting with Ryan Rees.

Inside the place they decided on – more out of necessity than anything else – there was a withdrawn atmosphere, despite extravagant prints on the walls and luxurious seats and tables, their surfaces as reflective as mirrors. The handful of men scattered here and there were nursing hangovers, their faces as pale as their coffees were black. A piano sat in a corner, looking like it hadn't been touched in years.

They found a spot to themselves and she ordered profiteroles, an act that immediately, in the context of the general desolation, acquired the bright ring of health.

'So,' she said, 'soon the words you speak will make you famous. You'll be important. Will you desert me when the photographers cling to you like pigeons?'

'Never.'

'That's just as well. Though I might have to desert you.'

'What do you mean?'

She ignored his question and said, 'Oscar, if you're going to be paid just to open your mouth on this discussion program, you'd better make sure what comes out is good. Do you plan to represent the voice of the common man? That won't do, since you aren't particularly common.'

'Nothing so ambitious; I'm just going to contribute to a discussion about love.'

'And what do you know about love?'

There was a slight pause.

'Well ... I'm not ready yet. I have to get my ideas down on paper first.'

'Well, I won't press you.'

'Do you think it's stupid?'

'Of course not. Correct me if I'm wrong, but I had the impression you wanted to be a painter. That, if you remember, was why you started modeling.'

'I haven't got the talent; I've come to see that.'

He thought about how Bloch's story had mythologized him as a great painter: could it be this part of the fiction would not find its real-life counterpart, that he would never paint again? Could it be that the story's capacity for doing good in his life was all used up?

'You know, Nicholas offered to exhibit my work the day I met him. But I told him I had nothing to give him. I want to have an effect on people. I can't do it with canvasses and paint. Perhaps you can. In fact, I know you can. That red nude on the sofa, both versions, were magnificent. You should try and mount a show as soon as you can. Why don't you ask Nicholas? Or is that a bad idea?'

There was another pause in the conversation, during which the profiteroles arrived.

'Have you been to the Earl Gallery yet?' she asked, a hint of tension creeping into her voice, tenuous but undeniable.

'Yes, as a matter of fact. I was quite struck by the show there. Nick Naidirem. Have you heard of him? He's really very good.'

'Very good?'

'Very good, sometimes more than very.'

'Oscar, do you know what my second name is?'

'No, I don't. Do you suddenly feel the desire to tell me?'

'It's Meridian.'

'That's nice. Unusual.'

'Can you tell me what Meridian is spelt backwards?'

'It's ... N ... A ... I ... D ... I ...'

He stopped short, shocked.

'It's ... God ... it's Naidirem.'

Her smile of affirmation made him dizzy momentarily, as the truth prized its way into his brain.

'They were your paintings?! What about the signatures?' He suddenly remembered there weren't any since she always signed her canvasses on the back. 'What's this all about? Why are you exhibiting under that name?'

'I needed there to be some distance between me and the public.'

'What?'

'It's ... the truth is ... I don't ... Nicholas only agreed to the exhibition ... he was getting his stupid revenge ...'

'I don't understand ...'

'No, I didn't think you would.'

She lit a cigarette.

'I used to beg him to take on my work, he never did because he was jealous of me. He said so a number of times. He'd pretend he was joking but he meant it really. He said as an excuse that my paintings were too grand, too garish for his modest little gallery. But then, later he agreed to exhibit my work on one condition.'

'That you used a different name?'

'Right. He made a slight concession, that the surname could be an anagram of mine. I can't get a dealer – apparently I'm too old-fashioned. I couldn't get an exhibition anywhere. I was desperate, so I agreed. I certainly didn't want to rent out some gallery, tiny and cramped, for pots of money. I know the Earl gets reviewed – whatever else you can say about him, Nicholas *is* well connected – and the place pulls in the punters. In fact, I ended up getting a rave review in the *SGJ*. They said I had feminine finesse. Well, at least they got one thing right.'

'What a disgusting thing to do, to rob you of the glory. People have a right to know it's you.'

'Oh well. Who cares, in a way ... if people get to see the paintings, get some pleasure out of it, does it really matter? They come, they go, as do all the piss-artists. I think of it as my *nome-de-plume,* you see. That comforts me. By the way, Nicholas would never have made you such a generous offer – have offered you a show – unless he had something nasty to gain by it. He probably thought it would kill me if he offered you – a stranger – an exhibition, when I'd been his girlfriend and he hadn't given me one. He probably also reckoned it would cripple our relationship, whatever its status. His thinking is so bloody crude.'

These further revelations knocked a large dent in his skull, and it took him a moment or two to recover. He couldn't believe how mendacious Nicholas had been, though he realized Najette's explanation made perfect sense. Why should Nicholas have been so generous in making that offer all those weeks ago? Only to employ him as a pawn in his battle against Najette.

'It's so strange ... that they were your paintings. At the time I just wasn't making the connection.'

'That's disappointing, I was hoping you knew me better than that.'

'Know your work better, you mean?'

'I am my work, my work is me. And if you couldn't see me through the screen of a false name ... I'm suddenly sad.'

Oscar tried to recall the shape of that afternoon in the gallery, the delight the paintings had spread in his mind, and tried to gauge the nature of his reactions to them. They had cast a spell over him, but could he really have been expected to know that it was her work? Maybe. But after all, he had only seen two of her paintings before his visit to the gallery. Feeling both moved and disturbed, he tried to sustain a healing silence.

Finally he said in a low voice, 'Why does Nicholas hate you so much?'

'I don't think he does hate me. Not really. He's scared of me; he knows I have something he's always wanted. He's tried to persuade himself he has it too. With Turkish cigarettes and cultivated eccentricities and refined words, he can be a bohemian. But deep down he knows he's just affectation without a shred of talent. When we were together he admired me and resented me in equal measure. He could have helped me, but he didn't because it would have been another nail in his coffin. When I broke with him he knew it was because I'd seen through him, realized how hollow he really was. In a way it makes perfect sense that he should have agreed to exhibit my work on the condition that it wasn't my name that was used. He was giving me what I wanted and at the same time qualifying it with what I loathed: a lie. But I went along with it. What else was I going to do?'

She paused and took a deep breath and it seemed as if she was on the verge of some great confession, then she lightened slightly and resumed.

'Oscar, so now to us ... you have to be patient with me; I need everything *andante*. I'm tricky, you see. It all has to come out at the right time, perfect, like a soufflé.'

Oscar registered this with tentative joy, because the words seemed to announce the possibility of intimacy between them; but he was not sure if he had heard them right. He wanted to ask her to repeat what she had just said but to have done so would have destroyed all the subtlety he knew she was straining for. Besides this, her words had sprung from a specific moment, and the realizations that had been forming in Najette's mind during it. That moment was already past.

She understood the meaning of his slightly baffled look but chose to ignore it and started at last on her profiteroles.

'You can't imagine the joy contained in this plate. I never want it to end. Perhaps that's my problem; whenever I see perfection I want to bottle it up. Why do I ask the impossible from God? Is it that I think he has a special ear for me, and me alone, and that I'm his favorite? In another life I think I'd be nailing butterflies to wood, not painting them.'

A smartly dressed man walked out of a door marked 'PRIVATE' and sidled up to the piano, his movements jagged and reptilian. But as soon as he started to play his body became engulfed in calm, as if a sedative was calmly feeding into his body via the keyboard. A Chopin waltz was unwinding; and its cadences summoned up the specter of loss. The music was not so much played as summoned, an impression confirmed by the pianist's now trance-like state. Najette glanced over, then said softly, 'I didn't spot the piano. It's easy, isn't it, to miss what's in front of your nose?'

He felt the remark applied to his own perceptions, or lack of them, so he tried to make small talk in order to avoid any possible clash between them.

'Do you play?'

She said nothing and assessed the state of the other customers. The remaining men were continuing their descent into mental twilight. A little way down someone was being forced into a dinner jacket.

The music dislodged the sadness that had settled at the bottom of her mind. It floated to the surface and stirred lazily. She looked around and tried to disregard how the music revealed the fragility of everything, of life. Her circling gaze came to rest on Oscar. Inquiry widened his eyes, defiance curved his lips. Coming now as it did in the midst of her escalating feelings of loss and the music's pathos, Oscar's face embodied life. Fearful of that life's extinction, she craned her neck towards him and studied the still unclouded features which placed him apart from the dispossessed men around them. He watched as her eyes locked onto his, eyes that startled him with the intensity of their gaze, eyes that turned her face into a centre of magnetizing beauty by finally shedding their veils.

She kissed him fiercely.

# II
# A KITE TORN BY THORNS

# 9

The sun was setting, casting streets and buildings in a magical haze. Earlier it had rained, and the trees still held droplets of water which, from time to time, were released by sudden breezes, gently dousing those walking under their branches. It was growing quiet, and the evening's progress altered the texture of consciousness. People coming home from work looked forward to the balm of food and alcohol, and the rejuvenation of night.

Daniel Bloch had just been on the telephone with Barny Crane, his agent, who wanted to know if there was any sign of a new book. Bloch told him it was out of the question, that he was only writing fragments of an autobiographical nature, not meant for public consumption. Barny played along, suspecting he had just caught him at a bad moment, assuming Bloch was exercising that capriciousness he had come to expect before the genesis of a new novel.

And now, while London wound down like a gigantic spring, he stretched his tired body out on his pink double bed, propped himself up, and arranged the half dozen pillows and cushions around him until he felt comfortable and secure. Only then did he begin writing words on the thick wad of sheets next to him.

*Autumns and summers and winters have come and gone and I'm still here. Oscar is young, he has his life in front of him. I am past the zenith, the peak shrouded in snow.*

*I wish I could recall the past more clearly. How did I fill each day? One day I woke up and found I was an adult; suddenly I'd been thrust onto the milling stage. Have I embraced the responsibilities of being a man;*

*have I advanced onto the battlefield in full regalia; have I, one of those about to die, saluted my maker? God is still up to his old tricks, a foolish old man muttering as he pulls rabbits out of his hat, while a building topples here, a love dies there.*

*Talking of love, I ache to see her again. But she's three-thousand miles away, she's no longer in the neighborhood, as it were. We left each other like segments of an old rug coming apart at the seams. She was a lovely tapestry crowded with mysterious figures, indecipherable hieroglyphs but I failed to be an adequate Egyptologist, venturing into subterranean caverns with my flaming torch. She was rich, it's true, but her riches made me poor.*

*To see Natalie with a child was wonderful. An unfeigned sincerity spilled out when she was with a child, when she could leave aside that Amazonian womanliness, complete with underwear, stilettos like daggers and industrial strength eau de cologne. I never quite felt at ease amidst her various splendors. She seemed to have been born with a silver make-up case in her mouth, since she was always pampering her features and readjusting the contours of her face, a protean face that make-up made more protean; she had a soul of rare expressiveness, she was a free spirit, and I ended up paying for that freedom.*

*I still recall the wooded walks. Sun-filled spaces where the dust from platitudes could settle. The confusions we have cultivated for time immemorial could be dispersed. Then we were alone. And there was time for she and I to stare into one another.*

*But then the abyss ...*

*So dark down there; the well, from where water sprang and gushed and finally caused me to drown. Drown because sometimes I would be caught irretrievably inside her, losing my own sense of self.*

*At other times her long locks were alien to me, strands from a body I regarded with indifference: do I really know this person?*

*At others still we were so close, closer still, closer and closer until I thought I had the key in my palm, but it clattered onto the cold ground and was sucked away and the chained door rattled.*

*And we became ghosts once again. Diminuendo.*

*She had a landscape for a body. And conjuring with it every night (and then not at all) made me perceive the wonder of being alive more than anything else ever managed to do.*

*And once or twice, over breakfast, in the garden, under the stars, after sleep, it was sweet, so sweet I cannot name it.*

*I must keep writing; I must get this out of my system. I want no interruptions this time; I want to say what has to be said.*

*I am expecting my father tonight. I have no idea how this will turn out; I hope that we will be civil to each other. This would be something. Actually, it would be quite a lot.*

*I am closing in on myself, I have declared a new mode of introspection, I no longer want to go out, I no longer want to negotiate with etiquette, I want merely to crawl into my shell, and hibernate. Perhaps I should apply for Oscar's old job...*

He leaned back on the pillows and undid the top button of his pyjama top. Images churned around in his mind. His eyes closed and his body turned automatically, forming a fetal position. He pushed away the sheets of foolscap, which spilled all over the floor, settling into fan shapes as if by design.

He was standing on the roof of an impossibly tall building. The wind was whipping itself into a frenzy. As he looked around he could see he was all alone there. Beyond was a gigantic glass door through which people in carnivalesque costumes were visible, drinking and dancing. Then the scene changed and he was walking along a long, narrow corridor. At its end a shadowy figure was tucked away. Try as he might he couldn't see its face. Then, other faces and bodies sprang up and pressed onto his body until he was being squeezed by a circular mass, a crowd exerting a monumental pressure. He felt his own body losing its form, becoming volatilized. His mind broke free and he was looking down from a spiritual, lofty plain, glimpsing himself still pressed between the others.

Something from outside began to demand his attention and a signal led him back towards consciousness. His eyes snapped opened. Staring down at him was Oscar's blank face. Bloch started up with a fright.

'How ... how did you get in?' he stammered, as if to a hostile intruder.

'The downstairs door was open. So was your front door. I've shut them both.'

'I ... I was sleeping.'

'At this hour? You should be frolicking in the park. It's a Mediterranean evening.'

'Is it? I think I'm ill or something. Or else my mind's gone to pot; I can feel bits of me rattling around my skull. I just had the strangest dream.' He began rubbing his eyes vigorously.

'Are you up to having a conversation?'

Bloch nodded slowly. His eyes were bleached by fatigue. Oscar, sensing the weight bearing down on him, and in turn finding himself wading through sluggish waves, thought it might be a good idea to pick up the sheets of paper scattered over the floor, as if this would somehow energize them both. He did so and placed them on the side table next to the bed, noticing the growing pile of books under the table lamp: tattered volumes on Buddhism, Tantra, Plato. Prompted by a complimentary impulse, Bloch reached over for an ashtray to anchor the sheets with but he misjudged its weight. It fell and broke into three hearty pieces, which went hopping across the floor. Oscar was about to retrieve them when Bloch bawled, 'Leave it; stop making such a fuss.'

Oscar tried to cover up his discomfort by making small talk. As his lips moved Bloch, who wasn't listening to a word, noticed that Oscar's skin glowed in a slightly synthetic manner; he looked waxy. Bloch buried his nose in the smell of his pillow.

'Perhaps you need a doctor?'

'A quack? To examine and poke me? Get me a duck. It can do the quacking.'

'What's the matter, exactly?' asked Oscar thickly, nearing the open windows of the bedroom. As he reached over to rest a hand on the frame the sun's dying rays struck the tenement building and a pearl-colored light flooded in, reshaping the room by revealing previously hidden corners.

'Nothing … I'm dying,' came the weary response.

Oscar hung his head out of the window. His dark hair flopped over, as if electrified. A young girl, perched on some steps, was blowing soap bubbles happily. He watched as they hovered and popped in orbit around her small figure.

Bloch wished Oscar would come away from the window before he tumbled to a disemboweling death.

'I said I'm dying.'

'I heard you,' Oscar half-shouted.

'Is that all you have to say? My life is ebbing away and I have no idea why. Perhaps you could shed some light on it.'

'I'm not used to shedding light. That's your department.'

'Since when? Why am I suddenly the source of all wisdom? I'm nothing special, just another mid-life crisis merchant, peddling his wares on street corners, hoping someone will hand him a  powerful enough loud speaker to shout his insults through.'

Oscar walked back from the window and declared, with a certain urgency, 'I could be your loud speaker, now that I'm turning into a television personality. Only joking.'

'What are you talking about?'

'That's what I thought we might discuss.'

Bloch squinted up at Oscar, puzzled. He was finding it harder and harder to connect the person standing in his bedroom with the person he thought of as Oscar Babel.

'What do you want from me? Blood? You keep coming here, why?'

'Do you want me to go?'

'No, forget it. It's just that .... you and I .... we seem to be – hanging on to nothing, except each other. Yes, I know you want to go out there, into the big bad world, to do battle with it, confront it, to wave your sabre around like a lunatic. As for me, I've had my fill; I'll leave you to be glitzy, to taste the strawberries and blow raspberries. I'm tired of all that shit.'

'I think you need a holiday. Why don't you – '

'Because I'm not going to find whatever it is I'm looking for in the company of boarding passes and suncream! I need inoculating. I need to hibernate, meditate, forget Natalie. But she's still there, blowing kisses. How cruel of her to have spent all that time fine-tuning that landscape body, avoiding red meat, flossing twice a day, waxing her legs, cycling till her tires blew up .... what a performance! And then that old fart comes along and the next thing I know I'm dying for a cuddle in the middle of the night. But tonight I'll get my revenge. Love's a snake-pit.'

Oscar had a dozen questions about Bloch's private references, but didn't know where to start. As Bloch's phrases buzzed in Oscar's head, Bloch thought of the words he had written before falling asleep; they already seemed ghostly, fragments destined for the dustbin. What is the secret to weighted words? He sat up, legs crossed, head held in enclosing hands, his fingers typing as if at the keyboard.

'When you say love's a snake pit – what – I mean – now that we're on the subject ...' Oscar muttered vaguely.

'Love?'

'Listen, can I ask your advice about something?'

'What now?' Bloch mumbled through the wall of his hands.

'Are you comfortable? Can I get you anything? A glass of water?'

'Actually, yes; I mean no, get me a gin and tonic. Gin's in the kitchen next to the teapot, tonic water's in the fridge. I think there's ice in the freezer.'

In the kitchen Oscar washed and rinsed a couple of glasses. As he did so a second question he had been trying not to ask clawed at him, promptly erasing the original one. He hoped that posing it from another room might render it more palatable.

'I was wondering,' he called, 'did you ever get round to writing any more of that story ... about me?'

Bloch's face instantly shed what animation the last moments had mustered.

'No, I didn't get round to writing any more,' he lied, as he had in fact started the third chapter and never shown it to him. 'I'm afraid that piece has been spiked, as the journos say. I didn't really see a way for it to go, and I couldn't find it ... it was all ... maybe some other time, when the mood's right ... the thing is Oscar, I really don't want to think about it anymore ... my head might explode. When I was writing it ... I thought Big Ben would stop chiming ... that cakes would bake themselves in the middle of the night .... that Oxford Street would fill with sardines.'

The gin and tonic fizzed and hissed as Oscar dropped the cubes into the glasses. Giving them a stir he shouted, 'Well, one thing's for sure, or rather a couple: I still don't like Wagner, and I haven't managed to paint a stroke. I think it's too late.'

'That's just as well, then ... Isn't it?'

Oscar returned with the drinks and Bloch took his glass with an air of incurable boredom.

'You referred to love as a snake pit just now ... I had the impression it wasn't so ... ' said Oscar.

'So *what?* What kind of love are we talking about anyway? Filial, paternal, platonic, sexual?'

'Sexual.'

'Maternal, divine, unrequited, unconditional ...' Bloch continued.

'Sexual. *Sexual* love.'

'I was afraid of that. That's the tricky one. Because it contains elements of all the others, potentially. I was thinking ...' He trailed off.

'Why don't you tell me about Natalie? You never really speak about her. Get it off your chest. Or is that a bad idea?'

'I shouldn't have brought her up – the reason I did is because, before you rolled in, I was knocking together some scraps about her. Fag ends. Nostalgia. I may be romanticizing the past, but looking back on it now when I was with her – and only her – I felt more truly alive than ever before or since. Consequently, I've been asking myself this question: can that freezing of time – that strange something acquired in the act of copulation, screwing, bodily irrigation – help you live your life more creatively? In other words, can sex be a gateway to some higher perception? As in Tantric teachings, which I've been imbibing. Perhaps. The real thing might come close, but not the kind of fucking that goes on behind the bicycle sheds.'

'How would you define that kind?'

'Sticky, mechanical. It's fading into memory even when it's happening. A non-event.'

Oscar was slightly unnerved by how dismissive, even misanthropic Bloch's remarks were. But he nonetheless produced a notepad and began scribbling all over it, as he moved his chair closer to the bed. Bloch was growing more animated.

'But if you were in love, whatever that means ... if intimacy made a wind blow through your body, turned water into wine, turned the pimples and freckles on her face into diamonds and brocades, almighty emeralds from the Maharaja's private collection, giving her reality the stamp of great art ... that, to me is what love could mean when it's really soaring: a revelation, a manifesto of how to live. That's what it was like with Natalie ... I think ... sometimes.'

Oscar stopped writing, looked up; he had an intimation of having heard something vaguely momentous.

'That's ... beautiful,' he whispered.

Bloch was suddenly light-headed. Perhaps it was the gin. And his hearing had grown more acute. The noise of the traffic from outside seemed greatly magnified, the sound of slamming doors floated up through the floorboards. He could hear the kitchen clock ticking very distinctly. For a moment the activities of the world were with him, in a room which had turned into its echo chamber.

'All my life,' Bloch resumed, 'I don't know why, but I've managed to make a mess of the love that the romantic love magazines devote a thousand-and-one paragraphs to each day, the love everyone's dying from lack of. For me it took two forms: the promised land, or the land mine. Love should be beyond judgment, though it hardly ever is. It should be unconditional but who can truly love unconditionally? We all expect some return, ugly little egos always getting in the way, fouling up the works. By the way, orgasms are deceptive; their tiny moments cajole you into promising eternity.' Oscar had resumed his note taking.

Colors, shapes, contours were becoming more defined. He felt roused by a fevered eloquence.

'And why the hell, tell me, does love usually come with the imperative of wealth? But I grant you that, sometimes, very rarely, it turns out like a fairytale. And, as I say, when it's working, really working, it can even stop time, gloriously fuck up its springs. Then everything shimmers.'

He rested, took some deep breaths.

'But this is all very lofty, very grand, isn't it? Look at me, I'm so good at preaching, but it's pissing in the wind. I mean, can you think of anything more humiliating than having your wife leave you for your father? I can see the salmon swimming behind me, struggling to keep up, poor little salmon, big cruel whale churning in the ocean. Natalie saw the salmon as well; no doubt why she eventually opted for the beached whale that is my father.

'But aren't we all deceiving ourselves with these weak words? Oh yes, words can make everything all right, neutralize pain, give the gravedigger something grand to think about as he shovels earth. When they find me here, what will they say about me? What words will they disturb the leaves with? I'm tired, I'm spent. Leave me now, leave me; I'm not fit for company at the present time. Or take me to the water, I want to be beside the sea, Oscar; if I'm to die, I'd like a last glimpse of the sea. Do this for me, Oscar, let me go gracefully like a fish in the tide, not struggling in the net, but still in the silence of the sea.'

Oscar stopped scribbling.

'What ... what are you saying?'

Moved by the pathos of Bloch's words Oscar reached his hand out and held Bloch's in his own for a time. Bloch squeezed his eyes shut and slowly whispered, 'Why is my imagination swamping me? Why now?'

Oscar didn't have an answer. Bloch, his eyes still closed, speaking more softly, with a voice so small that it seemed afraid of disturbing even the air, said, 'You're young; you're not like me. You're not judgmental; you're not bitter, like me.'

Oscar caught himself peering out of the open windows and studying a line of *terracotta* rooftops, stretching into the distance. In the last few moments the light had been changing imperceptibly; now it was the color of whiskey, turning the room into a warm and golden sanctuary. A baffling, spell-binding stillness enveloped everything. Then, as if on cue, the skyline began to coalesce into a haze of cobalt and magenta serenity. What world out there awaited him?

'Oscar, you're young; you're full of beans,' Bloch repeated.

'I owe everything to you.'

'Like what?'

'Without you I think I'd cease to exist.'

'Oscar, I've something to tell you. I feel – I feel like it might be hard for me to get out of this bed for awhile. You really might have to be my foghorn, while I'm busy getting sucked into the swamp.'

With these words sudden, indiscriminate exhaustion knocked him sideways and his face caved in. Even as his face assumed an odd fixity, the pose of a death mask, his remarks ushered in oblique, skewed freedoms.

Oscar was on the verge of saying something but he was stopped short by the startling sound of the buzzer. At once Bloch's eyes were wide and manic. He yanked Oscar's arm so violently that he cried out in pain. Bloch wailed, 'My father – he's here already – Oh Christ – shit – I've got to get dressed – he can't see me in my pyjamas – he can't see me like this – quick, let's talk about the something real – practical – I've got to flush my mind out.'

Oscar backed off, massaging his arm. Bloch got up and shoved some clothes on over his pyjamas, feeling increasingly disassociated from his actions. He was connecting with reality spasmodically, one moment finding himself aware and the next in thrall to oblivion. He pressed a button on the intercom jerkily.

'Get the door, get the door; keep him happy, keep him happy.'

Oscar waddled into the hallway and opened the front door with his undamaged arm, holding the other close to his chest. He heard slow footsteps. An angular, distorted shadow was climbing up the wall in advance of its owner. After a minute, the figure of Webster, the antiques dealer, emerged. He was panting and wheezing. At last his breathing steadied and he was able to form words.

'Hello, we met at the swimming baths,' he said, squeezing the words out of the corner of his mouth, as was his habit. Then, gripped by embarrassment, he collapsed into helpless laughter and his face went red.

'Come in. Bloch isn't feeling very well,' Oscar said drily.

Their host appeared from the bedroom, looking as if he had just crawled out of a tumble dryer.

'Oh. Webster. I thought you were my father.'

'What? Oh. Sorry to hear you're indisposed. I wanted to ask a favor. Could I use your bath? My boiler's on the blink, has been for weeks. I'm refusing to pay the rent, to make a stand. All landlords are mean – first law of real estate.'

Oscar said, 'Mine's in love with a bag lady, so he's turned nice.'

Webster ignored this and muttered, 'I've brought you some dough-nuts.' He rummaged around and produced a paper bag which could not have been more stained or wrinkled. He offered the bag to Bloch with a limp hand.

'What do you say? I'd love a soak.'

Bloch snatched up the bag of doughnuts and snapped, 'Shall I put these in water, as well as you?'

'What do you mean? They're not flowers, you know; they're for eating. They should go in the fridge. Let me do it as you're not feeling too sturdy.'

'That's awfully kind of you Webster, but that will hardly solve my problems.'

Webster stared blankly, feeling more and more uncomfortable, trying to think of an appropriate response. He carried on automatically, 'They're nice doughnuts. I got them from this patisserie in Little Venice. The owner's a friend of mine. She makes the best coffee cake I've ever tasted.'

Bloch, determined to wrong foot him again, said, 'That's wonderful. I've always considered that to be the defining hallmark of a good woman. That and a vagina smelling of Earl Grey tea.'

Webster made an inchoate sound while Bloch peered inside the brown bag and saw two or three sad looking lumps.

'Do you think I'll ever see Natalie again?' he asked miserably.

Oscar looked at Webster, Webster looked at Oscar.

'Have you ever missed what's in front of your nose?' Bloch continued.

'No, because it's usually a pimple. I have quite bad skin, you see, and it's irritated when I don't wash,' said Webster, quite proud of the way he had slipped in the suggestion that he needed to bathe.

'I'm speaking of what life's about, of the inner meanings. The least you can do is maintain a semblance of intelligence! Straight from the horse's mouth come pearls, and you just sit and salivate.'

'Daniel, Webster didn't mean anything by that.'

'Not you, as well. Don't start, don't start. Isn't it enough that I've set this mad process into being; isn't that enough for you, and now I'm splintering; isn't that enough, haven't you got all you need from me? Aren't you happy now?'

By now the hallway was feeling extremely uncomfortable and Oscar, for his part, had the odd impression that he was no longer in someone's flat but in an airplane as it plunged screaming towards the earth, seconds away from igniting into a fireball.

'You have to go now ... both of you ... I have to wait for my father,' Bloch mumbled, turning away, his voice fading, his back slouched. He shuffled into the sepulchral bedroom, leaving in his wake two dazed forms, hanging like scarecrows in the gathering shadows.

They bounded down the stairs and into the open air, both shaken by the vehemence of Bloch's remarks, the sense that he had been on the brink of an eruption.

'He's not himself today, you see,' Oscar muttered as they walked.

'So, who is he then?'

Oscar made no reply.

'Bloch despises me, doesn't he? Thinks I'm an idiot? A dolt.'

'No, no. It's all right. I'll have a word with him. Let's go to the park.'

By now the sun was no longer visible. In its place there was an afterglow of color, red and tangerine. All around, as far as the eye could see, the skin of the sky was being stretched and tightened. The walk continued in silence. They were conscious of fragrant smells of honeysuckle and jasmine, swimming at the threshold of awareness.

Oscar felt more and more dazzled by his friend, as if by a marvelous waterfall. But there was no doubt that Bloch was behaving strangely; he was raging against the world. Perhaps, Oscar thought, he could communicate his friend's observations through a less savage persona, a more gentle prism. But then fear re-asserted itself, the fear of being conspicuous, criticized, or exposed. He was embarking once again on something utterly alien, but what was the alternative? To go back to projecting films? To go back to life modeling? To get a job washing dishes?

As they slipped through the gates of Regent's Park Webster mumbled, 'I really need a pee.' He tumbled towards a tree and furtively unripped his flies, watching to make sure no one was within range. As he urinated, willing his bladder to empty itself quickly, he remembered the time as a boy his cousin had spied on him in the lavatory and he felt a stab of pain.

Oscar spread himself out on a patch of grass beside a large oak tree. The grass was still warm from the sun. His eye followed the curving line of trees, some close together in clusters, others dotted about singly. His gaze came to rest on a rectangle of large-flowered carmine tulips in the distance. The tulips summoned up images of Lilliana pottering about in her shop. He thought fondly of her, but felt slightly guilty because he hadn't been in touch for so long. He liked her because she appreciated people for who they were and not because they necessarily struck chords with her life or shared her own opinions or feelings.

Oscar felt a sudden desire to spend the night in the park, in a spirit of non-conformity. As he was thinking about this Webster returned, peering around nervously.

'Webster, what about sleeping in the park? Wouldn't that be wonderful?'

'I'm not so sure, I've just had the 'flu.'

'Don't be such a baby. Where's your sense of adventure? Stay and keep me company.'

Webster sat down and muttered, 'Well, maybe for a little while, but I have to pick something up later from Basildon. A Japanese vase. Basildon's enough to piss off anyone. It's 19th-century, you see. I mean the vase, not Basildon. I don't know when Basildon dates from. Probably the dark ages. Still in them, if you ask me. What a royal bore. I'm in antiques; you know that, do you? Got a stall on Portobello. Drop in, you'll find me at the Admiral Vernon arcade. Chinese exports, Arita porcelain.'

Oscar ignored him and kept his gaze firmly fixed on the changing sky. The moon was visible, hanging sadly, a pallid disc growing gradually more distinct.

'What line are you in; what do you do Oscar?'

'Right now, not an awful lot. I'm hoping that might be about to change.'

'Well, I wouldn't count on it.'

'You think? If there's one thing that's been consistent in my life lately, it's change.'

'I need a change. And a new boiler. That useless landlord. I can't even have a shower, I've been having to shower at the gym.'

'That can't be so convenient.'

'It's ok. For some reason the clientele consists of fat men dangling their bits. From the way they carry on you'd think they had the bodies of athletes, not beer bellies and double chins. I wonder how their wives can bear to be touched by them. So they probably don't. In which case, I expect they visit ladies of the night.'

'And what do you feel about that?'

'Not a lot. It's not my cup of tea. I wouldn't go near a trollop with a barge pole.'

'Would you disapprove of a man who did?'

'Don't know. Don't think so. Would you?'

'I'm not sure.'

'So would you ever go? To a brothel?'

There was a pause.

'Actually, I went to one the other day,' said Oscar, looking directly at Webster, 'though I'm not likely to go again.'

'Where was this?' Webster demanded in a slightly hoarse voice. He wasn't sure what motives lay behind this question.

'Greenwich.'

'Were you on your own?'

'No, I went with someone I've since decided to have nothing more to do with.'

'Why's that?'

'Because he's manipulative and nasty. But at the time I didn't really know that. From the way he described this place I had to admit I was curious.'

'What did he say to you?'

'He told me it was like some *fin-de-siecle* bordello, the kind of place you could normally find only in Budapest or Cairo, and yet here it was in London, known only to a few experts and special clients, of which – he assured me – he was one.'

'I see. Doesn't sound that amazing.'

'No, it wasn't.'

'So go on, then, tell me what happened. That's if you don't mind.'

'Actually, I've been wanting to tell someone.'

Beside him, from his supine position on the grass, Webster moved around restlessly, never quite managing to settle down. He could find problems, obstacles in everything.

'I'm just getting comfortable. But you start.'

Oscar cleared his throat, feeling slightly self-conscious.

'All right. Well, we had to catch a train from Waterloo.

'During the ride I was pretty nervous. Nicholas produced a flask of whiskey, so I guzzled on it. It's amazing how alcohol can alter your perspective on things, don't you find?'

'I suppose so.' Webster was now making inroads into his left ear, excitedly excavating the bolus of wax lodged inside. Later on he planned to pick at the dirt in his finger nails.

'Is this boring you? Are you sure you want me to go on?'

'Oh no, I mean yes. Just ignore me. I'll settle down in a minute.'

'If you say so,' Oscar said with a certain exasperation. Now, as he told the story, his gaze drifted away from Webster until he was staring in front of him, addressing the open spaces of the park. He found it easier to look away, given the story's delicate nature.

'When we got to Greenwich we walked for about half a mile. The house was out of the way; it stood at the top of a hill, so we could look down on London, a mass of lights. I could see the line of the

Thames, silvery with moonlight. It was very picturesque.

'Nicholas rang the bell and after a while a doorman with the face of a bulldog materialized. Normally he would have made me nervous, but because the situation was so unusual, his pockmarked face struck me as appropriate. He looked like he wasn't happy about my being there, but after Nicholas had had a few words with him he showed us in.

'Inside it was like something from another time, as Nicholas said it would be, though nowhere near as spectacular as he'd made out. The wallpaper was covered in rococo patterns and there were shaded lamps hanging from the walls, casting a lot of red light. I could see lithographs of what looked like illustrations from the *Kama Sutra*. There was a rather flashy staircase in the corner and, up above, on the landing, I made out a line of statues. Nymphs, they seemed to be.

'On the ground floor there weren't any doors, just red drapes; we pushed past some and entered a kind of waiting room, filled to bursting point with cushions. There must have been about twenty candles burning. We planted ourselves down. Then I noticed, for the first time, a dwarf at the far end. He was puffing on a long thing like a pipe which coiled round into a bottle.'

'That would be a hookah; I used to sell them,' Webster interjected.

'Yes, a hookah. The dwarf was staring at me – he didn't seem interested in Nicholas. He had thick glasses and I could see his eyes magnified through the lenses. It was odd seeing this giant pair of eyes peering at me out of a tiny body.

'Nicholas offered me a cigarette. I took one, not because I really wanted it, but because I wanted something to focus on, and the dwarf was making me nervous. He just wouldn't give up. He could have outstared an eagle. He sat back on his cushion, puffed every now and then on his hookah and pinned me to the wall with his eyes. I wondered whether he was a regular client.

'I asked Nicholas what we were waiting for. He told me to "look seasoned, like you've done this before." "Done what?" I asked.

'The drapes fluttered and a woman – in her fifties, I suppose – came in. She wore a red dress with a long slit in it, and I noticed she had varicose veins. She sidled up to Nicholas and they moved away, chatting for a few minutes about all sorts of subjects, including me, as I gathered from eavesdropping. Meanwhile the dwarf got up to receive one of the girls as she made her entrance. I felt incredibly relieved that I was shortly to see the back of him. She wore a very unusual outfit; I don't really think you could call it a dress. Four or five black hoops were joined together in a vertical line down her body. There wasn't any material in between the hoops, just thin bars of plastic keeping them together. The hoops hovered slightly whenever she moved. Other than that all she had on was a black bra, black leather boots, and black gloves up to her elbows. Her pubic hair had been trimmed into a heart shape and her belly button was pierced.'

Oscar cleared his throat, then resumed.

'Anyway, the dwarf stomped off with this girl and Nicholas introduced me to his friend, who turned out to be the madam. She wanted to know something about my taste in women so I muttered a few words about how they had to be tall. I could see I was revealing my inexperience and Nicholas shot me a nasty look. Then, out of the blue, I heard this really strange sound. Someone was moaning, but it had an edge to it; it was impossible to say whether or not the person was in pain. Then there was a man's voice speaking – in – I think – Chinese. The voice was absolutely bizarre ... it sounded like the man was speaking out of a hole in his throat.

'I said in a hurry, "Do you have any girls with red hair?" This seemed to please the madam and she replied, "I've just the thing, she's very sensitive, like you; come with me, darling." My heart was pounding as she led me away. As I pushed through the drapes a woman in a toga brushed against me, headed, I supposed, for Nicholas. I was about to say goodbye to him but thought better of it.

'We climbed the stairs and she showed me into a bedroom overflowing with the smell of menthol. The bed was massive and covered with green taffeta, with gigantic phalluses embroidered all over it. There was a mirror above the bed and more lithographs on the walls, more explicit than the ones I'd seen downstairs. I also recognized a print by Hokusai, which was very eerie: it showed an octopus making love to a fisherwoman; she was held down in its tentacles.

'My hostess told me to make myself comfortable and that "Julie" would be along soon. I slumped onto the bed and tried taking some deep breaths. After a few minutes I decided a drink might help. I tip-toed into the corridor; there was no one around, just a set of closed doors, as in a hotel. I could hear moaning and words like "just there" and "harder, harder." I crept over to one of the doors to listen. After that I didn't hear anything.

'Back in the room I fiddled around in the side-table and found a few packets of condoms and not much else. There was a knock at the door and a tall, big-boned woman with red hair came in. She wasn't much to look at, it has to be said. I forgot to say there was a fireplace in the room, a large, open fireplace and as she came in I found my-self staring into the dead coals and wishing they were lit. I had this strange idea that a fire would have made everything all right.

'She was wearing a transparent satin shirt and her breasts showed quite clearly. She had jeans on, and they were cut so short that I could see the arcs of her buttocks. In fact, she gave me a little twirl just to make sure I didn't miss this feature. Her stilettos had laces that climbed up her legs like ivy, and she wore a single black ribbon round her neck. Her hair was loose, and it looked like she'd just stepped out of the shower, because it was damp.

'"What's your name, then?" she asked, sitting down by me on the bed.

'For some reason I told her my name was Max.

'"I'm Julie, Max," she said. She took my hand. I was surprised how light her touch was. Then, for the first time, I looked into her face directly. As I did she started talking – about nothing in particular. I think she'd sensed my nervousness and decided she'd try and make me feel at home by chatting for a little while. But when she spoke there wasn't any expression to her voice, she just sounded dazed. Sometimes she trailed off into these giant pauses and looked at me, but then she managed to pick up again. Half the time she didn't really make sense and kept on using the wrong word; listening to her was like trying to read illegible handwriting.

'Then I began to think she wasn't really human, or that she was a copy of a human. It was something to do with her eyes, which were like the eyes of a doll. Dead. In fact her face, when I really thought about it, and I had a lot of time to as she droned on, was completely expressionless; it was like the face of someone on very strong tranquilizers. She was a void. It felt as if the thing that makes a face alive, that spark, had been blown out of her, that actually every speck of life had been crushed out of her. I knew I had to get out of there, that I wouldn't be able to stand being with her for much longer. I thought that if she smiled everything would be different, that everything would suddenly make sense. But she didn't, it was as though she wasn't actually able to.

'Then something happened. She asked me what I'd like to do first. I didn't make any reply. There was a sound, another moaning sound. But it wasn't made by a person. At first I thought it was coming from next door and I wondered whether some of the clients liked to use animals. Then I realized it was coming from the chimney. There was something trapped inside it, a pigeon or something. She noticed, stuck her head up the fireplace, turned back and said, "It's just a crow, we get them all the time, it'll clear off in a minute. Shall we get on with it?" Her voice was still dead, flat.

'But this croaking wouldn't stop and it really began to get on my nerves. Here was this woman who was dead and this crow which was stuck, making this sound.

'I said, "Look, I'm sorry, but that's really putting me off." She told me it was nothing and that it was an old Victorian house, the kind crows liked. "Well, shouldn't we try and get it out, free it? It sounds like it's dying," I insisted.

'Then, angrily, she grabbed my hand and forced it down her blouse. I have to admit it was nice, feeling her breast against my palm. She was moving my hand around slowly in a circle, directing it for me. But I broke away and told her I couldn't go through with it with that bird trapped in the chimney and that we had to go somewhere else.

'"You're worse than a woman," she said. "You know this is costing you, don't you?" For the first time some kind of emotion penetrated her voice.

'I nodded. She'd see if she could get us another room. She went off.

'I tiptoed out, and ran down the stairs. As I opened the door the footman sniffed around me like the bulldog that he was, sensing something was amiss. I tried to look composed, knowing that Julie might be down at any moment. He growled, in his thick voice, "I trust you obtained relief." I told him I'd found the experience very gratifying, but you could see he didn't believe me. I made as if to go but he grabbed my hand and leaned up to me, quite close and whispered, "There's a girl in there, she's my daughter; if you've upset her, I'll make sure you never walk straight again." I tried my best to reassure him that I'd upset no one. I was really frightened now. "She's my own flesh and blood, she's a bright girl; if you've done anything to upset her, I'll stick you in a bath and chuck in a live toaster." I shouted: "Look, I haven't touched anyone, all right; I haven't even done anything." As he gazed at me with psychotic eyes, I tried to see if there was any physical resemblance between him and Julie. Then, suddenly, crazily, he started laughing, and then he barked, "You're all right; now fuck off home before you get gonorrhea." I broke into a run after I'd put some distance between me and the house, peering around every now and then to make sure he wasn't chasing me. I was gulping air down quickly, like I was gulping down food. The streets of Greenwich looked very wonderful. I don't know if you know what I mean, but as I ran for the station, through the night,

I felt incredibly excited just to be able to hear sounds, just to pass by the houses with their lights on. Wherever I looked there seemed to be something I could celebrate, the twigs from trees, plastic bags floating in the wind.

'As I slowed down I took to thinking about her ... but I just couldn't deal with that blankness ... I couldn't have slept with her; it would have been too weird. I don't know; maybe I'm using that as an excuse but –'

Oscar stopped abruptly. He turned to look at Webster.

He was snoring. It sounded like the noise made by the final swirls of water as they are sucked down a drain.

'Oh well,' he said.

It was dark now.

The park gates were locked. A few stars were scattered here and there and the moon was shining brilliantly. Everything was profoundly still and – aside from Webster's periodic snoring – silent. The trees were visible as filmy outlines and silhouettes. In the distance clusters of bushes stood out like the outlines of strange animals in the moonlight.

He thought of his story. He was glad he had had the chance to tell it; it amounted to a kind of confession. But why confess to Webster, whom he hardly knew, and who was not exactly noted for his sensitivity or intelligence?

His thoughts drifted aimlessly for awhile until at last they led him towards Najette. He visualized her face, matter-of-factly beautiful, and her transforming smile, offering an antidote against anxiety. He wished she was with him now. And then he was re-living once more their kiss in the cafe. It seemed to him that as they kissed her beauty had miraculously blossomed, grown supernatural, and his centre of gravity had shifted until he was falling, falling through great chasms of pleasure, leaving the detritus and boredom of life far behind ...

As he stretched out on the grass these thoughts plugged him straight into sleep.

## 10

After Webster and Oscar had left, Bloch climbed back into bed. But as soon as the covers were over him, he jumped up. He was determined to tidy the flat. He picked up the pieces of the broken ashtray and threw them in the waste bin in the study, whose floor was littered with books, ashtrays, cups of congealed coffee, newspaper cuttings, fax rolls. It was only by a massive effort of will that he was able to pick up the cups and ashtrays and put them in the kitchen sink. A vase full of dead roses sat in the corner, its water foul. He pulled one of the stems out gently and examined it. Its petals were sunken and dry, and a grey-green sepal hovered above the petals like a small jellyfish uprooted from its home and frozen. He placed the stem back in the vase, shuffled back to the study, collected a mound of dirty clothes which had piled up in the corner, went back to the kitchen and shoved the clothes inside his washing machine. He didn't see the scraps of paper with ideas scribbled on them – since they were dislodged between the clothes – so they also journeyed into the steel barrel. He took a deep breath, feeling very sick, but a little buoyed up by the space that these random maneuvers had created.

He closed the bedroom windows, blocking out the corrosive sounds of the street, climbed back into bed and – under the covers – tore off his clothes and the pyjamas underneath. When the buzzer sounded minutes later, he thrashed around with his clothes once more, as if locked in combat with them, until he was dressed. By the time he reached the hallway he was drenched in sweat. He mopped his brow on his shirt-sleeve, opened his front door and waited, listening keenly to the slow footsteps which – he noted – were abnormally loud and resonant.

And then at last a tall figure emerged, a mane of salt-and- pepper hair falling around his ears, wiry eyebrows jutting out like the remnants of a bird's nest.

The two men regarded each another painfully, but it was a long time before anyone spoke.

Finally, Samuel Bloch muttered, 'You look awful; what's the matter?'

The sight of his son's face was a terrible shock. His eyes were bloodshot, his lips had all but lost their color. His hair was more thin and grey than he could possibly have imagined, despite the long passage of time since he had last seen him. And the sweat pouring from his forehead looked like amniotic fluid.

'What's wrong, Danny?'

'Nothing, I'm fine.'

'Get back into bed.'

'How did you know I was in bed?'

'Never mind that now.'

'No, I don't want to get into bed. We'll talk in the living room.'

Bloch was determined not to appear weak in front of his father. He slumped into an armchair while his father eased his generous frame into another with an air of slight distaste.

For a man in his late sixties, Samuel Bloch was remarkably fit. In fact, as he now realized, he was in considerably better health than his son, though he liked to make out he was a martyr to old age. He insisted on having a morning dip into an ice pool every day. His diet was extremely spartan – bread, cheese, cashew nuts, avocados, eggs, fish, olives, yoghurt and figs. Occasionally he allowed himself the luxuries of bacon and coffee. He also drank red wine, but only from the most expensive bottles.

'Have you called a doctor? I think someone should take a look at you.'

He spoke in a gruff baritone, often becoming a mumble which

could only be deciphered with the utmost tenacity.

'You seem suddenly concerned for my welfare. What's brought this on? This strange gush of benevolence. Quick, let's bottle it and find a cork; it might trickle away.'

'Danny, please, no games, this is more important. Let me call my doc.'

'I despise doctors. None of them know a bloody thing. Drink?'

'I'll get it. Some brandy might perk you up. Where are we – kitchen for the libations?'

'I'll do it.'

Bloch forced himself to his feet, but his body wobbled and toppled over. His father rushed over, lifted him up and steadied him. He was at once phlegmatic and practical.

'Right, let's get you into bed,' he said calmly, and, wrapping an arm around his shoulder, they were able to shuffle into the bedroom, forming a curious couple. As Bloch fell onto the bedclothes his father rapidly punched buttons on the telephone.

'Who's that?'

'My GP; don't worry, he's excellent.'

While his father explained the situation to his doctor Bloch loosened his clothes as gently as he could manage. He was panting and his pulse raced.

'He can be here in an hour. I think brandy's probably not a good idea right now.'

'You may be right.'

'What happened to you?'

'I don't know.'

There was a difficult, interrogative silence. Then his father said, with surprising gentleness, 'You should look after yourself, you know.' Bloch stared into his eyes. How little he knew him, how welcome were these scraps of a love normally hidden in inaccessible places. He was suddenly seized with a desire for him to stay a few days, but he couldn't bring himself to say anything. Pride sabotaged his vocal chords.

He started to feel a little of his strength returning and his breathing gradually steadied. The conversation resumed abruptly.

'Daniel, I'm expecting someone in a minute or two.'

'What?'

'Well, put it this way; she's my secretary.'

'What?'

'She's a mobile secretary. She's also my ... companion.'

'You mean your mistress.'

'I wouldn't use those words.'

'"Mistress" is one word. How long is it since we've seen each other?'

'Five years, isn't it?'

'Couldn't you have kept your love life out of this? Couldn't you have exercised some self-discipline and not brought the cigar butt with you?'

'Don't talk like that.'

'Mistress, more cakes and ale, more wine and roses, more fucks behind the bicycle shed ...'

Fortunately, just as he was getting into his stride, the buzzer went again. This time it lasted for a longer time, as if the person on the other end was deliberately trying to annoy them. Bloch indicated the intercom with a sagging index finger. His father walked over to it and pressed the button which released the front door of the building.

Once again conversation seemed impossible. Until Bloch launched into a fractured tirade.

'Is this how you want to do things – all your life? Without the remotest conception of what's appropriate? I mean – you're meant to be here to see me, me. That means I don't want some hundred-words-per-minute bimbo to interrupt. I don't want – I don't want sex to get in the way of our friendly re-union. Or perhaps I'm not worth that basic respect – perhaps I'm just a little interlude between the next check-in at the next hotel lobby. Dad, life isn't all saunas, jacuzzis, velvet bottles of – '

There was a knock: very clean, efficient.

His father, with some relief, scrambled into the hallway. The moment that Bloch had alone in his bed was delicious.

A minute later, from his prone position on the bed, Bloch was able to see a large woman standing at the door, clutching a battered brown suit case. She presented quite a spectacle.

Her breasts were in a state of such mobility he feared they might divide from her body and start hopping across the floor. Her turquoise dress was barely coping with its contents, stretching and curving and twisting at her hips and waist, acquiring elasticity to deal with her recalcitrant curves. Platinum blonde locks tumbled down to her hips and her blood red lips were locked in a perpetual pout.

'Who the hell is this?' Bloch bawled.

'This is Miss Van Veuren.'

A bizarre pattern was now established as father and son proceeded to speak in a manner that suggested Miss Van Veuren was not actually there with them, or as if she couldn't hear what they were saying. She didn't seem to mind their disregard and maintained her air of statuesque docility.

'Would you ask her to leave?'

'No can do, Danny,' Bloch senior called. 'She takes care of all my arrangements and she has my tickets and everything.'

Samuel Bloch emerged from the shadows projected by her ample body. He ushered his secretary forward and they ambled into the bedroom. Miss Van Veuren put the case down, found a chair, wiped it with a large purple handkerchief embroidered with hearts and sat down. The smell of her perfume drifted over to Bloch who regarded her with something between loathing and lust. Then he demanded, speaking rapidly, 'Miss Van Veuren, do you find that there is a resounding lack of heart in the hearts of people today? Are you not struck time and time again by their inability to respond to anything that does not utilize a maniacal consumerism?'

After a pause Miss Van Veuren smiled, revealing her perfectly aligned incisors, but uttered no words.

'Look, Daniel, for God's sake, the girl isn't a professor.'

'I can see that, dad. By the way, what the hell happened to my ex-wife?'

'She left me. I told you that.'

Bloch chuckled softly.

'That's good.'

'I suppose I deserve your laughter. But I don't think we should talk about her now, not when you're lying here like this.'

'No, let's do talk about her, an excellent idea. It will be...diverting. Now that you've made the pilgrimage, perhaps you could grant me a few insights. How is she?'

'The last time I saw her, nearly a year ago, she'd developed a thing for her tango teacher. I don't need to tell you what she's like.'

Miss Van Veuren crossed her legs, and Bloch lapped the sight up greedily. She momentarily acknowledged his curiosity; something registered in the movement of her eyes. Then she was impassive again, supremely disconnected from everything going on around her.

'No, you don't need to tell me about her wicked ways; I know all about them. Still ... a remarkable woman. I got closer to her than you ever did.'

'I don't deny it. I never meant to hurt you.'

'She liked you because you were a real man, weren't you – the genuine article, the big whale showing off its bulk, making noise, being confident, with no sub-text of doubt, not even a smidgen of doubt, just self-confidence, no anxiety or angst. No sad swimming salmon hiding behind you, you were hundred-percent whale meat, through and through.' Weary of these rhapsodic stabs, Bloch abandoned them and said evenly, 'You could have said no.'

'You know that's impossible with Natalie; she doesn't take no for an answer.'

Suddenly impassioned Bloch blurted out, 'Oh, please, can't you think of something more original?!'

'I'm not original; I never claimed to be, Danny.'

'Except in one particular. Your love life is very original; your choice of partner practically earth-shattering. It shattered my world, anyway.'

'Danny, please, I couldn't … she seduced me; did you know she spiked my drink?'

'With what? Fertilizer? A pity she didn't spike you.' The effect of this last remark was so excruciating Samuel Bloch's brain erased any trace of it the moment after it was uttered.

'What's wrong with you, anyway?' his father asked, shakily trying to change the subject.

'I don't know. Burnt out, knocked for six, if you must know. But I'd love to see her again. I remember when it was bliss just to be around her, just to be in the same room as her. Not even to say anything. Why does that feeling go eventually?'

'You're the writer. Don't ask me.'

'I am a writer, of sorts. After forty eight years of life, my writing's evolving into something new. It's actually getting serious. That's something. It's strange, as my body turns into an old mattress, my mind bounces like a trampoline. Can't quite work it out. Oscar, I think.'

'Who's Oscar?'

'An old cunt-friend.'

'And what's he been up to?'

'Anything I can dream up.'

'What?'

'Let's talk about Natalie. Tell me, did she ever show you her trick, when she would pour hot wax on her nipples? The Amazons would have welcomed her with outstretched arms.'

'Hot wax on her nipples?' Miss Van Veuren interjected in an unidentifiable foreign accent.

Bloch stared at Miss Van Veuren incredulously, then bawled out, 'It's a miracle!'

'Oh please, Daniel, don't go on.'

There was a lull. Miss Van Veuren began filing her nails mechanically.

'Did I ever tell you about the time Natalie and I were on Port Meadow?' Bloch asked. 'There was the most stupendous thunderstorm. Stupendous. The whole meadow became a million-watt bulb. I pushed on, soaking, while she and her pal lagged behind. I was pissing my pants, trying to get to safety, convinced I was about to be reduced to a pillar of ash, when I caught a snatch of the conversation they were having. And do you know what she said? She said, "If lightning tried to strike me, I'd deflect it with my fingernails." Fantastically stupid, yes, I agree, on one level, but you had to admire the nerve of it, the sheer grandeur, to defy nature, to shake a fist, a fingernail, at it. It was sublime; she was so fucking unflappable. Of course I suppose I wasn't, and you, in your way, were. That was Natalie, glorious, unruly, mad Natalie. She was wasted on you … why am I singing her praises anyway, turning her body into a source of awakening? You both issued me with a castration order.'

'Danny, listen, I don't want to be cruel, but you have to face up to the fact that your marriage was over long before she and I …' He stopped, stumbled into a void, pulled himself out of it, his eyes manic, and resumed, slightly desperately, 'I didn't cause the estrangement between you; it just happened, and what happened afterwards was a terrible mistake. But I'm not the reason she drifted away from you in the first place.'

'So what? As if that makes everything wonderful. I know you weren't the reason. I also know the real reason, don't worry. She caught a glimpse of my frailty, that's why.'

'There must have been more to it than that.'

'I think deep down she just wanted someone who could surf on those gigantic, bending-over-backward tidal waves in New Zealand. The best I could manage was a bit of punting on the River Cam. Listen, Dad, don't bother being analytical, stick to your balance sheets and interest rates.'

'Well, she's gone now. She's taking tango lessons.'

'Day and night, eh? Dancing between the sheets, eh? She must have warmed to a man a third your age, papa.' Bloch uttered the words with icy emphasis.

Samuel Bloch's eyes betrayed something – pain, bewilderment, self-pity, perhaps all three, but then they became expressionless. These exchanges, having taken on the character of a slanging match, with Bloch clearly gaining the upper hand, browbeating his father into submission, came to a halt and once more the bedroom was still. But the conflict was not over yet. Bloch decided to try out a different strategy.

'Tell me Miss Van Veuren, how much does my father pay you for your services?'

Miss Van Veuren glanced at her employer (and lover) for a moment and then back at Bloch. She smiled, revealing her beautifully bleached teeth.

'Don't be shy, spill the beans,' Bloch intoned.

'Well, as his personal secretary and assistant Mr Bloch pays me £1500 a week. Bonuses include the use of his jacuzzi so long as he's in it at the same time. Also, the joyride in the Mercedes 280 SL convertible, which can reach speeds of up to 210 miles an hour, plus every now and then a bottle of vintage wine – '

'Stop! I'll pay you £2000 a week, and you may have access to my divine body at all hours of the day and night, depending on my mood ... and you may also be my own personal nurse maid. I will set you up in the East wing where you will have your own bidet, with the complete works of Spinoza thrown in.'

'Danny, don't do this. You're being ridiculous.'

'I think that Miss Van Veuren is quite old enough to make up her own mind. Now then Miss Van Veuren what do you say, wouldn't you like to work for me?'

'I'm not sure. I have to think about it,' she said, wriggling in her chair.

Then Bloch senior squirmed about in his.

'Perhaps we should leave you to rest, Danny.'

'Not so fast, Dad. It's my turn to do some poaching.'

'What are you talking about? I've told you, I didn't poach Natalie; she came to me.'

'You're not leaving, not until I've had a chance to woo Miss Van Veuren.'

'Are you serious? This is ridiculous. I mean, what would you possibly –'

'See in her? I'll tell you: precisely what you do. Nice arse, great tits. Those go a long way in my book.'

At last, in operatic distress, Miss Van Veuren rose from her chair. Bloch had done it – had succeeded in evoking a reaction, not just a tepid show of interest, but something far more significant.

'I'm not just a sex object, thank you!' She glanced nervously from side to side, searching to see if she had made an impression.

'You're right, Miss Van Veuren,' said Bloch. 'Indeed you are not a sex object; it's only men like my father who think you are. So don't let him.'

'That's nonsense, Danny. Don't tell me you're –'

'What?! The fact is it's *you* who reduce life's poetry into commerce. Yes, you are all whale, through and through, because you've never doubted anything in life. Everything was ordered, had its place –'

'Danny, what have you got against whales anyway? And what is this obsession with them – and other fish?'

'Whales aren't fish, they're mammals. I have an obsession with the sea and what – other than seaweed – floats through it. Maybe it all began with Humphrey.'

'Who the hell's Humphrey?'

'You don't remember?'

'No, I don't.'

'Humphrey. The goldfish I had when I was little. The one that went down the plughole. My goldfish! We got it at the fun fair. In Ealing! You bought it for me, it made me happy. I used to feed it. Watch it.'

'Oh, *that* Humphrey! I never did understand how the loss of a goldfish could be so traumatic.'

'You didn't understand much. And you weren't exactly around that much either. You turned up and I used to think: who's this character? Is he or isn't he my father? I loved that fish and after it went part of me went with it.'

'I see – the fish was reliable, was it? Dependable? Trustworthy? Whereas I wasn't. Well ... I mean ... didn't I buy you another one?'

'It wasn't the same.'

'Well, it looked the same.'

'That's not the point.'

'Yes, but I mean, it was only a bloody goldfish.'

'I was only six! Oh what's the use; you'd better go, we're not getting anywhere. I can't string another sentence together.'

Samuel Bloch stood up and approached the bed hesitantly. He glanced at Miss Van Veuren. He wanted to go over and give his son a hug but he was worried he might not want to be hugged. Finally, in a soft murmured undertone, he asked Miss Van Veuren to leave the room for a moment.

She smiled, revealing her pearly white, flossed and scrubbed, spotless teeth. After adjusting strategic corners of her dress she sauntered off, her hips swaying, her body rehearsing for a walk down a catwalk that would never exist.

In a little while both men realized that her being in the room with them – while barely announcing her presence – had actually made it easier for them to talk to one another. She had somehow given them free rein to express emotion, had warded off mute solipsism and the silence that would otherwise – eventually, inevitably – have come. And now they were silent and couldn't think of a single other thing to say to each other. With each passing second the silence grew more weighty, like clay hardening and setting. This silence was not becalming; it was barren, and as the minutes passed it became harder and harder to break it. They both found themselves wishing Miss Van Veuren would return. But then the question Bloch had been trying not to ask came back, re-surfaced once again. He tried to find a niche, an appropriate corner into which the question might fit, but nothing presented itself. So in the end he blurted it out discordantly, shocked by the sound of his voice, which seemed alien and unfamiliar.

'Tell me – truthfully – why you did it. Why on earth did you have to fuck her?'

There was nothing and then, in one breath, with lightning speed, his father half-shouted, half-said, 'I knew that if I didn't I'd kick myself afterwards!'

All at once his father looked very old and frail. Bloch's face didn't betray any emotion.

'I suppose you'll want me to leave now,' his father mumbled, his eyes turned away.

Speaking very slowly, Bloch whispered, 'No, I don't want you to go.'

Samuel managed the weakest of smiles. Inside him pain and pleasure were bleeding into each other, fusing until they were one. Each moment contained whole worlds of kaleidoscopic feelings.

'I've no more words ... ,' he said, his big head hanging.

Bloch also turned his eyes away.

'It's funny isn't it,' Bloch sighed, 'after all the noise ... there comes a point when a conversation turns real, all the smokescreens clear and all that's left ... is this ... two voices in the wilderness ... Do you know what I mean?'

His father's giant frame seemed to have been hammered into the ground. In a tiny voice he mumbled, 'Danny, I really need you to forgive me for what I did to you.'

He was crying now.

Bloch's face, pulled by conflicting forces, was opaque and clear at the same time.

He was suddenly aware of the artificiality of his indignation, a residual sense of contrivance. Had he been acting out the role of someone who was wounded, full of accusing anger? He realized that he was more pleased than he cared to admit that his father had made contact with him. The strange thing was – he now saw – that those spars and verbal parries had been enjoyable; despite the enormity of his father's violation Bloch still found him amusing. Something was stopping Bloch from really giving vent. But was that something the product of a transcending magnanimity? Or did it suggest that he had finally severed his links with life and didn't really care about anything at all?

After Bloch had gestured for a scrap of paper and written down *I forgive you* on it a great weight lifted from Samuel's shoulders, some color returned to his cheeks, and he felt a strong desire for food.

# 11

Ryan Rees carried three cellular phones with him at all times. He gave the number of the first phone out to people he didn't want to speak to and so this phone was always switched off; those trying to get through could only leave messages on it. People Ryan Rees didn't want to speak to included lawyers out to sue him, two ex-wives, and those who wanted Rees to generate publicity for them: aspiring musicians and actors, people with 'remarkable' life stories, and other hopefuls. Rees had given them all this number so that they didn't feel he wasn't co-operating with him or that he was avoiding them, but at the same time he used the screen of voice-mail to have nothing to do with them. Their many e-mails would receive replies but they would never be written by Rees himself. For some in this unfortunate camp Ryan Rees was a duplicitous snake who hid behind technology; for those who were less worldly-wise he was simply a very difficult man to get hold of.

He gave the number of the second phone out to all the clients that he represented. The second number was also in the possession of certain journalists. For example, Lee Crackstone of the *Daily Mail.* Crackstone had once been described by his former editor as "the vilest, most spineless, toxic, evil smelling piece of scum to have ever crawled from under a rock where he takes his place with all manner of writhing and greasy worms. Whenever he opens his mouth the entire surrounding area should be fumigated and geiger counters installed to test for levels of radiation." Crackstone had – in the interests of the pursuit of the unalloyed truth – come up with the idea of having the homes of high-profile celebrities installed with minuscule cameras (which were accordingly secreted into lamps and lightbulbs by the celebrities' maids, the latter having been drilled and bought off by the *Daily Mail*). Crackstone had also hacked into the mobile phones of victims of crime, hoping to listen in on some glaring inconsistency which would reveal what *he* thought had actually happened. Interestingly, when Crackstone's own phone was subsequently hacked by Rebecca Murdeck, a rival journalist at the *Daily Express,* he went instantly to the police in a state of righteous indignation, and asked Ryan Rees to dig up or make up any dirt he could find on Murdeck, as he planned to sue and ruin her.

Rees' second phone number was also in the possession of the formidable Acquanetta Stilton, an editor at Shankly & Windup. Her tastes in fiction were quite esoteric; her greatest passion was reserved for novels about sado-masochistic practices among the Mormons. Another editor Ryan Rees was on friendly terms with was Miles Curfew of Nema. Their most heavily-promoted book that summer was *Toothly Intuitions,* which was about a dental hygienist whose secret, breathless dream is to be a health inspector. In addition, Rees chatted regularly on his second phone with the Director-General of the BBC, the Chairman of the RAC, the Head of the Inland Revenue Daffyth Ratchet, the shipping nabob Adonis Contomichalos (Contomichalos and Ratchet were good friends and Ratchet had stretched out many a time on one of the Greek's famed yachts), and the noted West-End actor, heart throb and drug addict Rufus Cerventino. He also used the second phone to converse with his staff, which consisted of Johnson Manger, his copywriter; Arnold Bateman, his accountant; and Donald Inn, his vulpine associate, and a fleet of secretaries. Rees would concoct and embellish stories with Manger, brainstorm ideas with Inn, and work out costs, budgets and hire fees with Bateman. He had no friends as such.

Rees made a point of never antagonizing newspaper editors. But when it came to the journalists he considered run of the mill it was usually his custom to show them two faces, softening them up when wanted something from them and demonstrating almost pathological coldness when they wanted something from him. But he had an uncanny ability to charm his way back into the lives of those he had alienated in the past, striding through their misgivings, quashing their queries with great gusts of laughter, showering them with expensive gifts.

The third phone was reserved exclusively for calls with his private banker in Liechtenstein.

Ryan Rees liked to ride in black cabs. He was riding in a black cab at the moment. He was scanning Tom Beard's review of last night's television on his tablet.

Beard was a feature writer on *The Guardian*. He was an intelligent, erudite man, but he had problems. He had begun his journalistic career by espousing the highest of principles, always reviewing a book honestly, researching his stories scrupulously, taking editors to task for changing his copy. As the years rolled by he found the energy required to swim against the current, to oppose the will of those interested in maintaining the lowest common denominator, begin to wane. He developed a serious cocaine habit after his wife left him for a younger, less complicated man. At about that time he no longer bothered to check facts or read up on people he was interviewing; when reviewing a book he confined himself to its first thirty pages. He became soft, unsure of his opinions, and accrued debts everywhere.

He had joined *The Guardian* after coming from *The Times,* having been sacked by the latter after his drug habit had come to light. At *The Guardian* Beard was paid a third of the salary he had enjoyed as a feature writer at *The Times.* Rees had approached him a few days ago, and treated him to lunch at the Café Royal. He told Beard that if he could review the forthcoming edition of "After Meditation" and mention Oscar Babel in a glowing, even ecstatic, light he might be able to secure him the lucrative position of restaurant critic on the

*Evening Standard* since Martin Maclehose was going to the Bahamas for three months to get a really good sun tan in readiness for his new life as a talk show host in Los Angeles. Rees had propositioned Beard after a couple of bottles of claret and after slipping him a small tin marked 'Strong Mints.'

The tin had in fact been stuffed with cocaine.

Beard agreed, after some hesitation, to write a favorable review.

Later on Rees gave Beard a contact number – that of his first cellular phone.

As he finished scanning the review he rolled one of the windows down and popped his head out. They were stuck in some traffic on the Victoria Embankment. Behind them was the dome of St Paul's Cathedral; in front the slender line of Cleopatra's Needle. Beside them, to the left, like a long, gelatinous blanket, lay the Thames. All along its length boats and ships were eerily still, as if embedded in the water. The grey façades of south bank edifices, office blocks and concert halls were lent a certain vigor by the bright morning sun. Rees watched commuters scurrying back and forth along the Hungerford bridge, the dilapidated trains behind them creaking into slumberous life.

Ryan Rees loved London, its messiness, the sense that it had been spliced together from so many different parts. He loved its color and dust, its history and pubs – rumbustious, dingy, warm, squalid. He loved the city and its cut and thrust, the giant mechanisms of business and banking. He loved Trafalgar Square and the figure of Nelson presiding over it. He loved Canary Wharf with its futuristic layout and Soho with its cluttered one, the serenity of Green Park, the clamor of Oxford Street. He loved the fact that telephone booths, buses and post boxes were red. He even loved the parking meters. In short Rees' love of London was like everything else about him: the product of demented energy.

At last the cab began to move and as it did so Rees read the review of "After Meditation" with care. Released from a set of traffic lights, they turned into Westminster Bridge with a spasmodic burst of speed.

# Last Night's TV Tom Beard
## Turning Pimples
## into Diamonds

Summer is of course the time of year when courtship thrives, as the inhibitions and clothes associated with the other seasons are shed. It is around now that people think about having flings, men expose their anaemic legs, and women wear skimpy dresses. So it's timely to find a program dedicating itself to the thorny subject of sexual love. Sexual love has an uneasy ring to it; no one quite knows what it is, but everyone knows it's highly desirable. Sexual love is wonderful, we are told, whereas sex without love is just empty; and love, well, that can be downright boring on its own.

On last night's inaugural edition of BBC2's highly trumpeted new discussion forum *After Meditation* some respected minds tried to define what sexual love is. The various luminaries included A. S. Meredith, the novelist, Stephen Rialto, critic and raconteur manqué, and Christopher Carey, professor of English at Cambridge University, in his streetwise leather jacket. During the course of an unexpectedly entertaining program these were the highlights. Meredith – tragically – confessed to never having said, "I love you" to anyone because of the danger of misinterpretation. Carey, in an uncharacteristically acute line, remarked that society today was geared towards creating maximum sexual longing and minimum sexual

satiation. Stephen Rialto noted that the byzantine contortions of internet pornography had had a disastrous effect on our sense of what we desired in a partner. No one could really define the term sexual love with any real precision. It was left to the token member of the general public who was present, one Oscar Babel, to shed some light. Clearly the following had been painstakingly rehearsed but what he had to say deserves to be quoted in full.

'I think that if a person was really in love, reaching out, if that intimacy was blowing through your body, turning water into wine, turning the pimples into diamonds, giving the loved one's reality the stamp of great art ... the sexual act could be in this case a revelation, a manifesto of how to live your life.

'But instead erotic love is usually sold as a promised land, or seen as a land mine. Love should be beyond judgment, though it hardly ever is. It should be unconditional but who can truly love unconditionally?

'These days the idea of love comes with the imperative of wealth. But sometimes, very rarely, it turns out like a fairytale. When it's working, really working it can even stop time, so that everything shimmers.'

Unfashionable stuff, I grant you, but I found it bold. Babel was obviously drawing on Tantric doctrines about sexuality, while giving them a slant that is all his own. Meredith told Babel his remarks were labored and vague, and then the others all put the boot in. Everyone was quick to dismiss Babel, to belittle his con-

tribution. Perhaps we were witness-
ing an outbreak of the Bitching Virus. Who can say? I think we should
watch out for Babel. He is clearly
destined for something, though I
don't know what yet. My sources
tell me that he used to life model,
and spent many years studying Sanskrit, while traveling widely in the
East. Maybe that's what greatness is
made of. Who knows?

(Someone else who read the review with care was Najette, but her reaction to what she read was rather less positive than Rees's. A day afterwards she had a dream about Oscar. He was perched – or stuck – at the top of a silver birch tree; he was calling down to her, 'There's an amazing view from up here. How do I get down?')

The cab, having turned around via Westminster Bridge's round-about, was duly able to enter Parliament Square where tourists were busy snapping photographs of Big Ben and the Houses of Parlia-ment. Rees's gaze drifted towards the bronze statue of Churchill in its corner, his left arm tucked inside a pocket, his right hand leaning on a cane, his gaze fixed and resolute. As they moved towards Vic-toria Street he turned round to catch a last glimpse of the austere, faintly hunchbacked form. Rees liked statues – they were emblems of solidity, of unwavering firmness, judging and absolving. They em-bodied something human beings lacked: magnificent detachment.

The cab was moving quickly now and as they chundled along he put the newspaper aside for a moment and extracted a digital music player from his case. He placed the earphones into his ears and fid-dled with the keys. A second later an ear-splitting medley of animal cries and bird calls assaulted him. He was listening to a recording that a travel journalist had edited for him, assembled while traveling in Kenya. Here was the plaintive trilled whistle of the Green-winged Pytilia, and the diurnal song of the Common Drongo. The latter sounded like a banjo as it rasped and twanged. The White-bellied Go-away-Bird called in a nasal whine, not unlike the bleating of a sheep. There was also the pig-like cry of the Maribou stork, spasmod-ic, stopping abruptly. Rees carried the recording with him wherever he went: it allowed him to be transported, to leave his immediate sur-roundings behind. He also listened to it whenever he felt particularly excited, as he did now.

He closed his eyes, his lips drawn back in a crooked smile. Na-ture was pure, amoral, uncluttered, he reflected. Nature and statues: these are the ideals. That review was good, really good. He lit a cigar. What a stroke of genius, what a minor miracle it would be to turn Oscar into a modern myth; to take this nobody and make him into a somebody, give him status and worth for no good reason, other than because it would be good fun to fool everyone.

Rees – though attracted by the thought of ultimate financial gain – wanted to mould Oscar into an icon. He would be there, by his side, the ring master proudly introducing his lion. Deep down he aimed to produce a hybrid of freak and god. In his experience there was an exquisite pleasure to be had in fooling the population at large, in milking their gullibility and juggling with their perceptions.

They had just turned into Grosvenor Place. Rees had an appoint-ment with Jura Proskovira, a Russian millionaire, at The Morgue, a fashionable restaurant on Brompton Road. Here, in a discreet corner, guests were encouraged to pluck off wads of sushi carefully laden onto naked, exotic looking women stretched out on slender tables. Rees was helping to publicize Proskovira's new nightclub – Baby Go Go. What this promotion amounted to was dropping the name during radio interviews and mentioning it to journalists whenever he felt inclined to do so. For this Proskovira was paying Rees £15,000 a month. Rees thought Proskovira harmless enough, though he knew his club didn't have any chance of gaining the cachet of the most well-known establishments, despite his assurances to the contrary and im-passioned guarantees that in three months from now the name Baby Go Go would be on everyone's rouged up lips.

He puffed on his cigar, the thick smoke enveloping him, obscur-ing his face. He removed his earphones carefully, pulled out one of his phones and dialed a number, all the while studying Beard's television review, his eye searching for usable phrases.

Speaking into his phone at breakneck speed, he said, 'Donny, we need to sort out some posters. Then get them up in every library, coffee house, public place you can think of. But mainly I want a few billion on the underground. You'll need to get in touch with the Transportation Display for permission. Tell them we'll need it for four weeks minimum. You can sort it out with whoever's the account manager for W1. To target, shall we say, an adult, central London audience? I don't know how long they usually take to come up with a design but my guess is weeks so sort something out with Jurgen. I'll dictate what they should say. Ready? ... What do you mean Jurgen might be tricky? For fuck's sake, don't piss-arse around. Ready? "Is love inseparable from wealth? Is love a fairytale or the wailing of the damned? The cure will follow." Got that? Now, read it back to me.'

The cab came to a shuddering halt, halfway down Brompton Road. Outside Harrod's elegant-looking women were studying their even more elegant counterparts locked in stasis within the windows, disquieting prototypes of perfection. The summer afternoon crowds moved along, driven by a mad compulsion to spend, to burn money, as if to do so would be to breathe more easily.

'That's good, sounds just right, wouldn't you say? I want the words in 164 Bodoni MT Ultra Bold. Now, in addition, I want you to make up another set of posters. Five thousand, do the same, yes, exactly the same. All I want for those is the following: "Who is Oscar Babel?" Got that? ... That's all, yes. Tubes again. And everywhere else. I don't care, bribe grannies, put them in bistros and boutiques, anywhere that will have them. Up vicars' arses, for all I care. Right. Don't foul up. How's the website coming? ... That's right, get Johnson to mention the ashram in Kerala, like I said. And all the rest. Sanskrit, blah, blah, blah. *Au revoir.*'

The cab moved on unsteadily, as if buckling under the weight of Rees's loquacity.

# 12

Albertine's restaurant, off Regent Street, looked like a conservatory. Dozens of resplendent, sub-tropical plants sat in the corners, serpentine stems flourishing. Hibiscus hung from the ceiling, anchored in slowly twirling *terracotta* pots. Their white petals were so luminous that they seemed to cast a counterfeit light.

On first taking their seats the radiance of their surroundings practically overwhelmed the diners. There were sleek, brightly polished mirrors everywhere so that wherever the eye strayed it met with a cluster of animated faces advancing happily through the menu. The walls were painted in a dazzling off-white and the floor consisted of orange and black ceramic tiles. Many people found that the mere fact of being in the restaurant lifted their conversation to previously-unscaled heights. Invariably, later on, they could never recapture the magical quality of that evening's performance, or find within themselves the same reserves of wit, intelligence and charm.

The reason he had booked a table here (with enormous difficulty) was because he thought it would please her, given how the decor chimed with her life.

As they sat there Lilliana realized she still didn't know his first name.

This insane scheme was actually going ahead, it was no longer just an abstract concept. She felt faint and cold. Before it had all been theoretical, but now she was dangerously close to that moment when reality would start summoning its own agenda, with all the anarchy and loss of control that this implied. What if they asked questions to which she could give no answers? What if she was revealed as an impostor? What if their accounts conflicted? The only thing they had rehearsed was how they had met: at a poetry reading.

Furthermore, all that she really knew about him, she realized, was all that she could not dwell upon: that he was a homosexual, and a charlatan.

She considered the enigma of not having properly prepared her role; what could she have been thinking, why hadn't she seized the available time to make sure she wouldn't now be feeling like this, terrified of making a mess of everything? They had kept on postponing a meeting and in the end had only managed to exchange a few words on the phone about tonight's performance. She glanced round at the other diners, all enjoying themselves, dressed in white summer jackets, shimmering, flimsy dresses, and expensive denim. Conversation was flowing like a frothy, everlasting river. But the baroque surroundings only added to her agitation. She looked at him. He was fumbling nervously with his toupee.

'Mr. Sopso, I still don't know your first name.'

'What?'

'What's your first name?'

'Well, you must know that by now,' he insisted in his high-pitched, diminutive voice.

'I really don't.'

'Really? How strange that neither of us ...'

'There's a million things I don't know about you that I should know, but I think it would probably be a good idea if we could manage to establish your Christian name before your parents get here.'

'Of course, of course, but why didn't you think to ask me before? And when we spoke on the phone – '

'It was something to do with the sign on your door. You know: "Mr. Sopso, Fortune Teller." I always thought of you as plain old Mr. Sopso.'

'How interesting. You were probably ... My first name's ...'

'Alexei!' a voice bawled out with incredible force.

A few heads turned in amazement.

'Alexei! Alexei! Alexei!'

It was like some primitive battle cry.

'Oh dear God,' Mr. Sopso whispered, then turned slightly pale.

Two figures were advancing from the far end of the restaurant, moving with startling speed.

He and Lilliana had arrived at eight; he had told his parents to get there at eight-thirty, to give Lilliana and himself enough time to get settled. His parents were early by twenty four minutes.

Lilliana glanced at her companion. His bearing had completely altered – his body had locked itself into a defensive spasm. She turned back to watch this elephantine couple brushing against the plants, dislodging napkins from tables, scaring small children.

Mrs. Sopso was dressed in a fur coat, a pair of glittering, gaudy boots, and a vast, billowing skirt. Sopso senior was wearing brown cords, trainers and a green combat jacket. Mrs Sopso's make-up was so thick and fastened onto her face that it looked as though only surgery could have removed it.

Lilliana and Mr. Sopso stood up awkwardly to receive them.

'Hello, Mum, D-d-dad, let me introduce you to Lilliana, my fiancee.'

Lilliana stretched her arm out but Mrs Sopso was already reaching for a kiss which landed awkwardly on her cheek.

'At last our son's getting hitched,' she said. She seemed agitated, as if she had left a pan on the boil somewhere and would shortly have to go and attend to it. Mr Sopso shook Lilliana's hand, then said to his son, 'Fine-looking woman. Not a bad place.'

Instantly Lilliana was feeling extremely uncomfortable.

'Yes,' she said, doing her best to appear responsive to Mr. Sopso's last remark, 'it's a lovely place Alexei introduced me to ...'

'Oh, you call him Alexei too? I thought it was only his mother who called him Alexei,' said Mrs. Sopso, donning a slightly wounded air.

'She alternates between Alexei and Alex,' said Alex Sopso.

Lilliana nodded, assimilating this information quickly and decided that 'Alex' would be better, considering the pain etched onto his mother's face.

'Well,' said Alex, 'let's all sit down.'

'Oh, Alexei, aren't you going to take my coat for me, that's a good boy,' said Mrs Sopso.

'Alex, take your mother's coat. You know how she likes to have her coat taken. That's one thing, Lilliana, about her; she likes people to help her both on and off with her coat. Don't ask me why.'

Alex duly assisted his mother while Lilliana monitored his growing discomfort, which in turn fueled her own. Having wrestled with the coat he didn't know what to do with it, so he waddled off in search of a waiter, welcoming the chance to escape the radioactive presence of his parents.

They sat down, Lilliana doing her best to look calm and composed.

'So, Lilliana. Nice name. By the way, has Alex told you our names yet?' asked Mr. Sopso.

Oh God, it's starting already, she thought.

'No, I'm afraid he hasn't.'

'Well, that's not very good,' said Mrs. Sopso.

'I'm Harvey and my wife's name is Nina. Has Alex told you about Geoffrey?'

Lilliana decided it would probably be best to lie at this point, having failed to pass the first test.

'Oh, yes ... Geoffrey ... yes, he has.'

'What do think of him then?'

'Well, he's very nice.'

'So you've met him then?'

'Well, not exactly.'

'And yet you say he's very nice.'

'Well, he sounds nice.'

'What do you think of his profession?'

'Remind me again what it is ...'

'For God's sake Harvey, give the girl some air,' said Nina.

'He's a priest! How could you forget! What could be more noble?'

'Oh course, a priest, very ... very ... virtuous.' She suddenly remembered that Alex's parents were religious.

'Virtuous, that's a good word for it; a word I might have used.'

A waiter, with hair as dark and smooth as blackcurrant jam, arrived with the menus. This created some space in which to breathe. Alex had yet to re-appear. At that moment he was splashing cold water over his face in the men's room.

As they were looking over the menu, written in French (which annoyed Harvey excessively) Nina spewed out words as a machine gun spews out bullets.

'Have they managed, my dear, to stuff the whole of the hanging gardens of Babylon into this restaurant? I don't think I've ever seen such a magnificent collection of flowers. There's as much of God's creation here as there was in the garden of Eden, I dare say. All these plants remind me that while I'm in London I must find some China roots.'

'Oh, I know a good place, a health food store, very near where I met – ' She stopped abruptly.

'Where you met? Who?'

'Oh, just a friend of mine, the other day. It's off the Tottenham Court Road.'

Alex re-appeared, his shirt and collar conspicuously damp.

'Sit by Mummy, Alexei dear, that's it, and what about a little hug? That's better; it's been so long since we had a little hug, hasn't it?'

Alex wore a pleading expression in his eyes, as of a man being told he is about to be fed under a set of giant rolling pins. Lilliana stared at him pointedly.

'They say they're a miracle cure for arthritis ...' said Nina.

'What's a miracle cure for arthritis?' Harvey said, looking up from the menu which he was attempting to decode, with negligible success.

'China roots! Don't you listen to a thing I say? A miracle cure for arthritis and syphilis. I'm only interested in the first of those ailments, though. Eucalyptus is also very good. I used to go to the Eucalyptus room at the spa in Dortmund before they knocked it down. To make way for an internet cafe! It did wonders for my sinuses, unblocked them. Not the kitchen sink! For that you need acid, though it can leave a nasty stain. How I like to talk. The menu looks interesting, doesn't it? Probably delicious. French food always is. But we must resist temptation. Do you like french fries? Of course I can't eat the sort of things I used to. Great godfathers! Great big banquets, rich sauces, lobster thermidor, steak *au pauvre,* french fries. My doctor won't allow it. I've a fragile stomach. But hush, I shouldn't mention it, or it might go off again. And I've only just managed to get it to quieten down. That's what comes of eating well for thirty years.'

'You mean that's what comes of me taking you out to restaurants for thirty years,' Harvey snorted.

There was a lull. The colorful surroundings could do nothing about the jaundiced mood fast taking hold.

Lilliana asked, 'Have you been married all that time?' She had decided that the only way to make the evening bearable would be to shift the focus completely onto the parents, while trying to keep a very very low profile.

'Thirty years, that's right,' said Harvey, 'and why not? What are your thoughts, then, on marriage?'

'Oh, I doubt if I'll ever ... if I'll ... be able to wait until our wedding,' she spluttered, the gaps in her sentence causing Alex to practically fall off his chair.

'That's nice. Alex told us you were a religious girl.'

'Did he now?'

'How far have you taken that religiousness?'

'Well ... I go to church every now and then.'

'Only every now and then?'

'Lilliana doesn't like to discuss it, she thinks it devalues it,' said Alex, springing to her aid.

Harvey considered this viewpoint, clearly one he had never encountered before. He considered a counter-attack, decided against it, returned to his menu and belched with staggering force.

Nina said breezily, 'That's nice, not discussing it; I like a bit of mystery myself.'

Alex smiled knowingly at Lilliana, a smile that luckily escaped the attention of his parents. It was going to be all right.

The waiter re-appeared with a selection of bread rolls and a jug of iced mineral water. A rigorous series of questions from Harvey Sopso about the menu began. At first the waiter was more than happy to comply. But when the questions touched on cooking time, ingredients, and the state of the vegetables a labyrinth appeared through which he saw no hope of finding his way. Finally the waiter muttered, 'Perhaps you'd like a few more minutes,' and withdrew.

'Lilliana, didn't you think that waiter was a bit rude?' asked Nina.

'Yes, I suppose he was.'

'By the way,' said Harvey. 'Do any of you know who Oscar Babel is?'

'What?!' Lilliana very nearly spat out the gulp of mineral water she had just taken.

'I keep seeing these signs everywhere, on the subway, in cafes, and all these things say is, "Who is Oscar Babel?" Well, who the hell is Oscar Babel anyway? I mean what is the point of a poster that just says, "Who is Oscar Babel?"'

'I know who Oscar Babel is,' said Lilliana, dabbing her mouth with her napkin.

'She's very well up on current affairs,' said Alex, trying to summon up a suitably proud look.

'He's a friend of mine.'

'Really?' said Nina, 'tell us more.'

'I met him at the flower shop ages ago.'

'So why the hell is his name everywhere?' Harvey demanded.

'I hadn't noticed. I don't get out of the shop much.'

'What shop?'

'The Sun Well; I run a flower shop.'

'Alex, you didn't tell us your fiancée owned a flower shop. Imagine, Lilliana, all he said was that you were a good cook. Alexei, why are you always so secretive?' Nina demanded.

'Oh yes, the shop's a beautiful place – full of asparagus – parsley,' said Alex in a fluster.

'Well, we'll have to see about that.'

'Well, mum, you haven't got very long in London and – '

'No, no,' said Lilliana, who decided to agree to avoid problems, despite the fact that consenting now would inevitably lead to more problems later. 'That's fine, Alex; of course your parents should see the shop.' She had decided she could and would master these obnoxious people.

'That's nice, a flower shop,' said Harvey. 'Better than being a fortune teller. Alex, why couldn't you have been a priest like Geoffrey, or a dentist, or an accountant or something like that. But no, you had to go swanning around with Ouija boards and God knows what – '

'Dad,' said Alex, his voice reaching breaking point, 'let's try not to make this a bore for Lilliana, all right? And you know that I don't have anything to do with the occult. I just indulge in occasional palmistry and tarot readings.'

'At least,' said Harvey, carrying on regardless, 'when you were in the art world, you were respectable, but what kind of vocation is fortune telling? You'll be reading the entrails of cats and dogs next, or monitoring the movement of sea gulls and crows. I can't understand why you can't find another, proper – '

'Please shut up, Harvey,' said Nina with unexpected majesty.

A new waiter appeared (the original waiter had begged his colleague to take his place) and another prolonged process of inquiry got under way until at last the orders were trotted out with a collective sigh of relief. Some kind of peace reigned. Alex looked as depleted of energy as a minutes-old mother.

'So, tell us more about this Oscar character,' said Nina.

'Well, as I explained,' Lilliana began, starting to feel rather sorry for Alex and beginning to realize the extent of the sufferings he must have received at the hands of his parents, 'he's a friend, but I don't know why these posters are up everywhere. When I last saw him he told me that he was doing some nude modeling.'

'Nude modeling? More of the devil's handiwork. What is it with men of today? Are they all turning into women? Since when has exposing yourself been a proper pursuit for a young man? It's an abomination. I mean to say, why don't they all go home and read some St. Augustine, or something, or tuck into the Bible with a cup of tea,' said Harvey.

'Forgive me, Mr. Sopso,' said Lilliana, succumbing to a rare degree of irritation, 'but wasn't St Augustine a self-confessed sinner who then found salvation? Shouldn't one be less hard on those who haven't yet seen the error of their ways? I mean, doesn't the Christian viewpoint preach forgiveness and tolerance? Didn't Christ say judge not lest you be judged?'

This seemed to have a profound effect on Harvey. He lapsed into silence, though his mind reeled with a thousand insults. I mean, who exactly did this nonentity, this nobody, a flower girl, for God's sake, think she was? Did she think she could sit and lecture an old man?

'Hear, hear! Lilliana,' said Nina Sopso. 'You know, Alexei, I like this girl; she's different from all your other girlfriends. Well, the other one anyway. You'll have to come and visit us in Dortmund, my dear. I like you; you have spirit. Now, Alexei don't go and lose her, will you, she's an angel. And she has the most beautiful white skin, doesn't she?'

'I know,' said Alex, 'I know that she's an angel, gazing up at all the stars. That's why I gave her that painting; you know, the one of the two saints.'

'How lovely,' said Nina. 'I've always had a soft spot for that painting. It's by Picasso, isn't it? Alexei always loved it. I'm glad it came to you, Lilliana.'

Lilliana felt flooded with different emotions. She felt a sadness for the measly quality of Alex's father and at the same time a growing affection for Alex as she saw him in a new light and realized how special the painting really had been for him. Her eyes were moist with tears which had welled up but were not full enough to drop, so that they glimmered in the light of the restaurant. And now for the first time there was silence, a welcome alcove which Lilliana huddled into.

'Did Alex tell you how we met, Mrs. Sopso?' she asked after some moments.

'I was just going to ask you sweetie!'

'It was at this pa – ' Alex began.

'Let me tell the story, Alex!' Lilliana interrupted emphatically.

For a horrible moment Alex thought she was going to tell them the truth, tell them how they had really met, and that he was a liar and a fraud, that the evening had all been staged.

But she had another, more mysterious agenda ...

Ever since she had walked into the restaurant an afternoon from her past had kept on returning to her, the memory of which she had always treasured, when life had revealed itself in all its richness, when it had been bliss just to breathe. A man had arrived at the end of that idyllic afternoon, a man she had been strongly attracted to. Sadly, she had never set eyes on him again. Now she decided to let Alex Sopso be that man for awhile, to let him occupy that special place in her mind. And, in so doing, she hoped to forge a large dent in Harvey Sopso's armor.

'Yes, I'll tell you how I met Alex. It's a good story.

'It was in the summer. Last summer. I was coming back from the countryside where I'd been visiting a girlfriend. I remember it was a boiling hot day. The concrete on the station platform was hot enough to fry an egg on. The station bordered a field of daffodils, and they swayed slightly each time the breeze blew. It was beautiful. There wasn't a soul; you know country stations – they're always deserted.

In the winter it's horrible but on a day like that an empty railway station is sort of magical. I could have waited there, for a train, for hours.'

She took a sip of water. Alex stared at her, wondering where this story was leading.

'After a while the London train pulled in. I walked down to the last carriage, and climbed on. All the windows were down and the wind poured in. Quite wonderfully, I had the carriage all to myself.

'Never-ending fields flew past. The sun popped up as we rounded a corner, blinding in the sky. I was feeling incredibly happy. Maybe that mixture of movement, sunlight and solitude came at exactly the right time. You see, the friend I'd just left had made it possible for me to buy the flower shop by lending me some money. I'd just quit a job in a cockroach-infested restaurant. The world seemed full of promise. I'd changed my life, not enormously, but it was something. So it felt like things were coming together in that ragamuffin carriage.

'I stuck my head out at each stop. No one ever got on, the whistle just blew and we clunked off. Then a mother and her little daughter shuffled in from the next carriage. They made me think of the outer and innermost sections of a Russian doll. Whenever her mother spoke the little girl repeated her words; whenever she made a movement or adjusted her hair, her daughter mimicked her. It was just unbelievably sweet. And funny. I watched them secretly from my corner by the window.

'No-one else got on for the rest of the journey. We pulled in to King's Cross. The joy of the train ride was still with me so to celebrate I decided to have a coffee and a cake. As I waited in the queue in the cafeteria I noticed a man sitting on his own. He was reading a novel: *The Flight of the Innocent*. It's by a writer from the 1930's, Catherine Lyle. The first time I read it was at school. Hardly anyone's heard of it, so I was rather amazed to see it in his hands. It's not especially great or anything but whenever I pick it up it takes me back to when I was fourteen. So it has sentimental value, I suppose. It's the story of a young girl growing up in Looe. She spends her time playing truant from school, wandering around the Bodmin moors, flying kites, making dresses, listening to the sound of the waves breaking. Eventually she makes friends with one of the young fishermen. They have a love affair and he breaks her heart. That's it, really, pretty predictable. But there's something in the way she writes about adolescence which is very vivid, real. She captures the awkwardness, the dreams, the body's confusion.

'I don't know why; maybe it was my feeling of optimism and confidence, or maybe it was the fact that he looked kind or maybe it was just because he was reading that particular book, but I had the overwhelming urge to speak to him, which isn't something I'm normally brave enough to do.

'At first he looked puzzled, but then as we began discussing Josie – the heroine of the book – he asked me if I'd like to join him. Then we talked. We talked for hours. He missed his train, though I begged him not to. We talked until the cafe closed and they had to throw us out. I told him I thought Josie was someone you hoped would grow up to be this wonderful, intelligent, beautiful woman. But you were also afraid she might not fulfill her youthful promise and just marry some dull man she'd be forced to suppress her identity and dreams for. Then I told him about my dreams. He was wonderful, intriguing, gentle. I told him about how I wanted my shop to look, about the place I had in mind to buy and do up, about how I wanted a spiral staircase. I waxed hysterical about oriental lilies. I told him about the temperate room in Kew Gardens where there are these massive, frightening Javanese banana trees which look as if they're going to start moving. I bored him silly. I told him about the hydrangeas in Madeira. When you first see them you think they're fruit because they're so ripe and solid. They look like peeled pomegranates or crimson cauliflowers.'

She paused and took a sip of water. For a moment she looked

drained by some buried sadness. But then her eyes grew defiant.

She murmured slowly, 'The man's name was ...' but trailed off.

With a trembling voice she whispered, '... Alex Sopso.' Then, with sudden conviction, and smiling broadly, her face reborn, she said, 'I think Alex is very special. And his heart is very big.'

There was a period of digestive silence.

As she had told the story in her slow, careful way Alex gazed at her in wonder and became overwhelmed by a feeling of infinite fragility. Lilliana's story was like a snowflake which she had plucked from her pocket and offered up to them, miraculously intact and unmelted. He wanted to preserve that moment in his mind, the story itself, which was perfect and so unrepeatable, a moment as wonderful as the ones she herself had described. Her words created great longing in him for her; he was bewitched by the poetry of her tale, but also filled with the pathos of knowing that the story was not about him. He wanted to ask whether or not she had ever seen the man again.

'So that's how it was,' she said.

Harvey Sopso, very slowly and weightedly, asked, 'Are you sure we're talking about Alex?'

Nina Sopso said, 'Of course, that's my dear little Alexei all right.'

For a moment Harvey Sopso suggested a fatally wounded bull, heaving and rasping in the throes of a death agony. With an effort he summoned up a more dignified expression and grunted, 'Alex, that good-for-nothing?'

Nina said, 'Harvey! Don't start in on Alexei, I've told you before; he's very sensitive. How can you talk about your own son like that? That was lovely ...'

'Tell me something,' Harvey continued, 'didn't his wig bother you?'

Lilliana decided to steel herself further, to counter his nihilism more outrageously, more ridiculously, and merrily declared, 'Oh no, in fact that was one of the things that attracted me to your son.'

'What? No one's attracted to a wig!!'

'Mr Sopso, forgive me but I feel that you're far too hard on your son. Has it perhaps ever occurred to you that many of his problems might have stemmed from your own overwhelmingly strong opinions?'

'What-is-that-supposed-to-mean?' And here Mr Sopso became rather angry and knocked over a wine glass. 'Are you trying to tell me my business, are you trying to tell me I've been a bad father?'

'No, Mr Sopso, but it's clear to me that you're not the easiest man in the world to talk to.'

'Lilliana,' said Alex, 'don't worry, don't bother; it's all right, it's fine.'

'It's not fine, Alex, it's not fine, and it's not all right. I think that these things have to be confronted; I don't think you should put up with the kind of treatment your father metes out to you. And I think that – '

Nina, her voice assuming that shrill pitch that Lilliana had noted when she first came into the restaurant, and her arms becoming airborne, said, 'Darlings, darlings, let's not have a fight; we haven't even had the starters yet, it will spoil our appetites, won't it? I mean, I for one am very happy for you both and I just want us all to be – '

Harvey interrupted with, 'If Alex has anything to say, he can say it to me now, to my face, which will be fine by me, and better than saying it to me when I'm in Germany.'

Alex, whose body all this time had been as tightly wound as piano wire, his face agonizingly contorted, said, 'Please, let's just drop this. There is nothing I wish to say to you; you are a fine father and I ... I ...'

He caught a glimpse of Lilliana watching him intently. The movement of time slowed. The noise of the other diners seemed to fade away.

Her story – its delicacy – the things it revealed about her formed a collective thread. Had she told the story, so romantic and dreamy, in order to nudge his father towards the negative remarks he would inevitably make, remarks that would prompt Alex to defend himself?

Had she foreseen what would happen? Was she trying, obliquely, to force him to confess his sexual persuasions to them, to do him a favor of sorts? He glanced at her face, convulsed with feeling. She seemed to be saying, with her eyes, as she stared at him, that she was there for him, that she would support him, that she wanted him to defend himself, to be himself, to oppose his father's violent will. How could he be sure though? He could not ask her now, could not confer with her now, in the presence of his parents. He would have to act alone.

'Dad, I have got something to say to you, and to you, mum.'

Even before he had finished his sentence panic and dread were casting jagged shadows across the table. Lilliana found her palms were instantly bathed in sweat.

'The thing is ... I'm, I'm ... there's no easy way of saying this ... this isn't easy – '

'For God's sake, Alexei, don't tell us she's up the spout!' Nina Sopso interrupted, with a notable absence of tact.

'No, no, the thing is ... I ... this isn't about Lilliana at all ... or about us ... it's about me ... just me ... and ... it's about my personal ... personal ... the thing is ... how can I put it? I ... well ... I ... I like men.'

'Big deal. So do I,' said Harvey.

Nina chimed in with, 'So do I. Or at least I used to.'

'No, that's not what I mean. I mean ... I like men ... I mean I'm ... I'm a ... I'm a homosexual.'

At that precise moment the waiter appeared to ask if everything was all right.

'I'm a homosexual! I can't ever have a wife!' Alex screamed at the waiter.

He scuttled off like a spider.

Mr Sopso's face became a mass of wrinkles and all the world's pain flooded into his eyes. Mrs Sopso looked staggered, but beside her husband's face her own was the picture of contentment.

Mr Sopso began sobbing like a baby. All the tension of the evening, all the tension of his life began to thaw and this was the result, a great unstoppable torrent of tears. The four of them sat huddled together in a silent hell. While the emasculation of Alex's world proceeded the other diners told stories, laughing and howling.

Finally his father stammered, 'What … what have you been telling me all these years? What is all this pigshit? Has it all been lies? That you just haven't met the right girl? When I think of what you've been telling me, has it all just been lies? What kind of a son are you? Answer me!'

But Alex couldn't form words. He wasn't feeling very well.

'And what about this woman here … who is she … what about this cock and bull story she just told? I mean what is going on?'

He turned to Lilliana and began to direct his aggression toward her.

'What have you got to say for yourself; how can you sit there, and speak to me of trains and *The Light of the Innocent* and God knows what and all this time – '

Finally, Alex managed to piece splattered words together. 'Dad – don't blame her – it's me you should be blaming – I asked her to do it. I wanted to make you happy, I wanted to tell you that I'd met someone – '

'To make me happy! What could you have been thinking? And you, what should I call you – a courtesan? You make fun of a poor old man, sitting there, like a duchess, and you have the gall to dictate to me about what is right and wrong, and you've been lying through your teeth, lying in front of God. Yes, God sees everything, everything, all comes under his gaze, and you just –'

'Dad, can you be quiet? She's not to blame, I am. But it's good that you know now, know the truth, this couldn't have gone on for ever. It's better this way.'

'No it isn't, it's not better and I'll make sure that it isn't better.'

Lilliana couldn't bear anymore. She shot to her feet, her chair screeching as it was dragged backwards from under her, her eyes streaming with tears. As she rushed towards the exit she brushed against a bunch of orange amaryllis and one of the stems was flung outwards violently. In her confusion she stooped to pick it up. For a moment she allowed herself to stare at the delicate, gauze-like texture which had an almost human expressiveness, its curves appearing in that moment terrifying, its beauty made of nausea, making her long to find a place purged of all feelings. Not knowing what to do with the stem, she put it in her jacket pocket. Some of the other diners stared at her as she scrambled to the door, fumbled with it, and stepped outside shakily.

What have I done? I've ruined everything. He only said what he said because I started criticizing his father, because he thought I would be there for him and now I've just walked out and left him in the mess I created and I shouldn't have said anything to his father and I shouldn't have told the story and it's all my fault, it's all my fault, it's all my fault.

Walking at a frantic pace she reached Regent Street in less than a minute. As she hurried down towards Piccadilly her brain rioted. She was not in any real sense aware of her surroundings. Only of screaming thoughts. She heard some sounds, but they were inchoate, vague. She took a step and then another, some impulse in her compelling her to cross the road. It would be good to cross, I could be on the other side. Further away. The road would be between me and the restaurant. I'd be further away from the restaurant ...

*safe* ...

A black hole opened. Consciousness tumbled down it sickeningly ...

*Something's got my wrist.*

A car hurtled past, its horn blaring horribly.

*Oh God.*

A hand was pulling her wrist, stopping the flow of blood, dragging her backwards.

*My hand. The car. It hurts. Turn round.*

There is a man standing next to her. They are standing near the curb. The man lets go of her hand. The blood begins to flow. The man is tall. He is dressed in white. He has green eyes.

'Are you all right?' he asks, registering the sight of her flooded, bloodshot eyes, her smudged mascara.

'What? What? Yes, I'm all right, thank you, you ...'

'Are you sure? What happened?'

'I didn't see it coming. I didn't see it.'

'Didn't you hear the car?'

'No, I didn't hear it coming.'

'Are you sure you're all right?'

'Yes, I'm sure, I'm sure.'

She walks off as if in a trance. As she does so the meaning of what has just happened begins to sink in and she realizes how odd she must have seemed. She turns back to thank the man, properly this time. But when she returns to the spot by the curb he's already gone.

She stands there, a solitary figure, the wind from the speeding traffic causing her hair to swirl fiercely. She tries desperately to remember what he looked like, the shape of his face. But he is gone.

Some way down along the pavement petals from the amaryllis stir in the wind.

She stares at them for an hour.

Then she begins to make her way home.

# 13

## Oscar Babel: *the Invention of Wisdom*

HOME | ARTICLES | IMAGES | ABOUT

image not currently available

*A* recent portrait of Mr. Babel

**'*When love is working it can stop time so that everything shimmers.*'**

## Who is Oscar Babel?

Oscar Babel is a free thinker and pioneer, who may well develop into the most influential speaker of the day. He is still only twenty-six years of age. He stands well over six-feet tall. And he is brilliance personified.

He has no preconceptions, no limitations. His mind is open. He is free when all around others are handcuffed by greed, hypocrisy, money and misery.

*You too can be free.*

### Be the dream!

Oscar Babel
c/o Ryan Rees Publicity
39 Great Portland Street, London W1 4RT UK
Tel. +44 20 7336 7876  Fax. + 44 20 7336 7875
e-mail. ryanrees@oscarbabel.com

**Facebook**       **Twitter**       **Blotdrop**       **Gadoo**

## How Ryan Rees Discovered Oscar Babel

Ryan Rees is always on the look out for fresh talent, for people who can be promoted because of their exceptional charisma, because of their compelling personalities. Because Ryan Rees is only interested in one thing: excellence. His credo might be: 'serve the people, feed the real.'

Ryan Rees discovered Mr Babel's original, extraordinary mind during a chance meeting in a Tapas Bar in West Kensington, London when the publicist overheard Mr. Babel holding forth. He was so struck by his fellow customer's brilliance and erudition – despite the sound of flamenco guitar music – that he immediately offered his services.

Within a short while Babel had appeared in a documentary on life modeling and the late night chat show "After Meditation."

Babel's manner is quiet and unassuming but he has something to say. The truly unique aspect of Mr. Babel lies in his unclassifiability. He is not a politician, nor an artist. He is if anything a teacher who seeks to educate and instruct. He is what might be described as an Urban Messiah.

Oscar Babel will be speaking at The Duchamp Prize for the Most Controversial Artist of the Year in ten days' time at the Kensington Hilton.

## The Background *************

Mr. Babel is a very shy man who needs his privacy as he is not used to socializing, having just returned from the Modylmyr Ashram in Kerala, India where he read widely and meditated for up to fourteen hours a day.

He studied Sanskrit at Oxford University. He took a first and briefly considered a career as an academic before realizing his calling lay elsewhere. He saw academia as an embroidered dead-end. Running circles around others no longer held any interest and conventional methods of teaching left him cold. The world beckoned and he travelled widely in Tibet and India. For a time he came under the influence of a guru in the Caucasus – Seer Nayar. Then he lived amongst the Aborigines and acquired psychic abilities. For example he could predict with *uncanny precision when a coffee machine would break down.*

## A Note on BabelSoap

Mr Babel became obsessed with **volcanic earth,** which he travelled the world to acquire, developing different kinds of **volcanic soap** from it, for medicinal purposes. Babel's soap, when applied to people's skin, could in some cases cure them of racism. Though his theories have not been backed up by scientific evidence many people have testified to the **effectiveness of the treatments.** One woman in Gran Canaria even claimed that the application of the soap had healed a **14 year old rift with her mother,** which had started when the two had argued about the best way of removing **facial hair.**

## ** WAKE UP CALL
*by* Oscar Babel **

---- forthcoming title by Babel to be extracted soon on this website, concerning the real self and how to find it, and the possibility of freedom from the chains of consumerism and desire. In order to change your life, you have to want to change your life.

"Most people are asleep; I think I can wake them up if I shout loudly enough."

Facebook    Twitter    Blotdrop    Gadoo    Godpage

181

# 14

Bloch had been lying for days in his bed, not getting up, dried out. He looked like a man who had been granted a vision of hell and as he lay in his somnolent state, disconnected thoughts moved through his brain like a drunken dancer.

Several physicians, including his general practitioner, said he was suffering from nervous exhaustion, and needed to have a period of complete rest, even suggesting he be admitted to a private clinic; but Bloch had refused point blank. So, here he stayed, with Webster looking after him, whom Bloch had invited to move in. In the end his GP had declared himself satisfied with this arrangement, and concluded that Bloch didn't pose a threat either to himself or others and wasn't showing suicidal tendencies.

Webster had been evicted from his flat so Bloch's offer was timely, even though moving in meant adopting the role of nurse. Webster had been refusing to pay his rent to protest the fact that his landlord still hadn't had his boiler repaired. It all came to a head when the landlord called in one morning with the eviction notice in one hand and in the other a letter from Middle Maintenance Services confirming a new boiler would be delivered the day after Webster was to be thrown out. Mr. Conk had said evenly, 'If only you hadn't resorted to such an unfortunate line of action, you could be bathing with your rubber ducks next week.'

Webster, besides keeping the flat clean, shopping and cooking also picked books up from the library and drugs from the chemist: valium, painkillers, vitamins, and rehydration treatments.

One doctor had tried to persuade Bloch to go to the countryside but the prospect made him even more agitated. So he just languished in bed, reading when he felt up to it, mainly books on Eastern mysticism, and in particular Tantra. But because he was spending so much time in bed all sorts of unforeseen ailments descended on him. Bed sores appeared on his feet; he became chronically constipated; and he started to get stomach cramps. He ate irregularly, and invariably never managed to finish a meal. He resorted periodically to valium, which did nothing to stop his mind's feverish activity, while making his body feel heavy and sluggish (and so even more at odds with his mind's perpetual motion.)

*

Webster was in the kitchen, watching the washing machine as it advanced towards its rinse cycle. As it ground on, to Bloch the sound it made came across as oddly distorted, battering him into submission. Unbeknown to him, sheets of note paper, full of ideas and plans, were being destroyed mercilessly in the machine's steel barrel.

'Webster!' Bloch yelled from the bedroom.

Webster groaned. Though Bloch's flat was comfortable, though the sofa bed was preferable to the mattress in his van, his host was impossible, to put it mildly. He couldn't always be at his beck and call. He would have to say something, and now was as good a time as any. Not that there was a good time with Bloch.

He waddled into the bedroom. Slumped on the bed, Bloch was clutching an ancient, retrograde cassette player and microphone, with which he'd been recording his thoughts, since he was too tired to write them down anymore.

'Do you play chess?' he asked.

'Actually Bloch, I need to talk to you about something.'

'Yes?'

'Well ... the thing is ... I don't think I can go on looking after you like this.'

'Why not? Aren't I paying you enough?'

'No, you're very generous. It's not that, it's just I don't think I'm really the right person for this kind of thing.'

'What do you mean?'

'Well, I don't know what I'm doing. I'm not a trained nurse or anything. You want soup, and when I make it it's either too hot or too cold; you want fresh bedsheets and then I have to use that bloody machine all the time just to keep the supply of clean linen running smoothly. It's exhausting. And I mean to say, don't you think you should be under medical supervision so that doctors can monitor you? I mean a private hospital would be nice.'

'Webster, don't pester me. I'm not a virus that I should be monitored.'

'But you need taking care of! And I'm not the right person for it. I have to think about my business schemes.'

'Isn't that a rather grand term for flogging bits of china?'

'If I spend all day here,' said Webster, ignoring him, 'looking after you I can't order things, buy things. My stall needs me.'

'But you can use the phone. I'm not stopping you.'

'I know, but it's not enough.'

'It's not as if you don't have any free time. You can go out.'

'Yes, but sometimes I need to be out all day, and that doesn't seem to be very convenient for you. I need to do the rounds, meet people, catch the auctions at Christie's, go to Bermondsey market, Camden Passage, Covent Garden. Buying and selling, I can't afford to be out of the game. I can't stay in all day taking care of you. I have to go down to the V and A, Basildon. I need to – '

'If it wasn't for me you'd have no home! Is this the thanks I get? I take you in, I'm paying you good money, you're sleeping in a luxury flat. You can eat cheese cake when you want to, coffee cake when you need to.'

'Please, Bloch, don't be angry.'

'You short-sighted bumpkin! You're a buffoon, a penny farthing with one wheel missing, a clown with a green nose. I can get along without you. Go on, leave then, get back to your precious pottery, if you've got your heart set on it. You'd better get your things together.'

'What? But where will I stay? Where will I sleep?'

'Well, you should have thought of that, shouldn't you?'

Webster's state of habitual sluggishness and slurred perceptions were whipped up and shaken. Like someone driving down a motorway, excited to think he will soon be home, only to find he has failed to take the correct turn-off and is hopelessly off course, he was stopped short. Had he been going the wrong way all these years? Thinking he was headed for home when in fact he'd been going further and further astray? What was life? And why didn't it come with a set of instructions? Panicking now, paralyzed by these unfamiliar thoughts, he wrenched his mind back into a practical mode, reviewing all the things he had to do: I've got to pay the parking fine; I've got to ask for a free picnic hamper from the bank for messing up my card; pay the phone bill; buy new foot soles and long johns; cash the cheque from Antiquarius; get coconut soap and razors from Sally at Portobello; go down to Basildon and barter like a maniac for those Chinese lanterns; get my ears syringed, and find somewhere to live.

Feeling calmer he said, 'I forgot to tell you, Barny Crane rang while you were sleeping.'

'That parasite – what did he want?'

'He wanted to know if he could drop by.'

'What did you tell him?'

'I said it probably wasn't a good idea.'

'He just wants me to write more crap. Enough! No more banality! No more mediocrity!'

Webster shuffled about from foot to foot; the conversation was becoming unbearable, as it had so often been during the last four days. He wanted to be conciliatory, to please Bloch; even to impress him, but he didn't know how to; didn't know if it was actually possible.

'Listen, Bloch, I'll stay; I take it all back. I'm happy to look after you; you need taking care of; after all, you're poorly.'

Bloch gripped the blankets tightly with both hands and pulled them over his face, and let them fall. Webster stared at this lumpen form, this woolen sculpture. Nothing was said. Was this retreat into the bed meant to communicate Bloch's acquiescence, or his desire for Webster to leave? He had grown used during the last few days to trying to decode Bloch and his silences, to interpreting his signals; perhaps hiding himself under the blankets was to be his latest gesture of opacity. Bloch began speaking from under the covers in a muffled voice.

'It's no use.

'I can see that. It's no good.

'You should go ... because ... I have to think things through. I have to be dedicated, solemn, like a priest. So no room for small talk; I have to have peace. I can't wrestle with another ego, be reasonable, compromise, negotiate.

'I need to be alone for this housebound odyssey. To go into the forest. It's true I've turned into a monster. You should be spared the monstrosities. And you have things you have to do.'

'But if I go who's going to look after you? Will you ask the doctor if you can have a nurse?'

'I'd love to have a nurse, but she might not love to have me.'

Webster nodded sadly, as if Bloch was able to see him through the blankets. Then he shuffled off out of the room, mumbling, 'I know what you mean.'

Bloch re-emerged, fluffed his pillows and sat up. He flicked the RECORD button on his cassette player and began speaking into the microphone. At first Webster ignored the sound of his voice, but then, as he caught some of the words, his attention was seized and he tiptoed closer to the bedroom. It was striking how Bloch could plough on, regardless of the upheavals of the last few moments.

'I have said before that Natalie allowed me to perceive the wonder of being alive more than anyone I've ever known. Now – the landscape of her body – I concede it was an especially flawless body which, even after I'd first made its acquaintance, climbed aboard it, been tossed on its stormy seas, been shipwrecked because of it, been rescued by it, even after I'd been led gently onto its desert island, stayed there for days during which time lost all meaning, tasted its mangoes and papayas and basked in its sunsets, even after all that it still made my jaw drop. Perhaps that's why we grew apart because I never actually achieved any degree of naturalness with this woman who nightly shared my bed. Do I make myself clear? The theory I have put forth is that when I was with her I was aware of her every stirring, the marvelous mechanisms of her flesh, aware of each mole, scar, vein. Now, here we go: if everyone applied that awareness to their every act, prayer, gift, etc. If they could transpose the sensibilities that come to them in lovemaking onto the daily commerce of this dreary planet, would not the world be a happier, more creative place? An erotic relationship with the world. But the world does not offer that which another presence, and only that, can give. Not possible! I hear you cry, it would prove too exhausting, and besides, not everybody's lover is as exciting as Natalie was, or can breed as much love, lust and the capacity to jettison sperm as she did; nor do they have that landscape body she did. Another gigantic flaw: I daresay too many people see sex not as a path to the divine, but as a fuck.

'And yet ... it has something I keep going back to. The whole of creation as a gargantuan lover's body. Bring the sensitivity to your lover that comes in good lovemaking to bear on humankind and see what happens. If we all did this, all did this, imagine! Unity as achieved in coupling, barriers breaking, what if they broke in every situation? Between all people. No, it can't be. And we remain fatally apart from one another, not linked by a molten, cosmic conduit. Only in sex can we create the illusion that we are infinite and boundless. My little theory: just another tattered footnote in the book of idealism. '

He paused, cleared his throat, and had a rest. Meanwhile, Webster cast his mind back to his last sexual encounter, which had been a fairly disastrous affair with a nanny some eight years ago. He had last slept with a woman in a different decade of his life. Desperate situations required desperate remedies. He would get his hair cut and buy a new jacket. He'd spend a hundred – no – fifty – no – twenty pounds. Or less if he could find something nice at Bermondsey Market.

'But in the golden age,' Bloch resumed, 'with Natalie, you should have seen me. She was Shakti, I tried to be Shiva, destroyer and creator, dancing in the circle of flames. Oh, can I help it if, in my limited way, I see the time we had as a time of unity? When I lost myself in her arms I experienced at least a semblance of that ego-transcending consciousness that Eastern mysticism is always banging on about. Getting beyond yourself, seeing the interpenetration of you and it – the world. Atman as Samsara. Or maybe Atman as Brahman. That kind of thing. Yes Tantra thank you – you have given me a framework within which to place Natalie and that time together before the whale. Yab Yum. She and I swapped stories and whiskeys; we drank our way into the hidden arteries of each other's hearts, and when the hangovers lifted we made all forests and woods our own.

'Foolish, foolish, to do this to myself when I'm an invalid hack writer who churned out books as a chicken churns out eggs. Is the chicken proud of the eggs as they plop? Slimey shell. Was I proud of the pages that rolled through my typewriter? This is what I should have been saying all those years; this is the voice I should have been using, but why has it come to me now? Why now when it's too late? Perhaps Oscar has done me a favor by helping me discover these melodies and we are both adrift now; he is poised for fame and I am poised for death.

'Here I'm left alone with the bare bones of life. The life that lies beyond the network of distraction, reaching total boredom, total vacuum; the route I take is humble, lined neither with gold nor opium. It culminates in the same cul-de-sac as does the Buddhist's in the monastery. But he is at ease with his vacuum. He rejoices in his meditative stillness, whilst I flow with dark rivers.'

He flicked the PAUSE button impatiently.

Webster stood there, as confused and disturbed as he had ever been. The feelings and words seemed so new and strange. Was Bloch insane?

Webster had glimpsed a whole other parallel world which rendered his own small and empty. He wondered at the pain Bloch had endured, tried to fathom his suffering. But his mind was not big enough.

He decided to sleep in his van, which *was* big enough.

# 15

The evening after Webster moved out Oscar came home to find that the walls of the hallway had been stripped, and the carpets removed, revealing floorboards with gaping holes in them, leading to a subterranean world of cobwebs; that the power points had been pulled away and sad little cables now dangled from the walls in their places. Half a dozen workmen in filthy overalls were smoking roll-ups and discussing what was next on the agenda: the general consensus seemed to be that they were long overdue for a tea break. Some of the men's trousers were so loose that they revealed the spaces between their buttocks, crammed with debris.

He walked on, in search of his landlord. He knocked on the door of his maisonette, which was ajar, waited, knocked again and walked in cautiously.

Act II of *Tristan and Isolde* was playing on Grindel's old record player.

He was surprised to find that the living room had been carefully tidied, cleaned and dusted. He also noticed that the heating was off and the windows were open – a welcome development since it had been rather difficult to breathe during his last visit. He turned his attention to a bookcase and read some obscure titles: *The Beauty of Overcoats; 101 Recipes with Crab; Business as Salvation; Big Business.* He picked the last one out and flicked through it, after finding a chair.

After a minute he closed the book, as he found it utterly incomprehensible, and took a moment to listen to the music, instead of blanking it out as he normally did. As he sat listening, he reached an alcove of peace, a still point. Then somewhere deep inside him there was a subtle shift, something resolved into an unexpected and yet familiar pattern and at the same time he felt a numbness spreading slowly along the axis of his body.

He listened intently as the man's and woman's voices ebbed and flowed, veering towards and moving away from an ecstatic union. As they came to rest another woman's voice took up from where they had left off, ushered in by shimmering arpeggios from the harp.

This new voice was icy, and sounded as though it came from far off, from outer space. As it carved out a luminous path the strings and woodwind introduced a recurring subject, and the resultant web of sound attained a trance-inducing level of beauty.

He was nonplussed. He wondered how it was that this music, which he had been indifferent to, could now hold him so strongly. His arms, neck and face were misting over with cold.

Then he closed his eyes, as if stirring at the touch of an invisible lover. Thought fell away and he sank into purifying fire, all the while rooted to his chair.

At last the record reached its end and began to hiccup in its groove. This pulled him out of his reverie and he looked about him, beginning to take in his surroundings again.

Grindel eventually appeared but it took Oscar a moment to realize that it was actually his landlord. The first surprise was that he was cleanly-shaved. He had never seen him without his stubble and he was startled by how youthful he looked. Not only was his face free of its perpetual half beard, but his body was also kitted out in entirely new – and fatally ill-judged – clothes. Grindel might conceivably have been dressed for a fancy dress party, but he had no party to go to; or costumed for a pantomime, though no theater expected him. He wore a pair of pink shorts reaching down to his knees, revealing mottled, lumpy calves, and a nylon shirt splashed with every possible color, depicting a giant octopus, its tentacles stretching along the length of his sleeves. He was clutching a cheap parasol in one hand and a golf club in the other. The transformation (or humiliation) of Mr Grindel was now complete.

'Mr. Babel, what are you doing here? Can I help you?' He slotted his parasol and club into an umbrella stand, walked over to the stereo and dutifully returned the record to its sleeve.

'That music was amazing,' Oscar mumbled, still taken aback by Grindel's idiotic sprightliness.

'It's not half-bad, is it? How can I be of service?'

'I'm sorry; I'm a bit dazed. I should apologize for inviting myself in like this, but as the door was open and as it seems to be open season around here; I mean, with all these workmen everywhere; I was wondering, why are they here; in other words, Mr. Grindel, what's going on exactly?'

'Mr. Babel, I'm a changed man.'

Oscar said nothing, staring blankly at Grindel's flabby face.

'I see things through my lover's eyes. I want to be clean and tidy from now on, like her. I want to be able to cut bread smoothly, dust and scrub efficiently, change sheets, wrap up leftovers and eat them before they go off, defrost the fridge. She's taught me so much, you see. Can I open up to you?'

Oscar nodded.

'You see, before, I was disgusting, filthy ... I had no notion of how to make life beautiful, but Androola has shown me the way. Now I can remove a stain from my trousers; I can boil an egg beautifully. It might not sound like much to you, but for me it's the dawn of a new era. I used to be afraid of life, Mr Babel; I needed constant heat and my overcoat; I needed my windows to be permanently shut. With tenants I was rude and negligent; I distrusted them, but now .... You see, I have great plans for this place; I have such plans! That is why the workmen are here, Mr Babel. I am having this place cleaned up and dusted. New wiring, new wallpaper, new carpets and curtains in the hall. Oh, and of course a new mattress for you, Mr. Babel.'

Grindel's address left Oscar feeling drained. He wondered if he would be able to put together a coherent response, since one was eagerly awaited, judging by the sight of Grindel's bulging eyes.

Oscar mumbled, 'That's wonderful … So you're … in love, then?'

'In love, on love, with love,' he chanted.

That's going a bit far, thought Oscar.

'Do you have anyone special in your life, Mr Babel?'

'Well … there is someone … she's … I last saw her a couple of weeks ago – '

'I know what you're thinking; you don't think I can keep it up. Don't worry, Mr Babel. I'm telling you; I'm different now. I've put it all behind me.'

'Yes, I can see that.'

'Oh, that reminds me; I've got a package addressed to you, Mr Babel. I picked it up this morning to save it from the paint.'

Moving slumberously he passed through a small passageway; after a while he returned with a parcel wrapped in brown paper. As Grindel held it close to his chest Oscar couldn't help noticing a possessive, protective air about him, as if he was holding a baby rather than an inanimate object. He seemed reluctant to part with the parcel, as he sagged into an armchair.

'You know,' said Oscar, 'I was wondering …'

'Yes, Mr Babel?'

'Have you seen my cat anywhere?'

'No, Mr Babel, I'm afraid not.'

'I let her out sometimes into next door's garden and then she climbs back; I let her out yesterday and I haven't seen her today. I'm worried she might have gone missing.'

'Well, Mr Babel, that's a bit of a blow. I liked that cat. She must have been a great comfort to a bachelor like you.'

'Yes, she was,' Oscar said.

He walked across to retrieve the package.

'Can I have the parcel?' he said, pointing to it with a hesitant forefinger.

'Oh, I clean forgot.'

Grindel stood up ceremoniously, still hugging the package tenderly. As he did so Oscar was struck by a very distressing thought. Had Grindel murdered Dove? And was his cat now inside the package he was so reluctant to part with? Had Grindel's old, vile ways secretly re-asserted themselves?

'Mr Grindel?'

'Yes, Mr Babel.'

Speaking slowly he said, 'Do you know what's inside the package?'

Oscar stared at it lodged in Grindel's hands – the box was certainly large enough to hold Dove.

'No, I'm afraid not Mr Babel. It came this morning with the first post.'

'I see. You're sure you haven't seen my cat then?'

'Yes, I'm sure, Mr Babel; I would certainly have told you if I had.'

'Mr Grindel, can I have the package now?'

'Of course.'

Very slowly, ritualistically, he handed it over. He could have been parting with a priceless gem, a sacred artifact. For a fraction of a second Oscar thought he looked irritated but then Grindel smiled politely and bowed his head.

Once in the hallway Oscar took a couple of deep breaths. He was anxious to open the box in the privacy of his room, but frightened about what he might find. As he ran up the stairs the workmen, having cut short their tea break, chose that moment to begin beating their hammers, sawing through wood, drilling through concrete and the resulting ear-splitting level of sound annihilated thought.

Once inside his bedsit he bolted his door. A strong wind was blowing from the window and the curtains were swelling and billowing wildly. He looked around for Dove, scrambling under the bed, searching inside the cupboard, tossing aside the blankets in her basket. There was no sign of her. He was just about to open the parcel when the phone rang.

'Hello,' he said, sticking a finger in his ear to block out the sound of the drilling.

'Oscar.' There was no mistaking that manufactured, unctuous voice, which delivered its every utterance with undue rigor and emphasis. 'This is Ryan Rees.'

'Can I call you back?'

'I'm about to be cut off as it is.'

'Well then, call me later.'

'Oscar – '

The line went dead. Oscar sat down heavily on his bed, which sagged and squeaked, and stared at the parcel. He took a couple of deep breaths. The curtains subsided with the wind and became quite still.

He was afraid to open the parcel; opening it might enclose him, might cause him to fall apart.

From below the ruinous sound of the drills refused to abate. To Oscar it felt like his bedsit had uprooted itself and settled down onto the exposed tier of a building site. There he was to spend his days in a bracing outdoor setting. In the winter time he would be rained on, hailed on, spat on by workmen, in the summer the sun would make him wilt, until at last, slowly, all around the building would begin to take shape, girders fall into place, windows slide downwards, scaffolding be dismantled ... and he would be buried alive in a pitiless steel structure.

He was yanked back to the presence of the parcel. He tried – calmly and rationally – to account for his fears, which, he was amazed to find, still persisted. Grindel's continued benevolence made him nervous. His new persona struck him in some way as unreal, collapsible. Had Grindel secretly committed a senseless act of evil to make up for all his recent acts of kindness? Was he now attempting to give himself up?

If Oscar's cat was inside that parcel the world would no longer make sense, and anything could and would happen; Oxford Street would fill with sardines, as Bloch had said; Big Ben stop chiming. He had to ready himself for what he was about to see – harden his heart. Images flooded into his head of Grindel howling and cackling like a lunatic as he prepared to carry out his monstrous practical joke, brandishing a carving knife. He saw Grindel's jowls quivering, his beady eyes locked in a hideous leer, his lips drooling with saliva. He saw Grindel being carted away, handcuffed and straitjacketed.

He started unwrapping the paper. Then he opened the box.

Dove was not inside it.

Of course she wasn't.

"Thank you, God; thank you," he said evenly.

Instead of his cat he found a pile of magnetic tapes stacked up in two columns. There were flecks of a white substance lightly dusted over them. Licking a finger, he hesitantly tasted a trace of the unknown.

It was icing sugar.

He stared blankly at the box for quarter of an hour.

Then the phone rang again.

'Hello, Oscar speaking,' he said nervously.

'It's Ryan Rees. Sorry about that. The network went down; how's the prophet of London?'

'Please don't call me that.'

'Why not? It suits you. I'm ringing about the Duchamp banquet.'

'I'm not going. You didn't even ask my permission. When did you arrange it anyway?'

'About a week ago if memory serves.'

'What am I meant to be speaking about?'

'The future of painting.'

'I don't know anything about its future. Why should I? I'm not a painter. Or rather I'm a failed painter. I'm not even that. I'm not even a failed painter anymore. I don't want to do this anymore.'

'Do what?'

'Pretend to be something I'm not.'

There was a moment's silence. He could hear Rees' rasping, carnivorous breath. Oscar sensed that a new line of attack was taking shape inside him, his brain clicking and blinking like a computer.

'Oscar, you're an interesting man,' Rees started again. 'You have energy, charisma, classic good looks and something valuable to say.'

'Look, cut the shit; what do you want from me?'

'What do you want from me?'

'Nothing.'

'That's a pity, because I can give you almost anything.'

'What was the point of plastering those posters all over the place?'

'Oscar, don't be so hard on yourself.'

'And what about all that ridiculous crap you've been devising on the internet? You shouldn't write such things.'

'I'm not sure I know what you're referring to.'

'You said that I've been to Oxford and studied Sanskrit. And the rest. That ludicrous volcanic soap. All that horseshit. None of it's true.'

'The truth's boring, Oscar.'

'Well, I don't want to be associated with all your elaborate lies.'

'Oscar, it's just a bit of harmless fun. People want to meet you, hear you speak. My office has been flooded with e-mails asking about you. And by the fucking way, I think we could make a killing with BabelSoap, I've got a guy on the case right now; he's this anorak geek, got a chemistry lab that he blows himself up in from time to time, but he knows soap like the back of his hand. Or what's left of it.'

Oscar ignored this and barked, 'How did you arrange this Duchamp thing anyway?'

'Monty Bell's a friend of mine.'

'Who the hell is Monty Bell?'

'A juror for the Duchamp Prize. He told me that Mac Llewelyn, who was meant to be speaking originally, has got a fistula on his backside. So I pulled a few strings and I managed to get you in instead, since you have expertise in the field of painting and since your backside is fine. It's a high profile event, media coverage, celebrities, and you could shine.'

'Tell me something; why are you bothering with me? I'm causing you expense. I'm not making you money.'

'That's true, but I like challenges. You know Oscar, can I tell you a few things about myself?'

'I get the feeling you're going to regardless of my answer.'

'I'm what, if you were to ask them, people would describe as a man of influence. I command respect in the media; I'm feared. I dine at the Ritz and swim at the RAC. I have done it all, seen it all, eaten it all. So I want another challenge, something to make the public bite its lip, to give hope to the morons who get drunk daily on beer and soap operas. I thought to myself, "why not take a man like Oscar and make something of him."' For a moment he seemed to flounder, his slick rhythm eluding him, but then he picked up again. 'Now, don't get me wrong, you have substantial qualities of your own, of course you do, that's plain to see. That's why I want to give you a voice but I want it to reverberate courtesy of modern technology.'

'But I keep telling you I've nothing to say.'

'What about your little speech on love? You read Tom Beard's review. He practically called you a genius.'

'What if I told you that everything I said on that program was derived from someone else's head?'

'Oscar, Oscar, don't be so naive. Do you think there's such a thing as originality anymore? Everything's recycled from everything else. Besides, the idea that an idea is untouchable is a sick one.'

'I'm sick as well, but not as sick as you are.'

Great gales of laughter blew down the telephone line. Oscar had to move the handset away from his ear. But even then the roars were clearly audible. This was laughter like no other. It so utterly, so crushingly nullified his riposte, announcing that Rees's mighty imperturbability remained unscathed. After a while the guffaws began to subside.

'Oscar, do you really want to stay a nobody all your life? Here I am offering you the chance to do something beautiful. Don't you want respect and love and adoration? I can give you those things. And women will flock to you, Oscar. And gourmet meals and fine wines will be yours. And you will have caught a flash of glory before it ebbs away.'

'And what's in it for you?'

'The sense that I have contributed to the community and that I am personally fulfilled, my boy.'

'That's royal duckshit,' said Oscar.

'Don't be a fool, Oscar. Speak at the Duchamp Prize. Speak about anything you like. Fuck the future of painting. Lay into those fools. Think of it. You can do it; you can cut through the pomp of the art world, the postures and airs and graces. Tell them, Oscar. Moses at Sinai. Jesus in the temple. You can do it, Oscar. You can do it. Pay them back, the no-talent, mediocre elite, swigging champagne and settling back for evenings of fun and games. Tell them that we're all destined for hell, that we've managed to make a mess and call it art, managed to drink and call it sophistication, managed to get lost and call it charm. How can you miss this opportunity? Who's got the real backbone? Most just a few vertebrae, the rest cotton wool. You can make a difference. Don't you want to soak like a sponge in all the attention? This speech won't be about the art world, it will be about the truth!'

Rees was enraptured by his own words – he had surpassed himself – what spell-binding precision – how skillfully made were those gold dust sentences!

'I thought you said the truth was boring,' said Oscar flatly.

'Oscar, don't split hairs. I've got to go now. So what do you say?'

'I'm not sure; I'll have to think about it.'

'Oscar, it's just a speech, that's all; I'm not asking you to steal the crown jewels.'

He returned the phone to its cradle and turned to stare at the box again. He took all the cassettes out, and examined the bottom of the box for something to explain its contents. Nothing. He opened up all the cases and finally, in the last cassette, to his relief, he found a small note. He unfolded it carefully.

*Dear Oscar,*

*Enclosed are some tapes full of my thoughts on life, love, art, the whole thing. You may find what I have to say of interest. You're free to use what you like as you wave your sabre. If these various grunts and moans are of help to you, I'm glad. Feel free to shred them otherwise. Please don't come and see me anymore. Webster is with me. I'm unfit for company and would like to enter a long period of hibernation in the middle of this glorious summer. Just like me to be so contrary.*

*D. Bloch.*

*P.S. ON NO ACCOUNT SHOULD YOU COME AND SEE ME. OUR FRIENDSHIP HAS PLAYED ITSELF OUT. THE LAST MEMBERS OF THE ORCHESTRA ARE PACKING UP THEIR FIDDLES. LET SLEEPING DOGS LIE; BETTER STILL SHOOT THE MUTTS. I CAN'T GIVE YOU ANYTHING ELSE – I'VE DONE MY BIT – IT'S UP TO YOU NOW.*

Snatches of *Tristan* returned to him. He tried to put them out of his mind. And then he felt tears well up in his eyes. Through their cloudy veil he re-read the note disbelievingly. It was unimaginable, to exclude him like this. Why was he doing it? Had he really become so unbearable to Bloch?

Somewhere under his bed he still retained an old portable cassette player. Like Bloch he had tried hard to resist acquiring the latest technology. He scrambled around for it, struck by the notion that if he heard Bloch's voice all would suddenly grow clear, or he might gain some insight into this act of severance and be able to come to terms with it. He unearthed the battered and dusty machine, made a perfunctory attempt to clean it, then slotted the first tape in and pressed PLAY, turning up the volume above the sound of the drills.

Bloch's voice, cracked and old, sounded.

*Who will water me?*

*I have decided to speak of light, to be positive, if disconnected. Therefore, please grab your parasols. It's time for a sermon, because I have words huddled up in my gullet, eager to come running; because I have time to kill. Ah yes, that says it all: time to kill. Why is it that some fortunate souls experience time only after it has run its course, while for me time was always something to be lived through, to be killed?*

Oscar pressed the PAUSE button. No – there was nothing in that voice, those words to reverse the effect of the note or to make things clearer. Clearly Bloch had done all the explaining he wanted to do; he knew the recordings would not be touching on their relationship.

And now Oscar felt rage rise up and seize his insides and wring them as a pair of hands wrings a wet towel. He wanted to harm Bloch, to hurt him badly.

He read the note for a third and a fourth time. On the fifth reading one phrase stood out and he kept repeating it questioningly.

'It's up to you now, it's up to you now, it's up to you now.'

The words, he thought, were like a call to arms. What was up to him now? But then, for an instant, Bloch's rejection ceased to be painful, became in fact rather irrelevant while something else, ancient and mysterious, slid into view.

As he was trying to keep a track on all these different, conflicting thoughts the drilling stopped abruptly, giving him some peace.

He decided to telephone Rees but just as he was on the point of picking up the receiver the phone went again.

'Hello,' he said in a depleted voice.

'Who is Oscar Babel?'

'I'm sorry?'

'It's Najette. Why's your name all over London? Literally?'

'I don't really know.'

'In the fortnight since I've last seen you you've turned into a product. What's happening to you?'

'I think I'm growing.'

'Into what?'

'I'm not sure; it feels like things are happening.'

'Oscar, I'm not sure if it would be such a good idea for us to continue being friends.'

'But ... but I thought we were more than friends.'

'The thing is ... is it really you? Are you real or not? I'm not interested in shadows, because they have a habit of vanishing. I'm worried about you, you have to find out who you are. And I don't think you're a philosopher or a spiritual teacher and it's going to burn you out if you try and pretend you are. I need sincerity, not playacting.'

Oscar pushed his fist into his mouth and bit down so hard on it he drew blood. On moving his hand away he saw teeth marks enclosing the skin in reddish, scorched circles.

'Najette, please ... we all wear masks ... now and then ...' he said hopelessly.

'Yes, but yours is getting stuck. Listen ... I'm going away for a few days. I might give you a ring when I get back; that is, if you're not in the East, studying Sanskrit. I'll see you around.'

She rung off.

And now, as he sat there, dumbstruck all over again, he began to think loss bred loss, that Bloch's rebuff had somehow brought about Najette's rebuff, that this double loss was too unfair – it should have been spread out over days, not minutes, so he could have absorbed the blows, and he began to think that perhaps if he hadn't opened the parcel and read the note Najette might not have called just then to tell him what she had told him.

That night he didn't sleep at all.

# 16

The photographers standing in the foyer were like bees gathered round the entrance to their hive; they made a lot of noise, they were alive with appetite. The nominees for the Duchamp Prize were obliging some journalists with ad-hoc interviews, posing for the cameras, smiling and running their fingers through their hair ostentatiously. Cyril Vixen, a corpulent, prominent figure, clutching a bunch of white carnations, (a further two were pinned in his hair), was elaborating on his non-existent theory of art. He talked in a heavy, droning voice which never seemed to have enough energy for the completion of sentences. Vixen had been nominated for a series of subversive photographs. He had managed, by some sleight of hand, to procure the feces of several very well known female fashion models and taken pictures of their respective waste products. The names of the models had been inserted under the compositions, grainy and austere in black and white. He was, he claimed, trying to explode the myth of beauty by revealing the ugly underbelly of the body's normally invisible mechanisms. After the exhibition had finished several of the models denied that they had ever taken part in the project; they claimed that they had never offered him their stools and that Vixen had photographed his own. Some writers had suggested that it didn't matter whose waste products had been photographed because 'it was all the same shit anyway.' Vixen's career had blossomed and he had been nominated. In fact he was the favorite.

Another nominee was holding forth in a corner. She was a performance artist who would declaim, scream, sing and speak her erotic verse while couples simulated what she called 'symbolically-charged sexual activity' on stage. She said she was interested in the juxtaposition of the imagery of sex with the abstraction of poetry. She was famously promiscuous and never wore underwear because she felt it interfered with the flow of her artistic energy. Her mother had given birth to her in someone's living room, while her boyfriend strummed the guitar. After being arrested once in Covent Garden for indecent behavior (she had fellated a man during her street show *Menstrual Nights*) she had acquired greater fame and more admirers as an artist who was categorically unwilling to hold back. Her name was Rada Bhat.

The pink champagne that went floating around the foyer was being consumed at lightning speed and waiters were hard-pressed to ensure its smooth availability. A dinner gong sounded in the distance but no one seemed in the least interested in retiring to the function room a little way down the aisle, where the speeches were to be made and the prize to be awarded at the end of the evening.

A solitary figure, dressed in a cream suit, a white boater tilted stylishly on his head, stood apart from the fray, feeling slightly odd. This was Alastair Layor. Until recently he had been quite a prominent theater director, staging shows at off-West-End venues, particularly the plays of Jean Genet, and championing works by new playwrights. As a director he had sought to bring a shifting quality to the delivery of the text, a sense that each and every word was being articulated differently. He was trying to combine extreme stylization with spontaneity. But lately his productions had lost that quality of density he so valued. He found he no longer knew how to direct his actors; he no longer knew what they should be doing when they weren't speaking. His staging had grown tired, and rehearsals never really came to life. So he had opted out of the theater and was now trying to make a transition into psychotherapy. He was poised on the edge of an abyss. So far he had managed to avoid falling into it. As he sipped his orange juice he was haunted by an image which had been continually surfacing in his mind: the image of the woman whose life he'd saved on Regent Street, a woman whose pocket had had a single amaryllis sticking out of it. Once again he found himself wondering who she was, and what had upset her so much.

Philip Crumb, the third contender for the Duchamp prize, was dressed in a flamboyant orange silk shirt and a giant nappy. On his feet he wore tattered sandals. He had got into a lot of trouble recently for grave robbing. His primary purpose had been to try and obtain a different bone of the body from a different grave with a view to constructing a skeleton assembled from two hundred and six dead humans – the number of major bones in the body. He had managed to procure enough bones to piece together the upper half of a skeleton. The work – entitled "206" – was exhibited for a week at Tate Britain before someone heard about his nocturnal exploits. Crumb was promptly arrested and tried. After he had spent three months in prison he announced his new project to the world: to publicly slit his wrists while lying in a hot bath. This he referred to as "The Hot Toddy". Unfortunately the project had had to be cancelled when he discovered he couldn't stand the sight of blood. "206" had earned him tonight's nomination, despite public outcries and much vilification.

Pebald War, the final nominee, was telling someone about his latest work: a collection of ninety nine coat hangers made out of different kinds of pasta. Later he had plans to construct a cutlery set out of his own frozen semen to be called 'Life Utensils.' The general consensus was that War was the weakest of the contenders for the coveted prize of £50, 000.

And standing on his own beside a small waiting area, away from everybody, was Oscar.

After Najette had hung up he had listened to Bloch's tape recordings, cobbling together a gargantuan transcript throughout the night, watching the reels of his old cassette player turning slowly. In the morning he tried calling Najette but her phone was continually engaged. Then he looked for Dove sleepily, but couldn't find her. He placed adverts in local papers, on trees, even on the buses running through Elephant and Castle. By searching for Dove he could do something, take action; whereas there was nothing he could really do about the phone call with Najette, at least not until some time had passed; and the letter of severance from Bloch couldn't have been more final.

As he stared at the glamorous people in front of him he wondered whether his speech would be a complete disaster or whether he had an outside chance of winning the crowd over with eloquence, an eloquence derived from Bloch's recordings. Though much of what Bloch had uttered on the cassettes made no sense and seemed to be on the edge of madness Oscar also came across words of great clarity and insight. The tapes were like the testament of a man who kept passing from light to darkness, from profundity to anarchy. Within the transcript he found – rather serendipitously – material relevant enough to yield the basic content of the speech. He had cut, cleaned and curtailed, sanitized and summarized, stripped Bloch's observations of their excess and incoherence, confident that he had at the end a striking, poetic, and meaningful statement.

But Ryan Rees and Johnson Manger, his copywriter, had insisted on looking over the speech, like builders examining a wall for cracks. They then produced a series of damning observations on the nominees and their work. Rees had said, 'Find a way of getting these comments in there; otherwise it's a bloody waste of time.' Oscar had had to completely restructure what he had until at last both he and Rees were happy with the final draft. Over the last few days he had learnt it off by heart, and rehearsed its delivery obsessively and painstakingly.

He continued to study the crowd. There was something strange about the way people were behaving. After a few minutes he realized what it was. While everyone seemed interested in their interlocutors, they nonetheless kept one eye on the promenading figures in front of them, eager to acknowledge those who drifted along, watchful to identify and perhaps make contact with an especially famous or important person. This state of frantic receptivity paradoxically made everyone unreachable and detached in the end. Conversations were aborted before they had had a chance to move beyond tired opening gambits and introductions; remarks went undigested, and, like windswept leaves, people hurtled halfway across the foyer to greet someone else, only to leave them seconds afterwards.

Oscar motioned nearer to the crowd, like someone lowering himself into a hot bath. At the same time a young woman broke free and walked up to him. She wore a crimson sarong patterned with images of dollar bills, and a brightly-colored waistcoat, her exposed arms covered in a fine sheen of glitter. She smiled at him playfully and the way she raised her eyebrows suggested she might have been a little drunk.

'I'm Anna; you're Oscar Babel, aren't you?' she said.

'Yes, how do you know?'

'Someone pointed you out. What are you doing here?'

'I'm meant to be making a speech later. I'm a bit nervous.'

'Have you had enough to drink?'

'No.'

She intercepted one of the roving waiters, slid her empty glass onto his tray, picked up two full glasses and handed one to Oscar. She sipped at her champagne, her free hand gesticulating, chiming with the rhythms of her speech.

'You need to unwind. Self-consciousness is fatal at this kind of do; they'll show you no mercy. The only way you'll get through this evening is by staying near the booze taps.'

'I'm sure you're right. Perhaps you could guide me around the hot spots.'

'Tonight, I'm already acting as someone else's nanny.'

'Nanny? How do you mean?'

'I'm hanging on to the tails of some of the fat cats.'

Her smile was growing more tantalizing, her movements more exuberant. She was on the verge of breaking into dance. Oscar feared she might glide away from him. As he smiled back at her he sensed her eyes settling on his lips, and darting away again. He glanced from time to time at her waistcoat; it hugged her elfin form tenderly.

'So, what's it like being famous, Oscar?'

'I'm not really famous,' he said.

'Your name's plastered all over the underground. That's the summit, isn't it? Or do you have to get your face on postage stamps to really make it?'

'I'm just holding the fort. I'm not sure I like being in the limelight.'

'Then get out of it.'

'You're very frank, aren't you?'

'I just bring up the rear.'

She grinned mischievously.

'How do you happen to be here tonight?' he asked.

She took a deep breath.

'Well, this is strictly between you and me. I shouldn't really be telling you, but I feel I can trust you. You see that guy over there' – she pointed to a big, bearded man in a brocade jacket embroidered with silver galloping horses – 'he's my boss. I call him the Bear. He pays me to be seen with him. He's as thick as pigshit.'

'Do you have to go to bed with him?'

'Oscar, I think you may be even franker than I am.'

'I'm sorry, you don't have to answer that question.'

She pulled out a cigarette from a pocket of her waistcoat and lit it. After a long, languorous drag she exhaled and rotated her head slowly so that the smoke was released in a trail that moved in tandem with her head.

'The Bear's asexual; the only thing he cares about are his stallions. He'd rather ride those than women. He's stinking rich.'

'Doesn't he have a wife or someone?'

'He has a wife, but she's divorcing him because he spends more time in the stable than the boudoir. I'm her public replacement.'

'It sounds like a very bizarre arrangement to me.'

'Perhaps, but I get to eat and drink at fancy places and meet exotic people. Ernst may be dull but he's in with an interesting crowd.'

A steward came out of his corner of deference and made a succinct announcement, requesting that people start making their way to the function room for the banquet. Practically everyone ignored him.

'Anyway Oscar, I have to get back to him. And it's feeding time. Good luck with your speech. Maybe I'll see you later and we can chew the fat.'

She slipped away, not before giving him a dazzling wink. He needed another drink, several drinks – she was right. But he didn't want to get too inebriated. As she secreted herself into the crowd a man latched onto her predictably.

He went up to the seating plan, which was propped up on a silver easel outside the function room, and, after studying it, strode in warily.

His table, like all the others, had achieved a perfect marriage of kitsch and opulence. Twelve bottles of wine stood on it, forming a regal circle amid glittering plates and endless sets of cutlery. Starched cotton napkins, folded into hourglass figures, were planted in gigantic wine glasses. A bouquet of artificial flowers sat in the centre, partially obscuring butter dishes and baskets of bread. Name cards were mounted in gold-plated frames. In the middle of each plate there sat a miniature work of art, offered to each respective guest: a statuette of Venus, a wax thumb standing erect on a slide, a three-dimensional version of Goya's Saturn devouring one of his sons. Oscar's plate gave a home to a tiny teddy bear wearing a dinner jacket. He noticed that his name had been spelt incorrectly: he was now Oscar Bubel.

A small man, balding and energized by alcohol, slumped down next to him. Under his breath, Oscar said to himself, 'From a hovel to the Hilton.'

The small man said, 'What was that?'

'Oh, nothing.'

'We haven't met. I'm Willy Nargall. Hack.'

'Willy Nargall Hack. That's a funny kind of name.'

'No. My name's Willy Nargall. And I'm a hack, even though I say so myself. Who the hell are you?'

'Oscar Babel. You won't know who I am. Actually I'm not sure I do.'

'Good, I like that; shows you're not afraid to be vulnerable. In the circles I move in  vulnerability's hard to demonstrate, so I like a bit of vulnerability in others. It keeps things in balance.'

He produced two fat cigars, cut the ends off with an elegant looking clipper and handed one over to Oscar, taking it as a given that he smoked.

'Married?'

'No.'

'Good. Girlfriend?'

'Well – no.'

'Are you an uphill gardener?'

'Eh … oh … no.'

'Good. Why are you here then?'

'I'm speaking about the future of painting.'

'Shitty subject. What future? Maybe two centuries ago. Now the only paint that counts is the emulsion on your wall.' Nargall examined the art work he had been allocated – a tiny cheese grater made of tin foil – scrunched it into a ball without hesitation and chucked it onto another table. It landed in a butter dish. He lit Oscar's cigar and Oscar spent the next few minutes puffing and coughing in equal measure before finally giving up and stubbing the cigar out.

The other guests for that table began taking their places with much chattering. A middle-aged, sun-baked woman moved in drunken orbit around the seats, searching for her name card. After she had found it she switched it with another at the opposite end and sat down breathlessly. Then she rang her hairdresser on her cellular phone and spoke to him for fifteen minutes about possibilities for new hair styles. Nargall, observing her closely, whispered to Oscar, 'That old soak's had more facelifts than I've had paychecks.'

Oscar chuckled. Nargall had for some reason taken a liking to Oscar and continually nudged his arm to deliver more verdicts about someone dangerously close. The presence of Nargall was somehow comforting. His outspokenness weighted the evening, and as the others took their seats Oscar gradually began feeling quite good.

A young woman, dressed in a sleek white dress of classic design, sat down next to him. He guessed she was a model. Her coal-lustrous mane of hair resembled a great snake coiled around itself. At either side two pig tails dyed in vermilion had been coaxed out of this fibrous loop and flopped outwards. Eight large hair clips, inserted at vital points, kept the whole, intricate structure intact. All around the circumference of her forehead, falling down to her eyebrows and ears, were isolated strands of a waxy fringe.

There was no denying her beauty, though beneath her exquisite facade there ran an antiseptic strain and after some time Oscar found her studied perfection cloying. She was talking and laughing with a well-dressed man with lean, tanned features. There was something about the way they spoke to one another which announced their privileged inclusion in a club which coolly denied entry to outsiders. This made him want to deface her beauty, to rip out the invisible wall she placed between herself and those who weren't part of her circle and that warned people not to come too close.

When he had a chance to, he said, in his most resonant voice, 'We haven't been introduced. I'm Oscar.'

She looked at him ponderously, with an air of indulgence but made no reply.

So he asked someone for a cigarette.

'Do you mind if I smoke?'

'Not at all,' she said quickly, in a staccato rhythm.

'How do you happen to be here?' he persisted.

'I'm sorry; would you excuse me.'

Her smile as she turned away was as hollow as the barrel of a gun. Then she was laughing and joking once more with her tanned companion. Oscar felt unreasonable pain. As he recovered from her snub, he almost marveled at how unfriendly she had just been. It was transparently obvious, he thought, that she was only prepared to talk to people she considered important. And those she deemed insignificant she swept away as she would an annoying insect.

The food had yet to arrive, though no one seemed to mind. Instead, all around wine was being zealously, religiously poured and drunk. And as more and more tumbled down people's throats less and less made it into the glasses, spilling decoratively onto the tables.

As the master of ceremonies introduced the evening from a sleek, raised platform at the far end, Oscar began to find the whole affair faintly ridiculous and decided to concentrate on his menu. His eye gravitated towards the words that interested him. Grilled trout, rochette salad, avocado and prawns, white pickled cabbage and lamb, saffron poached pears, orange creme brule. A waiter deposited a salmon about three-feet long on the table, surrounded by almonds and lemons. Little pots of tartar sauce wrapped in red ribbons framed the display. Nargall stared at the fish in deranged anticipation.

'A handsome fish. Lots of room to maneuver with there. Pass me the garden shears.'

Oscar chuckled. The waiters began serving little plates of *hors d'oeuvres*.

Now the immaculate table was raped slowly and methodically. The fish was devoured, the wine bottles were drained down to their last drops, and the plates practically licked clean. By the time dessert approached the table cloth was a mess of color, stains and fragments of food. The waiters laid out a fresh cloth efficiently, like nurses changing bedclothes for a sick patient. They brought order and hygiene.

Various luminaries delivered their speeches while the puddings were picked over, devoured or put aside by those who were too bloated to eat any more. Oscar knew that very soon it would be his turn to speak. He felt a cavity open up in his abdomen. He turned to Nargall and whispered a few words.

'It seems a bit gratuitous, Mr. Nargall.'

'My dear boy, I guarantee everybody here considers themselves terribly deep and complex and important. Little do they know how trivial they are in the grand scheme of things. Those picayunes and pygmies. I only came for the booze and grub. I won't be staying for any more speeches and I couldn't give a donkey's testicle who wins the fucking prize. He or she won't manage to string two sentences together anyway. I don't care to celebrate further the abortions of these charlatans. I'm off. I feel ill and I've only had two bottles of inferior claret.'

'But I'm next on the list. Won't you stay to hear me?'

'Well, if it will make you happy. But I know what would make me happy. If you could speak the truth. That would be a first. Imagine – someone for once getting off his talc-encrusted arse to tell these walking facsimiles that they don't deserve to drink Picasso's piss. Don't sugar the pill, poison it.'

The words were like the sting of a tarantula.


A stopped figure came up to him, took his hand and guided him towards the platform. Oscar felt his body pulsing with adrenaline. He climbed the stairs to the platform and waited as the emcee spoke some words which were lost in the fog the place was suddenly immersed in. He took a few deep breaths. What did he have to lose? He wasn't really anybody, he had no reputation that could be tarnished, no status to be stripped of. He peered into the gathered assembly, the faces slurred with alcohol, the brilliant lights, this group of sophisticated, beautiful people. He did not envy them. The scene before him swayed, perceived as it was through the distorting lens of his heated mind. Here he was, at the epicenter of London's art world; by some miracle he had been accorded a place in it. He had marched in and no one had objected; no one had pointed to him and demanded he leave. Here he was, ensconced in privilege. He could see himself, standing on that stage, see himself as if he had separated into two entities and his doppelganger was monitoring him from afar. What world out there awaited him? Now was the time to find out.

'Actually, I don't want to talk about the role of the painter; I don't think it's important. Painting bores me. It's light I want to speak about.'

Willy Nargall's head snapped up – a jump-started car. Others were roused out of their state of inertia, and their heads lolled around, as they tried to focus.

'But first I want to tell you what I think of you all. You're all a pack of frauds ... and before you accuse me of being judgmental ... mirror, mirror on the wall, I'm the biggest fraud of them all.'

Murmurs of alarm spread across parts of the room like forest fire.

'The light of the moon. A voice singing in a chapel. The reciprocal smile of a lover. The morning light of summer. And the dance of shadows.

'There is no fraudulence in these.

'In the beginning was the turd. Then followed the ichthyosaurus, the ice age, and now ... here we all are in the Hilton, having forgotten our ancestry and animal urges, which crop up behind us from time to time, ambush us, and remind us, no matter how hard we try to cover them up with words and sweet perfumes and stained glass windows and art. Or should I call it fart? Is art just a big fart that's been sweetened up? Is it just the whining and moaning of the uninvited guest dressed up as objective and detached? Methane wrapped in an outer shell of cinnamon? Perhaps.'

Savage laughter issued from Willy Nargall. When he realized no one else was joining him – since no one else was anything other than appalled – he opted for silence. The room felt cursed suddenly, as if drained of oxygen. Oscar regarded the shocked faces fastened together in a frozen tableaux. He was determined to go on with his speech even if it killed him. Sheer willpower, coming from nowhere, pushed and drove him through the mounds of mute dissent.

'I think we are dying, ladies and gentlemen.

'I think we are dying. We need a new song to sing.

'I wish there was something I could say. Not these tawdry words, not this crude flesh and bone, wrapped in scarves and eau de cologne. Somewhere in eternity buses carry free-floating souls across the ages, depositing them like nuggets of gold. These souls that float before and after time, before birth and after death, they are housed into mortal incarnations and frames, but diminished – their true nature distorted – by man-made dilutions, man-made pollutions, fixations. Hiding the luminosity within and without. Hiding the love.

'We should choose love over fear; I want to be plain about this.

'If, as many men have pointed out, we are asleep then it is important to wake up. But maybe it is too late and the sleep is all about us, like a viscous fluid.'

Oscar was settling into his rhythm now, finding some measure of composure; and his assurance acted like a sedative on the crowd, which was actually starting to listen to what he had to say. And as he said it, as the speech moved on, parts of the audience grew intrigued. Feline women slid their designer glasses on and studied Oscar curiously, jaded men pondered the meaning of life. The mood became tinged with something approving, something congratulatory, very faint and yet unignorable.

'Perhaps we have lost the sense of wonder that should accompany our acts of love, our prayers. But we have to reach out and grasp wonder, hold it close, court it, keep it flowing like a stream.

'But now, after all – it can't be helped – it's time to get down to the nitty gritty, the specific. The nominees and their works. I'll begin with spirit. There seems to be a fundamental lack of it – in photographs of people's shit. Yes, it's amusing; a nice little gimmick. But does Cyril Vixen really think he has anything to contribute? The best that can be said of him is that he's shallow; but the truth is that, at the end of the day, his images are as bloated and dull as he is.'

Cyril Vixen muttered under his breath, 'What a little cunt; how dare he?' Someone at his table grappled with a bottle of port.

'Mademoiselle la Bhat, on the other hand, likes to recite poetry while couples couple. It may be edifying for her but it isn't for the rest of us. Let's not confuse hobbies and charming eccentricities with something which is meant for public consumption. She is a talent-less anachrid who should think about a career change, and perhaps open up a brothel – '

Rada Bhat stood up and shouted, her face very red, 'Who the hell do you think you are?! What gives you the right to – '

But she was cut off as more parties joined the debate. Others pulled out their smartphones and began to film the proceedings with impeccable discretion.

'He's right; what the hell is the point of what she does, or what any of us do, for that matter?' Alastair Layor, the retired theater director, shouted. He welcomed this friction, this conflict – it was infinitely preferable to the usual lassitude of prize-giving ceremonies. He welcomed Oscar's unfashionable endorsement of wonder, his willingness to risk making a fool of himself. It was the same kind of risk-taking Layor had once championed as a director. He felt something very like excitement, like danger at the moment. And the crowd also was turning volatile, getting into its stride.

'Get stuffed; are we all turning against ourselves now, the only ones who ever supported us? We have to stick together; we're all in the same game ...' a plump woman squealed in response to Layor's uncomfortable question.

'Mr Babel's only attacking the charlatans amongst us, not those with talent,' Mark Redhill pronounced. He was a film director, whose debut *Tea and Valium* had been received catastrophically by critics and crowds alike, turning him embittered. Willy Nargall shouted,

'Hear, hear,' and clapped, solitary applause that drew attention to his table for an instant, before promptly dissipating.

Redhill continued, 'Yes, after all, pictures of shit are still, when all is said and done, pictures of shit. I suggest that Cyril just confines himself to not flushing his toilet.'

'Ladies and gentlemen, please let Mr Babel finish!!' the emcee yelled in a slightly strangled voice. For a moment the hubbub, the anarchic energy of the room was contained. But then there were sharp intakes of breath all round as Mark Redhill and Cyril Vixen strode up to one another. People couldn't quite believe their eyes. Things were getting out of hand. As if to reward himself for trying to establish order, the emcee sipped on a liqueur but unfortunately it went down the wrong way and he proceeded to cough with much self-consciousness. Oscar, who was at his side, stared at him for an inert time, realized that he should try and help him, and began to pat him on the back as his face turned a shade of burnt sienna. As he continued to gag Redhill and Vixen gazed into each other's eyes like gladiators in the moments before a bloody conflict.

The emcee settled down and Oscar poured a glass of water for him, but he did nothing but look at it, too worried now about a repeat performance. Then he turned his attention to the distressing scene down below. Cyril Vixen had poured his saffron poached pears all over the director's head, and the sauce was now mingling with his hair wax. In retaliation the film director produced a tiny can of deodorant from his inner pocket. Cyril Vixen stared helplessly, rooted to the spot, for some reason unable to move when he should have been bolting.

Redhill, having shaken the can with incredible vigor, pressed its button, releasing its fragrant spray into Vixen's eyes. Vixen doubled over and started to scream in agony, shouting out something about blindness. He then assumed a fetal position on the floor, growing smaller all the time as friends flocked to his aid. These friends took one look at Redhill's demented eyes and backed off, sensing that they were about to meet the same fate. One man, however, who was un-commonly big and strong, remained undaunted and walked straight up to Redhill, snatched the can of deodorant, and crushed it in his bare hands. Redhill stared in amazement. He was about to speak when another very large man, deciding that the first very large man was showing off, resolved to teach the latter a great and edifying lesson. A meaty hand sliced through the air, and slammed into the first giant's chin. This sent him reeling and crashing into a nearby table, which shivered under his immense weight, its contents flying here and there colorfully. Redhill made a furtive bid for the exit. During all this time Cyril Vixen was in convulsions on the floor, great porky knuckles thrust into his excoriated eyes.

The first giant picked himself up and in the manner of a sumo wrestler, charged his opponent, arms akimbo, his fists locked into plier shapes. He found his opponent's stomach and heaved both arms around it, squeezing tightly. In a few seconds the two were locked into a single unit of trembling, thwarted movement. The expend-ed energy was tremendous but they didn't really seem to be getting anywhere, rearing up like two bulls, their legs locked into the floor by virtue of the opposing force coming from the other. As the two continued their monumentally pointless grappling, a succession of grunts and angry cries issuing from them, other men tried interven-ing but their efforts were just as pointless and the two central titans barely even noticed their ineffectual pawing and pulling at their legs and shoulders. A further set of men then joined the original set to assist them. It was like some multiplying tug-of-war. In the end some ten or twelve bodies had fused into a fragmented lump reminiscent of a rugby scrum. They heaved, they shoved and still the central hub of force held. All the while Cyril Vixen lay slumped underneath, half-crushed, moaning and gnashing his teeth. The orb was being as-sailed by centrifugal forces that threatened to tear limbs from limbs, to dismember bodies. Something had to happen, something had to give way.

The crowd, having been shocked, fascinated, and appalled in quick succession, had now lapsed into utter silence, trying not to look, but looking; trying not to be caught looking, trying to temper their eye-popping gawking and failing to. This was insanely compelling and fatally addictive. People squeezed their legs together, so that their distended bladders wouldn't release their contents, desperately trying to postpone the moment at which they would have to go to the toilets. Camera flashes ricochetted around the room. TV producers' minds buzzed with ideas for new programs, journalists scribbled notes – there was no way of embellishing this story, it was already thoroughly mad. The final debasement of art, the end of civility, ladies and gentlemen, dear readers, last night I was privy to what must rank as the single most extraordinary media spectacle I have ever beheld, a debacle of such proportions, a fiasco so farcical in its character and yet so terrible in its implications, no play, no film could have matched the blood sweat and tears the viscera the drama the conflict as a fisticuff turned into human meltdown at the Hilton, as centuries of evolution went down the drain in one fell swoop as

'For God's sake, somebody stop them; somebody do something!' somebody shrieked.

Whereupon, momentarily letting down their guard, the two giants keeled over. The others tumbled onto each other, and legs and arms fanned back and forth, dissipating all the detonated energy and pain. There were cries and curses, shrieks and moans.

Finally, Mr Vixen's bulldozed form was carried out by the now repentant giants.

The others staggered to their seats, walked away in search of water and collapsed in heaps.

Then, exploding in a frantic jumble of sound, everyone boiled over. They all spoke at once, practically at the same instant, all at once, and a great tapestry of words was instantly weaved with lunatic dexterity and speed. Everyone had an opinion, everyone had a point of view. Some expressed mere incredulity, others tried to put the thing into a proper context. But one thing emerged that was consistent: no one listened to anyone else; they pretended to but just waited for the other person to finish so that they could start again. Roughly one-thousand text messages were sent in the space of two minutes. Alastair Layor watched it all dispassionately...

'Well, that wasn't very sensible; it's always best to keep one's cool ...'

'Mark Redhill will never make another film, and he'll probably go down for GBH...'

'He looked like he was going to explode; I wish I'd had a camera ...'

'I think it's refreshing; I would have done the same if I'd thought of it ...'

'What about Ruby's remarks about how we should stick together; do you think she had a point?'

'Who cares? The important thing is that it was entertaining ... and we have Babel to thank for that, even if nobody has ever heard of the little prick.'

These remarks and many others poured out for several minutes, in a cacophonous whirl. The emcee had long ago given up the attempt to restore order and he just looked sadly at Oscar, with an expression that, infinitely more eloquently than words, spoke of equal parts despair and futility. Oscar tried to smile back, filled with baroque levels of guilt.

The uproar that had had its origins in Oscar's speech now gave everyone an opportunity to express opinions they would normally have shied away from. Mudraking and the unbridled expression of disgust had a context which made them permissible. All the pent-up fury, jealousy and dissatisfaction that normally remained repressed found various outlets and the unsayable was said.

'Mark Redhill's film was so bad I heard even the projectionists were refusing to run it.'

'Pebald War's spaghetti coat hangers are about as interesting as my mother-in-law's dandruff. I think he should leave his brain to science – *before* he dies.'

'Philip Crumb has soiled his nappy. Get Vixen to squeeze in a few shots.'

'That reminds me; Twitter should be called Shitter.'

'If I get a showing at the Earl, I naturally expect an offer from the Norbury because they both like that kind of soulful stuff that I do ... and I *am* a genius; my work drips with derelict luminosity.'

Alastair Layor looked on dispassionately.

Willy Nargall, still seated at his table, stared into the remains of his cappuccino in disbelief. He examined the rim of the cup. An incredible concoction, he mused. The frothed-up milk, the encrusted edges of the cup that are revealed as the coffee is depleted, a moon's surface of contours, a dinosaur ... He was lost in abstractions. He glanced back at the platform.

That was good, he thought, that was really fucking good.

Photographers were blinding Oscar with flashes.

In between flashes Oscar looked ahead dumbly. To the right, near the stage, a man was fondling a woman's breasts. To his left, towards the exit, a woman was feeding a Labrador some quiche lorraine. Oscar's eyes rolled from side to side. The emcee spluttered into the microphone. 'Ladies and gentlemen, ladies and gentlemen ...'

Then the PA went dead.

At that instant Ryan Rees, who had been watching the whole thing on CCTV, rubbing his hands together, entered the function room, accompanied by a stocky henchman in his employ named Edwin. Oscar was retrieved from the stage and marched off. Everything was suddenly very confusing: the continuing camera flashes, Ryan Rees at his side, babbling incessantly in his ear (when does he ever switch off, thought Oscar; is it that, at the end of his busyness, there is nothing?) the presence of Edwin, his flaccid face looking on stupidly, the floor splattered with food and wine, the bawling voices. But in another moment Oscar was gone, safely ensconced in the toilets.

While Oscar emptied his bladder, Rada Bhat and someone else were in the middle of a heated exchange.

'He's obviously a nut job. What pretentious steaming duckshit. Did you understand a word? Who the hell is he? Has anybody ever heard of him? No. Has anybody ever seen his work? No. I'll turn him into *taramasalata*.'

'He's a buffoon, a dolt. What was he trying to say? It was so ... boring! So ... what's the word? Boring, that's it. Who the hell invited him? Is there any more of that *grappa*?'

Others spoke more positively of Oscar, among them Anna, dwarfed by Ernst, the lover of horses. She was with some journalists.

'I got talking to him before the meal. I thought he was very nice. I didn't expect that performance, though. I'd heard of him, seen him on TV. But I liked what he said. It woke all the fat cats up. It was unexpected. I think we should give him a marzipan medal. He's either a loony or a genius.'

Willy Nargall was holding forth magisterially.

'I suggested that he do a bit of lashing out and I have to take credit for that, but I can't deny he did a very good job. And allied to some mystical tish-tosh that was rather effective, under the circumstances. The man obviously thinks he's some kind of messiah. Let him. At least he wasn't a bore. The same can't be said for the rest. Cuban Cigar?'

(Willy Nargall's version of events not only exaggerated the importance of his role, it also left out the fact that he had been asked by Ryan Rees to sit next to Oscar, to befriend him, and – finally – spur him on into rubbishing the whole evening, in accordance with Rees's wishes. Rees had been worried Oscar might get cold feet and he knew that Willy Nargall's remarks would help to keep Oscar on course. Nargall and Rees were bosom acquaintances.)

The debate about Oscar raged on.

He was eventually whisked away in a stretch limousine to a party in Hampstead. The banquet broke up at two in the morning, the photographers drifted away, pleased with the evening's harvest, the celebrities continued to drink at nearby clubs, and the waiters were left to clean up the mess. By the end everything had fused into a bloated, drunken quiescence. Eventually this dissipated into sleep. The journalists submitted their copy to their editors, and London promptly heard about Oscar's performance in the morning. And pictures of him were plastered all over the papers and the internet. Some of the phone footage was posted online and clever people re-edited the footage in clever ways and the wrestling match was slowed-down and speeded-up and fragmented into repeating loops of ever-increasing manic energy, accompanied by the configurations of demented drum machines and screamed lyrics about dismemberment.

The most controversial artist of the year did indeed turn out to be Cyril Vixen. He eventually used his prize money to pay for his hospital expenses.

*

Alastair Layor, the disillusioned theater director, left the Hilton feeling disappointed. He would have liked to have spoken to Oscar personally. A feeling of futility enveloped him as he climbed into a taxi. During the ride to his house, in Kentish Town, the feeling deepened and settled. He couldn't seem to shift it. When he got out of the taxi he walked off without paying. The driver caught up with him, as Layor fumbled with the keys to his semi-detached house, and demanded his fare. Layor gave him a fifty-pound note, murmured, 'Keep the change', and walked off, as if in a trance.

Once inside his house, a house filled to bursting point with possessions, saturated with echoes from the past, existing, as it were, more in the past than in the present, loaded down by objects and books and letters and papers and photographs and dust – a house that was already a museum – he felt significantly worse. Oscar's speech was very much on his mind as he sat down in his armchair and lit a cigarette. This man Babel, he thought, is right. It is time to cut through the pretense, the gimmicks, the absence of soul, the marketing tricks. What we need is some chastity, some order, sober mathematics, some Bach. Men like me, he reflected, have added to the confusion, creating visions of nihilism in theaters, unwittingly making suffering glamorous. Enough of this impurity; it's time for a change, some simplicity, the simplicity of a corpse in a living room, with a halo of seedy light around it, the light cast from a suburban lamp.

He sat very quietly in his chair, the smoke stirring round him like a slowly-spreading cancer. He inhaled on his cigarette, got up and walked towards a mirror. He stared into it, studying his face. A pair of sunken eyes, like grapes sinking into cream on a hot day, a slightly anaemic complexion, wiry locks of perpetually unkempt hair, a long, thin nose whose nostrils were disproportionately large. In his face a constant war was waging between alertness and lethargy.

After staring for a few more moments into the mirror he began to ask himself if he really knew his face, its contours, crease, curves, patterns. Does this face embody me? Does it represent me, the caverns inside containing the past and the inscrutable workings of my life? How I hate this house. How I hate the dungeon that this place has turned into. It used to teem with life and people and talk of changing the world, dreams and plans for revolution, for an artistic nucleus of like-minded spirits. Now every night, when I walk through that door, I feel stale air shooting down into my lungs.

He sat down in his chair again. He stayed there, his brain misting over, his thoughts amorphous and meaningless. But when he eventually crawled out of this cavity of time a solution came to him, an act of desperation masquerading as a solution.

He got up, roused himself, and, moving quickly, started gathering a few things, scraps, photographs, books, papers and bundled them into a suitcase, barely large enough to contain everything. What was it that Babel had said? Perhaps we have lost the wonder that must accompany our acts of love, our prayers.

He began writing a note to himself full of dark eloquence.

*Dear Ali,*

*The time has come to jettison the past. If your eye bothers you, pluck it out; if your past bothers you, pluck it out; if your house bothers you, burn it down. Conventional morality dictates that pyromania is wrong; my morality dictates that this house is wrong. This house is a prison of memories and past brilliance that now hounds and tortures me. Isn't psychoanalysis always trying to make us come to terms with our past? Isn't it always the past that causes our present problems; it mangles new relationships, new projects. If we are scarred we are scarred not by the future but by the past, so we must disengage. I want my innocence back; I want my wonder back. The wonder that accompanies acts of love, as Babel said. A taste of wine. A voice singing in a chapel. A new beginning. That's what I want.*

*When I was at the Gate doing* The Balcony, *doing* The Nursery, *I was happy recreating emotion, but wasn't it ultimately just synthetic, unreal? Who cares about improvisation if the performance is solid without it - why build up histories for fictitious characters? Why have fictitious characters in the first place?*

*It's time to do something honorable. Pick up litter, save a whale, feed and clothe a child, plant a tree. I can no longer see the value of making people stagger to the bar in the interval because they have been moved and need a whiskey. Why do people cry when they watch* Hamlet *and not when they see a man dying in the street? Why this readiness to respond to art and not life? Let the critics pursue their trainspotting; let the academics pursue their learning; let the actors pursue each others' orifices. I can't do it anymore, take part in this. I've had enough. And in order to make a clean break I must shrug off conventional morality. No one will be hurt I promise; I'll call the fire brigade as soon as the flames are up and running. As for the damage, nature will take care of it, reinvent itself; it always does. I'll keep a few fragments for myself. Then take to the road. I have no strings to hold me back.*

*Finally I wish to make it clear that if I set this place on fire I do it out of self-preservation. I want to kill the demons; who doesn't, except all those who live off them in some capacity.*

*Yours fondly,*

*Ali.*


He found some old newspapers. He found a box of matches. He lit one shakily, dropped the flame into the papers, grabbed his case and moved off. As he was stepping over the threshold into the corridor, the telephone rang. It was coming up to three in the morning. He was suddenly in a panic, not knowing what to do. Should he answer it? Why not? The fire would take a little time to get going. Very calmly, he walked down the hallway to the little table where the phone sat and picked it up.

'Ali? It's Nero. What did you make of this man Babel?'

'I liked him. He was different ... different.'

'We're over at this place called "Baby Go Go." Want to join us? I'm with some of the models.'

'Which models? The models of temperance and virtue?'

'Can you drop by?'

'Must go; something's burning.'

Smoke was gathering in the corridor.

He stepped outside, walked some paces down the street and watched the house in horrible fascination. Was there still time to save it? As he was considering the full temerity of what he had done he glanced up at the sky. A few stars were twinkling. The expanse of the sky was otherworldly and serene; an extraordinary silence reigned. The silhouettes of the houses reminded him of backdrops in Balinese theater.

There was a loud explosion, the sound of breaking glass and the first eruption of the fire had happened. Smoke seeped out of the shattered windows of the living room like liquid from a cracked bottle. Layor took out the hastily written note and cast an eye over it, reassessing its strange logic. He threw it aside and walked back inside the house. Inside, from the corridor, he peered into the living room, now a spectacle of swirling brilliance. He was coughing violently, his lungs felt as if they'd been dipped in soot. He watched the fire for a few more morbidly-alive moments. The generated heat was fantastic, causing everything in turn to ignite even though the flames had direct contact with only a part of the room's contents. A chair became a ball of light, his bookcase dissolved in a golden blur. A marionette, delicately made and grasping some flowers, succumbed to the flames and Layor watched as its face perished in the blaze. He grasped the wooden door handle and yelped – it was scorchingly hot. Yanking out a handkerchief he pulled the door to with its assistance, then dialed 999.

An age went by until he was finally able to say, 'My house is burning.'

'Address, sir?'

'32 Montpelier Grove, NW5. That's Kentish Town. Please come quickly.'

'And your name, sir?'

'Why do you need that? My house is burning down.'

'Your name sir?'

'Ali Layor. L. A. Y....'

'That's all right sir; the fire engines will be with you as soon as possible.'

Layor slammed the phone down. He rushed into the kitchen and filled a bucket with water. Spilling most of it, he hurried back. As he opened the door he was confronted with flames of a different cast, stronger and wilder. His eyes were stinging and streaming. He couldn't believe the speed with which the flames had spread. He poured the water into the inferno, and it had precisely no effect; he slammed the door, from under which blackened smoke oozed upwards. Hacking violently he staggered out into the street again. He drew an agonized breath of air. In the seconds it had taken him to shut the door and get out, the fire, as glimpsed through the broken glass, revealed its true, infernal dominion over matter. Panic hurtled through him, sabotaging his brain, turning his body hollow.

A few people had congregated and were watching the display excitedly. They came up to him.

'What happened?,' someone asked.

Layor kept his mouth shut. In another moment the whole of the ground floor was its insane billowing grip. He thought he had it all under control. This was not what he'd intended. He would have been miles away, having phoned the fire brigade from a safe distance. Now here he was, at the scene of his own crime, splintered by shame and remorse. All he wanted now was to save his house. He had made an awful, mind-boggling mistake. How could he have lit that match? He found it hard to believe that something so terrible could have had its origins in a single safety match. Suddenly he realized that the note he had written to himself had to be found. After all, what it said was incriminating. He scrambled around for it.

More and more people had emerged out of their sleep. Layor hated them – they were so inconsiderate, so vulgar and prying. He reflected – bitterly – that even now he had created a piece of epic theater for the masses. He had laid on a glamorous spectacle for them, non-paying customers. At last a fire engine came into view. At the sight of it he regained some calm. There was still time to save his house; they could do it. He looked around again for the note but couldn't see it. In his turmoil he thought someone had picked it up and would shortly use it as evidence against him. My beautiful house, my lovely house, what was I thinking? There was another loud shattering as the first floor became a swirling pulse of light. Black smoke swept upwards, with swaggering power. Even then, when his life was being redefined in front of his eyes, when he was confronted directly with the fragility of things, Layor could not overlook the awe and beauty of this natural force, towering above infinitesimal (as he thought) men like himself. He felt humbled. He felt scared. He felt alive. He felt he could work again. He felt innocent before the sight of destruction. He felt a million things.

The firemen got out and set up with remarkable speed and soon their hoses were spewing thick jets of water into the fluttering pit ahead of them. One of them came up to Layor and looked into his eyes.

'Any idea how it started?'

'No, no; I was upstairs and I smelt something burning, and I wanted … I came down and the front room was already in flames, I only just managed to phone.'

'No one inside?'

'No, no; I live on my own. You can put it out?'

'It's already pretty far advanced; that doesn't help. We can stop it, but we may not be able to limit the damage much. The other problem is that by the looks of it, there's a lot of wood in the house. We should be getting some back-up in a moment.'

Layor nodded respectfully. He felt immensely grateful to the firemen, a gratitude that had no borders. Then his eye saw the crumpled note. It lay by the front door, next to some stray leaves. In another moment the flames claimed it.

From their ladders the firemen directed the jets into the upstairs rooms. People had begun to walk away, though a few remained in a file close to Layor. A woman walked up to him. After glancing at the various faces she could tell from his that he was the owner of the house. So she put her arm around him. He was not at all surprised. The fire freed them both from the straitjacket of etiquette. He looked into her eyes. She looked luminous, not quite of this earth. Neither of them could bring themselves to say anything.

It was Lilliana.

## 17

Inside the limousine Rees talked incessantly, telling Oscar it was important for him to be noticed at the party they were going to.

Despite the sound of Rees's voice – rendered less irritating than usual in the sepulchral calm of the limousine – Oscar had an impression of incredible well-being. He could study the occupants of the cars moving alongside them through tinted windows which ensured his own invisibility. He was surprised to find he was thrilled to be riding in the limousine. There was something vaguely illicit about the experience and he abandoned himself to it. The car's motion did not actively impress itself on his senses; rather it was felt subliminally, like a tremor, an imagined sound of thunder.

It was midnight by the time they arrived.

The limousine turned into a private, sumptuous avenue free of cars and full of some of the grandest houses Oscar had ever seen. The predominant impression the street gave was of whiteness. Every exterior looked as if it had just that moment been painted. The limousine stopped outside a house whose stucco facade was magically lit by golden floodlights. It made Oscar think of a gigantic wedding cake, tier upon tier reaching heavenwards.

They walked up to the entrance and were greeted by a footman.

Inside, as Oscar marveled at the grandeur of the hallway, the Bohemian crystal chandeliers and the sumptuous staircase, he was aware of Rees only vaguely as if the latter was locked in a misty bubble from which he emerged from time to time. In the hall a group of Indian men in loincloths were playing sitars and tablas. A few people were scattered about listening, sipping blue, green and pink cocktails. It was sparse, refined music – it did not demand to be listened to but its recurring patterns, its percussive continuities were calming. Rees and Oscar climbed the stairs, brushing against some of the guests coming down in great droves, and came eventually to a gargantuan ballroom with paneled doors and a ceiling crowded with figures who seemed to have stepped out of Renaissance Florence, their gravitas contrasting, as Oscar thought, with the abandon of the people jostling together in an untamed throng. Outside, a stone balcony looked out onto the silent street. There were more guests gathered there, squeezed between spectacular geraniums. Eerie, otherworldly music was playing in the ballroom. At the far end there was a long, sleek table with a brilliantly polished mirror for its surface. A pyramid of cocaine was piled up on it and various men were crushing it up with credit cards and other flat surfaces. They reminded Oscar of dealers, cutting cards at casinos, and had that same air of skill and bravado. All around the table people were snorting the white powder through little gold tubes and rolled up bank notes.

No one took any notice of Oscar and Rees as they made their way towards the bar and the small plates of food that sat there, unmolested. Rees was talking, babbling but Oscar refused to listen. He wished he would go away. He needed endless energy to be around him; Rees' every utterance was designed to prove something, to persuade or to sell. The barman poured Oscar a glass of red wine and Rees a Bloody Mary.

'Oscar,' said Rees, 'make sure that you get around, sample the different characters. Don't be shy.'

And with that he strode brazenly into the crowd. Oscar was as surprised as he was delighted.

There was a truly astonishing mix of fashions, faces and characters now claiming his attention. Many of the men looked Latinate and wore their hair slicked back, the lines drawn by the comb still intact. Others were less suave, but were uniformly smart, with their starched shirts, and immaculate trousers. But it was the women who really held his attention, in their kimonos and embroidered negligees, catsuits and saris, with their predatory, ornate, aggressive footwear, their black onyx beads, gaudy rings and searingly patterned stockings. Oscar found himself thinking of these people not merely as strangers, as he would normally, but rather as individual selves, with rich and complex existences. He wondered what their lives were like, the shape of their histories, what it was they did, who they loved, who they hated. It was thrilling to soak everything up, to speculate on the usually hidden layers of people's lives but he was afraid his head would burst like a bubble crammed with too much oxygen.

Tucked away in a quiet corner a girl in torn jeans crouched on a chair. She held onto the arching armrests with gangly arms, while her legs were crossed over each other and planted into the large cushion underneath. She was bending her sinewy hands into the shape of binoculars. She fastened them onto her face and peered around through this imagined lens, looking this way and that, making sharp movements with her head, like a robot. Then suddenly her head was swaying wildly, following the rhythms of the music. Then it was hanging limply, her hair flopping about, reaching her knees, a cascade of disarray. She was like a crazed marionette. About her there hung a kind of poisoned *joie de vivre*. She was like a kite torn by thorns. She lit a cigarette and took some puffs in quick succession until she was hidden by smoke clouds.

Oscar found her mesmerizing and was intent on speaking to her. He walked up to her. She was peering through her hands again.

'What do you see?' he asked.

'The planets. The stars. Supernovae,' she muttered.

She spoke so quietly that Oscar had to strain to hear her. Her face was close to his and he stared into green eyes whose pupils were abnormally dilated. She was indistinct, as if she could only be perceived through tracing paper.

'The planets. The stars,' she repeated in a colder, shriller voice.

'Can you see that far?'

'No, not really. I'd just like to go that far.'

She dissolved into sulfurous laughter, and for a moment it yoked back together the splintered fragments of her psyche, but as it died away she was a lost soul again.

She moved her lips together, as though she had just applied lipstick and was smoothing it over her mouth with a final flourish.

'Do you like the way I look?' she asked.

'You're beautiful.'

She smiled sweetly and once again for its duration she seemed fine. Someone catching her smile would have seen an expression of unbridled joy. Then the smile disappeared without trace and her face became a melancholic mask.

'I think I'm going to leave this party. It's such a bore.'

'Where will you go?' Oscar asked.

'Oh, you; you and your questions! You do nothing but ask questions! Well, now I'm going to ask you one.'

'Go ahead.'

'By the time this party is over the universe will have expanded in all directions by many miles. How many would you say?'

'I really couldn't.'

'A billion. A billion fucking miles. Did you ever think about that? Once? We're on this tiny planet spinning away – and we think we're so important – we think we're the cats' pyjamas. Well, we're not. And I'm never going to see with my own eyes what's out there. I'm going to die never having seen the edge of other galaxies, never having seen the final moments of a star's life as it explodes. I'm going to die never having gone through a wormhole or travelled at the speed of light. Instead I have to be happy with all this ...' She pointed to the bacchanalian display around her.

'It doesn't interest me – this sludge doesn't interest me. It's such a fucking bore.'

She walked away with a motion both agitated and natural.

Then she was gone. When Oscar turned round to find someone

else to talk to a woman in a leather skirt and beret was standing near-by, clutching a wine bottle.

'You must be Oscar,' she said.

'Yes. How did you know?'

'Someone pointed you out. There are some people from the Du-champ prize here. I would have liked to have heard your speech. I'm sorry I missed it.'

'Please, don't be.'

'I heard you caused a riot.'

'Does news travel that quickly?'

'The people I spoke to were quite impressed.'

'I didn't mean to cause a riot. Actually, I'm not sure *I* did.'

'Relax.'

A man dressed in tweeds was shuffling past slowly. The woman grabbed his arm and dragged him over.

'This is Oscar and Oscar, this is Malcolm. He's a lecturer.'

'Pleased to meet you, Oscar,' said Malcolm evenly.

'What do you lecture in?'

'Anthropology.'

Malcolm's eyes were glazed over and he blinked incessantly. In fact he looked thoroughly exhausted and ill and barely had enough ener-gy, it seemed, to remain standing. Standing next to him Oscar had the feeling that he too would shortly be struck down by exhaustion or paralysis.

'My name's Kim, by the way. So tell us what you said in your speech. Tell us what caused all the commotion.'

'I can't remember.'

'You can't have forgotten. It's barely been that long,' said Malcolm.

'I really can't remember. I've had a mental block.'

'While you're thinking about this, perhaps I could ask you some-thing,' said Malcolm.

'If you like.'

'Are women capable, do you think, of rational thought?'

Kim gripped his hand tightly, indicating that she didn't want him to do this, to be intense and contentious with a stranger.

Oscar considered the question for a moment and then said calmly, 'Of course, but they don't ascribe such a high value to it.'

'Oh, I see; they're in touch with their feelings and all that baloney.'

'Malcolm, do you really have to alienate every new person you meet?' said Kim.

'No, I don't, but it saves time, seeing as we'll be falling out later anyway. Best to get it over and done with before you become friends; then it's less painful, don't you find, Oscar?'

'Perhaps.'

'The way I see it, there is no objective friend, a friend you're destined to meet, no standing outside-of-time lover, no innately- right partner. We choose who we're stuck with, who happens to come along. People press a few buttons and hey presto people fall in love, get married. One day they choose Susie, the next Sally. One day they're with Tom, the next Malcolm.'

Kim snapped, 'Then Malcolm's days are numbered. I'm sorry about this Oscar. Malcolm doesn't believe in anything and takes every available opportunity to say so. He likes to dress up his nihilism as something else but – '

'What's that, my love?'

'As wisdom.'

'Nothing so grand as that, surely.'

'Piss off, Malcolm.'

'You see, Kim likes to see herself as a dominatrix, but she wears slippers instead of boots. Well, how do you see the love thing, Oscar? Are these conclusions of mine misguided?'

'Love's a snake pit,' said Oscar evenly, undoubtedly intrigued by Malcolm.

'That's nicely phrased. Kim and I are in the pit; we're stuck there and to each other, millstones around each other's necks.'

Oscar studied Kim's face. The whites of her eyes were clouded and murky, her cheeks sallow and sunken.

Malcolm continued. 'There's no time now for this, is there? I have to be light and frothy; I have to forget the world's ills as I sip cocktails. Never mind; no time, not the right place for this sort of talk but stick around, Oscar. We might make some progress, you and I. I feel I can confide in you. She accuses me of living in a diseased world and she calls herself an artist. Do you know what's in that bottle she's clutching, like her very life depends on it, which it does?'

'Wine?'

'No. But close enough, if you're a Christian. She thinks she's Christ you see, and what could be more diseased than that? It's her blood in there. I repeat, her blood. Her latest project. She's been drawing her own blood out with hypodermic syringes and filling bottles with it. Her body can't make blood that fast to replenish the supply so guess what: she's anaemic. She faints. She loses weight. And why does she do it? So that some gallery in Shoreditch can exhibit bottles of her blood every week. The bottles are meant to accumulate as the weeks go by. But what can I do? What – '

Kim slapped his face and screamed, 'What do you know about me, you shit? You don't know how I suffer! When I suffer I suffer with my whole body, every nerve ending, every vein, every artery. I'm trying to get my career going and all you can do is pronounce on – '

'You're killing yourself! I don't want you to die! I don't want – '

'If I die, it will be your fault. I'm an artist! I'm trying to alter the parameters! I'm trying to say something!'

'And what's that?' Oscar asked politely.

'I'm making a statement about the way we live today – it's about martyrdom, the necessity of sacrifice – I have to sacrifice my blood so that people can see how precious it really is! To make people honor their bodies. Because we don't – we feed it with shit – with processed shit – with chemicals – with pesticides – and everything becomes interchangeable, valueless, fake. It's all the same, don't you see? Of course it's destructive; it's meant to be. So is a Buddhist priest burning himself to death.'

'Talk to her, Oscar; tell her she's spouting incoherent crap.'

'Perhaps Malcolm is right. Perhaps you should think of your health.'

Kim pulled out a long comb with sharp, gleaming teeth and swiped it across Malcolm's face viciously. He winced in pain; she had taken some skin off. His hand shot to his cheek.

Kim stormed off and was instantly swallowed in the vortex that the room was rapidly turning into.

Oscar pulled out a handkerchief and handed it to Malcolm.

'God, are you all right?'

'That's nothing,' he stammered, as he dabbed his face, 'she's just teasing.'

'I'm sorry I wasn't able to – '

'Forget it. She has to learn on her own. We all have to learn on our own, that's the thing. Of course I know as well as you do that the social message is baloney. It's a slow suicide, pure and simple. She gets needles from "acquaintances" of hers and then carries out her ghastly work when I'm not at home. She's crazy; she needs to be under sedation, so she can't harm herself, but what can I do? I do love her; I actually do, in my own sick way. She's been sectioned three times. After the third she refused to see me for a year, a whole year, said I'd betrayed her, said I could have stopped it. I'm at the end of the road myself. And who's interested in listening to her? It's just a tiny blip, her inch of gallery space. There were a couple of features in a couple of papers and that was that. The world isn't bothered. The world will just grind on and she'll be fucked up somewhere in some hospital. But I have to prevent that from happening. I have to. So many people have tried to stop the world from turning; all they've managed to do is toss a cloud into the pathway of the sun. Excuse me.'

When Oscar's gaze reverted from Malcolm's face to the scene around him he was surprised to find that the conversation had been all-absorbing, so the crowds now infringed onto his consciousness as if for the first time. More and more people were spilling into the room. He could see a man and a woman heading over. There seemed to be something joining them together, but Oscar was not sure if he trusted his eyes. He was beginning to feel the effects of fatigue. He glanced again at the pair. They wore matching shirts, which revealed navels pierced with large golden rings; a bright chain ran from one ring to the other, connecting them: a silver umbilical cord. He stared for a few more moments and said out loud, 'Maybe it's better not to get so attached to people.' He didn't think his remark had been heard by anyone, but a man dressed in a single flowing robe glittering with countless sequins turned to meet him. He had intoxicatingly blue eyes, the skin on his face was glowing, but there was something about his appearance that suggested he was not quite real. He smoked the longest cigarette Oscar had ever seen.

'Do you think?' the stranger asked.

'I'm sorry?' said Oscar.

'Do you think that it's better not to get so attached to people?'

'Oh, I was joking; a little dig at that couple over there with the chain.'

'What couple?'

Oscar looked over but the place where they had been standing was now occupied by someone dressed in an orangutan's costume.

'What couple?' the man repeated.

'They've gone,' Oscar said.

'Oh well; they'll be back and you can tell me all about them. By the way, do you like my face?'

'It's very nice.'

'Good, it cost me nearly half a million pounds. I presume you're familiar with the latest developments in plastic surgery?'

'No, not really.'

'Let me tell you. In twenty years of course things will be much more sophisticated – now it's all a little crude. I keep telling my sister to have her breasts enlarged, in the easiest way, which is through the navel. Moving parts of the body around seems like fun too, but it may be a waste of time in the long run to have one's thigh forming one's upper lip. I tried that, didn't like it. But think: soon everything, organs, blood, skin, muscle will be replaceable. Isn't it wonderful?'

'Wonderful. But, on the other hand – and forgive me if I sound old fashioned – isn't all this all a little macabre? The body's a temple. I learnt that when I was life modeling.'

'My body used to be an abandoned pig sty. *Now* it's a temple, I've turned it into one.'

'I've always been worried that people are too similar, too made up of the same thoughts and ambitions. Won't we just rob the world of the little individuality that does exist by turning ourselves into synthetic dolls?'

Oscar's tone was impassioned. He noticed that others were flocking towards them, taking an interest in the conversation. An intense looking young girl was nodding enthusiastically as Oscar spoke, agreeing with his every word.

'No, no, my little man ...' began the man in the robe.

The girl interjected, 'He's not a little man. He's a wise man and you should crawl back to the laboratory that spawned you. Come with me, Oscar. This is Oscar Babel, you moron. He's a visionary, a poet. He knows what the hell is going on with the world, even if you don't.'

She gripped Oscar's arm tightly and gave him a friendly smile. She made Oscar think of some rare, delicate animal that the world had not yet caught and catalogued.

The man, who was not to be beaten so easily, snapped back with, 'So, if you're such a visionary, what are your plans for improving things? What do you suggest, that we all go back to the dark ages, throw out sugary drinks and drugs, and take up witchcraft?'

At this point a man in a dog collar and balancing several drinks in his hands felt the urge to say something, however irrelevant. The skin on his face was stretched thinly, like a fine pastry.

He shouted out, a half-spent cigarette bobbing up and down between cracked lips, 'I'd like to make a point. I want a penis as big as a tree trunk. My mind's too small; it needs bigger and bigger things to keep it amused, you see. I'm not like you, deep people, profound fuckers. Bigger and bigger chocolate. More and more fireworks, more puffs of the cigarette death machine. I may be deluded. More and more color and carbohydrates and blisters of noise to hide behind, to fill in the big zero.

'More and more stimulus like the body's become immune to painkillers so that only morphine will do and then not even that. Give me bigger and better pornography, juicier and fatter steaks, sicker and sicker entertainments, more and more bloodletting in the galleries.

'Roll on man, roll fucking on!'

He staggered off, as if the fact of having spoken had finished him. Oscar moved away, anxious to lose the devotee of plastic surgery. The girl followed, holding his hand affectionately. For someone so young, Oscar thought, she certainly had enough confidence.

The party had entered a new stage of abandon, having reached in the last few minutes a plateau fueled by raucous, heavily percussive music. People were dancing orgiastically, thrashing about, limbs bending backwards, their spines threatening to snap in the search for greater expressive freedom. The evening looked like it could go on forever, its frantic rhythm never tiring.

A man in dreadlocks, struggling with a large amplifier, an electric guitar slung round him, was making his way onto the balcony. A small crowd joined him and awaited the solo concert. The girl squinted at Oscar and said earnestly, 'Shall we leave this party and go somewhere else?'

Oscar stared, slightly bewildered, into the central pit before him. Again he was struck, as he had been when he first entered the room, with the complexity, richness and mystery of those gathered. He was on the point of answering when someone shouted out his name. He turned to see Ryan Rees leering at him in the distance. The next thing that happened was that a small brown object headed for him. Oscar ducked and caught it. Another and then another catapulted towards him. Oscar caught the first but not the second, which in landing, announced what it was, as it became a mass of shell and fluid, yellow and transparent. An egg. In the distance Rees grinned and moved on with the bawled words, 'Just keeping you on your toes.'

He slid away but Oscar could hear his vile laughter issuing from afar. He turned back to the girl but she had gone. He made his way towards the balcony for some air. The guitarist had started playing and the street echoed to the sound of distorted notes and chords which periodically gave way to the wailing of feedback. It was phenomenally loud. Oscar consulted his watch. It was two-thirty. Had he already been there for two-and-a-half hours? Surely not. It's strange, he thought, how the experience of time is so changeable. Sometimes it's like treacle; now it's thundering along and taking me with it. Perhaps it's all these people, all these personalities who turn time into a black hole, so that my sense of self is wiped out by their sense of selves and the time that normally drags because of my self-consciousness, doesn't, and I forget myself, because I've lost myself in the heat of others.

A little further down the balcony two men were occupied in dropping wine glasses onto the street. They kept saying, 'Beautiful' and 'Wow.' The guitar wailed and screeched. All the while the guitarist wore an expression that suggested he was in considerable pain. The men popped back inside and re-emerged a minute later, this time armed with bottles, glasses and plates. They stacked them up on the stone wall, which was scarcely wide enough to hold them, and they hung there precariously. The pile wobbled from side to side, until one plate took the lead and dragged everything else with it into the void. The shrill sound of breaking echoed across the street with crystal clarity since the guitar had come to a standstill an instant before. Apparently, the men's joy was boundless. Oscar stared at the mess below and then up at the street lamps, small yellow halos. It was a warm summer night, a perfect night. The phosphorescent moon, one of its corners slightly blunted, the endless expanse of the sky flecked with one or two stars, the sleep of the silent houses, the sleep of those inside them, sealed off from this party that continued to mutate. He felt happy.

He went back inside. Everyone was a little more sweaty, a little more disheveled and dizzy. There were by now so many people bearing down on each other that it would take several minutes to get from one end of the room to the other. Oscar started shoving his way through. As he got wedged in the mass of alien bodies, pressing intimately against him, he reflected on the evening, his speech, and the uproar it had caused. And as he arrived once more at the point of time he now occupied it was a surprise to find that his thoughts had allowed him to be transported from the party which he, at that same instant, now perceived not only as claustrophobic, but also as empty.

He stood there, unable to move. The party had come to a halt, it had clotted. Oscar's chin was nuzzled against the chest of a man so tall he had to strain his neck to see his face. As he tried to push through he felt some fingers caressing his hair from behind. He turned round to look. He blinked at the face staring back at him, then realized who it was.

'Anna, how did you get here?' he shouted above the thick membrane of voices.

'I took a cab with the great Bear,' she yelled.

'No, I mean, what are you doing here?'

'I'm enjoying myself.'

'When did you arrive?'

'About an hour ago. I got bored at the Hilton. I liked your speech. I told the reporters you were either a lunatic or a genius.' Oscar had to strain to hear even though her lips were practically touching his earlobe.

'Shall we try and go outside?' he bellowed.

'Sure, I'll follow you. You seem like an experienced navigator, midshipman Babel.'

They struggled together and after a crushing interlude during which they crawled past some masked figures ceremoniously clutching spears they found an opening and walking quickly reached the paneled doors and practically fell into the corridor. Anna started twirling about. She led the way and soon they were outside, crouched on some steps, glancing up at the stone balcony.

'Where's the Bear?' he asked.

'When I last saw him he was downing shots of vodka, drinking to each of his fillies, with this paunch king with a stalactite grin. I kept wishing he would freeze. I'm glad I bumped into you.'

'Likewise.'

'Your speech was pretty wild, but what followed it was wilder. Everyone will hate you now.'

'I really hope not.'

'But you'll be the talk of the town. For a day or two. You chewed the hand that fed you tonight.'

'No I didn't. I just made a few disparaging remarks about certain people. They can take it; they're adults.'

'And you, what are you? I think you're a bit of a puzzle, Mr Babel. Are you the sensitive type who gets excited by flaxen hair, but lets the dishes pile up, goes easy on the mustard and always leaves a tip? Or are you good in a fight; do you hail taxis with a single whistle, drink to excess, and kiss girls and make them cry?'

'I'm whatever you want me to be. I'm your mirror. And a sponge.'

She threw him a coquettish smile. She seemed bewitching to him now, a poetess in her dollar bill sarong, the skin of her face made diaphanous by moonlight.

The street was gradually filling with some of the other party guests and he wondered whether there would soon be a complaint from the neighbors. But, he thought, if the sound of an electric guitar at full volume is all right then anything probably is.

'You see, where the guru goes the people follow. Pied Piper Oscar.'

She slotted a cigarette into his mouth and another into hers. She lit her own, inhaled, exhaled, the released smoke turning with her head in that characteristic way. Then she lit Oscar's cigarette with the glowing end of hers, still poised between her lips.

'You've led me to oxygen,' he remarked.

Pounding, throbbing music started shaking the building.

'Nicotine tastes better than oxygen. But after this farewell smoke I should probably get back to Ernst.'

'How can you stand it, being at his beck and call?'

'Don't make a fuss, Oscar; now you sound like David.'

'Who's David?'

Her eyes lit up.

'David's my big sticky pudding, my late night tipple. He's what I wrap myself up with on chilly nights, my spark plug, toad in the hole, my one-night-stand-for-every-day-of-the-week. Lover, beau, and paramour.'

'You've got a boyfriend?' said Oscar, trying hard to hide his disappointment.

'You're quick off the mark. And who do you have, Oscar?'

'No one. My recent spell in the spotlight has pushed her away.'

'Jealousy?'

'Oh God, no. Najette would never get jealous. She's too principled.'

She laughed mockingly and ruffled up his hair. More and more people were pouring out of the house and Oscar could see that others from the neighboring houses were joining in, clutching bottles of wine which had apparently just been located. The previously deserted street was now teeming with life. He wondered whether the police would also be joining the party shortly.

'What does she do, this turtle dove of yours?' she demanded.

'She's a brilliant painter.'

'Has she had much success?'

'She did have an exhibition recently but it wasn't very ... fulfilling.'

'I see. And you're telling me there isn't the slightest chance that she's envious of the fact that you've been on television, been quoted in *The Guardian*, have had your name plastered all over the London underground, and have just spoken at one of the most prominent art events of the year and caused it to implode?' She was as assured as a preacher and yet as light as dew.

'Well, she doesn't know about the last of those of course, but she's really not like that.'

'She must be a saint.'

'And I'm a fake.'

'Oscar, you're not a fake. How many people would have had the gumption to stand up and say the things you said tonight?'

'Can we change the subject?'

'Sure. But before we do, promise me you'll ring her.'

'I promise.'

Above, the pounding music stopped and babbling voices rose on a wave. Oscar glanced up at the stone balcony. He could make out a face peering down at him. It was Rees. He had his earphones on and was listening to the Kenyan bird medley, drawing sustenance from that shrill soundworld.

'Can we move over there?' he asked Anna, anxious to be out of the line of Rees's vision.

'Anything you say,' she said, winking flirtatiously.

They found some other steps to perch on, beneath the stone cover of one of the adjacent houses, and watched the crowds milling about. Oscar savored the stillness of their communion, the sense that in words there was communication but in silence there was a deeper intimacy. Very slowly and gently he moved his hand towards Anna's and held onto it. He felt her fingers wrap around his.

There was a rumble of thunder. They looked up into the sky, illumined with eerie light at its edges. Thunder but no rain, though rain suddenly seemed quite possible. He wished it would rain, it would be good to feel something cool against his flesh after this sultry night, this night of relentless, blurred impressions.

'Who will water me?' he asked out loud.

The thunder roared again like a dinosaur caged in some remote chamber of the sky. This time it was louder and people turned their heads, shed some of the skins of intoxication, held their breath. The semi-delirious figures, swigging bottles of beer and speaking volubly, creating an ambient buzz of sound, had transformed the avenue into a pleasure dome. Despite the fact that it was the middle of the night it might as well have been day and the idea of sleep remained just an idea; indeed it had already been established that this night was to be sleepless, was to be a series of leaps from one snatched pleasure to another.

The first drops of rain started to fall. There was an almighty flash of lightning.

A moment later the cloudburst, the deluge had happened. In seconds the rain was forming swirling rivers that flowed from the pavement, ran into the gutters, seemed to churn the cobblestones. Oscar stared, enraptured by the criss-crossed, fractured lines, straining to see beyond the meshes in the storm's giant net.

From where they sat, protected on the steps, Oscar and Anna imagined that everyone would rush back indoors in a confused bid for shelter. But instead, the numberless throng, with a collective yell, threw its arms up in the air and was instantly drenched. They danced and turned and clutched each other and opened their mouths to receive the streams of water hurtling towards them. Now Oscar and Anna, unable to resist, joined the loops of bodies claiming the road for themselves. Oscar looked around at the drenched, exhausted faces; for once he could cling to what drew him towards them, and not to what forced him apart. There was still something waiting for him, he knew, there was still some alchemy hidden in the shadows. It's up to you now, Bloch had said. The rain was falling harder than ever, and every now and then lightning flashed, creating equal amounts of doom and wonder. The street had been sieged, sabotaged by irreverent life. Daylight seemed to be an age away. Instead it was the trajectory of the present which everyone was locked onto, as sensation climbed higher and higher into a place stripped of cares.

So this is life, Oscar thought.

# III

# THE ORGY

# 18

After the party Oscar's existence evolved and mutated and regressed in different ways; he felt as if he was moving through a hurricane which uprooted him of his bearings, possessions, certainties. He felt as if instead of walking, he was always running. He felt as though a fierce wind was slamming into his face and rushing down through his half-opened mouth down his gullet into his lungs, causing him to swell with euphoria, but then as that wind subsided and left his body he sagged and flopped into a place of stupefaction. The earth was turning and he was turning with it, but stripped of the gravity which kept others securely grounded in their lives, where the certainty of sunrise ushered in other, countless, certainties, like a loving husband or wife, or a well-peeled orange, or a carefully clutched and presented bus ticket.

Many things now happened in quick succession.

Firstly, he was both vilified and celebrated in the press for his performance at the banquet. He was now visible in a way he had never been in his life. Secondly, he was moved into a hotel in Chelsea. With his sticky fingers Ryan Rees plucked him from the squalor of his bedsit and deposited him into fully-blown, unreal luxury. Oscar said goodbye to Mr Grindel who agreed to forward his mail. His landlord's parting words were, 'I shall miss telling you of my love, Mr Babel.' Oscar thought: I won't miss hearing about her.

The reason Rees was willing to put him up at the hotel was because he felt Oscar now needed to be more centrally based, and to be associated with a glamorous residence. Visiting journalists would be treated royally in royal surroundings.

And the third thing that happened was that he became obsessed with *Tristan and Isolde*.

The living room overlooked the King's Road and from the tenth floor Oscar could virtually see its entire length, which simply wasn't possible while he was walking down it. It was stirring with life: shoppers hopping from butcher's to supermarkets to delicatessens, stopping for coffee breaks at the Stockpot; devotees of high street fashions appearing as listless, moving emblems of color – figures swathed in handkerchief neckline dresses and chiffon shirts, leather jackets and green jersey trousers, silver hoop earrings and purple sandals – receding into tiny points, and then being replaced, as it were, by more prospective candidates for the most beautiful person on the street, until clusters of slowly moving rollerbladers eclipsed them with the grace of their motion, making Oscar envious, since their acrobatics turned existence into a nonchalant game, a sport to be played in perpetual sunshine; but as he further considered them, some half glimpsed sight of strife or friction – a quarreling couple outside the Cafe Picasso, tortured by the specter of infidelity, a screaming driver blocked by a detested rival, the homeless in their patches all but invisible to the shoppers, fashion slaves, rollerbladers and drivers – made him forget his envy and leave aside his longing to waft through life like an idiot.

He turned away from the windows, and puffed on a cigarette, its wafting clouds intact with the density bequeathed to those who don't inhale. The windows were so large they occupied virtually an entire wall, giving the onlooker the feeling of being giddily interconnected to the emptiness outside. Indistinct impressions and memories of his old bedsit returned. Sitting there, staring at his new, elegant, surroundings he couldn't entirely free himself of the suspicion that soon someone would have him evicted from them. He was fearful of staining an armchair with smudged fingers or of breaking one of the glasses or wetting the bed at night, the pink double bed which felt as different to his old bed in Elephant and Castle as a kiss feels to a punch. He had so much space he didn't know what to do with it –the living room alone was ten times the size of his bedsit, an enormity with alcoves in each corner bathed in the light of zinc-galvanized steel lamps. The walls were colorwashed in a rich red over cream which blended with the burgundy of the muslin curtains, and the sleek paintings hanging on the wall – depicting landscapes of rich, fecund greenery, enigmatic figures amid screens of foliage – were not so much windows into other worlds but mirrors bringing the room back into itself, forcing the spectator to confront the equally lush landscape of the room. Everything was eclectically stylish: a Viennese secession screen; a bent beechwood rocking chair with a caned back; crystalline ashtrays looking as if they had been chiseled, like tiny embryos, out of the Strass crystal chandelier; a modernist cream sofa. But the centerpiece of the living room was the drinks cabinet which resembled a miniature chapel; a squat, brightly-polished mahogany square with small doors open at either side, inviting the onlooker to covetously behold the neatly arranged bottles within. The miniature bottles of spirits (spirits whose potency was masked by the daintiness of their vessels) were tightly clustered together and chimed like bells when one of them was removed. Behind the glass shelves, where wine and brandy glasses were lined up, a mirrored, brightly-lit wall illuminated the contents of the cabinet while creating the illusion that its stocks were inexhaustible.

But Oscar's favorite part of his suite was the gold-plated bathroom, always sparkling as a result of the miracle of a daily clean. It was wonderful to bathe in a tub not only free of the communal grime of Grindel's house but also large enough for him to be able to submerge the full length of his long body.

A melodious ringing. Oscar stubbed his cigarette out in one of the dozen or so ashtrays near to hand. In fact he had, in a display of profligacy he now regretted, used seven of these for the collection of respective units of ash. The ringing continued with polite insistence. That was another thing he had to get used to: connecting such an agreeable sound with the telephone.

'Hello.'

'Did the woman from "Cherubs" turn up?'

'I'm fine, thanks, Rees. How are you?'

'When she gets there, tell her to call me – '

'It's a beautiful morning, I quite agree; I was just about to have some breakfast. Eggs Benedict and – '

'By the way, don't worry about the tse-tse flies buzzing around you. No-one can reach you there, in reference to the Duchamp prize or anything else – '

'And croissants and some gorgeous looking figs – '

'Look, Oscar, why do you insist on being facetious? I've put you in the lap of luxury.'

'And pears and ... and – but I suspect it's a gilded cage.'

'It should be; you're my prize parrot. So remember to go over your party pieces. They're fucking priceless. *Au revoir.*'

He walked over to his breakfast. On the table there sat a silver coffee pot in which he could see his distorted reflection, a plate of eggs Benedict, butter croissants and muffins, fresh orange juice, pears, prunes, figs, frozen yoghurt and cinnamon toast. There was enough there for three people. He tried his best to eat most of it so it didn't go to waste. Everything tasted delicious, the coffee felt velvety and aromatic in his mouth and he was reluctant to let it finally slide into his stomach but when he did so he felt a shiver of well-being. As he was beginning to tackle some of the fruit, feeling a bit puffed-up, the phone went again.

'Hello.'

'Is that Oscar Babel?'

'Yes.'

'Sorry to bother you Mr Babel. My name's Mark Anderson. I'm from "Art Attack." I was wondering if I could ask you a few questions about the Duchamp Prize of a few days ago.'

Hadn't the tse-tse flies been turned away at the door? So – Rees's iron grip on the media wasn't as iron as he'd reckoned. He was delighted to find the über-publicist had finally got something wrong. Good for Mr Anderson.

'Sure, but isn't it a bit old hat now?'

'Did you know Cyril Vixen is planning to sue you?'

'Me? Wouldn't it make more sense to sue Mark Redhill?'

'He says your remarks at the banquet sparked off the attack on him.'

'But that's silly, it was Redhill who sprayed deodorant in his eyes ...'

'Yes, but he's very upset with you. I suppose you know he was admitted to hospital a few days ago; well, on the night of the banquet in fact?'

'What's happened to Mark Redhill?'

'He was held overnight in a police cell. Then a shrink turned up; there's something about a report and how he recently tried slashing his wrists – the same old jazz – aborted razor suicide. Apparently he's got a history of slicing himself up – I think he should go into performance art; there's a big market for that sort of thing. you know, you must have heard about that German guy who stands on stage and hacks off bits of his body? He sent his big toe to his girlfriend in Munich on Valentine's Day. The things we do for love, hey? Anyway, Redhill was depressed about his film. I don't really blame him – it was monumentally dire.'

Oscar started cutting up a pear into roughly equal segments. There was a knock at the door.

'Look, can you hold on a minute ....'

Oscar yelled a slightly hoarse 'Come in' and a small, stooping Portuguese maid, her left hand overflowing with keys, her right arm wrapped around a pile of pillowcases, bundled in. She greeted him with blood-curdling liveliness and moved quickly into the bedroom, displaying all the purposefulness of one who is utterly wedded to her work.

'Where were we?' Oscar asked.

'Litigation.'

'But he can't sue me. On what grounds?'

'Defamation of character, I imagine. I just wanted to hear your thoughts on the subject. Oh, he also called you a charlatan who talks shit.'

'Whereas he just photographs it. Maybe we should sue each other; that would be droll.'

'Would you care to refute his accusation?'

Oscar's gaze drifted towards the window – the glass was so transparent he could imagine passing his hand through it. He started chewing a piece of pear. From the bedroom came scraps of a Portuguese love song; even though the maid couldn't really sing Oscar found her voice unexpectedly affecting. Then she scooted back in and out into the corridor, reappearing with a mop and bucket in readiness for her assault on the bathroom.

'Mr Babel. Are you there?'

'Yes, I'm there. I'm everywhere.'

'Quite. I just hope you don't hire body doubles to lure the press away from the original. He called you a charlatan. Are you?'

'Yes.'

Anderson was confused – he no longer knew how to play this game at all. He could deal with charlatans – the world was full of them – but he wasn't quite sure if he could deal with charlatans who said they were charlatans. He cleared his throat and decided Babel was being icily ironic.

'Did you want to ask me anything else?' Oscar asked.

'What did you hope that little protest of yours was going to lead to?'

'Nothing much. It's the papers which are making it into such a big deal.'

'And what do you think about that?'

'I suppose it just demonstrates that people will go to any lengths to give space to conflict, especially if it concerns the famous. The planet could be exploding and they'd still be worried about filling the gossip columns.'

'But isn't all this rather good publicity for you?'

'I'm not very important in the grand scheme.'

'But still – you're getting some fine exposure.'

'What happened the other night had nothing to do with me – I was just a channel for someone else's thoughts.'

'That sounds suspiciously like you're refusing to take responsibility. It was actually you on the podium speaking, wasn't it?'

'We should stop making such a fuss all the time about nothing. I'm not that interesting – children are interesting – the sky's interesting, but nobody looks at it anymore because it's not in a gallery and doesn't have a price tag.' Before he knew what was happening, unbidden words from Bloch's recordings were rising to his lips, drifting up from his viscid unconscious. 'There are too many sounds, too much information, too many images. Look around you and ask: what in all this dross, this infinite supermarket that the world has become; what in all this mass-produced bile truly has the right to exist and doesn't just amount to the blood and mucus dripping from a newly ejected baby?'

'Well ... em ... I mean ... now you've put me on the spot ... eh ...'

Here – Anderson mused – was someone who wasn't bothered about towing the line, about being co-operative, and playing by the rules. Oscar was getting under his skin, earning his respect. By repeatedly emphasizing his insignificance he was acquiring significance. He was strong or bored or mad enough to call a spade a spade.

'Do you think you could just repeat that little speech – it was kind of quotable.'

The maid emerged from the bathroom, as energetic as ever. She stomped off, still singing merrily.

'Mr Anderson, I should go now.'

'OK but can you just repeat the bit about the supermarket and the baby, that was great, what was it?'

Oscar said nothing.

'The bit about the supermarket. What was the word you used? Hey? The bit about the baby? The supermarket? Are you there ...?'

Oscar sighed, replaced the handset quietly, and shuffled off to run a bath. After he'd turned the thermostat to the required temperature he opened the tap, then walked over to his cassette player and rummaged around for Bloch's recordings. He was on the point of slotting a tape into the player when he was stopped short. An inanimate object – a piece of plastic and tape – a breakable trifle, but in that rectangle was the essence of something; the best of his old friend, an incorporeal reality which he could preside over. Then, on the heels of some mental adjustment, for the first time he found the idea of his spurious guru role appealing. It was as if a constricting jacket had widened out, and suddenly fitted. Bloch's act of severance had brought pain, but now he didn't need him – he had his voice, his thoughts, his interesting theories about life and death, love and sex. He could *be* Bloch.

The voice started speaking. Oscar caught slow intakes of breath, and every now and then an asthmatic wheeze. As the voice continued he sank back in an armchair, listening impassively. For a moment he had trouble connecting the voice with the person.

Once again, the door was announcing that someone was on its other side. Who was it now? The valet? The barman? Or Cyril Vixen hobbling on crutches and out for revenge? He pressed the STOP button.

'Hello – Mr Babel? Mr Babel – I'm from "Cherubs and Co" –I've got a few ideas – I had a bit of trouble finding you – gosh, what a fabulous room. Those curtains – are they chintz?' she said in one nervous breath, hurrying towards the curtains and dropping her portfolio. Oscar stared at her, scrambled after her, picked up her book, and tapped her on the shoulder while her hand lovingly caressed the curtain's length.

'I could do something with this,' she said dreamily as though she was alone. 'This could be fabulous. Oh – did I drop that?'

Asking the question confirmed (in a sudden flash) what Oscar already suspected: that his new visitor was a scatterbrain. But he would humor her, at least until he'd established what it was she wanted.

'I'm always dropping things. I'm a little bit nervous – I've heard so much about you – I'm Cressida.'

'Of course you are. I'm sorry, but what exactly do you – '

'This is a fabulous room – gosh it's so – what's the word I'm looking for?'

'Big?'

'Yes – but – I'm sorry – shall we sit down. I've got a few ideas.'

'So you said.'

'Well, that's what the book's for. Why don't we sit down? Is it me or – gosh, that painting's ... It's so – what's the word?'

They sat down. Oscar took the time to study her. Everything she wore – tights, skirt, shawls, jacket – was purple. As were her eye shadow and lipstick. She intrigued him – despite the trying air of clumsiness she also transmitted some essential enthusiasm which stopped him from losing patience with her. Her eyes flashed, winked, smiled; her lips curved, pouted, fluctuated; her skin blushed and glowed; but when she laughed, as she now began to, there was no sound – her body bended and her face distorted in the usual way, at laughter's bidding, but there were no accompanying chuckles, sniggers or giggles. It was the laughter of a mime artist. On recovering her powers of speech she murmured, 'I'm sorry; you must think I'm a nut case.'

'What's so funny?'

'Nothing. The thing is, I'm – I've had the most godawful terrible morning. You won't believe what I've been through.'

'I'm all ears.'

'Oh, I wouldn't say that. Only joking. Can I tell you about it?'

He nodded slowly.

'Well, first off, I was woken by a car alarm – three hours before I usually get up. Then I couldn't get back to sleep. When I got in to work, after nearly being run over by a motorbike while I was crossing a one-way street I found out that all the costumes I'm hiring for a fringe show are going to cost me £1500 more than I'd been led to expect – so now I have to come up with a completely new design. Then I spilled coffee over my hand – see. Now it's burnt, which will make it very hard for me to sew. Then – get this – on the tube a man tried putting his hand up my skirt. I screamed and no-one did a bloody thing. Then, as I was walking along the King's Road, a tramp went mad because I didn't give him any money. So I'm in a bit of a state. And I wanted to make a good impression. Oh gosh.'

'Would you like an alcoholic drink? As you can see I'm well stocked.' Oscar gestured to the cabinet with a lean finger.

'I'd love to, but I don't think it would be right before lunchtime. Anyway I'm starting to calm down now. Would you like to take a – take a look at my book?'

'Do I gather you're here to dress me up then?'

'Oh, I'm sorry, didn't you know? Mr Rees said – '

'Never mind what Mr Rees said.'

'Well ... anyway, I've got some photos here which give you a pretty good idea of what I've been chewing over. Now, for the guru look – '

'What did you say?'

'The guru look.'

'"The guru look"?'

'Yes.' She moved her left hand over her scorched right hand, in a protective impulse.

'But – it's not a "look" – I mean – you talk as if there's a "guru look" being worn in Paris and Milan this summer. I'm sorry, but I really don't think this is a very good idea.'

Now she was blinking rapidly.

'But couldn't I just show you what I've got? I've been looking forward to showing you.'

'Oh Christ, all right then.'

'Well, I thought we might have you in something like this – ' she flicked forward to a scanned photograph of a cassock, 'but I have a feeling this is too obvious, too – what's the word? – passé. On the other hand, with a bit of nipping and tucking at the sides we might make it look quite sexy; or there's this jacket here – sorry about the photo – which is actually made, would you believe it, out of an antique Russian carpet, circa 1880; an oriental rug for a jacket, imagine that! Or, if you prefer, we might have you got up like the Bedouin in this cotton thobe, which, by the way – '

'I'm terribly sorry, but this is just too depressing. How can I possibly say the things that have to be said when I'm dressed like this – it's just too theatrical, like I'm an entertainer. No one would take me seriously – you can understand that – oh shit the bath.'

He darted off and wrestled with the tap. The water was just beginning to spill over the sides, at gravity's instigation. Rolling back his shirt sleeve he pulled the plug out. When he turned round Cressida was standing next to him – a purple shock.

'But what am I going to say to Mr Rees?' she asked in a small, pitiful voice.

'Nothing. I'll tell him.'

'But I can transform you; I can make you look wonderful. I mean, not that you don't already look wonderful, I mean – '

'I know what you mean, but I just think it's inappropriate.'

Oscar, fully expecting another persuasive maneuver was surprised when she just muttered, 'You know, I don't think I've ever met anyone like you before. You've got integrity.'

'Please don't say that – I've got to have a bath.' From the way he joined the two statements together it sounded like having integrity ruled out the possibility of bathing.

'Do you want me to go?'

'Well, yes. Ultimately. Actually – now would be good.'

'I like the sound of your voice; it's strong but at the same time supple. This is a fabulous bathroom. I'm so sorry you weren't taken by any of my ideas.'

'That's all right; please, don't take it personally.'

'I hate it when people say that. How else am I meant to take it?'

'Listen, I really have to do some work now, so thanks for the – '

'What about a drink? After all, you did offer. Then I'll plod off, I'll –' But her sentence gave way, her voice gave way, then she gave way. Her tears were so copious he thought she must have tear vats, not ducts, behind her eyes.

'God, I feel like such – fool!' she sobbed, words and syllables being sacrificed as she struggled to get the sentences out. 'I'd heard – so much – you. I wanted – impress you – you think I'm – stupid ninny. Well, I'm gg – bb – m m – h g …'

'Please don't cry, Cressida. Please, look, come here, let me get you a drink.'

Oscar glanced over at the bath – it had just emptied itself soundlessly since he'd forgotten to replace the plug. He was loath to run another – perhaps to punish himself for his ineptitude. I can't even run a bath. Taking her hand he led her back to the living room and set her down on the sofa. He went over to the bar, momentarily stymied by the wealth of choice there. His eye scanned the assembled bottles of whiskey and stopped at a bottle of Talisker single malt. He poured her a glass. Then he poured himself one, threw in some ice and brought the tumblers over, swirling them around easily.

'There you are. Drink this; you'll feel better.'

'Thanks,' she sniffed. Oscar plucked some tissues out of a silver box and dabbed her eyes with them – a repetitive, nervous movement.

'You're very kind. I'm sorry; I don't know what came over me. I've had such a terrible day.'

'Let's have some music.'

'Ooh – that would be nice.'

Oscar walked over to one of the zinc-galvanized steel lamps, switched it on, and drew the curtains. The walls grew muted and mysterious, the alcoves melted into shadow. Sounds became more defined and an indeterminate blend of excitement and stillness was formed. The room's vast dimensions, so clearly discernible in daylight, were muffled, rendered less indigestible. Watching Oscar through the tranquilizing prism of the fiery whiskey she noticed how confidently, how purposefully he moved and orchestrated his remedy. He was like his voice, she thought. Supple yet strong. Unhurried. He drifted towards a stacked-up stereo sound system and found the disc he was after.

'I hope you'll like this,' he said in a low voice. 'For a long time whenever I heard this music it left me cold. I don't know what it was – I just didn't care for it. Then, one day – this was when I was living in Elephant and Castle – I listened ... and it was ... amazing.'

Then – from the depths, almost imperceptible at first but gradually rising, the first notes of the prelude to *Tristan* were exhaled. Oscar sat back next to Cressida and closed his eyes. From the start, with those opening chords, the world slipped away, and he was immersed in the music's soundworld, and the incessant striving of life was stilled.

'Gosh,' Cressida whispered.

But she wasn't really listening to the music – she was aware of it, and it made for a pleasant backdrop. What really struck her was his willingness to reveal something about himself, something other than the size of his waist or the fact that he preferred corduroy to denim. After sniveling like that, she thought, after that pathetic display, he hadn't grown stiff and formal and awkward as most men would have done. His words gave her back some of her dignity, and made her feel valued. She tried to picture him as a boy, with a mop of dark hair, discovering girls. And then, adrift in the room's incantatory light and shade, seated next to someone willing to be nice to her, she felt, in spite of all the bruises, the sweetness of life after all.

They stayed like that for a while, not speaking. He didn't feel like speaking for a while.

*

From where he squatted Ryan Rees studied the intricacy of the cathedral's facade, its lofty bell tower, its alternating bands of sandstone and red brick (forming a texture which reminded him of St Mark's Basilica in Venice). As an architectural achievement the cathedral was not very impressive, he reflected, but it was a welcome, surprising injection of color alongside the grey bureaucratic buildings framing the piazza. Here is history; tradition, Rees thought, and I shall shortly be thumbing my nose at it. There were still a few people dotted around, walking to and fro, placing the building in its historical context, admiring it, ignoring it. It was getting dark but Rees knew that the floodlights weren't due to go on until later.

The sturdy transit van he and his employees were currently squeezed into was parked on the curb directly opposite Westminster Cathedral. Inside, while Rees exuded his customary Olympian calm, two scruffy men in dungarees scurried around and searched for light meters, arranged slides, acted as if they knew what they were doing which was only partly true. One of them repeatedly failed to strike a match until Rees obliged with a single stroke; a memory stick was extracted from an aluminum case; a lever was yanked violently. A source of power came on, humming with oppressive life.

Outside, stray tourists continued to take photos, munching hamburgers, relishing the gherkins especially. A man held a mobile phone in front of him, filming the transit van, hoping he was about to catch the opening moments of a heist. He preferred the image that shook and hovered in front of him to the reality firmly grounded around him. Some pigeons in the square took flight with sudden synchronized ease. A lady rocked her pram back and forth mechanically, and from within, at regular intervals, howls were heard. A girl sucked on her lollipop, then plopped its sticky disc onto her little brother's nose where it hung ignominiously. He started crying. The girl started laughing. A man in a teeshirt, seated on one of the bollards, tried to clear his sinuses and triggered a violent nose bleed instead. He pressed buttons fitfully on his phone and tried calling his GP. His GP was in his consulting rooms telling a patient that everyone coughs blood every now and then and it was perfectly normal and nothing to worry about. The double-decker buses toiled onwards. Society kept up its dull, plodding rhythm.

Glancing up at the sickle moon Rees considered the folkloric connection between full moons and madness. He had read somewhere that obstetricians tended to believe pregnant women were more likely to deliver during full moon cycles than at other times during the lunar cycle. These thoughts suddenly brought back memories of a bizarre passage from *The Golden Bough* that an unhinged, misogynistic school teacher had demanded all his charges learn by heart: "According to Pliny, the touch of a menstruous woman turned wine to vinegar, blighted crops, killed seedlings, blasted gardens, brought down the fruit from trees, dimmed mirrors, blunted razors, rusted iron and brass (especially at the waning of the moon), killed bees, or at least drove them from their hives, caused mares to miscarry ..." The passage's blend of magic and insanity instantly appealed to the pre-pubescent Rees and he began to entertain fantasies of bringing about similar ruination at his boarding school. Shortly afterwards he established a reputation as a formidable and elaborate practical joker – passing oranges round under the desks during the senile Mr Wiseman's history lessons, setting nails down on teachers' chairs, gluing coins to the pavement and watching passers-by struggling to retrieve them, and majestically breaking wind during assembly. These triumphs left him breathless and euphoric. In a sense all his subsequent enterprises had been an attempt to re-capture the intoxication of those first heavenly coups. At that time he had been known universally as "Orley", after his then-name of Donald Chorley. He changed his name at the age of twenty-one when he got his first job in advertising.

It was getting darker. In the square, standing somewhat apart from the others were three or four impassive, smooth looking men. They were editors: features editors, literary editors, arts editors. Ryan Rees had invited them along – a friendly gesture. He strategically wanted to keep them sweet and happy, as they might have proved useful to him at a later date. Rees regarded the editors very much in the way he might have regarded a screwdriver or a hammer: they simply had their uses, they were tools which could facilitate the assembling of something far grander and more important than they were.

Inside the van there was a piece of equipment whose most vital part was worth £100,000: the lens. This piece of equipment could project an image of up to 100 feet square in size. It was about two-feet high and five-feet wide. It ran out of a diesel generator, the source of the relentless hum.

'Mr Rees, we're ready to go in five,' said one of the men in dunga-rees, 'Terry, get the door.'

The laser projector was so powerful it needed fifteen minutes to heat up and twenty to cool down. Its lens was aimed directly onto the timpanum and central facade of the cathedral.

Ryan Rees rubbed his hands together.

'This is going to be beautiful.'

The sliding doors were opened and Rees stepped outside, strode up to the editors' corner and handed them all in turn some Brazilian cigarillos (*palomitas*) he had recently had shipped in from Sao Paulo. Their sweet, chocolatey smell not only lent the scene a certain aromatic exoticism, it also seemed to act as a tonic on the editors; their manner changed, they became friendly, deferential even. Though neither of them trusted Rees, they all had a certain grudging respect for him, considering him a dangerous man to cross. Not only could he manufacture reputations he could destroy them. As they puffed, the editors were obscured by thick smoke until a slight breeze gradually carried the clouds across the square, thinning them out.

A mighty beam of light from the van cut through the central limbo of smoke and smashed into the cathedral's facade. Everyone in the square stopped what they were doing, stopped their rocking of prams, their licking of lollipops and dialing of numbers, and stared with dropping jaws at the fifty foot square of gaudy color, bathing the cathedral in strange light. It was simply gigantic. Those parts of the facade which weren't completely flat caused the image to bend. Along the bottom of the square ran a black strip about as tall as a person. There three separate massive sub-titles flashed up and alternated with each other in an unending cycle.

**Is love a fairytale or the wailing of the damned?**
**Oscar Babel has arrived and it's time to wake up.**
**This journey terminates at Enlightenment Junction.**

Oscar was speaking, but what he said remained deliberately inaudible, his lips moving fluidly, about the size of a canoe. His face was pinned to the facade, brilliantly lit, filtered through greenish-blue filters, shot on 16-millimeter, which had been transferred onto beta-tape, the sub-titles inserted in post-production. This gargantuan face speaking to no one, and for no one, its eyes as big as portholes, the cavities of the nostrils like entrances to vaporous caves; it was horrible and beautiful. Those few whose eyes were currently popping would have uneasy dreams tonight populated by giant things – massive tables and oversize chairs, scurrying, gigantic spiders, lips like boa constrictors on the run from faces which squelched up behind them in flapping confusion. Oscar had been turned into a behemoth. A freak created by technology.

Those inside the van weren't sure how they felt about the loquacious and yet silent icon they had constructed; striking, yes, it was certainly striking; but there was no denying it was also a little eerie. The human face could not possibly withstand such magnification –

faces were not meant to be that high or wide. Subtlety was shredded, Oscar's sanguine eyes became oppressive, his lips turned to rubber, his teeth into ivory weapons.

The editors were oddly impressed – they sensed the story's strange potential. They said 'Shit!' and 'That is big!' every now and then. Small children darted up to the cathedral and pawed at spots within the square of light, half-expecting to be turned into frogs or pillars of light. They ran away and shrieked in delight. Rees, for his part, was tentatively pleased. Judging by the members of the public's faces three things had probably been accomplished so far. Oscar's face had been ingrained in their minds, curiosity about him had been sparked off, and controversy assured. How dare they defile one of London's houses of God? Why oh why? He could already hear the voices of dissent. He chuckled happily.

But the show wasn't over yet. Out of nowhere, a freelance photographer rolled on like a bowling ball hurtling towards its skittles, his body apparently undaunted by the shipment of cases and paraphernalia he had slung around his bull neck. He moved with profligate energy, darting this way and that, taking long shots, medium shots, like someone who had just swallowed a dose of amphetamines, which he had, shooting the image from every conceivable angle, bending over backwards, standing on steps, ensuring the face was snapped to death. On finishing he strode up to Rees to have a few words. While Rees confined himself to monosyllables, remaining perfectly still and impassive, his mask-like face giving nothing away, his interlocutor jittered and twittered, touched Rees's arm, his elbow, his hand, (all of which contact Rees found revolting), and spoke in sentences jostling with meaningless jargon. At last the photographer, with diminishing energy, carted himself and his gear away. The photos would be printed, syndicated to the press, cropped and published. (Rees's copywriter had written a modest press release to accompany them: "Now the words can be fitted to the face. For this is Oscar Babel, spiritual teacher and enemy of pretension, the man who recently exploded the

London art masquerade. If you want to hear what it is he's saying all interested parties will have the chance shortly at the Grosvenor Hotel during a series of innovative lectures. For further information contact Ryan Rees Publicity.")

Meanwhile, on Victoria Street people were shoving and pushing their way out of buses to try and see what all the fuss was about. Wallets and purses slid out of pockets and became irretrievably tangled up. Arguments started as elbows accidentally collided with groins. Those who elected to stay on board took pictures from the top; others wished they would stop blathering on and sit down and shut up. Civil servants, rushing towards the tube and the bus stops were stopped short and wondered who it was they were looking at. They concluded it was some pop star and marched off. It was at this point that a helicopter, which had been gradually approaching, finally coincided with the piazza's latitude and longitude, and out of it, like shards of hope to lost souls, dozens of leaflets spiraled, swam and rocked downwards, so in seconds the ground was covered with tokens of rhetoric: "Oscar Babel's here. It's time to wake up." Then, as an encore, a cargo of small red balloons stamped with Oscar's face were ejected and as they began their celebratory descent they created a beautiful effect, irradiated in the beam of projector light. Some got caught in the wind and drifted towards Pimlico. (One of the balloons steered itself, with great skill and tenacity, all the way towards an Italian restaurant in Rochester Row, and came to rest, without fuss, on the plate of a solitary customer dining al fresco. His back was turned since at that moment he was admiring the swaying bottom of a woman walking her dog. As he turned back to his plate of *tagliatelle ai funghi porcini* and jabbed automatically into it the balloon popped, his body spasmed, and he and his chair lurched groundwards. He didn't even bother to pick himself up from his crumpled position, his legs threaded through the chair's, his head resting on the concrete. He lit a cigarette, resigned to his fate. Passers-by stared at him disapprovingly.)

Some way back, leaning against Victoria House – the chilly steel building directly opposite the cathedral – watching through dark glasses, wrapped up in a cream-colored raincoat, was Oscar, his head tucked into an uncomfortable corner. As he watched from this shrouded spot, it seemed to him the face he was staring at was not his; the face up there was really that of an actor's who resembled him, an expert mimic perfectly able to reproduce his facial expressions. But after he had stared so hard that the image burned itself, like the imprint of the sun, onto his retina, he had to accept it really was him up there. His consciousness grew numb and he felt as though everything around him, the buildings, shops, commuters, cars, the station, coaches, buses, the newsstands, the people selling the newspapers, the newspapers in the newsstands, the faces on the newspapers, had been fatally diluted, abdicating their capacity to exist as signifiers of reality. It was only by keeping his eyes pinned to the nothingness of the sky that he was able to stop this feeling of unreality from engulfing him completely.

And now as people picked up the flyers and waddled off with them, fanned themselves with them, scrunched them up and kicked them, and as the children claimed the balloons, and the rest bobbed and stirred all over the square, the cathedral floodlights winked on, thereby swallowing up the face which nevertheless persisted as a faint, ghostly form.

*

From *The Independent*
10 August 200 -
## Oscar Babel projected in silent PR stunt
### by EMILY EVANS

OSCAR BABEL, who recently came to prominence for insulting the nominees of the Duchamp Prize, has now succeeded in offending the Church. Last night an image of him was projected onto Westminster Cathedral. Though Mr Babel's lips moved what he had to say remained tantalizingly off-screen.

Cyril Vixen, who is recovering in hospital for injuries sustained during the Duchamp banquet, has denounced Babel as a charlatan. After being informed, the Archbishop of the Diocese of Westminster, who had just attended the premiere of a new West End musical about the story of Christ, described it as "an act of blasphemy and barbarism."

*

From *The Daily Telegraph*
11 August 200 -
## Altar Ego

SIR - As you know, my church, Westminster Cathedral, was recently subjected to what amounts to an act of metaphorical rape. The image of Oscar Babel's face was projected onto its facade for nearly an hour. I am the first to appreciate publicity stunts, but institutions like the Church are sacrosanct symbols of authority. In this age of the image and the internet it becomes increasingly easier to build a monument to oneself, but I need scarcely remind you that the infamous dictators of this century were all masters of the art of self-aggrandizement, surrounding themselves with blind followers. I would urge Mr Babel to curb his narcissistic enterprises before he trades in his soul for the sake of being grotesquely visible.

MICHAEL ENGLAND,
Archbishop of the Diocese of Westminster.

(A letter submitted to *The Daily Telegraph* and turned down for publication)
12 August 200 -

*Sir,*

*The projection of Oscar Babel onto Westminster Cathedral made for an extremely beautiful visual effect. I was there. To imply parallels with dictators, as the Cathedral's Archbishop has done, is surely far-fetched. Babel is just someone who likes to irritate the establishment – and why not? It's healthy in a democracy. He's a lot more vital than those whose job descriptions require them to be, including the Duchamp prize nominees.*

*Stephanie Duncan*


(A letter submitted to *The Guardian* and turned down for publication) 12 August 200 -

*Dear Sir,*

*Oscar Babel reminds me of that anonymous figure in Bosch's Garden of Earthly Delights with the flower stuck up his backside. Just substitute "flower" with "himself" and you will get an even clearer idea of my view of this excuse for a human being.*

*Rada Bhat*

*

Now everything got scrambled together; time was stripped of its continuity. There were no longer beginnings, middles or ends in Oscar's life; just isolated frantic episodes, giving way to long stretches of toil, contemplation or boredom.

The cathedral coup and the subsequent controversy made Oscar more appealing to editors and this fact was not lost on Ryan Rees. He had decided, since Oscar was extremely photogenic, even when his face was caught on badly scanned, shaky newspaper images (or indeed grossly enlarged), and since Rees wished to protect Oscar from difficult questions, that film was by far the most appropriate medium with which to forge Oscar's "innovative" lectures. His plan was to have him filmed giving talks on life which would be referred to as the "Imagures", (an amalgam of 'lecture' and 'image.') He wanted to use the same man who had shot the footage used in the projection, a director whose studios were down at York Way in King's Cross. The films would be shot on a super 16-millimeter camera, in tandem with a Nagra, a portable sound deck the size of a small case. Then Rees planned to invite selective writers to view the screenings in private, at the Grosvenor hotel, laying on champagne and delicacies, unveiling a new communicative medium, whose author only existed in a celluloid form. He fell in love with the idea, as he usually did with his ideas.

So from now on, on-and-off during the next fortnight, by day Oscar listened to Bloch's recordings, mined them, edited them, selected usable material. He had to work very hard, writing his speeches and learning them off by heart and regurgitating Bloch's views on art, solitude, love, the nature of human relationships. He acted as a kind of editor. He tidied up, expanded, structured. The more outlandish sections of the huge transcript were left out. Deep in the currents of Oscar's mind was a sense that at least this masquerade allowed Bloch to reach an audience he would otherwise be denied. But at the same time Oscar knew he wasn't giving Bloch any credit, and was altering the nature of Bloch's idiosyncratic thoughts. His subsequent guilt triggered a series of uneasy and unsuccessful attempts to contact him by phone. But Bloch wasn't answering calls ...

After these films had been edited and the sound mixed in post-production a video projector and screen were installed in Oscar's suite, the curtains drawn, the champagne poured, the *hors d'oevres* passed round, and the digital voice recorders switched on. The projector beamed out the crisp, high-quality image onto the wall; the film cut energetically, jumping from extreme close-ups of parts of Oscar's face, to burned-out overexposed long shots of him, to his face filling the frame, then dissolving into distorted silhouettes of his face speaking against changing backdrops: of brick walls, detonating hydrogen bombs, crimson sunsets, weddings, naked mud-wrestling, and anything else which could be construed as portentous or symbolic. These backing images had been slowed down so much that they moved at imperceptible, soporific rates. Throughout, Oscar's voice flowed uninterrupted for the duration of the eight minute films. He spoke and the journalists listened, their faces redolent of inquiry, amusement, boredom, and indifference, their bodies lulled by alcohol, their stomachs silenced by cucumber-and-salmon sandwiches. They were being let into another world – that was the promise which accompanied the imagures – like explorers entering neglected caves full of hidden treasures. On film Oscar was calm, he acquired a kind of presence and power which he lacked in real life. The camera liked him. His voice exuded god-like serenity and patience, the patience of one who might watch a snail for hours and find its slow movements compelling; the patience of one who might rejoice in a traffic jam, a delay on the underground, a stalled elevator, finding in that stasis a chance to escape the earthbound. This effect had been achieved by careful mixing in the audio studio, use of reverberation and delay, 'gating' the top end and boosting the bass frequencies, creating a spacious, alpine resonance. Some – those men and women who all their lives had treasured hard facts, had seen the world only in terms of data tossed their way, the insignia of reality stamped on their minds as literal, unquestionable – now began to question those instincts that said all was as it should be, that all was ordered and rational. Tiny cracks appeared in the fabrics of their minds, then widened. Others rejected what he said outright, and made a note to ridicule him when it came to writing their copy, certain he was a fraud. Some had an experience vaguely analogous to psychoanalysis as puzzles about issues in their own lives were resolved or slotted into wider contexts as they listened to Bloch's re-dressed words. And so the imagures ran in hushed, mythic, manufactured circumstances, their author never present.

When Oscar wasn't working on his speeches or filming, he went for walks in Hyde Park and tried to sunbathe, though he could never remain still long enough to get a tan; drank excessively in pubs donning dark glasses, approached every now and then by strangers who recognized him; listened to Wagner in the dark; read about Tantra, prompted by Bloch's references to it, and grew entranced by its visual art which he studied in monographs; sat in the hotel's Turkish hot rooms and Russian steam rooms, where heat paralyzed action, running his fingers through his dark, damp hair, taking with them the sweat which had accumulated on his brow; waded slowly in the plunge pool, feeling distinctly nervous about exposing his genitals in front of fat businessmen who waded with him (at such moments he couldn't believe he had once life modeled); savored the momentary loss of self as the cold water he doused his head in caused his brain's neurons to fire and spark, but then, as the effect wore off, as he dried himself, as he rode in the elevator back to his room, and went for walks, fed the ducks in Hyde Park, versions, fragments, whole chunks of Bloch's recordings went spinning round and round his head, unceasing echoes from another life, another mind spliced into his own.

He tried to call him but Bloch wasn't taking calls ...

*

From *The Times* and *The Guardian* online
15 August 200 -

# Hats off Gentlemen, a genius!
## Quentin Verrico-Smith

*Question:* What do the London underground, the Duchamp Prize Banquet, Westminster Cathedral and a version of video art that goes by the awkward sounding name of "imagure" have in common?

*Answer:* OSCAR BABEL. His name adorned the first, his words sabotaged the second, his face defiled the third. I'm not so sure which constituent parts of Mr Babel go up to make the fourth but more about that later.

Babel's website tells us he is a scholar of Sanskrit, has studied meditation in India and Tibet, and is the personification of brilliance. As such the website promises something like the arrival of a new messiah who can set people free, wake them up, etc, etc. We've heard it all before of course. Gurdjieff, Khrisnamurti, Rajneesh all tried to wake people up, to see reality clearly, to espouse consciousness-expanding philosophies. Some espoused consciousness-expanding drugs as well. It's too early to say whether Babel will have any impact on London society, beyond being a source of rather tired controversy. What I can say, having been one of the privileged viewers of the "imagures," is that Mr Babel is, in my view, almost certainly a genius. During the screening of the first imagure at the Chelsea hotel Babel currently resides in, I sensed something I have rarely felt in my life. That I was present at a historic occasion. What is remarkable about these imagures is that Babel has utilized a fledging form – the short, eventless film – for the development of philosophical ideas. Detractors have said: why doesn't Oscar Babel appear in person? Why doesn't he appear live, not hiding behind a camera? Is he an orator who refuses to speak in person because he doesn't want to be saddled with awkward questions? It's a fair point.

But my understanding of the imagures is different. Firstly, they are brilliantly in keeping with the zeitgeist: they utilize image knowingly, playing with the medium. Secondly, the fact that Babel isn't willing to appear in person just goes to show how he is happy to let his audience take from the imagures what they will. On film he isn't subject to the whims, prejudices and preferences of one audience's questions and agendas over another. He can just say what he has to say. Clearly it is a philosophy of a non-confrontational stamp, hardly surprising for someone trained in the East where passivity and placidity are more highly valued than they are in our more belligerent, adversarial society where winning is everything and truth can often go by the wayside. And the image part of the imagures has thrown up some beguiling sights: a burned-out overexposed Oscar, his lips in extreme close-up, a pair of rhapsodic eyes, and the face hovering and fluctuating in silhouette, while a mellifluous voice intones on the soundtrack. It was all very effective and topically packaged. As an appetizer there now follows a snippet of Babel's cogitations:

"Society asks individuals to surrender their color and richness as soon as they enter into their livelihoods. What began as infinite possibility is reduced to predictability. As children we are free to express our eccentricities and dreams but as we grow we are forced into narrower paths and avenues. And our behavior is judged in terms of consistency, conformism and material success. To be sure these are valid criteria but they are only one set of criteria.

"The lucky ones find a niche that allows them the freedom which others enjoy only in private moments - away from the boredom of the factory floor, the antiseptic office. Others enter into a double life, wearing masks for their employers, and taking them off at night. Sometimes the charade is played out harmoniously, but often the strain is too great."

I will admit the remarks are hardly original but that's not the point. The point is that they demand to be listened to, in a highly unusual context. I am the cynic par excellence, but I venture to say that when Mr Babel makes his first public appearance demand for seats will be high.

# Oscar Babel and Accidental Resonance
## Mark Maynard

A week ago nobody had ever really heard of Oscar Babel. They say a week in politics is a long time. In the skewed, surreal world of celebrity, perhaps it's even longer. These days fame can be manufactured out of nothing, in the manner in which a magician merrily pulls rabbits out of a hat. The case of Oscar Babel raises some interesting issues. When a young, attractive man walks onto a stage in London and rubbishes those who are present we love it because it has a hint of the prodigal son, the ingrate and the rebel. It's so unruly – I wish I could have done that, we think. But the sad thing is we elevate such an act to a level it scarcely deserves, scraping the barrel, masticating and chewing and sucking. And so a non-event gets surrounded with talk, hype, conjectures, theorizing, social commentary. The same goes for the siege of Westminster Cathedral. Oscar Babel isn't really anything – he's not a singer, a writer, an athlete, an actor. He claims to be a self-styled guru – but of what exactly does his teaching consist, to what philosophy does he owe allegiance, what is his solution to the world's ills?

Oscar Babel is now well placed to contract what I shall call ARS –accidental resonance syndrome. My suspicion is that he is a complete nonentity, a blank canvas others can scribble and paint on, adding great splurges of graffiti, crayon doodles, speculative whirls of color. Every now and then an innocuous, though attractive individual comes along who for some reason people seem to take an interest in, once the initial shove has been given, by the media and its lackeys. And this individual, by courting an insipid kind of controversy and by having just enough in the way of non-conformist credentials to stand out, is given a vastly disproportionate amount of attention which he simply isn't interesting enough to merit. And here I am adding to the fuss, just another cook spoiling the broth. Which leads me to the next point. There's a new socio-political problem creeping up on us these days. It is becoming impossible to comment on something let alone criticize it without somehow lending it a greater, more bloated importance. So if I want to say something about Oscar Babel I had better shut my mouth.

In the age of cyberspace we now have more access than ever in history to knowledge, art, thought. But instead of learning from the masters of the past – the true spiritual leaders, Jesus, the Buddha – we turn to derivative, bogus, muddled, simple-minded thinkers. I am sure Oscar Babel will be a success because he is all of these things. Babel's recent lectures – the "imagures", so called because they are relayed entirely on film – are about as absurd and vacuous as they sound. (Transcripts of these exist on the internet should you wish to be cured of insomnia.)

Are we more likely to turn to false prophets today? I think so. It's because we've forgotten the value of having to work at something, to let insights come over time like a carefully nurtured seed which eventually grows. Real thinkers, on the other hand, require hard work. But we're not prepared to put in the graft. We want it all and we want it now, at the click of a mouse. And in the final count we haven't the time or the inclination to distinguish between the real and the fake.

*mark.maynard@guardian.co.uk*

# 19

The fire was still raging.

Others had replaced those who had walked away, drawn by the fate of Alastair Layor's house.

A gas pipe announced its destruction as a new line of angry flame was born. Dissonant, harsh sounds filled the air and reached into the heavens, then mercifully dissipated in the nothingness of black-bruised night. The new flames merged with the old and together they tightened their grip on what remained of the house.

She was still holding him, her cheek against his, and it was mysteriously consoling. He recognized her as the woman he'd snatched away from the car on Regent Street and he was not sure (he was wondering about this only on some buried level) if it was this or the fire which allowed for the ease of their union.

Neither of them uttered a word.

She, too, recognized him. There was something deeply right about holding him. When she had walked up to him – minutes earlier – she couldn't believe it was him, since she had the chance to thank him now, but how could she say anything after realizing the house in flames was his? She knew it was his because when she turned to the other faces none were grief-stricken. His face bound him to the house; the other faces were bound to the spectacle.

Watching the fire, he was not really aware of the sounds of scrambled activity around him, of the jagged movement of firemen and people. He had to resist the impulse to jump into the flames, not in order to end his life but just to do something, to counter the awful passivity of watching.

Flames jumped and raced and fluctuated in the cavities of the shattered windows, the smoke blew angrily, black and dirty white; the guttural, tormented sounds of destruction were already familiar. She wanted to drag him away and take him somewhere else, anywhere else so long as it was far away from there.

But she knew he would never go. So she waited there with him. Waited while he was crucified. The strange thing was, she felt his pain, experienced it as if it were hers.

One of the firemen was visible inside, a shadowy figure in oilskins, indistinct through the *chiaroscuro* patterns flickering around him. He directed the hose into the flames and they were momentarily quashed, only to rise and grow strong again immediately. Just then there was a loud explosion. The fire had found another gas pipe and a long, spray-like flame rocketed along the side of the house. This undid the firemen's work and the last few minutes, in a flash of time.

In the confusion few people noticed the arrival of another fire engine until the frenetic, jumbled activity alerted them. Hoses were wheeled out, ladders climbed, more foam and water jetted into the house. One of the firemen just managed to elude tendril-like flames stretching out towards him as he scrambled down the ladder, taking two steps at a time, very nearly losing his footing.

By now there were faint bars of purple in the sky, intimations of a dawn still some way off. Their beauty was the more poignant for appearing on the fringes of the inferno and the promise of dawn they carried made Layor even more of a hostage to pain. With the idea of dawn came the suggestion that this was all a nightmare, or would be perceived as such when it finally arrived. But he knew daylight could not re-write the history of the last, calamitous half-hour.

New parts of the house were being ravaged and explosive cracks and thuds sounded and it seemed as though the fire was beginning all over again, recreating itself like a mutation on the rampage, a disease immune to all the defenses humans try to mount against it. The air was full of the smell of burning; the street had turned into an open oven.

In the inferno the firemen became murky, cloudy figures. Water burst on one side, flames and smoke rushed and clawed at the air on the other. Light and dark, water and flame merged into a continuous pulsation.

Lilliana whispered into his ear, 'Let's get out of here.'

Her words had no effect.

There was a rumble of thunder. It sounded like artillery fire in the sky, evidence of some distant, mythic war. He looked up to see the sky illumined with eerie light at its edges. The moon was shining, a disc of purest white, one of its corners slightly cloaked. He wondered why it wasn't splitting up or shedding cosmic tears. How dare it still be hanging there?

One of the firemen came up to Layor and yelled, 'Rain, that's what you need, sir; some of that.'

Layor nodded, without really understanding. He nodded out of habit, which had its roots in the conditioned impulse to convince those around him he was in control, that he understood. But he was not in control. He did not understand. He felt he too was going to ignite, to burst into a ball of flame, spinning away, a skeleton carried by the wind.

A crack of fork lightning flashed and died across the sky. The ensuing thunder, for its duration, rivaled the roar of the fire. A large part of a wall came crashing down; the dust that would have bloomed was lost in the debris continually being created. At the moment of the flames' writhing life there came the evidence of its handiwork; no time needed to elapse for the effects of the fire to be measurable. He turned to look, tears rolling down his face, at the residual audience. They were not so bad; oddly, he now felt comforted by their presence, and then he turned to meet the eyes of the woman beside him. As he glimpsed her pale, porcelain skin and crimson hair, he found her mild, gentle features sustained him. He reached for her soft hand. He tried to imprint the shape and texture of her face onto his mind. Her hair was sticking to her forehead in little curls, sweat causing it to cling, the patterns of the fire reflected in her limpid, mild eyes. She had been unravelled by the trauma of the night; emotions the air was heavy with had latched onto her and made her strikingly beautiful.

So a frail river of joy formed from the sea of his pain. She watched him, alert to the sense that he had awakened, from a deep sleep or dream. Then she took to thinking of her flower shop and of how she needed water and light for her flowers. And of how water was what the human body mainly consisted of. And that the moon must therefore control humans as the moon controlled the tides through the pull of its gravitational force and humans were like the tides; they were high and low ...

As she was thinking these things, she didn't feel the light, imperceptible tingling on her skin and she didn't hear the hiss of drizzle and she didn't see the people in their pyjamas peering up at the sky, didn't see them dispersing, darting about, taking shelter.

A ear-splitting crack of lightning burst out of nowhere; its sound was terrifying, a metallic, shattering intrusion, and its target was a part of the roof, which instantly ignited. The whole of the street was chillingly illuminated for a split second. It was almost as if nature was showing off its greater power, provoked into life by the domestic fire it now mocked. But just as the new flames born of the lightning danced wildly they were stymied by pelting rain. The rain was of such a tropical cast – in seconds it was forming warm, swirling rivers which flowed from the pavement, ran into the gutters, seemed to churn the cobblestones – that he half-expected to turn around and see tapirs slithering out of the gutters, chimps swinging from roof to roof, or some exotic, multi-colored bird bank out of the sky and glide towards him. These thoughts raced, imitating the perpetual motion of the rain whose lines were brilliantly brought out in the glare of the flames, so they became a million broken, oblique shards of light. All at once, the fire lost some of its momentum and trembled uncertainly, a giant in the process of being felled. The rain was beating it into submission, confusing it. Burnt out parts of the house were revealed. Everything was swirling, the elements indistinguishable. He heard laughter beside him and turned, astonished, to Lilliana whose face was re-shaped by a tentative smile, the rain streaming down her face. The firemen had moved away from the house; they were shouting inarticulately, their faces coated and caked in dirt.

'It's going out,' one yelled above the hissing. Alastair Layor nodded at him and stared at the half of his house gradually being revealed, the half still standing. The flames were dying, shuddering with final flourishes. In a few more moments, in the moments it might take to water a plant, to address and seal a letter, to cut a cake into equal portions, the fire was spent.

Oily smoke coiled and writhed, alternately concealing and revealing ravaged outlines. Wooden stumps were on the point of disintegration; ashes and wires dangled, planks hung suspended, having nothing to connect with, no floor to be incorporated within. On the right side of the house a faint specter of domesticity persisted: a window frame, a bed and a painting discernible inside. It was strange to see through the pattering rain this collapsed, ravaged shell hanging onto its intact other half.

Layor, soaking now, his hair greasy and shapeless, couldn't digest the damage, couldn't take it in. His relief at the fact of the fire's extinction was instantly quashed by the unchanging reality before him. Somehow what he was now looking at was even more terrible; while the fire had lasted the hope of its being put out sustained him; now that it was out, the flux had hardened into this – unalterable wreckage. Through the rain his house stood decimated; in the sunshine it would be no different.

The firemen were standing, sitting around, getting their breath back, sipping at mugs of coffee, their oilskins glowing. The blue lights on the fire engines revolved, blurred by the rain. Layor looked around him; by now, most people had gone home. He searched for

Lilliana. She already seemed so important to him now. Eventually he made her out, approaching with a blanket and an umbrella, her dripping hair all curled around her face. Her dress was glued to her so the delicate lines of her torso were clearly outlined through the rain dance. She wrapped the blanket around him, and very gently took his hand. He stared ahead of him, struck by the alienness of these once so familiar surroundings.

'I think we should go now,' she said. She thanked the firemen repeatedly and profusely and told them she would take care of him now; they assumed she was his girlfriend and nodded easily.

She started to lead him to her house, a few minutes' away, both of them huddled under her umbrella.

'I live round the corner. It's hard to believe it's really you. I was asleep – I heard all this shouting. Thought I was dreaming. I came out; everyone was heading for your street. I went after them, saw the fire, then I saw you.'

He said nothing – he looked pale and sick. In his eyes there was a sightlessness which worried her but she strode resolutely into the night, tapping into hidden reserves of energy and certainty. She knew words weren't possible at that moment so she was silent, but his hand felt good in hers. In chancing upon the man who had chanced on her, in this accidental encounter she also found something to sustain her. The tentative knowledge that she could love someone. At the same time she was freed by the immense realization that love was not quantifiable. And if love was transient, so be it. If her life at best would contain only a handful of moments of intimacy, and nothing more, so be it. She knew that the sweetness of this umbrella-cocooned union would stay with her, she would be a richer person for it. Alex Sopso's face came back with sudden vividness. Her guilt about having deserted him lightened – perhaps it was being siphoned off while her hand continued to link with the man's beside her. And then she knew her touch was consoling.

Perhaps she wasn't such a bad person …

The rain had eased, though it was still weighty enough to drum on the umbrella. He felt secure under the small black dome. It seemed to him as though the rain had melted the scaly surface of the streets, the edges and faces of houses, the street lamps. The splashing puddles, the dampness in his shoes – everything was working to a distinct end, though he could not give it a name.

As he moved he glanced every now and then out of the corner of his eye at Lilliana, too scared to look at her directly in case she would become self-conscious, in case the bewitchment of their second brush with each other would be lost. He felt like he'd traversed those stretches of time in which her past was housed, moving closer and closer towards her essence; he felt able to say, if he wanted to, "I know you." But he didn't want to say it, or to say anything at all; and, when he realized this, words had never seemed so light and meaningless. What possible words could he stick together, what verbal constructions could he unearth from the ruins of the night?

Now the rain dwindled to the occasional random drop, which joined those millions already lodged in the trees. Lilliana closed the umbrella. Trees that seemed no longer trees but men, huge, silent giants with great heads of hair. Serene and sleeping.

The streets were utterly deserted; there was that peculiar heart-stopping stillness which grows deepest at the hour before dawn. Bereft of the glistening skin the rain had lent them the rows of houses looked drab and uninhabited. They were lost in the creases of London.

By the time they reached Lilliana's front door she no longer felt the need to be so decisive and strong. And she could tell, standing close by him, that he was feeling a bit better.

'Come in,' she said. 'I'll make us some tea.'

As they walked through Alastair's eyes fell upon a painting hanging in the hallway. It was the copy of the Fra Angelico panel which Alex Sopso had given her.

'That painting ...' he murmured. It was the first time he'd spoken to her tonight.

'Do you like it?'

'Very much.'

'Then you can have it.' To hell with possessions, she thought. Then she added, 'Because I think you saved my life on Regent's Street. There's a tradition: the current owner has to give it to the person who has saved his or her life.'

He didn't have the energy to ask her for a fuller explanation of what she meant, and stammered some thanks.

She commanded that they go through to the kitchen.

Along the way he took in the exquisite array of plants and flowers. Their presence reminded him of the good things in life. This person beside him, he thought, had surrounded herself with beauty – and invited him into her gentle world. He felt honored. He understood, in a way for the first time, what hospitality meant, what generosity of spirit encompassed. In the past he'd been fooled into thinking he'd sampled them, misled by their being packaged in the glamour of the theater. It was not that theatrical people were unfriendly. They were very grand at being friendly, but the grandeur was the problem. An excess of flamboyance, for Alastair, only robbed the air of oxygen in the end. Among exotic, stimulating people, people who could speak knowledgeably about claret or name the rings of Saturn there was certainly much amusement to be had, but very clever people (and he included himself here) often seemed to him to be finding ways of excusing their hypocrisy, finding ways of eluding loyalty, afterwards justifying their betrayals by stressing their awareness of life's dizzying ambiguity. But that was not the real, right thing ...

She was different. She had a constancy about her.

He'd heard about love, heard about about its transforming power. Could it be that up until now he thought he'd known love when he'd only ever known a pale shadow of it, and this pale shadow was something he had accepted as love, had gone along with, got by with, having nothing else?

And now?

He felt as though he was being ushered into a room full of subtle treasures, a room vast and never-ending.

And was this room love after all?

'You're ... my find ... aren't you?' he murmured.

She laughed, a little self-consciously, a blush welling up which she tried to stifle. They stood standing close to one another, in the large, clean kitchen, choosing to squeeze themselves into a corner, not bothered with chairs or comfort. As they listened to each other's breathing, breathing which detained the moments, they lingered in the caesura between linking and not linking, until their lips moved closer, searching tentatively, roaming in restraint. Then, when their mouths had circled, this dance of unrealized touch abated: she kissed him very softly on his lips, so softly he felt hers as his lips' shadow made palpable. She glanced up at him, to gauge his reaction. There was a fragile smile suspended there.

She drew up a chair for him, found a towel and dried his hair. She filled the kettle and pulled out a couple of mugs from the cabinet, and set them on the little wooden table which had nothing on it except a set of salt and pepper cellars.

She said, 'Are you feeling a bit better now?'

He nodded.

'It was you, wasn't it you?' she said. 'That time. On the road. I never thanked you properly. Do you remember? It was you. That time.'

'Yes, it was me.'

'You went off; I came back for you, but you'd gone.'

He smiled – a true, deep smile which reached his eyes and made them mild, re-awakened their sight, warmed him in a startling way.

'Would you like to have a bath?' she asked. 'Perhaps you should take a bath. Your clothes are soaked through. Your hair's caked in filth. We must both stink of smoke. Two ragamuffins.'

'We must stink; I'd be disappointed if we didn't.'

Lilliana gave a brief, happy chuckle.

'You're soaked, too,' he said. 'You should take a bath. But before you do, it's my turn to thank you – for being so kind. If it wasn't for you, I don't know what I would have done.'

'There's really no need. I think we're telepathic, you and I.'

He squeezed his eyes shut, held his fingers to his temples, as if testing out her theory.

'You may be right.'

The kettle boiled and she made two cups of strong tea, stirring sugar into his without asking if he took any because she thought it would do him good. They sipped at the cups, seated at opposite ends of the table. While they sat there in silence the curtains grew diaphanous, imbued with the glow of incipient dawn.

'You know, tonight I feel like I've lived three or four lives,' he said in a low, even voice. 'Perhaps I have. But what I really want to say is ... I feel ... earlier it seemed like I'd turned into an x-ray machine ...watching the fire, I could see through my house, see into it ... but I felt like I could see through life as well, and people, see how ghostly we all are. That's it. I'd seen too deeply, I'd drunk too deeply of this reality, this reality most people – they're smart – they manage to avoid. But here, with you, even after the fire ... I suddenly ... I have a life again ... I can't put it in words ... but with you ... you fill me with mad hope. It's crazy. I can't explain but I feel right being with you. I need you. Can I say that without scaring you, my sweet friend?'

Lilliana had listened very carefully, as she would to a confession. They had followed two paths, those subterranean tramlines had crossed once and now twice. It all seemed good and true and inevitable, right now, but she had been hurt before. She did not want to be hurt again. She circled her hands around her mug, savoring the heat creeping into her hands. She studied his milky eyes, the unkempt, dirty hair, his big nostrils. She slowly drew her arm across the table and touched his hand.

'I think we're destined to meet at times of crisis, you and I, my sweet friend.'

Now the curtains were aglow, the sky was growing luminous. Through the spaces between the leaves light was finding its way, flinging the promise of purity at the world. Soon Kentish Town would be waking, while those flocks of crowds adrift in sleep- heavy stupors, their limbs aching with the need for rest, were returning from the West End, seeing in the spaces between the leaves their lives blissfully trying to disappear.

'You can stay here with me tonight, if you like,' she murmured.

Without hesitation he said, 'I can't sleep alone. Can I sleep in your bed?'

Her eyes widened with unspoken reservations. She ran some fingers through a clump of damp hair. She took a sip of tea; it trickled down her throat. It felt blissful.

'My bed ... well ... I mean ...'

'Don't worry, we don't ... I mean, we'll just ...'

'It's OK ... you don't have to say it ... I'm telepathic, remember?'

He took another gulp of tea, noticing for the first time the sugar in it.

'Oh yes.' His nerves had temporary ascendancy and he gave in to a disconnected ramble. 'Telepathic. I'm grateful for your gift, must say a little prayer of thanks, get the prayer mat out. You know – this farmhouse kitchen of yours – have you ever cooked in it – has oil ever splattered those gas rings – have you ever left a dish unwashed overnight? I only ask because ...What's the secret?'

'No secret, no secret.'

The repetition slowed him down, stopped him. Her voice seemed to him to have grown more lovely,  enriched by fatigue and acceptance, had turned into a sleepy river of a voice lapping at his consciousness. She watched him carefully, intrigued by the way he watched her, so that for a moment they were like mirrors on opposite sides of the table, reading in the other reflections of their own serene curiosity.

'I haven't been up so late since ... since I don't know when. I always feel a bit out of step with nature when I can hear the birds singing and I'm still awake. Do you know what I mean?'

'I'm out of step, I'm out of pocket, I'm out of a house.'

She laughed at him – he was asking her to, she felt sure, and when she laughed he rolled his eyes around. She was glad that more crumbs of conversation had followed the hiatus of the question of sleeping arrangements; these last exchanges cleared the air, restored normality. The last thing she wanted was an atmosphere which was highly charged; she wanted unheard melodies to creep up on them; she wanted their hands never to lose the special union of that rain-splattered walk; she wanted soundless tranquillity before the familiar skin of sleep closed round them.

They finished their tea and she put the mugs in the sink. They went upstairs. They took turns to wash the dirt and rain out of their bodies.

But when they undressed they knew they would have to touch.

And when they touched they saw they would fall in love.

And when they slept they dreamt of each other's touch.

# 20

'Yes.'

'It's Oscar.'

'Oh. Where are you calling from?'

'A phone booth. Are you still disgusted with me?'

'I never said I was. But ... before you were a product; now you've been promoted, or demoted, depending on how you look at it. You're a puppet. I can see the strings.'

'I'm beginning to think the puppetry might have started with the life modeling.'

'Are you suggesting it's my fault?'

'No, no, no, of course not ... no, I just ... Listen, all my life I've been no one, and now I feel I have a voice, power ... I could give something ...'

'No, Oscar, you listen. You may be a tunnel through which visions pass, but I'm not especially interested in hanging around with a pseudo-messiah. I'm not holy enough. What's more, I've no desire to be. Which hotel is it you're stranded in?'

'The Grosvenor.'

'What's the food like? Does it come designer-wrapped? Or is that only you? How long do you intend to go on playing this game?'

'Najette, listen, I'd give it all up for you. The last time I saw you. I remember every tiny detail; I remember things you said. You were so ...'

'Oscar, what's the use of a good memory when all it does is help you lie to yourself and others?'

'You're right, you're right. I know. Would it make any difference if I told you I didn't really plan this – it just sort of happened. I just seem to have come under the spell of this man; he's just sort of taken over my life. I let him, I know; I should have resisted, but I mean, what was the alternative? I couldn't have gone on projecting films; I hoped the urge to paint would come back, but it didn't. Every time ... every time I'd sit in front of a blank piece of paper or canvas I'd just start panicking. I had so much to say that I couldn't even begin to say it, and it had to be perfect, and I knew it wouldn't even be mediocre. It had to be there, clean, with the umbilical cord neatly cut, you know, and I wasn't prepared to put in the work, the hours, to start and re-start and throw sketches away and then go through the basket looking for what I'd binned. I just don't have your dedication or talent. I don't feel good about this situation I'm in; I know I don't come out of this very well, but would you turn down a hotel when you'd lived in a series of bedsits all your life? Would you turn down the opportunity to have a voice? I could teach, be Daniel's mouth – I mean – '

'How presumptuous to imagine you've something to give the world.'

'You're right, but it's not I who's doing the talking; I can't explain ... imagine I've chanced on a treasure trove and I'm its caretaker.'

'What?'

'Never mind. Oh God, never mind. It's just too complicated. I'll just say that – in a weird way – I feel free ... now ... because I'm ... not free, no, that's the wrong word ... I feel this indifference, a disregard. It's as though I'm tied to the mast of a ship; it's on the verge of capsizing in a gale, I'm soaked, but while I'm up there, it's exhilarating in the way sticking your head out of an express train is exhilarating ... and I want to scream at the world.'

'Oscar, a prophet should be dispassionate, not desperate, and shouldn't be living in a five star hotel. He should be poor, not eating gourmet meals. He shouldn't be looking into the eye of the camera, but into eternity with a beatific smile.'

'God, it's so good to talk to you. You talk so much sense, Christ, and all I've heard lately is nonsense. Never mind. I mean to say, do you think ... I was wondering ... you're right, of course, you're right, you're right. Would you mind ... could I see you?'

'Listen, Oscar, I know what you want. You want me to sort you out, that's it, isn't it? You rely too much on others. You have to save yourself. I think perhaps it would be best if you didn't call me again.'

He didn't say anything. She didn't say anything. He stood there, clutching the phone, his fingers tightly curled around the handset, as if only this connection with drab plastic was staving off total despair.

Now Oscar was granted a glimpse into eternity but it was comfortless.

Najette murmured, 'I have to go now,' and hung up.

A minute later the phone in the booth started ringing but Oscar wasn't there to pick it up.

Afterwards he walked sadly, staring hard at the pavement. He thought of the time she'd kissed him.

One kiss.

It took on a frightful sacredness. If only the kiss had been caught on film, if only he could have replayed it, re-lived its intoxication vicariously. No. The kiss was already fading, would fade further, in time would vanish. Could it be affection left no visible traces? Just when a special part of her had started to unravel, like a ribbon twirling in the moonlight, the mood between them had soured. He could not really blame her – she was too defiantly intelligent to tolerate his willing participation in illusion, his compliance in a fabrication which distorted his humanity, blurred the edges of his life, ran the risk of making everything he said and did ridiculously meaningful, or meaningless. What should he do? Could he give up this life which had been thrust upon him? All at once, erasing these questions, came a simple, overwhelming desire: to see her.

So he hailed a taxi to take him to the grand, dilapidated house where she lived. But he managed to land himself a cab whose out-of-control driver (adorned with a grandly-fungal beard) tackled speed bumps as he would the level road, causing Oscar's stomach to dip and soar sickeningly. Not only was he torn between anxiety and hope, but he also had to deal with a man intent on killing them both, as he smashed his foot down on the accelerator like an angry child trying to crush a beetle.

At the end Oscar stepped out warily. He paid the driver, and the cab tore off in search of its next unsuspecting victim. He paced up and down, wondering what he should do now he was here. He walked up, stopping a few yards away from the house, crossed over to the far side, and watched. The large bay window which he remembered glancing out of all those weeks ago (he could picture the young boy learning to cycle) allowed for an unobstructed view of her canvasses and easel. Otherwise the room was bare. He grew more and more agitated. It seemed so easy to go up and ring the doorbell, and pour out a stream of words. But he held back. As he stood there she glided in and moved towards the easel, her face turned in profile. (She had had to give up her studio and did all her work at home now.) He was able to study her eyes as they in turn studied her canvas, to follow the taut curve of her arm running towards the precise hand and its sable brush. Without warning she strode off, and returned with a thick glass palette. For some time her back was turned to him and he assumed she was mixing paint. Then, with neither ceremony nor fuss, she resumed her work. She waited, waited for the paint to find its own form and space, to show her the way which was its way. He moved forward a little, now five or six meters off. He was taking an awful risk: if she happened to glance outside there was no doubt she would see him, but while she was still in profile, focused on her work he thought he would be all right. Now as she painted he found the mere sight of her made him happy – he no longer felt the urge to announce himself, recoiling especially at the idea of interrupting her work, which he realized, in watching her, was sacred, more sacred than anything in his own life was to him. It was clear how fired up she was, how engaged she was with her art. Only chains wrapped around her could have dragged her away. In her physical energy he saw a corresponding mental fertility: new ideas flowed, new perspectives and possibilities opened up. So her joy stifled his sadness. He took in the sight of her olive skin, her startlingly long eyelashes, her straight silky hair rearranged every now and then by the hand that was free.

Oscar had caught her at a moment when a study for part of a larger work was showing her how the latter might cohere as a whole. She wanted to find a new way of linking the apprehension of an object with the emotion it evoked. Studies and sketches of the shattered plant pot, its edges distended and swollen like a heavily pregnant womb, and the elegiac face of Lilliana, gone over in pencil, pencil and crayon, pencil and gouache, powdery charcoal, and finally oil, were the keys. It was her conception of the strange union between Lilliana and the blonde hairdresser in the Sun Well at the start of the summer. In her view the finished work would mark a new departure. For the final painting she planned to use maimeri, an acrylic paint with a high density of pigment, which glowed and sparkled, leapt out of the canvas with its luminosity. She visualized the work as being predominantly a dialogue between blues – ultramarine, cerulean, cobalt.

Now he was daydreaming, constructing scenes of love between them. He imagined her frictionless, unblemished skin, her draping body draped over his. He imagined her smiling eyes greeting his as he turned towards her in the morning. But the reverie came to an abrupt end as he had to step aside for a passing car. Then he was struck by the realization that he wasn't worthy of Najette, that her inspired state began where he left off. How right she was, he reflected, when he eventually drifted away, to keep him at a distance; and it was right that he hadn't tried to bridge that distance by placing his finger on her doorbell.

He hopped off the bus as it slowed down.

During the journey one or two people recognized him. They weren't interested in why he was a public figure – just that he was one; the fact of his fame was sufficient and they were drawn to it as by a fire on a cold night. They generated a kind of childish excitement around him, asking for his autograph, which he readily gave. And yet even as he scrawled out his name – the letters scrunched and compressed so as to minimize the time spent in writing it – he felt like he was engaged in an elaborate pretense, a ridiculous game.

He walked quickly as the bus turned into Tottenham Court Road. The evening was cool, and the air was tangy and sharp. He made out a line of cellular phone devotees dotted along the length of the Charing Cross Road. They clutched, cradled, and caressed their phones. They moved with their phones, paced up and down with them, turned with them, waltzed with them. Their phones were their dance partners and together they performed for the benefit of a non-existent jury and audience.

Boisterous groups, solitary men accompanied by canine companions, and giggling couples were headed for the public houses. It was a Friday night. The evening's task was to imbibe alcohol, the great liberator, the stepping stone to confidence, compliments and the harvests of expediency. Breathing deeply of the healing elixir, sampling the blurring of perception in a joyous haze, succumbing to the disorientation of an overloaded system: these would make up the successive stages of the evening, joined seamlessly through the conduit of beer, wine, cocktails or spirits, as these offered a network of possibility whose lines would terminate in anonymous fumblings in unfamiliar rooms, dreamless sleep, and vomit (colorfully adding life to the drab pavements of West London.)

He turned into Old Compton Street, walked to its end, and up Brewer Street, noticed the ghoulish girls in their neon booths trying to egg customers (men) into sampling the strip shows. Soho, with its fruit machines, sex shops, and cosmopolitan bars was like a cluttered, cramped village whose inhabitants were linked not by the familiarity of proximity but by a shared interest in abandon. The faintly rancid smell of this interlocking empire filled his nostrils. Every now and then men, usually with rounded bellies, thinning hair and glasses, stole into certain shops and crept out again, peering round furtively. Regarding these faded individuals Oscar felt a terrible stab of longing for Najette and her feisty, flamboyant embrace of life. As if in reaction to this latest recognition of her loss (which, despite being just another in a series of recognitions, imparted all the devastation of the original, leaving his heart freshly eviscerated) he too was seized with a craving for a drink. He opted for one of the ailing basement bars. Trotting down beer-sodden stairs, he brushed against a man in leather, with long, chalky hair, his jacket strewn with badges, one of which said simply 'POET - PAINTER - FILMMAKER - ASK.' He wore swimming goggles which gave him a sinister appearance. Oscar offered him a tentative smile but the man appeared to be frowning back at him. He had the feeling he was entering some kind of arts performance venue.

The bar's bleached brown walls and orange, plastic, shapeless furniture suggested the interior of an abandoned spaceship. The sight of a bass guitarist occupying a ramshackle stage and crooning the odd note at the skeletal audience confirmed that he was indeed there to be entertained. As the erstwhile musician finished his set, his hair flopping over his nose, the compere bounded up and told a joke about a hunter in the Black Forest paid by disgruntled spouses to set ravening wolves on their husbands or wives.

Since the place was so quiet only one of the two hefty-looking barmen was actually serving while his oversized colleague was busy tossing glasses into the air ostentatiously, darting aside to avoid the flying shards when the conjuring didn't always go according to plan. A few heads turned to register the periodic, violent smashes. Oscar ordered a double vodka and tonic, made short shrift of it, and ordered another. Tired applause coincided with his location of a seat.

The compere introduced the next act: a scruffy woman who went by the name of "Fierce Fatima." There were so many rings pierced along her lower lip Oscar could picture the rings holding up a shower curtain, its width interlaced through them.

'This is called "Fucked Up and Alone Again,"' she declared, and proceeded to rattle through her monologue as if having some kind of seizure.

'In a smoke free zone I begin to burn I'm a martyr see my stigmata. I'm a dishcloth for men I'm a tea towel for lovers. I'm on stage taking bows deafening APPLAUSE I look left and right how do you do how do you do how do you DO? Scene change. Life change. Touch my soul with your foot my arse with your heart. Night falls like a dead rabbit the moon hurts my eyes I'm moon BLIND. In the cafe I watch a woman slip a sugar CUBE into her mouth. She must be very lonely she has mascara in her ears. I'm a martyr see my stigmata. Boyfriend gets me to sign along the dotted rejection line. Says I'm past my prime that my tits sag like bin liners. My eyes fill with tears but I won't show, curses fill my veins I'd like to put rat POISON in his sperm but I say nothing smile politely because I'm a martyr so FEEL my stigmata.'

She bounded off the stage and into the compere.

As he tried to clap Oscar thought about how different a drink in his hotel room might have been, in the company of Wagner and the gossamer breeze from his giant opened windows. He thought about the "Imagures" and how silly they were. As he was thinking the man in goggles who he had encountered on the stairs re-entered and walked stealthily to the bar. The staff seemed reluctant to serve him but eventually one of the barmen started mixing him a drink. While he waited he glanced over at Oscar and Oscar had the distinct impression it was with hostility.

Oscar scrambled around for something to read, and found a flyer advertising a play called *The Rampant Gardener*. He tried to look engrossed so as to deter a potential approach, but the leather clad stranger, his hand curled around his beer bottle, sauntered over to him. The next performer appeared: an asthenic guitarist whose B string snapped two chords into his new song. He battled on heroically until someone threw a peanut at him.

'Mind if I sit here?' the man asked in a gruff, smoky voice. Oscar thought he could detect a hint of a mid-Atlantic accent.

'No.'

'Then I don't mind if I fucking do, friend.'

He started laughing, a slow, grim laugh which made Oscar uneasy.

'Enjoying the show?' the man demanded, having produced a small pouch of tobacco. He began rolling himself a cigarette with wiry, nicotine stained fingers. He was edgy, restless.

'I'm not sure.'

'Think you could do better?'

'No, that's not what I meant.'

'Then what do you mean?'

He lit his sleek roll-up and inhaled deeply, so deeply Oscar could imagine the smoke passing down the length of his lungs, into his stomach, and sinking into his intestines. Blue wisps eventually dribbled out of his nostrils.

'I'm not sure.'

'Cigarette?'

'No, thanks.'

'What are you drinking?'

'Vodka.'

'You Russian?'

Again the ashen, disgusted laughter.

'I'm a poet. Want to hear a poem?'

'Not especially.'

He took another long, predatory drag. Then his manner altered, his neck tilted, and he began to recite his verse in a curiously ineffective way.

'What do you look for? / Do you look for a silver lady under a poplar tree?/Do you look for a raven with elegiac eyes?/Do you look for a constant friend?/A house and car? /A life without end?/What do you crave?/A stolen kiss?/A peaceful exchange?/ An end to all your pain/ I have nothing for you /Except a palm lined with toil/ And a heart that's uncurled.'

Oscar was surprised to find the poem wasn't as bad as he had expected – though the last two lines grated slightly. He peered at him and said, 'That was very nice.'

'Nice? How many hundred-thousand words in the English language and that's the only adjective you can come up with?'

'All right; it was simply but powerfully phrased, and poignant.'

'Better, but still not good enough, my friend.'

'Please don't call me your friend.'

'Problem?'

'I'm not your friend.'

The poet took another drag, communicating throughout its duration an icy, barely-restrained fury.

'And,' Oscar continued, 'I didn't invite you to join me, and I'm not required to give you an analysis of your poetry.'

'But surely you can do better than that.'

'No I can't. I've got to go now, excuse me, it wasn't very *nice* talking to you.'

'Hey man, what are you getting so uptight for? Lighten up, I just want a chat. Let me buy you a drink.'

Oscar stared at him warily, then slowly sunk back into his plastic egg chair.

'My name's Vernon. Vernon Lexicon. Poet, painter, film-maker.'

'Ask.'

'What?'

'You forgot the "ask". I noticed your badge earlier.'

'Yeah, "ask." That's right.'

'My name's – '

'I know who you are. And I'm onto you. I'd just like you to know that.'

'You're onto me?'

'It took awhile for me to make the link. You're the one all the papers have been writing all the horseshit about. Tell me something, Mr Oscar Babel, how the hell does someone like you get through the night? Aren't you sick of seeing yourself being discussed by the critics? Don't you just feel your soul rotting each time another picture makes it into print, or when your mug goes up on a church?'

Though Oscar was distinctly unnerved by Lexicon's attack, he instinctively sensed a way of annoying him.

'You'd rather it was you on the facades of buildings; you'd rather be the one preaching, wouldn't you, Mr Lexicon?'

'Don't turn it around; you're in no position to mind read; you're no guru. You're a marketing by-product.'

'I think you're jealous. Jealousy's a terrible thing, Mr Lexicon, it eats away at your insides.'

'Spare me the homegrown wisdom, Babel. I've got an acid test for you. If you've travelled to Tibet and India, and studied Sanskrit, you should know all about Buddhism. And if there's one thing you should know about Buddhism, it's the contents of the Four Noble Truths. So – Mr Prophet, Mr Self-Styled Guru, remind me of them again.'

Oscar said nothing.

'Talk to me, faggot.'

By this stage Lexicon was emitting a ferocious level of aggression – the goggles had been torn off and heroin eyes revealed. He moved closer to Oscar and started pushing against him. One of the bar staff noticed and decided to intervene.

'Hey, Vernon, take it easy; don't do this to me again.'

'Piss off, I'm talking to my friend here; wait your turn.'

'Don't speak to me like that Vernon. I've told you before – if you get abusive with the customers, I'll turf you out.'

'Fuck yourself.'

The bar man, whose exposed, tattooed arms were bulging with muscle, found it very easy to stare Lexicon in the eyes. He said in calm tones, 'All right Vernon, you've insulted me now. It's time to go.'

'I insulted you earlier too; I want that to be taken into account as well Mr ...' He didn't complete the sentence, let it hang in the air for a while, then rounded it off with one of his own vituperative coinages, '... beefy fatface.'

The other barman came over, in a show of solidarity. By now all of the dozen or so drinkers had turned from the stage to watch the conflict. The first barman, with a hefty fist, delivered an almighty blow to Lexicon's stomach and he keeled over at once. Oscar stared in horror, revolted by this show of brutality. Someone in the audience whispered, 'Is this one of the acts?'

'Hey ... that's going too far ... please stop,' Oscar pleaded.

He was surprised when the barman snapped back, 'It's out of your hands, sir.'

Lexicon was writhing around like an agonized fetus.

'Please ... don't hit him again. He really didn't mean anything, I mean – '

'This isn't your problem anymore. This man has insulted me. I have to teach him a lesson. You don't understand, sir; this man is a disease; he poisons the air; in his presence things go bad; I've seen it happen time and again. Couples can be having a lovely time; he'll get talking to them; within minutes the couple's at each other's throats; he's managed to turn them against one another. He picks fights out of nothing; he lives to destroy. Enough is enough. He has to be taught a lesson.'

The barman's pedagogic impulses kicked in by way of his boot, and Lexicon yelled in pain, scorching, blood-clotting pain. Oscar, desperate to make him stop, started muttering something about his influence and importance and how he could make life very difficult for the establishment if he wanted to. At this the barman stopped short and took note. From the floor the poet admitted defeat, his words enmeshed with flying globules of saliva.

'All right – you – savages – you – goddamn philistines – I'm licked,' he spluttered. 'Mighty Caesar is fallen – you've – managed to bring down – the only good man – in the room. I, who have more creativity in my little finger than ... oh ... just ... fuck it ...' After a period of stillness, during which he was gathering his energies, the poet got to his feet and, foolishly, tried throwing a punch at Oscar. Oscar easily eluded him and Lexicon thrashed about madly, blurting out shrieks and squeals of frustration while the barmen held him back. He was dragged off in a tight diagonal, his legs refusing to walk, his boots squeaking across the matted floor. As he was thrown out he screamed in a tremendous voice, a voice which would haunt Oscar during the coming weeks, a voice scarcely human, 'IT SHOULD HAVE BEEN ME, BABEL! NOT YOU, IT SHOULD HAVE BEEN ME! YOU'RE FINISHED BABEL! YOU'RE FINISHED!!' His final word lasted for the best part of five seconds, and seemed to reverberate around the walls afterwards.

After a few minutes whatever ambience the bar had was recovered and the acts staggered on. Oscar felt badly shaken. He had another drink – a double whiskey – and was offered a cigarette by the more placid of the barmen which he smoked in brooding calm, his face blank and inscrutable. One or two people looked over in his direction but, finding nothing to encourage an approach, turned away.

Eventually he finished his drink and left. He walked quickly, his hands thrust deep into his pockets, his face turned down for fear of being recognized again, huddled into himself, as though he was trying to shrink, like a hedgehog curling into a ball. He felt a great desire to walk; to work out of his body and mind the agitation and confusion currently ruling them; to find some calm through the agency of aching legs and feet.

After nearly two hours of walking around he came to Sloane Square and sat down, a solitary figure in the middle of the square. Here and there buses were being boarded. Otherwise, there was little going on. He looked up into a sulfurous sky. This seemed to do him good, as the immersion in its emptiness freed his mind of the thoughts hounding him. But the moon was tired, a faded actress who gives the same performance night after night.

At last he began the walk back to the hotel. As he walked, more evenly and calmly than before, he peered up at the figures coming to meet him. Some were clutching each other happily, figures who seemed to have assumed an animalistic state of simplicity, mere strands of life, floating through his field of vision. Others were gripped by a nocturnal unease, anxious for the resumption of the sleep from which they had never truly awakened.

When at last he arrived at the glittering lobby of the hotel his mind was utterly drained of thought. He rode up to the tenth floor, unlocked his door, scrambled into bed, and fell asleep immediately.

# 21

Address: http://www.oscarbabel.com

19 August 200-

HOME | ARTICLES | IMAGES | ABOUT

## WELCOME TO THE OSCAR BABEL HOMEPAGE!

**<<Somewhere in eternity buses carry free-floating souls across the ages, depositing them like nuggets of gold>>**

**Oscar's tweet of the week**
I observe politicians in the same way
in which I monitor the movement of ants in the sand.

Oscar Babel currently has 576,987 followers on **Twitter.**

**Opinion** > HomePage > Imagures Transcripts > Public
Appearances > Recent Articles > Photographs

From what I gather I think Oscar Babel might be a good role model for young people. He doesn't smoke or drink; he's fit and he has very optimistic views on love. He could provide an interesting alternative to pop stars and politicians and thankfully lacks the former's unintelligibility and the latter's hypocrisy.

*Mark Armistice,*
*New Mills, Derbyshire*

Oscar Babel is such a moral coward that he will only air his views via film, not in the flesh. He is what our age deserves – a banal, mediocre cipher.

*Name withheld*

I admire Oscar Babel because of his normal, unsensational, honest, simple approach to life. My only criticism: he should say something about animal welfare.

*Nicola Snodgrass,*
*Hampshire*

If i had a kitten i will call it Oscar.

*Hattie Turnbull, London, aged 7*

**e-mail. ryanrees@oscarbabel.com**

Recent Articles
1-10 of 227/next

## "Just Who Does Oscar Babel Think He Is?"

The New Forum Jeremy P. Zouffler

"I was tucking into a plate of *pâté de fois gras* the other day ..."


## Art Attack: Diary 9 August

"Oscar Babel likened the art world to a bloody supermarket ..."


## 'A New Kind of Celebrity'; The New Statesman.

"The ubiquitous, insidious Ryan Rees, who has a finger in every soggy ..."


## "Does Oscar Babel take hallucinogenic drugs?"

Big Papa Scream/Wolf "Bunsen" Burner

"In order to qualify as a guru you have to talk to sycamore trees ..."


## "Hats off, gentlemen, a genius!"

The Times /Quentin Verrico-Smith

"Question: What do the London underground, the Duchamp Prize ..."


## "Is Babel Sound?"

Financial Times

"Kazooi-Template, noted for their unconventional advertising ..."

### "The Great Pretender"
The Observer/ Stronz O. Rebellato
"I was picking up my dry cleaning the other day, a dinner jacket ..."


### "The Social Significance of Oscar Babel"
*by* Lucretia Juniper Peretz
Essays in Evaluation (E. I. E.)
"De Quincey saw the Rameses II bust as personifying opium reverie ..."


### "Babel - does he prefer red or white wine?"
www. hallo!weirdguru. com
"They say he could levitate, but never after heavy meals ..."


### "The Final Inglorious Bellyflop is upon us"
M magazine Leo Khak Marenbonn
"I shall be using three words a lot during the course of this article ..."

**Essays in Evaluation**

www. eie. com/lit
of 2

page 2

So, in conclusion, what do we see when we see Oscar Babel? Is it not, as the French would say, *tout le monde*? In this frazzled world of ours; in this motor-neuron frenzy, this image-battery of inanition; this moisturizing, corporate, pummeling, thrashing octopus we are all being sucked up by, is he a speck of substance in the sea of alienation bequeathed by our forefathers (God and art and love are dead, long live TV and gherkins)? Here is the innocent as leader, matinee-idol as soothsayer, seer. Convergence of the meditative and public, confessional and devotional. Of course Mr Babel is a shrewd, astute operator, NOT an ingenue at all; and his recondite, esoteric, abstruse brilliance is the flip side of street acumen. Of course there will always be intellectuals, but will they also be at the center of vibrant, vital debates? Or just scribbling their yellowing tomes in libraries like so many stiffs? Like the Marlovian overreacher, Babel dares to look at the stars, to be percussive in his loftiness. The swirling words of the Imagures, interested in assiduous transfiguration, the tendentious cause which is wrapped in the clingfilm of modern, slick video art – a good trick this, Oscar, to introduce your serious pearls with some sleight of hand sensationalism (beginning with the Duchamp prize formula: a troublemaker gets media attention, on the back of that gets profound); you're a sniper who shoots from the hills since you know you'll be lost in the commodious fields. Do we not see Sisyphus fighting a losing battle? But is there not something heroic in the glorious attempt? Or Orpheus in the underworld – which is the overworld, our world populated with predatory, perfidious turpitude (soon to be turned into a motion picture). Oscar Babel, knowing that his own perceptions constitute the Alpha and Omega of experience. Marmoreal, mass-produced newspeak is our unfortunate birthright, so we must needs have, within the bounds of what is communicable, (the world as the temporally ambiguous motorway, great rolling landscapes exploded for the sake of convenience) the simple, rustic warbling of the farmer, the authentic accents of the mystic, the child who is father to the man, and Babel, in his self-consciously imagistic cell (uloid), daring us to get the hell out of ours.

Lucretia Peretz lives in London and holds two PhDs, one in Media Studies and the other in Victorian women's undergarments from the University of Wisconsin. She is the author of *Can We Have Knights as well as Dragons in the Modern World?* (Horton University Press) She does not like anchovies.

Opinion > HomePage > Imagures Transcripts > Public Appearances > **Recent Articles** > Photographs

**Facebook   Gadoo   Twitter   Godblog   Bogoff   Blotdrop Vagtalk   Deepfluff**

# 22

On 27 August, eight days later, Bloch was admitted to hospital.

Webster, who had been living in his van ever since he had moved out of Bloch's flat, had decided to check up on him, since the phone was never answered whenever he rang.

He was let into the building by one of Bloch's neighbors, climbed the stairs and hammered on Bloch's front door.

Nothing.

He knocked once more and was on the point of giving up when some unidentifiable feeling told him to persist. Then he heard what sounded like gurgling sounds coming from within. He rushed downstairs and found the porter and explained the situation. Luckily, he had a spare set of keys. They clambered up and the porter was able to let them both in.

Inside it smelled as if someone had died.

And the flat looked like burglars had left moments before, having violently rifled through everything in a search for plunder. Clothes were everywhere, every receptacle's contents had been upended and tossed across the floor. They looked in the kitchen, the study, the bedroom. They found Bloch lying in the empty bathtub, dressed in disgustingly dirty pyjamas which had glued themselves to his skin. He was emaciated, cracked: a shadow of a man. Since Webster had last seen him he had lost two-and-a-half stone. He had a week's stubble, his eyes were sunken; they transmitted no light. His cheek bones jutted out, and his skin was discolored and dry. His voice was squeaky and feeble. When they took off his pyjama top and made him put on a fresh one Webster could see the sharp outline of his ribs. He looked like some brittle, snappable bird.

Webster went for a glass of water. The kitchen, without his guiding hand, had gone to pot. The floor was scattered with broken bits of cork, bread, and tissue paper. In the sink piled-up plates were stuck together by decaying food. Strands of spaghetti clung to the wall, the color of mud. The washing machine was stuffed with scrawled and ripped sheets of paper. The wallpaper was peeling, the floor matting was peeling. Bloch was peeling.

From the bathtub Bloch wheezed pitifully, 'I was oppressing mind ... body ... with fasting ... to be bodiless. No more yes to dreary world ... timeless reality ... that's what I want.'

Webster forced him to eat a slice of bread, whereupon Bloch threw up all over the bathroom tiles. He took some water afterwards and managed to keep it down.

During the previous week all he had eaten was a cup of brown rice. The bed was showered with brown rice. On opening the drawers of Bloch's dresser to find clean clothes they found brown rice.

He thought he was renouncing the world, but he was renouncing himself.

Webster said, 'We have to get you to hospital. Can you walk?'

'No – no doctors ... fine. I just need ... to lie down.'

'You are lying down.'

'No ... in bed.'

With a superhuman effort he got up out of the bath, staggered to the bedroom and collapsed onto the bed.

'Bloch, there's no way you're staying here. For God's sake, you're ill, very ill. I'm driving you to Charing Cross Hospital; that's not far.'

'No, no ... not taking orders, you don't understand ... finally being set free. No more maya for me.'

'No more what?'

'Maya. Illusion. Now ... I can soar.'

'I'm not sure what you're on about, but you're coming with me.'

For perhaps the first time in his life Webster was authoritative, dominant. He instructed the porter to grab Bloch's feet and he took his shoulders and together they carried him into the living room. Bloch was too weak to resist, but as they trudged along he croaked, 'Hey, not an ox, where you taking? Steady, still got a bod ... Wait, keys, get my keys, in bedroom. On table ... get tape machine too ... tapes.' So they set him down on the sofa. Webster darted back to the bedroom, found the items, stuffed them in his pockets and took hold of Bloch once more.

Since he was so light it was easy to carry him down the three flights. They set him down inside the van, on Webster's mattress, next to his boxes of Japanese Arita porcelain. Webster started the engine, thanked the porter profusely and drove off, soon hitting the van's maximum speed of thirty-five miles an hour.

Webster persuaded one of the hospital porters to get him a wheel-chair, a rather retrograde affair under which three small wheels swiveled frantically in their brackets, and into this Bloch was installed, feeling extremely dizzy and ill. Webster wheeled him round to Accident and Emergency. They zig-zagged along, the chair apparently reluctant to cede control of its own destiny. But at last Webster guided Bloch into a harshly lit waiting area full of hordes of anxious people. As Webster explained the situation to the woman manning the reception, a stretcher was wheeled in and he caught glimpses of a face capped by an oxygen mask. Then doctors, stethoscopes and exhaustion hanging from them, rushed in and the stretcher was wheeled away. When things had calmed down Webster was told Bloch would have to wait for approximately two-and-a-half hours.

During the wait Bloch kept saying he wanted to leave, and that he felt fine. But at last his name was called and Webster wheeled him into a consulting cubicle. He was deposited onto a level surface, a curtain was drawn and he was left there on his own. After a while the triage nurse arrived, took one look at him, and realized he was critically ill.

'I'm terribly sorry you've had to wait so long, but we're under-staffed.'

'It's OK ... there's no time where I am.'

She stared at him, slightly puzzled by his remark, took his pulse, asked about his medical history, examined his mouth and gums, shone a light into his eyes and ears and tested his reflexes which were virtually non-existent. She sent him next door for a blood test. A hypodermic syringe was forced into three separate veins, none of which offered up any blood. Finally, a small jarful of blood was drained from the fourth vein. He was weighed, and given an electrocardiogram because when asked he admitted to having chest pains. Then a registrar, a packet of *Gitanes* cigarettes stuffed inside his coat's top pocket, appeared and asked Bloch some questions about his diet. Bloch told him he just didn't feel hungry, and wasn't interested in food anymore.

How long was it since he'd eaten a square meal?

'Can't remember ... maybe three weeks. But I had some rice ... the other day. After those first couple of weeks you really ... I really ... lost interest. Didn't want food.'

Had he been taking fluids?

'Yes ... lime juice, camomile tea ... lashings of black coffee, but ... I'm not really ... I'm just ... I've no time for trivia ... if you get my drift. All the peacocks have ruffled feathers.'

The registrar thought Bloch was in an advanced stage of anorexia. He went up to the desk and asked the nurse to see if she could find a free bed. He knew that if Bloch wasn't put on a drip immediately his condition would deteriorate very rapidly and he feared kidney failure or worse. As it turned out a patient had just been moved from the Ely Wing on the 3rd Floor to intensive care and his bed was now free. The registrar explained that Bloch was in a very privileged position: not only was there a bed free, but a private room as well. He started getting argumentative and bolshy. Webster begged and pleaded with the doctor to admit Bloch. The doctor explained that under the Mental Health Act in severe cases such as his, compulsory treatment could be enforced. He didn't want to have to force him to be admitted, however, and would rather Bloch agreed of his own volition.

Bloch asked Webster where he was living. Webster told him: inside his van.

'I suppose if I ... if I ... you could ... would it be good for you if ...'

'Don't worry about me Bloch; you come first. Don't worry about me. Just get into that bed so you can get better.'

'You can have the flat; here, reach inside for my ...'

'It's all right; I've got the keys here. You're sure? That's – '

'OK, doc, take me to the sick ... But I'm only going so Webster can have my gaff ... and I won't eat ... I won't ... I have to be ... pure mind.'

Webster said he would be in to see him tomorrow but had to go now. He left Bloch's tape recorder with the nurse. As he trotted back to his van, he clutched Bloch's keys tightly in his pocket, feeling badly shaken.

On the third floor the lift's doors snapped open and Bloch was wheeled through another set of doors and then another. He had to wait for a porter to come and lift him onto a bed. The porter helped him into a gown. He rested on the bed for awhile until a young nurse appeared – she looked at Bloch earnestly, and gave him a glucose solution to drink which he took without resistance. She said, 'Now then, what's the matter with you?'

'Oh well ... you know ... this and that. I'm up for auction.'

'I'm going to take your temperature, pulse and blood pressure.'

'They did all that downstairs.'

'I know, but I have to check again.' She stuck a thermometer under his tongue and rolled a black band around his arm and inflated it.

Afterwards her manner changed slightly; she frowned, then mumbled, 'I don't really understand this ... I can't seem to find your pulse. This is absolutely unbelievable. Your systolic is 60 and the diastolic is 25. That's the lowest blood pressure I've ever seen.'

'I don't need to eat. I really don't. It's fine. I'm feeling better now. I'll have some water if it's going. I've been drinking loads and loads of coffee.'

'But you're just skin and bone; listen to your voice, it's all squeaky. Now that's not right, is it? And your skin, it's dry and flaky; there's no color in your eyes. You know we'd all feel a lot better about you if you let us put a drip up.'

'Well ... why?'

'If we don't ... there's no real why about it ... we just have to ...'

'Let me speak to the ...'

Just then the sister arrived and conferred with the nurse; they went aside for a moment.

Then the house doctor appeared, the nurse and sister retreated, and the doctor said in a very sympathetic tone of voice, 'Now, if we don't put the drip up, there's a very good chance that – '

'All right, all right, do it, do it. Just stop being so nice to me!'

He instructed the nurses to prepare a solution of protein, carbohydrates, fat, vitamins and minerals.

They fitted the drip and left him to rest.

Later on that evening the results of the tests came through and they established he had no malignant or organic disease suppressing his appetite; that he was deficient in zinc, thiamin, calcium, and magnesium; was anaemic, severely dehydrated, and that his liver wasn't functioning properly. His stomach had shrunken to half its size. Unless such time as he could resume eating properly he would have to stay in the hospital.

The next day Bloch's condition had stabilized somewhat and the danger of kidney failure had receded, though he still refused food. He was given a blanket bath. At lunch-time he was visited by a dietician whose reasonable, sedate voice explained that he had to eat something, anything, as it was very important to get his digestive system and bowels working again. His brain was not functioning as it should have been. Bloch told him fasting was an ancient and honorable pursuit, practiced by saints, mystics and martyrs. After much cajoling he agreed to have a mixed salad and when it eventually came he ate a few lettuce leaves and half a carrot but because his system had been starved of food for so long he vomited again.

The dietician gave him a glass of milk and Bloch drank it slowly through a straw. This made him feel sick. Bloch asked if he was allowed to walk around the ward but the nurse told him he was far too weak. Once he began eating properly again he could walk as much as he liked.

In the afternoon the nurse arrived with a boiled egg and two slices of toast and left it for Bloch to eat in his own time. As he stared at the egg's small, brown, dome he thought about how, when he was small, he would love to cut the toast up into thin strips and dip them, carefully, lovingly, into the rich texture of the egg yolk. Then, as he stared at the egg, lying there in the bed, in the unfamiliar ward, attached to the drip, drifting through the vacuum of time, the memory receded into the past not of this life but of some other, perpetually hazy one which he had long ago inhabited. He whacked a spoon down onto the head of the egg, scooped up some albumen and rammed it into his mouth. This left him exhausted. And the egg felt extremely salty and invasive, as if it was a piece of paper or plastic. With an effort he swallowed the offending fragment and he felt it move, a pellet of intrusion, down his gullet, laboriously forging a path through his shriveled, waterless throat, down into the empty steel barrel which was his stomach.

Later on he had a visit from Dr. Kendall, the liaison psychiatrist. Dr. Kendall looked rather lost and one or two of the nurses asked him if he needed any help. Eventually he found his way to Bloch's bay. On the bald dome of his head there were a few sun spots. His eyes were knitted and creased in sympathy; they had bags under them which seemed to be the direct result of a lifetime spent listening to other people's problems. Dr. Kendall knocked on the door, stepped in, dragged a chair over to the bed, sat down and stared at Bloch intently.

'Hello, Daniel, how are you feeling today? They tell me that when you were brought in you were terribly ill.' His voice was friendly and surprisingly reassuring.

'I am not Daniel; that name no longer has any meaning for me. I have no name; I require no names. The region I currently inhabit is free of such tired trifles.'

Dr Kendall thought: negative symptoms, psychotic ideation.

'What would you like me to call you then?'

'No names.'

'Well, I have a name and it is Dr Kendall and I'd like to find out a little bit about why you seem to have lost your appetite. The house doctor is terribly worried about you, you know.'

'Pipe down, I'm not deaf; everything is very loud and clear; terrible clarity, as if I'm in 70 mill.'

Dr Kendall had a pencil and pad with him and he jotted down some notes. Bloch stared at him with peculiar hostility when his face was turned towards his notepad. When Kendall looked up again Bloch was all smiles.

'I see. How old are you, by the way?'

'As old as I feel.'

'And how do you feel?'

'Timeless.'

Dr. Kendall let out an exhausted sigh.

'Are you trying to scare us with this hunger strike, Daniel?'

'No, no, let me explain, I have no further use for the external world of objects, of petty comings and goings. I am rejecting all that is not eternal. I am developing my *moksha*. Surely as a doctor you must see the value of trying to join the great river?'

'I'm afraid I'm not sure what you mean ... would you mind terribly – '

'The river, the pulse, the cosmic, the electric. I leave the living to him.'

'The living to who? Would you mind explaining a little more what you ...?'

'Wormy.'

'And who is Wormy?'

'That's top secret, but I will say this. Wormy is the great disaster of my life, but he means nothing more to me now and there is nothing more he could hope to beg from me. The thing is I have achieved a transcendence men like you only dream of. Why do you think mystics don't eat? Because they have mental freedom as a result. It's simpler that way.'

Dr Kendall stared at Bloch in some agitation, feeling that his remarks had an edge of insight mixed up with more obscure references. It was disconcerting.

'Daniel, what do you feel can be gained by refusing to eat?'

'A soul, perhaps. Let me explain. I used to write books, formulaic books. They said nothing; they were tricks, manipulations. I decided to try and think a little, to meditate a little, to calm down ... And I find that ... I find that ...'

Kendall continued to scribble. In irritation Bloch said, 'Do you have to make notes? Are we not just having a friendly chat?'

'Yes, of course, if you prefer. But I have to say that your state of mind is not ... can I be frank ...? Would you mind telling me if ... have you been experiencing any hallucinations, aural or olfactory; that's to say – '

'I began to see that the only way out was to become transcendent, to achieve luminosity, to cut through all the junk we are fed, literally and metaphorically, you see. I am not mad, despite all appearances to the contrary. Do I have to stay here? Can't I go back to my flat?'

'I'm afraid you can't leave as we don't feel you're able to look after yourself at the moment ... you pose a definite threat to yourself – '

'I can leave if I want to.'

'If you decide to leave we might have to take other measures, we may have to have you sectioned.'

'Sectioned? What section? Section 22B, paragraph 13?'

'No, put into a mental institution. But before we could do that of course you would need to be seen by two social workers and two doctors officially recognized by – '

'Social workers! Social workers! Get me anti-social workers! Or get me hermits and anchorites; they'll understand! Get me outcasts. Why do you come here to talk rubbish to me? Look, I tell you what, Dr Kennel, if you're a nut doctor, why don't you go and see all the nuts?'

Disregarding this, Dr Kendall continued, 'The thing is, if you continue to abstain from food we may be forced to initiate force-feeding. It's a last resort, of course.'

'Oh? That sounds jolly.'

'It's ... I can assure you it's not.'

'What happens there then, Dr Kennel?'

'It's *Kendall*; my name is Kendall. Force-feeding involves ... well ... a gastric tube is inserted through the nose or mouth ... a nutritional solution is fed in, consisting of minerals and amino acids, and other substances. It wouldn't be very nice.' In part Dr. Kendall was trying to scare Bloch into eating when he said this – he knew that rapid re-feeding carried with it the risk of cardiac failure and was at the best of times considered highly controversial.

'Do you imagine this drip is very pleasant? I can't sleep because of it.'

'Force feeding is substantially more – '

'Look. I have no appetite. Yes, about a few weeks back I did crave food, but then, after a couple of weeks of zilch I craved no more and I felt empowered as a result. Can't I get it through to you that I'm not eating because I am penetrating a supreme reality; I am achieving a transparency of vision?'

Kendall wrote: *Patient is showing signs of autoscopic hallucination, he talks of a heightened sensibility. Whether this is due simply to starvation or something else is debatable.*

'Daniel, I think under the circumstances I am going to have to say something you might not be very pleased to hear: I think your state of mind at the moment is delusional. Normally I would prescribe drugs to treat this, but this would be hazardous, given the delicacy of your condition. But we have to get you eating again. The drips will provide nourishment but you must try and take a little food. The drip on its own isn't a substitute for the consumption of three square meals a day. If you – '

'Eeeeeh! I couldn't possibly,' he whimpered pitifully. 'My stomach's tiny; I'd explode.'

'But if you don't eat regular meals, if you just rely on the drip, all sorts of things will continue to go wrong with you. You're already anaemic; your red blood count is very low. The drip is deceptive; it provides nourishment and rehydrates the body, but it can't stop weight loss. You really have to eat proper, healthy meals. Just ask the nurse for anything you feel like. Now I think you should rest for a little. I'll come and see you tomorrow.'

'I don't want to eat. I don't want to eat! You can't make me. You're wasting your breath on me! I don't want you to come and see me. I'm attaining a higher plane.'

'Let's say you are, Daniel. But the world's on a lower plane, isn't it? Or at least it's full of rough and tumble and imperfections and messiness.'

'Don't even think about it. I won't be drawn into a philosophical debate.'

'You must learn to live in the world; you must engage with it as I'm sure you have done, very well, in the past. You must come down to earth, so to speak.'

'This all sounds familiar and I used to spout such stuff myself. Oh yes, I did it very well in the past. You'll be bringing up mortgages and golf next. That's right, try and make the world seem hospitable, ordered, friendly; try and make us all think we have our place in it, that everything is as it should be. Oh, what's the use; he's doing the living for me. Have you no vision, man; do you think all can be explained rationally? There are more things in heaven and earth than are dreamt of ... forget it. I'm surrounded with pen-pushers and bureaucrats.'

Dr. Kendall very quietly withdrew his chair and said, 'I'll come and see you tomorrow. In the meantime try and eat something. The food here isn't bad.'

'"The food here isn't bad,"' Bloch mimicked. 'Is that all you have to say?'

Dr. Kendall put his hand out and tried to shake Bloch's. But he withdrew into the bed like a frightened spider.

'No thanks; risk of infection, you see,' he mumbled from under the covers.

'Very well. Until tomorrow.'

Dr. Kendall walked off, perturbed, considering once again the strange quality of Bloch's remarks and the fact that they had a grain of truth in them which, try as he might, he could not now erase from his mind. But Bloch's "asceticism" was so pronounced as to be pointing towards death. And Dr Kendall feared that was the only thing which would satisfy him now.

He pulled out his digital voice recorder and mumbled into it as he trotted along the corridors, oppressive with the smell of disinfectant.

'The patient is clearly suffering from anorexia nervosa. It is difficult to tell whether his condition is primarily psychotic. Although the patient is able to talk reasonably fluently his body shows all the signs of inanition. He is clearly anaemic. It is also difficult to tell to what extent his negative features are innate. There is evidence of schizoid ideation as well and some indications of mania; namely, irritability and flight of ideas. I am undecided about what would be the best course of treatment for him. Clearly he needs to eat something. If he insists on refusing to take food orally the question of force feeding may arise but it is likely that he would have to be sectioned first. His ego appears to be in a state of flux, and I detect some evidence of an identity crisis; this does not, however, appear to extend to his sexuality. On trying to shake the patient's hand he recoiled. Obviously the thought of physical contact alarms him. He must start eating again, but I fear we will have great difficulty in persuading him to take anything by mouth.'

# 23

A week earlier Donald Inn had to make an important phone call. He toned up the poshness of his voice by several notches.

'Yes, I believe you've already spoken to my associate Mr Ryan Rees. I'm ringing in regard to the showcase event to take place in Kensington Gardens on 28 August of this year.'

'Yes, I have your details. Now. I have to scan through copies of the Health and Safety conditions – vis-a-vis materials deemed safe, the non-viability of certain kinds of plastic, which, when melted emit toxic fumes; these conditions will have to be met of course by your contractors who will also need to be approved officially, but we can go into that later. You do know, of course, that the Events Office of the Royal Parks Agency will not only require payment of the hire fee in two installments – that's £30,000 in sterling in total for hire of the gardens from 9 am to midnight on 28 August of this year – but a percentage of any profits which will go towards upkeep of the park and the Royal Bursary?'

'What percentage?'

'Twelve percent precisely.'

'Yes, that's fine. Now, about the public indemnity insurance – can you – '

'Yes – now – the name of the broker is John Smallcorn, I believe. Can you confirm I have that right?'

'Yes.'

'With Higgle, Hacking & Hereford?'

'Yes.'

'And you have drawn up a policy to cover accidental injury of any member of the audience by faulty seating or collision with any equipment or any other cause, collapsed, rusty seating – '

'We won't require any seat –'

'Which might lead to infection, gangrene, necessitating amputation of limbs, etc.; faulty sound and light equipment; freak weather conditions such as an electrical storms, hurricanes, tornadoes, earthquakes, sandstorms – no we can disregard the latter – hence, electrical storms, hurricanes, tornadoes, earthquakes; acts of subversive terrorism from terrorists; and, last but not least, sonic bangs, that's to say damaging pressure waves caused by aircraft traveling at sonic or supersonic speeds passing over the gardens at those times they shall be in use?'

'Yes.'

'I shall need to see a copy of the relevant Schedule of Insurance asap to confirm that everything is in order. You can send me a copy or drop one round at your earliest convenience.'

'My secretary can drop one round.'

'That's fine. He or she will need to go to the Old Police House in Hyde Park. Your policy provides cover for a projected maximum audience of how many?'

'3,000.'

'3,000. Once the insurance policy has been deemed to be in order I shall send you a copy of the contract of hire and once that's all up and running can you make a copy and send me back the original asap? Good. Then all that's left is for you to hire appropriate contractors. They must be officially approved by the British Contractors' League. British League-approved contractors' equipment, seating and lights all come with IS safety seals. We'll need to see copies of said seals and only then will you be allowed to go ahead with setting up light and sound systems and anything else you require. The area you have requested for hire – the square whose uppermost tip is near the Statue of Physical Energy – will be cordoned off three days before the event. I trust that is satisfactory.'

'That all seems fine.'

'I believe you have budgeted for half houses.'

'That's correct.'

'Could you also furnish me with three copies of said budget as it currently stands, and the breakdown of ticket prices. As I said earlier, the hire fee is to be paid in two installments, half prior to, the rest after the event. You may, if you wish, have the option of paying the second half within a week after the event so as to recoup ticket sales – which will give you time for cheques to clear and so forth. And can I remind you of the 12% profit percentage which the parks agency will require from all profits. And other profits are rightfully yours or your organization's, I should say. Which reminds me, can you confirm that you are a registered charity?'

'Yes.'

'And you are known as The O. Babel Showcase?'

'Yes.'

'And can you confirm that you do not require any licensed vans, trucks, or booths for the sale of alcoholic beverages, soft drinks or foodstuffs?'

'Yes.'

'And can you confirm that once the event is over any scaffolding or seating or lights or equipment, including sound and lightning booths, tents or control towers, and generators will be removed before midnight.'

'Yes.'

'I realize of course this is all clearly stated on the contract but it's as well to go through it all on the phone, don't you agree Mr Inn?'

'I agree.'

'Well, Mr Inn, I shall await the contract and may I wish you and your event the best of luck.'

'You may.'

*

Inn toned down the poshness of his voice by several notches.

'Ashby Concert Contractors.'

'Hello, this is Donald Inn. Can I speak to Mr. Corby?'

'Speaking.'

'Ah, Mr Corby, I'm ringing about The O. Babel Showcase to take place in Kensington Gardens. Did you get my fax?'

'Yes, I have it here. Though the second page hasn't come out. Could you send it through again?'

Donald Inn turned round and called through, 'Sharon, can you send the fax to Corby at Ashby Contractors through again, but don't mention it to RR.

'Fax is on its way, Mr Corby; so if you and your men can be there at 9 am sharp on 28 August. As you know, there are several entrances to the gardens on Bayswater Road and there are maps situated there. The park manager – Mr Nathan Griggs – will be waiting for you at the Statue of Physical Energy; that area will be sealed off for your convenience and you'll have the whole day to fix things up. You're sure that's enough time?'

'Oh, yee-ees, Mr Inn, more than enough; after all Mr Rees requested something pretty basic; just a stage with a radio mike, a basic PA and sound booth with cables, amplifiers and six follow spots which may or may not be used depending on light, and one or two states for the lights and the lighting and sound desks.'

'Now, Mr Corby, you are certain you'll have enough time to set things up?'

'It should be all right, Mr Inn. But I should just ask again – in regard to seating arrangements – you just want cushions and a ground sheet, is that right? How come you're not going for tiered seating?'

'No ground sheet either. Mr Babel wants it to be very simple, modest. Just cushions and grass.'

'How many are you hoping for?'

'Three thousand.'

'Three thousand! Christ, you might as well hire the bleeding Royal Albert Hall.'

'Can't. The Proms are on.'

\*

Tickets were sold over the internet; adverts placed in all the broadsheets; flyers sent off to everyone who had ever come into Ryan Rees's orbit – journalists, artists, concert promoters, critics, writers. Within hours posters appeared along the Great Western, Westbourne Park, Talgarth and Portobello Roads. Flyers were dropped off in university cafes, at performance venues, left in phone booths, slid under front doors in Notting Hill, Bayswater, Chelsea, Kennington and Shoreditch, stuffed under cars' windscreen wipers. The timing couldn't really have been better – columnists were still writing about Oscar; the internet was swelling with opinions and speculation about him; the texts of the Imagures were being avidly consumed. Even some of the tabloids carried pieces – interviews with his detractors.

As yet Oscar had never actually spoken in front of a sizable audience. His early appearances had been for the television cameras; the Duchamp Prize hadn't been available to the general public; the Imagures were for a few select journalists. It was precisely the fact that Oscar had, until now, been perceived through an elliptical prism which made him such a tantalizing figure. So, although people had been reading about him, seeing his photograph in papers, on the internet, though he was already a fixture in the public's consciousness he still smacked of something fabular. He had about him a touch of the Abominable Snowman or the Loch Ness monster – he was thought to exist but perhaps only in a mythical, inaccessible realm. How many people had really heard his famed eloquence in the flesh? Now there was the chance to be given solid proof that this orator really existed. This factor, allied to an interest in Oscar's philosophy and the promise of a better world liberated from the empire of suffering and conflict, combined to make the public curious. But beyond any of these explanations for the fact that all three thousand tickets were sold there was another phenomenon at work. While commentators dismissed him as lightweight, superficial, bogus, the public found that the intelligentsia's readiness to pour scorn on Oscar naturally awakened their sympathy for him, so he came to embody not only a sense of otherworldly elusiveness but at the same time assumed the mantle of the heroic underdog, who may be being lambasted but nevertheless has a hearty audience cheering him on.

*

The day after the lecture, which was a wild success, Rees planned to approach the Verdant Theater with a view to using it as a venue for Oscar to speak at regularly. He was on friendly terms with the Artistic Director. Oscar's presence in the garden, through ticket sales at £20 a ticket, had recouped the cost of the hire fee, the insurance, and the publicity had in fact, against the odds, made a healthy profit in the region of £45,000. This augured well for the hire of the Verdant Theater, especially since the latter's hire fee was a fragment of the garden's. Arnold Bateman, his sly accountant, had calculated that the amounts they stood to make were potentially vast, assuming they could get half houses for a three-week period. Rees viewed any future profits in terms of their paying back the money he had already lavished on his product. He also knew that it was highly likely he would make much more than the expenses he had accumulated to date. In addition, hefty offers from car firms for TV adverts and six-figure advances from publishing houses were thrown Oscar's way directly after the bizarre triumph of Kensington Gardens.

He went up to Oscar's hotel suite with Edwin, his stocky henchman, and told him to wait outside. He was clutching half a dozen newspapers which all had pieces discussing last night's lecture.

Rees was feeling unreservedly euphoric. He felt like he was at school again, ruling the roost, undermining the system. He knocked on the door and didn't wait for an answer.

*

Before the lecture, in the afternoon, Oscar didn't feel particularly nervous. He rehearsed his speech a few times until it was all right. He listened to *Tristan* in the dark. In a way he wanted the lecture to go badly, as though a disaster would finally free him, allow him to get off this merry go-round which continued to spin as a result of the agencies of Ryan Rees. Bloch's words had given him the strength to mount the carousel in the first place, when it was still stationary. Rees had caused it to spin at a sickening speed. He could only get off now by being pushed off.

A week earlier Oscar had asked Rees to get in touch with Cressida again, the designer from "Cherubs and Co." He had decided he now quite liked the idea of wearing something theatrical and grand. Perhaps there lay behind this a subtle interest in ridiculing himself or the event.

Cressida rolled into the suite just as she had rolled in before, but this time she was less agitated, less talkative. She was dressed in blue, not purple, but once again the color was everywhere – on her leggings, shirt, skirt, headband, eyelids. She still had her inaudible laugh. She took Oscar's measurements; together they came up with ideas. Oscar told her he didn't want to look like a clergyman or like the Bedouin or to wear a Russian carpet. They hit on something mutually agreeable and she said she would come up with it in time for the lecture.

In the end she delivered a gold tunic which reached to his knees and was made of jaspé cloth, a sturdy fabric with a woven texture. Its collar was studded with transparent blue sapphires, creating an effect of great splendor. On his feet he wore decorated sandals.

When Oscar tried the tunic on Cressida and her assistant surged around him like the billowing petticoats of a Victorian lady, making tiny adjustments. They almost swooned because he looked so striking and regal in it. Oscar spent a few vain moments admiring himself in the mirror. He felt the curves of his torso brought out in its tight, and yet comfortable, embrace. He felt confident and dignified. Highly-ornamented patterns were woven into the sleeves and these added to the air of gravitas that hung about the tunic and about him when he was inside it.

He looked like some latter-day Roman nobleman or senator.

*

The sun continued to scorch London, even though it was well on the way to dropping out of sight.

Three-thousand people were seated in a dense, tightly-packed circle. Collectively there came from their lips a great froth of conversation: overlapping observations, throwaway remarks, more searching, deeply felt meditations on the best way to de-scale a kettle; how, in making a Caesar salad croutons were not absolutely essential. Someone advised someone else about how she should avoid the sun between the hours of midday and two o'clock while in Kovalam; there was an involved discussion about bicycle pumps; a middle-aged man was trying to persuade another middle-aged man to overcome his fear of sushi; a party of young women was trying to establish whether or not the clerk in their office was a homosexual; a teacher was complaining about the lack of wall clocks in his school; an angler was telling someone about bait; an octogenarian sculptor was going on *ad nauseam* about his infatuation with a French *au pair* girl; a bus driver was describing a spectacular swerve he had had to make to avoid slamming into a locomotive on Praed Street; a mother of two was complaining about her nanny's nose stud; a research assistant was thoroughly boring someone with her thoughts on Swinburne's letters; a backpacker stopping in London for a few days was telling somebody about a mystical experience he had had in Findhorn in Scotland that involved jumping naked into a freezing lake; a young songwriter kept breaking into renditions of "O, Canada" every time his girlfriend brought up the subject of marriage; a general practitioner was recommending the best way of treating oral thrush; a woman was telling another woman about her infatuation with another woman she worked with at Christie's; a priest was telling another priest about lubricants; an anesthetist was confessing that he was more often drunk than not when he administered anesthetics; a journalist was predicting Oscar Babel's downfall.

And so it went on. The diverse crowd, its myriad voices creating fragmented structures of meaning, was shaking and vibrating like a pan on the boil. People were geared up in the expectation of a profound experience. It was a giant picnic but without hampers or food or even flies. Or shoes. People had been instructed to take them off at the gates. They were given tickets as their shoes were packaged into chic little plastic bags (stamped with Oscar's face) and piled into two large tents manned by attendants whose black tee shirts were inscribed with the legend "BABEL IS ABLE!"

From time to time a squirrel darted towards the big trees.

They sat, pressed down on, wriggled around on their cushions and pillows, getting comfortable. From certain quarters the reek of unwashed feet was offered up bounteously to the summer evening.

Seen from above the space comprised a massive circle teeming with people, sealed off with rope. A slotted-together stage forming half an H-shape, about two meters above ground level, pressed heavily into the grass. This stage cut into parts of the audience, a crude pier whose entire length Oscar could utilize if he so desired. Here and there a few sizable oak trees gave those near them some support for their backs. One tree stood somewhat apart from the crowd, just behind the line of rope; it was immense, perhaps five-feet wide, a gnarled, mighty tree carved with hearts and initials and graffiti. Though the evening was still light six follow spots mounted on scaffolding towers were posted around this outdoor auditorium's circumference, aimed at the stage in readiness for the dark. Running alongside them were malignant-looking speakers, and cables fed from them into a raised sound and lighting booth. An enormous, thick cable feeding from the sound booth sloped down past the Albert Memorial, some hundreds of yards off, towards a generator parked opposite the Albert Hall.

Further off, apart from the crowd, there was a caravan; inside it someone was making Oscar up. His hair was gelled back, droplets to make his eyes sparkle and flash were inserted into his corneas. He took a final look at himself in the mirror, made minute adjustments to his charcoal hair. He looked resplendent in his gold tunic and sandals.

He heard words coming from the speakers, spoken by someone in the sound booth.

'Ladies and gentlemen, Mr Oscar Babel.'

He took some deep breaths, stepped outside and was hit by the stultifying heat.

He climbed up the ten or eleven steps to the stage.

Mighty waves of applause crashed into him. What was that for? Then he realized, flabbergasted, that it was for him. He took a few steps forward, faltering. The sapphires in his collar flashed and glittered. Now he was among them the applause showed no signs of subsiding. He peered tentatively into this bed of humanity, filling the air, beaming at him – three-thousand strangers beaming at him. Three-thousand people who had come to see him. He felt a violent rush of nausea, and experienced a strong desire to void his bowels. Panic set in. What if he soiled himself? He feared he might lose control of his limbs, disentangle, become an incontinent wreck squelching around on the stage. He looked at the graffiti tree, trying to draw strength from it; he told himself the feeling would pass. He stared dumbly into the audience. For the public you must feed the tenderest cuts, Bloch had said somewhere. Working quickly his brain clicked and computed and he came up with a related image to hang onto, but before he could focus on it he had the distinct feeling his body was being dragged out into space, wafting over the audience, born aloft on mercury wings, in turn touching each body, passing like a ghost through these, as he thought, transparent entities, receptacles to demonstrate he could pirouette into and around consciousness, that he was gaseous, that he was god-like. Then, as he once more coincided with himself, he noticed again that three thousand people had noticed him; and his face, his form, just another face, just another form, was not just another face or form because he was Oscar Babel, because all this life had come and knocked on his door, this audience had requested an audience with him, because he had supremacy, and the just-retrieved image which sustained him, as megalomania simultaneously inflated him, was that he was a zoo attendant at feeding time, tossing out into this arena slices of meat, and though together the animals were frightening, he had something they wanted – these refugees from the middle classes were turning to him for answers, for guidance and illumination. This idea of himself as a purveyor of nourishment calmed him.

'I feel very honored to be here tonight,' he said, speaking into his radio mike, his voice reverberating with fearful clarity through the speakers.

There were whistles and yells, more applause, this time localized. It was carrying on. They love me. How can they love me when they don't even know me? The flight of reality was locked into an unknown trajectory. But now his nerves had vanished without trace, replaced by insane well-being, reckless nonchalance. He was firing on the electricity the crowd between them had mustered and plugged into his skull.

But then just as he was about to start, without warning, fanfare or introduction, another voice began speaking. It had a faintly American accent and it made unintelligible sounds.

'Swa yala huuuu cur mee. Eeeighhurr e wee ooo wee.'

This eventually gave way to precisely articulated chuckles. There was stunned silence. Heads turned, interrogative glances spread from person to person, eyes goggled. But no one knew where this wax-work laughter was coming from or what was provoking it. When Oscar tried speaking into his microphone he found his voice was no longer amplified. At last the cackling subsided.

'This is what happens when you look for meaning, ladies and gentlemen,' said the voice thickly. 'Darkness falls. Oscar Babel is an impostor and you must not listen to him. He is not noumenal, he is phenomenal. I am noumenal. Don't listen to him. Listen to me; let me take you someplace else. What do you look for? Do you look for a silver lady under a poplar tree? Do you look for a constant friend? A life without end? What do you crave? A stolen kiss? An end to all your pain? I have nothing for you except a – '

The voice got no further. There was a sound of scuffling, some-thing knocked violently against something else, there was a sharp cry of pain and nothing more was heard from Vernon Lexicon, who had managed to creep unnoticed into the sound booth, overpower the technician, take down the fader for Oscar's microphone and bring up the fader for the announcements microphone. At that moment he was receiving another of those ritualistic, savage beatings he had come to know and even love during the course of his troubled life.

Oscar declared, after a pause, 'One of my detractors; let's hope he finds his silver lady and won't bother us again.'

The evil chuckling having run its course, collective and dispro-portionate belly laughter now replaced it. Oscar felt rather sorry for Lexicon but at the same time he knew his response was what the au-dience expected from him – a dismissive levity which showed he was in control and wasn't daunted. And Lexicon's attempt at sabotage, far from undermining the public's faith in Oscar, had only strengthened it. He mopped his brow, feeling the heat.

Some layers of clothing, he noticed, were being peeled off. Jackets made way for shirts, blouses for slips. Given the hour, things should have been cooling off. Perhaps a meteor was headed for the Earth; the heat clung like some invisible oil to the pores of the skin; perspiration no longer seemed to serve any function. Evenly tanned skin revealed itself provocatively. He tried to avert his gaze as the sinuous arms of sinuous women were gradually exposed.

After waiting a moment more, waiting for the shuffling to cease and the bodies to settle down he began speaking in a measured, confident voice, accompanied by a physical language which expressed a mixture of poise and energy.

'I wonder for what percentage of our lives our eyes are truly open? I daresay it all adds up to a very small figure; maybe even negligible.'

Women fanned themselves with whatever lay to hand; a few people were using cushions to shield their heads from the sun; others were taking swigs from bottles of water and wine. He tried to summon up a tone of sincerity and fervor so that his next words would take another step up the ladder to the summit of the speech, and its final perorations, a long way off.

'How did humans, who have minds which might be infinite, come to see in such a confined way? Here's a tentative answer. An external voice seduced us, a voice calling and coercing with images of greed, in the dreary patter of consumerism. Man makes compromise like bees make honey; his natural state is one of passivity; neither good nor bad, merely indifferent. And though he can momentarily be moved by a face, by suffering, he'd rather slouch back in his armchair and go on switching channels. Or beat his brother, or speak viciously of his colleague while turning to smile at him as he passes him in the corridor, or turn trees into concrete, or turn language into jargon, or turn the earth into a sea of blood, or license murder in the cause of religion ... or politics ... or money ... even freedom.

'And yet, even today, even in the current mire of fashionable nihilism, it's still possible to catch glimpses of those moments of subtle promise which stand outside of time, which seem to play tricks on it, accessed through art. And meditation. And love. Or, failing that, narcotics. Gateways to the divine, that whole spectrum of unnamable flowering which has been marginalized, told to take its leave because it apparently serves no useful purpose, does not enhance Productivity or create Profit.'

He was finding himself as an orator, his hands crossing and opening over his chest dramatically, his head tilted in sincerity.

'Plato's forms, Hinduism's Brahman, share an insistence on a world of ultimate reality beyond the confines of our changing, inconstant marketplace. And the one idea that all religions have in common is that of transcendence, of touching an undifferentiated reality beyond the boredom and dreariness of man-made reality.'

He took refuge in another pause. The audience still wasn't relaxed. He wondered if he was boring them all to tears. Or was it just the heat? Eyes peered and squinted at him. Reams of sweat pored from him so he had continually to mop his brow with a handkerchief. He wondered if the earth was about to catch fire. He imagined this must have been what it felt like to ride in the shaft of an active volcano, on the verge of becoming mucilaginous liquid. He glanced at the sun, collapsing in blood scorched glory.

'I would like to offer a few thoughts on how to live,' said Oscar.

Near the outermost ring of the circle, her legs telescoped up to her chin, feeling out of place and ill at ease, was Lilliana. She watched Oscar intently, more interested in the change she perceived in him than in his words. She noted his grandiloquent gestures as his arms reached out with a preacher's ardor. She was gently amused by his preened, theatrical appearance and found it hard to take him seriously in a tunic. But looking at him now, after all this time, she missed his aura of innocence; in her eyes his worldliness, his success had made him less sympathetic. She knew she would be reluctant to speak to him afterwards because there was a gulf between them now. He was famous and she wasn't. And could she be sure they'd be able to converse naturally and easily as they had before? She glanced round at the expectant audience, and, turning to Alastair, whose hand was in hers, whispered, 'Do you mind if we get out of here?'

Alastair did very much mind, but as he looked into Lilliana's ardent eyes he abandoned his resistance and they slid away inconspicuously.

His insurance company had offered him alternative accommodation while his house was being restored to its previous condition but he told them he had no need of it since he was living with Lilliana now. He gave her the opportunity to explore commanding impulses too often overlooked by her. She stilled the writhing of his demons. Since meeting her his disappointments did not run so deeply; he could relinquish his cravings and those perceived injustices he might have once brooded over were forgotten.

Shadows began climbing round them, and as they drifted away their happiness found reinforcement in everything, in the trees and their veins and arteries, in the gravelly paths, in the way he could gaze on the edges of her smile and the way she invited him to gaze by smiling.

They circled round and came eventually to a round pond. Patches of water flashed with dappled sunlight. The deck chairs were stacked, the ice cream vans were packed and gone. A group of toddlers were scattered round the pond with their fathers, their sailing boats steadily advancing across the water, powered by radio-controlled boxes which they eagerly punched with small thumbs. Lilliana crouched down to study one little boy's face. He was lost in delight when the voyage showed signs of wobbly progress, and utterly despondent, his bottom lip curled all the way down, when the boat capsized as he applied too much speed. One little girl hopped up to Lilliana, having decided she was interesting.

'You're nice,' she observed in a tiny, croaky voice.

'Well, thank you very much.'

The girl pulled a hair clip out of her hair with a big, bright lady-bird fastened onto it. She started waving it around.

'Do you like my hair clip – my mummy buyed it for me.'

'I like it very much.'

The little girl smiled an ecstatic smile which encompassed her whole face, turned and waddled off chaotically.

'Children just make up their own rules, don't they?' she said. 'Come on; I want to show you my favorite spot.'

Lilliana led the way down to a lime-tree enclosure adjacent to a white, rectangular building, locked and silent. Within there was a wall of bushes and she found an opening in them and pulled Alastair towards the spot she was already perching on. They were looking into an exquisite garden, a series of rectangles within rectangles, separated alternately by narrow columns of grass and beds of dahlias and roses. The heart of the garden was a central square of water where three fountains were hissing. Little islands of funnel-shaped leaves floated on the water's surface.

'This is the Sunken Garden. It's modeled on the Tudor garden at Hampton Court. Isn't it pretty?'

Alastair nodded. A couple of bumblebees were hovering heavily around some daffodils. Taking his hand, Lilliana very carefully directed them towards the water; they stepped over spraying shrubs and came eventually to the paved ground which framed the window of clear water. They sat there together and listened.

She threaded her fingers through his hair, leaning close into his shoulder, her head nestled there. She whispered, 'These hands have healing power, my love.'

'Why? Do I need to be healed?'

'I'm responsible for you now.'

'I thought it was the other way round: that once a person saves someone's life he's responsible for that life for ever.'

'That's a Chinese saying isn't it?' The movement of her fingers slowed. 'That night, the night of the fire – ' Lilliana began in a low, husky voice.

'I went from hell to heaven,' he interrupted matter of factly.

She re-commenced the threading of his hair, her fingers magnetic fibers.

'I never thought I'd be able to give myself to someone, with such little fuss,' she reflected, 'it was really natural wasn't it? It's funny, all these years I've been alone, I've turned love into something so tangled, I think I've put all my fears in its one basket. But that night they all just evaporated. I can't understand it. Life's so unpredictable and beautiful.'

By way of reply he leaned over and kissed her, and she enclosed him in her slender arms.

'We should go away, you and I,' he said. 'Run a seafront restaurant in Tel Aviv; take an elephant ride from Bombay to Cochin. I want to see the Sahara through your eyes.'

'Why? Do I have better eyesight?'

'You know what I mean, dummy.'

'What do we do for money?'

'I've got money. Enough for a year. We can make money on the road. We could start in Istanbul or Marrakech or Cairo. We could wash dishes, wait on tables, teach English. I want to drink red wine in a cockroach hotel, to ride in buses with no windows. I want to see sandstorms; I want to get caught in one and spend three days getting the sand out of my ears and out of yours as well.'

'I see. You've got this all mapped out, then?'

'Sure. Don't you want to say good riddance to shopping malls and itemized bills? And CCTV? And newspapers? I want to climb onto a camel and fall off it twenty-seven times.'

'That might prove painful, but I'd stitch you up; I'd have you up and running. Give the patient a good seeing-to. Us women: Florence Nightingales through and through.'

'I think women are wonderful. Everyone should own one.'

She started tearing at his stomach with clawing fingers and he doubled up, trying to block the siege of his torso. In the end on-slaught and defense collapsed and merged into a giggling union.

Afterwards she murmured, 'I worry you've too romantic a view of camels. Or rather of travel. Perhaps you're searching for a paradise that doesn't exist. Or perhaps this garden is it. It's all in how you look at things, isn't it?'

An exhausted sigh issued from his core.

'I don't know; maybe I am looking for a purity that's never existed. And I like to think it does in some unmapped corner.'

'You can find innocence here, too. Purity.'

'In London? Where people daily drag out their prayer mats to worship money? Where people have become so narcissistic they can't even go to the shops without grooming themselves for the catwalk?'

'Isn't it important to look your best?'

'Not when it comes at the expense of everything else. You're not like that. That's what I love about you.'

'So it's my slobbishness which appeals?'

'You know what I mean.'

'But you should love me for what I am, not because of the contrast I make to others.'

'I do love you for what you are, but at the same time I feel like you're an antidote to all the rubbish. I can say that, can't I?'

'But I don't want it to be Lilliana and Alastair versus the rest of the world. I don't have that kind of energy.'

'Nor do I.'

He looked blankly at her, then asked, 'So what do you think about going away?'

'I think I'd have to think about it. I'd have to do something about the Sun Well. With the house – I suppose I could rent it out and have the money wired to me up a juniper tree in the Congo or wherever.'

'That's not a problem. I think this is what I've always wanted. I've tried to deny it, but I  think deep down I'm rather nomadic.'

Within a few minutes the idea had gone from being a tentative suggestion to a finalized plan. This troubled her. At the same time she was slightly in awe of this tendency in his character – his ability to carry things through, not just talk about them.

'Have you lived abroad before?'

'Well, I studied mime in Paris. Then spent six months in New York, trying to become the next Brecht.'

'It's funny.'

'What is?'

'We've sort of done things in reverse, haven't we?'

'How do you mean?'

'You've moved in with me and I'm only really finding out about you now.'

'Does that worry you?'

'Not especially. And did you always want to direct plays?'

'At first I was keener on acting. I did a few big roles on the fringe: Macbeth, Dr. Faustus. But then it gradually dawned on me I wasn't any good. So I tried directing. I did a version of *The Misanthrope* in which Célèmine has all her suitors poisoned. Molière plus gore. It was a mess but it got me noticed. The artistic director of the Gate invited me to stage *The Nursery*, which was about adult babies. It's set in this house put aside for the mollycoddling of disturbed men who like to drool in oversize cots, dressed in nappies, dummies stuffed in their mouths, getting squirted with milk.

'I discovered directing allowed me to be an enlightened despot; I had all the power, and could still disappear after the dress rehearsal and get drunk. After the first night plays no longer need their director, like children who've outgrown their parents.'

She let her hand sink into the water, savoring its coolness.

'So do you think you might direct again?'

'Not until I've got something to say. I won't do it when it's just going through the motions, which is what it had become. I was whipping out blancmange. There might be a way, but I have to find it first. I have to find it.'

She thought about Oscar: had he found his way, in his tunic and sandals? Her eyes grew distracted. Alastair started planting soft kisses all over her yielding neck in between murmured questions.

'What are you thinking about?'

'Oscar.'

'Oscar Babel?'

'Yes, we were friends; but we drifted apart.'

'Really?'

'Ah-hah.'

'What was he like?'

'I don't know; that's what I was thinking.'

He stopped kissing her.

'You've gone all sad.'

'Have I? I apologize.'

'There's no need to. I hereby decree a ban on saying sorry. No more apologies, because when I'm with you, I'm filled with something good.'

'Golly, little me does that? This non-creative pleb?'

'Shush. That stuff isn't important. What it is about you, it's – '

'My bellybutton? My earlobes?'

'Among other things. You're serious and light at the same time. You lift me, you pull me up to where you're pottering, though you don't think of that place as being different to anywhere else. But it is, my darling, it is. And up there I'm not so haunted.'

'I'll drink to that.'

She cupped her hands in the water and made as if she was lapping at them like a thirsty dog. He stared at her in bemusement and began laughing.

Afterwards she said, apropos of nothing, 'You know that night – the night of the fire – do you mind my asking – do you have any idea – how it might have started?'

A frown of disquiet passed over his face. The trickling of the fountains continued.

'Yes, I've got a pretty good idea,' he said.

*

'I would like to offer a few thoughts on how to live,' said Oscar.

'A way we might all live creatively, beautifully, fully, our eyes opened, our senses steaming, our sinews burning.'

The space left by the departure of Alastair and Lilliana was now filled by a large man who welcomed the additional room for his bulk.

'Here's my contention: during the act of love human beings are able to perceive with full intensity the wonder of being truly alive. Not always, certainly, and to be sure such unions are often no more than functional and ephemeral. But when a person is truly engaged with another being there can be an attendant loss of aggression, self-ishness and greed; in fact, all those things which constitute the dark side of the human personality. When we make love we are truly alive, open like a petal, in tune with our environment, which in this case is the other person.'

Behind the stage there was a large screen about the size of a small billboard and on it images from ancient Tantric art now flashed up, back projected: stone pillar-sculptures from temples, statues show-ing the gods Shiva and Shakti in blissful embraces, icons of bizarre and ritualistic couplings, and finally the face of the Buddha radiating a narcotized tranquility, all sights Oscar had encountered during his recent trawls through libraries.

He caught a glimpse of a young man with orange-bleached hair looking up at him, his face imprinted with recollections of distant grandeur. It was as though Oscar's words were reigniting forgotten dreams.

Accompanying Oscar's next words was a newly-won physical grace, a plasticity as his hands found patterns to support his meaning and his body joined forces with verbal energy to create a composite picture of sincerity and belief. He suddenly felt a love for humanity welling up, a genuine desire to give them all he had. And the sight of the young man's face made Oscar think he'd managed to get the crowd on his wavelength. He might even be able to reach the speech's end triumphantly ...

'When we are in the physical world of another we have access to their most personal, private territory. The caress gives consciousness a greater definition; our sensibilities are raised onto a new level through passion. This enchantment is also a process of awareness, of awakening, when you learn about yourself more intuitively, more clearly than at other times. In other words our perceptions are operating correctly during the sexual act. Imagine if we could apply that intensity of perception to our ordinary waking lives. Then we would become aware of the whole of creation as if it were a vast, lover's body stretching out in front of us and offering us the riches which we all too often cannot see. Might we then respond to the call of others, regardless of whether they were friends or strangers?'

A couple got up to leave. This time (unlike with Alastair and Lilliana) Oscar noticed and tried to work out if his words might have given offense. But he couldn't read their faces from where he stood. They slid behind the leviathan tree carved with graffiti.

'I'm asking you to imagine a world in which the sensitivity and responsiveness to another person during the act of love, that respect, is brought to bear on all other beings.'

An actor in a caffeine twitter embarked on an involved examination of his finger nails. They were too long – however hard he tried he just couldn't get them to stay for any given time at the right length. It was the same with his hair; for about two days out of the month it was just right, but then a corner started sticking out. Inevitably barbers, no matter how passionately he pleaded with them, would lop great wads off the sides, so drawing attention to his drooping ears. He had a vast supply of sprays, waxes, mousses, and gels, but none of them gave him any joy.

Meanwhile, on the other side of the tree it became apparent that

Oscar's words, far from offending the couple who had withdrawn, had created an appetite for each other which could no longer be disregarded. Quietly, efficiently, they removed each other's clothing, which didn't take long, as they both wore little. Since they were cloaked by the tree and took great pains not to make a sound their coupling went entirely unnoticed. They were dimly aware of Oscar's voice droning on.

'The thing that allows for perception, that allows the channels to be opened is, surely, vulnerability. When a person unmasks themselves, reveals their essence, then great things happen. Vulnerability in turn leads to transparency. If we might express this vulnerability in our everyday relations, not just in the rarefied world of the bedroom – what I am suggesting is that to do such a thing might lead to a world free of aggression, a world of unity and understanding. The way forward is to achieve transparency through vulnerability, understanding through union. What might be delivered is a world free of hatred, a world that fuses into one being, one consciousness just as in a sexual synthesis or in the ego-transcending moments of orgasm. The key to this is to find a means of transferring this vulnerability.

'Eastern thought, whether it is Buddhist, Tantric, or Taoist, teaches that everything is part of a cosmic whole, that everything affects everything else. We must transcend the notion of an individual self in life, just as we manage to do sometimes in sex.

'The key is to have an erotically open relationship with the world and people. Make no mistake; I'm not licensing a meaningless pursuit of pleasure, and pleasure only. I'm talking about using those perceptions eroticism can offer in order to melt barriers, barriers between races, creeds and customs. There must be a recognition that what we take to be other and external has its roots in an incorrect perception which in turn encourages ideological distortions and untruths, and later on, injustices and tyrannies.'

By now the spotlights had been switched on though it was not yet completely dark. Far off parts of the gardens were lost in shadow. It had cooled off a little. Oscar looked romantic and dreamy, his golden tunic dazzlingly lit in the spotlights.

But as he stared into the arena he was aware of his heart pounding; he felt a resurgence of nerves. He wondered if he could possibly continue. He could scarcely believe such lofty sentiments were issuing from his lips. Though he was some way into the speech the end still seemed an eternity away. By contrast, the audience was comfortable, and people were intrigued. And it really did look to them as though Oscar had acquired a mystical aura.

He cleared his throat, took a few steps forward, reached the end of the walkway and resumed. It was then that the copulating couple was discovered. They had been too intent on finishing their work to notice the small boy who stood silently watching their growing fever. As he stood there, staring blankly, his father appeared, and was on the point of retrieving him when his eyes registered this double-decker of shuddering flesh. He uttered a cry of surprise, grabbed his son and marched him back to the audience. But the father's cry had alerted those closest to the big tree and they craned their necks to see what was going on. One or two men walked over to get a better view of the lovers, who were vaguely conscious of these random voyeurs, but carried on, thrusting together towards the moment of release they so desperately sought. Oscar's elevated sentiments about the sexual act were eclipsed by this more compelling spectacle. Then more people gathered round, drawn by the familiar and yet hallucinatory tableaux before them.

*And then something happened.*

The sight triggered a flutter of impulses and realizations in the minds of those watching which terminated at last at a beautifully stark place. The hothouse, aromatic night; the open spaces; their proximity to each other, made sex transcendentally simple. Oscar's presence; his magnificent eloquence; his insistence on the riches sex could bring (after all he was a celebrity, a prophet) all endorsed unstated desire, nudged desire into becoming deed.

Where now were the tenets of interpretation and speculation, misinterpretation and hesitation, rejection and acceptance?

And where was the beauty, the mystery, the tenderness?

They were dying, they were dying ...

Cross-currents of hysteria rose, drove forward, lashed out like angry winds, were squeezed through the eye of time's needle, then dipped and leapt out of existence.

Oscar stopped forming words, stopped moving his lips. He carried on breathing, and he carried on standing. And watching. Slowly and inevitably a shape began to emerge. The shape of the stirrings that lead to nakedness.

Some wanted to confirm whether or not they did actually feel more alive during coitus since they weren't at all sure they did; some wanted merely to satisfy newly-sprung desire; some thought they must first have sex in order to then carry out Oscar's 'transference' (by reminding themselves of what was involved) and others, who under any other circumstances would never have been able to have intercourse (because their partners had long ago withdrawn into disinterest or because their relationships were dead) now could since this night, by some wondrous sleight of hand, had resurrected the life of their unions.

Oscar stood rooted in horror.

Flesh was unveiled, clothes tossed recklessly into the air. Torsos, bare backs, legs caught the light. Hairlessly trim or furrily lumpen stomachs were revealed. Breasts bounced. Penises stood at half-mast, dangled flaccidly or proudly announced their graduation with flying colors. A kind of sickly nightmare had been created by his words.

So soon grinding bones and flesh fed off flesh and bones; restraint and diffidence were cast aside and people started to squirm, in a composite of agony and ecstasy whose character was refined and adjusted with each pulsation. For Oscar, the words of his speech were visible in a new and ghastly light. Not one, not two, not three, but scores of couples were copulating. Those who weren't were watching those who were. In the stifling night the blinding imperative of sexual desire had triumphed, crushing every vestige of self-restraint and self-consciousness.

Bodies moved up and down, from side to side, like pistons, grunting, sobbing, screaming, rocking, heaving, thrusting, pressing, swaying, supine, suspended and nailed together by burning pleasure, seeking ever and again for a more total and engulfing sensual cohesion. All about them were the hallmarks not of some spiritual awakening, but rather a negation of everything except pure will. There was neither vulnerability nor poetry here. Instead there was a final, precise reductiveness, a rendering of human complexity into reflex, the iron rule of instinct, emerging after short-lived hesitation, growing now to fury. They were lapping at one another, using each others' limbs as triggers, as buttons to be pressed, to yield a greater arousal, flooding each other in delirium. Acrid smells passed through, above, and beyond the lovers, tossed like salads.

'I think the audience may have taken me a little too literally ... em ...' Oscar began ineffectually.

'I can see my words may have had the wrong effect. Or you may have mis – misunderstood ... I'm ... I'm sorry if I've misled you. Please stop. Hey .... look ... HEY!!'

Some of the lovers glanced up. But most of them carried on regardless, rocking back and forth, limbs sliding, slotting together, generating the white heat of friction, moans and groans spilling from them, lending the night the atmosphere of some blood-curdling occult ritual. Someone newly joining the lecture would have been forgiven for thinking a series of pagan sacrifices were taking place, until they digested the phantasmagoric truth.

Those not having intercourse were staring aghast, or looking to Oscar for guidance or laughing with nerves or embarrassment or abandon. This laughter of abandon could have been the laughter of demons, as faces turned purple, single, arching veins standing out of brows with scorching precision. As Oscar watched he feared the violence of the laughter would leave bodies headless. He visualized scores of decapitated heads lolling around bloodily, still cackling, lines of blood trickling through the green grass, attracting swarms of flies and maggots.

Yelling so loudly that his vocal chords burned Oscar bawled, 'Passion should not be confined to the bedroom ... eh ... and thank you for such a frank demonstration of this. It should be universal. No, scratch that ... We're all poets within the embrace of flesh. Let's be poets elsewhere. But not here, perhaps. You might frighten the squirrels.' He didn't really have time to adapt his painstakingly rehearsed speech to the recent developments. And as the speech fell to bits the crowd broke ranks, growing more and more excited.

He tried to avert his gaze from the antics of the lovers but just couldn't look away. Something, he mused, must have burst like a fountain and turned people into lusty baboons, proving that with a little in the way of mental re-adjustment, the jungle was not such an alien place for mankind and perhaps the day would soon come when people could take their place there with pride, initiating an era of evolutionary regression.

Looking beyond the tight circle, in the distance he could make out a cluster of policemen galloping over from the direction of Knightsbridge. He resolved to finish his speech before they blundered in. He went off at an absurdly quick trot. 'I want to bottle rapture up freeze it and preserve it like a vital oil in short I want us to remember we're humans carrying a torch holding it aloft not robots licking a boot we must never sink into a mechanized existence.'

Then in slower, more measured tones, he declared that, 'It might be an idea to postpone the fornication until the police have been and gone.'

This brief calm fled and again the words were tumbling out of his mouth. He was determined to rattle through the rest. This time I'll get to the end. Why am I never allowed to finish my bloody speeches?

'The external breaks down with friends it melts with lovers it melts away totally they become one as they say the divisions between lovers break down as they spill into each other become part of each other. Do you feel it? Are you made one? Hey? You out there! Or are you just lecherous bastards?'

He caught a glimpse of the full, preponderant moon. The sky was a mess. Overhead some traces of blood were flecked against the outline of amorphous clouds. There were dirty white cavities wherever his eye wandered: it looked like something had taken the fabric of the sky and literally dragged and wrenched it apart. Nature was convulsed with pain.

'Love shouldn't wear price tags. Or be confined to one's inner circle of friends and family. And love must give up power, not exercise it. To give without expecting anything in return – that is something to work towards. By the way, I am available for one-on-one discussion. If you have any queries ...'

The crowds clambered onto the stage and pulled him down from it. They wanted to pay effusive homage to him. One man, hopping up and down into his trousers whilst trying to zip up his fly (he looked like he was on a pogo stick), yelled into his ear, 'Mr Babel, thank you, thank you so much; my wife and I haven't been able to have intercourse for six years ... you've given us the confidence to cure ourselves.' Oscar heard himself say, 'Oh right; don't mention it.' He tore off his radio mike when he realized his voice was still booming through the speakers.

Another member of the audience, a shambolic, breathless figure in a waistcoat tried to get close enough to Oscar so as to shout important words to him, but he couldn't reach. He tried calling from where he was standing, being repeatedly pushed and shoved.

'Oscar! Hey, Oscar! Over here!' Webster yelled. 'Bloch's in hospital! He's very ill! Bloch was admitted to hospital yesterday!'

But Oscar didn't hear or see him and that part of the crowd Webster was lodged in now began moving sluggishly towards the Albert

Memorial. Webster shoved up against a man from whose every pore a foul, unholy smell emanated; after about five seconds of this he was gagging, close to that total loss of control which precedes vomiting.

Webster had not been one of those who had experienced sexual intimacy.

He managed to find a few inches of space away from the stench and took in some air, then turned round to see if there was another way of reaching Oscar. But he could no longer make him out. He muttered to himself, 'Sod this for a game of soldiers,' and waddled off down to Kensington High Street in search of a slice of coffee cake. He was cheered up by the thought that he'd soon be seeing his beloved Chinese lanterns, which had pride of place in Bloch's front room.

A squadron of television cameras had arrived and were busily being positioned in key areas to film those still mating. They were like athletes gasping in the final stages of a marathon run, the finishing line within sight. Lights were speedily assembled since the night was dark now. Young women clutching microphones were speaking rapidly in front of their cameras, which observed the lovemaking dispassionately. The images were relayed to thousands of homes by satellite (interrupting an item in the news about a young boy charged with stabbing his mother to death. The two had argued over a missing container of chocolate icing). In their lounges people were suddenly confronted with this eruption of decadence. Fathers took their microwave dinners down from their laps, and told their children to go to their rooms and filmed their televisions with their phones and tablets.

In the gardens the crowds were jubilant. Stupefaction had given way to celebration. People were like champagne bottles popping open. The entwined bodies rolled and turned more freely around the cushions, freed by the crowds' dispersal. One by one orgasms were detonated and the rhythm of the bodies subsided.

From the periphery of the circle Ryan Rees smoked a cigar and watched, mesmerized. Even he had never seen anything like this.

But now the police were threading through the circle.

They struggled to cover breasts and genitals with their helmets. They shuffled women into their coats awkwardly, their splayed out arms and contorted limbs locked in resistance. Couples still welded together were asked, politely at first, and then aggressively, to separate and get dressed as they were under arrest. After a struggle, some pleas for compassion and Babel-esque love, they had no choice but to comply. A few remembered they were missing their shoes and had to recover them from the tents. They threw out designer names to convince their captors of the seriousness of the matter. But the constables' ears were deaf to the cause of footwear and within a matter of minutes they – sheep herders – had gathered them all up and were leading them to waiting vans and cars. Oscar watched helplessly.

A few yards away an interview was being recorded for possible inclusion as a later news slot.

'Can you tell us what happened here?'

'Well, first of all I have to say: this is the most incredible night of my life. And I think Oscar Babel is right about vulnerability! We should all be showing our vulnerability! Vulnerability equals transparency which equals the absence of masks which equals more love and that is what this evening has proved: people are full of love but they never get a chance to express it, so eventually it just withers away and dies.'

'But what we were seeing tonight, surely that wasn't love; it was just lust.'

'Well, maybe, I don't know. So what? Well, it was real, wasn't it? As the man says why should love be confined? It must be and is infinite, and I think what we saw tonight was a rejection of the social pressures which rule most people's lives. We saw an eruption of energy, a glimpse of what life could always be like if we allowed it to be and ....'

'Thanks very much,' said the pretty young reporter, turned to her cameraman and, when she was sure her interviewee was out of earshot, snorted, 'We won't use that shit.'

She tried to get to Oscar but he was still hemmed in by a thick wedge of people.

He was beginning to wish they would just back off, stop touching him and generally suffocating him. He kept saying, 'That isn't what I meant! That's not what I meant! I just meant we should be more honest, more selfless ...'

Rees, with the assistance of his stocky henchman Edwin (whose appearance created tremors of fear) was able to push through to him.

'Isn't there anything we can do about these arrests?' Oscar asked him as a small woman tried to kiss his bare feet.

'Afraid not, Oscar. But fear not, we'll make the headlines.'

'Is that all you can say? Is that all you fucking care about?'

'No, it's all the general public care about, remember?'

In a little while the police's zealous activities had sobered up those who were still left, which was the greater part of the audience. Those who had not been arrested watched as more of their indecently exposing counterparts were chased – naked figures pursued by uniformed ones – and were caught and carted away. Sirens howled, their shrill screams impaling calm and grace.

After the police had gone things became a little calmer. The TV cameras stuck around in case of further developments.

And now the crowd broke up into various groups; some rushed back to the shoe tents and presented their tickets dutifully; others hung around and soaked up the atmosphere of receding anarchy; a little clan of smokers formed; others went for rambles around the gardens, some looked for squirrels. Now that the police had gone clans of hot dog vendors rolled in, with their handlebar moustaches (in whose environs it was easy to imagine dispossessed insects resided) and started peddling their wares, turning tubes of grease in their beds of grease, calling out, 'Hot dogs, hot dogs,' with abbreviated bravado so it sounded as though they were saying, 'Hogs, hogs.' From their lips moist cigarettes dangled and every now and then dollops of ash merrily joined the sizzling hot plates and their contents.

Meanwhile, outside the shoe tents, men were presented with transparent stilettos, women were handed black brogues. A mix-up of titanic proportions loomed into view.

And then someone suggested that everyone accompany Oscar back to Chelsea and the idea was received with great cheers of delight. And so, while the lights and stage began to be dismantled and the rubbish and cushions gathered, a procession began, a parade down the streets of Kensington. Kensington Gore presented no problems, but at Gloucester Road what began as a polite observance of street etiquette – a legacy of the recent chastening experiences, the crowd confining itself to the pavement – lapsed into a great splurge, as everyone took to the roads. The vastness of the numbers could not be accommodated anywhere else, it seemed, after the transition had been made, but this was only because people fanned out along the wider roads, thus giving the impression of an even greater multitude. The tide of traffic was stemmed by the forms of men and women, within whose protective compass Oscar strolled, as if already enshrined. Ryan Rees was having a ball, though as usual his face betrayed little sign of emotion.

Oscar felt light, so light he might will himself to rise and drift towards the moon.

The night was sweltering, a great vat of heat and humanity.

But just as the festive mood was reaching its apogee, the police popped up again. This time the vans and cars unloaded far greater numbers. Some were clutching riot shields, which, along with their helmets, made them look like androids. They re-grouped themselves with quiet efficiency and surrounded the crowds. Oscar clambered on top of one of those cars brought to a standstill and, ignoring the driver's protestations, yelled into the crowd which immediately strained to hear him.

'Offer gifts. Choose love over fear.'

As if by magic people began emptying out their pockets, giving all their available change to the slightly bewildered representatives of authority. Elsewhere the upholders of the law were poised, primed to attack and repel those who threatened to bring mayhem and small change to Kensington.

'We mean no harm,' Oscar shouted. 'My people and I are walking home, that is all. We come and go in peace. Why should machines have right of way over people?'

Oscar strained to hear a ruddy cheeked officer shouting in a savage voice, 'You're blocking the traffic. Move away or we'll move you ourselves.'

Things were stretched tight.

Unfortunately in all the confusion Oscar did not hear what he said and carried on, hoping it would be all right.

'My poor lost brother. None of us see clearly, not even I. These people are committing no crime. We are humans walking the earth's surface. Cars kill people and the air. Throw away these shackles. They interfere with heaven. There is only internal order, order of the soul. Why not embrace a higher reality?'

This last speech annoyed the policeman very much. He turned and gave an order and at once the crowds were violently driven back onto the pavements, thick truncheons ramming in and out of the air and every now and then bruising defenseless flesh. A few ribs were broken; stomachs were pounded. People were thrown into a whirlwind of movement and confusion. Some retaliated and threw whatever lay to hand at the helmeted men who they now saw as tyrannical fascists. A shop window had something hurled at it, the glass went opaque and the alarm went off for the tenth time that day while elsewhere people were rammed up against cars – bodies pressed against bodies, bodies cushioning bodies, as people, in reaction to the machinery of oppression suddenly up and running, sought to protect each other, not to flee into the night but stand by their companions while the helmets raged and thrashed. From where he stood, balanced on his metallic throne, Oscar felt at once frightened and exhilarated. And humbled by this terrible and yet inspiring moment. And now, with frantic devotion, all the car horns begun blaring. The resulting cacophony, born in and provoking panic, sounded like some atonal, experimental symphony as played by a hopelessly incompetent brass band. Oscar hopped down, thinking quickly. He marched blindly into the fray, walked up to one of the policemen clutching a loud speaker and planted a huge kiss on his cheek. The man reacted uncharacteristically. Not being of a tactile disposition his usual reaction upon being kissed by a man would have been to beat him to a pulp, but he just dropped his loudspeaker in stunned silence. Oscar picked it up and put his lips to it.

'People, move off; look away; let's disperse; go back to the pavements; don't hit back, we're unarmed, just be firm about showing our peaceful intentions.'

The words were enough to stem the tide of resistance, so preventing the situation from becoming truly desperate. People made it clear they were not about to fight back and the police were partially appeased. The crowds quickly rejoined the pavement, so breaking up their bulk and in seconds normal human motion was resumed. The line that separates pedestrians and the road was restored. The police were left unanchored to any specific course of action, left hanging, as it were. A few of them felt disappointed. Oscar tried to smile benignly at the de-activated, uniformed figures. Slowly they filed back into the vans and in another minute these drove off, taking with them a handcuffed handful of those who had lashed out. The traffic was able to move finally and drivers heaved sighs of relief, pleased not to have to be claiming insurance for damage sustained to their vehicles. Oscar still retained a loyal band of about fifteen followers, propelled by euphoria, and they pushed on to Chelsea with a light, airy gusto.

Rees, who had been keeping a low profile, appeared alongside him and said, 'Well-handled Oscar. That could have been very nasty.'

Oscar wanted to say, 'Not as nasty as you,' but he held back.

The little group advanced, coming up to the Fulham Road. Some of the women darted off to buy flowers from late-night stores, and offered him carnations and roses, which he accepted graciously, sending them into little shivers. Very soon his arms were swamped in bouquets and he had to siphon some off to perfect strangers approaching from the opposite direction, who as a rule either accepted them in surprise or refused them rudely.

A small girl, perhaps six years old, was playing a harmonica, in a little world of her own. People made way for her as she marched forward, like some emissary of a snowflake world of delicacy. The sight of her exquisite immersion in innocence caused Oscar's mood to swing, this glimpse of purity making him momentarily – and vividly – perceive his fallenness. He turned to meet the gaze of his disciples; he wished they'd leave him now but they looked like they were here to stay, and he was loath to offend their feelings.

But by the time he found himself outside the entrance to the Grosvenor Hotel only four or five remained. The elation which had bound them together was gone, and now only awkwardness prevailed. Oscar didn't really feel like inviting them up to his suite. Exhaustion had finally caught up with him, no longer held in check by adrenaline. He managed a weak smile and whispered, 'Remember – no price tags. Unconditional love.'

One of the younger men murmured sweetly, 'This has been the most amazing night of my life. We think you're incredible.'

Oscar looked at him earnestly. Speaking slowly he murmured, 'I'm really not, you know. I'm very unincredible. But, you're right; tonight was pretty good. I'm sorry but I'm just shattered. I must say goodnight.' He walked slowly through the revolving doors, turned round – momentarily trapped in one of the compartments – waved, and then he was gone.

The disciples stood standing for a while, struck down by an unreasonable sense of loss. Then one of them suggested they camp outside the hotel and try and have breakfast with Oscar in the morning. Surely he wouldn't be averse to the idea. So they settled down near the revolving doors while a girl darted off to an off-license for a few bottles of wine and some paper cups. The strange homage began and the extraordinary events of the night were discussed and dissected endlessly.

As Oscar entered the lobby he spotted a herd of journalists hovering near the reception; they instantly rushed towards him with chaotic precision. Struck with a sudden idea he tossed the remaining flowers over their heads; they ducked and raised their arms clumsily, while he scrambled inside the elevator, jabbing repeatedly at the button for the tenth floor.

Inside it felt good to have eluded them. He rode up a couple of floors and then, without quite knowing why, pressed the STOP button. The lift shuddered to a halt. He took a few deep breaths. Here he was isolated, he could take a break from the madness. In that little cubicle he was safe. The events of the night already seemed dreamlike. He couldn't quite accept what had happened. Just as he couldn't quite believe that in a few hours he would be really famous – or really notorious. In a few hours the events of the night would be irrevocably associated with him, talked about and analyzed by London, perhaps by Britain. Words would scurry down phone lines, e-mails would be sent, videos would be posted, signals would bounce off satellites, insane theories would get posted on the internet. Technology, the matrix of technology, had thrust its legions of fingers into every nook and cranny of the country, and the globe. Even as the elevator sat suspended the furnaces of the media would be roaring, its fires fanned by money and power.

He was in so deep, he was so enmeshed in this life which had scooped him up and claimed him. From that still point he perceived the events of the summer as misty, illusory. I've been spinning lies. And all the lies have set, they're as tightly knotted as the steel wires which stop this lift from hurtling to oblivion.

For a moment he wished it would fall, and take him with it ...

But at last he gave the order for the lift to clunk back into life and it rode up inexorably. The doors snapped open and he walked out. He slotted the key in the lock and turned it. As he stepped through he heard a voice issue from the darkness.

'At last.'

He assumed his mind had invented the voice, a supposition that didn't really surprise him, given the insanity of what had gone before. He reached for the light and was on the point of motioning towards the drinks cabinet when he realized he wasn't hearing things. Because there was a person standing in the middle of the room. In the half-second during which his eyes took in the lithe form his mind was blank, his reaction non-existent; in the next half-second, despite the fact that his key had worked, despite the presence of his clothes and the familiar landscape before him, he told himself he was in the wrong room, and it was only after the voice spoke again, in the third half-second, saying, 'You've been ages' that he realized he actually knew the person standing in front of him and that she was Najette.

The windows were all flung open and her violet dress rippled in the night's breezes. He stared at her in silence. The faint sound of traffic reached the room, telling him life was going on as usual.

'God, what – what are you doing here?' he stammered.

She had a drink in her hand. She was grinning now – a grin which waged war on rules and regulations. There was not the slightest suggestion in her manner of self-doubt or hesitation: her presence there was the most natural thing in the world. Oscar, on the other hand, was incredulous and confused.

'You're back from the picnic, then. Nice place you've got here. You must get a lot of light,' she said, jabbing at the windows.

'How – how did you get in?'

'I explained the situation to the steward; gave him a twenty pound note and a big smile.'

Though it was quite clearly Oscar, he looked alien to her. His face seemed flabbier, less expressive. As she studied him more keenly he struck her in the way a faded painting might have done.

'What are you doing here?' he managed eventually.

'Waiting for you.'

'In the dark?'

'Yes, I like it that way. Besides, the moon's not far off; tonight it's silver paint. Did you see the sky? It's acting up.'

'Why now? Why tonight of all nights?'

'I'll tell you after another drink. The immediate reason was listening to the radio, they were talking about you. So I got on a bus.'

He didn't know what to say. He walked up to her very slowly.

'I'm ... I'm thrilled to see you.'

'It's good to see you too, Oscar.'

'What are you drinking?'

'Rum and coke.'

'God, I'm whipped. I could use a drink. What a night.'

'Tell me.'

'Not yet; it's still too close.'

He fixed himself a vodka martini. Then he fashioned another rum and coke for Najette, set it down on a side-table, and said, 'That's for you, when you're ready.' She watched him closely. He moved easily, like someone who finds calm after grueling labour.

They were standing quite close to each other now. He looked into her eyes. Her loose, ebony hair was looking longer than before, reaching down her back, her face as full of unruly beauty as his dreams and memories suggested.

She found a corner of the sofa to perch on. He set himself down at the other end.

'Did you work out who you are yet?' she asked.

'Not yet.'

'Then what did you work out?'

'That everything you said about me was right.'

'Maybe. I rang back a few minutes after I put the phone down but no one picked up.'

'I was busy feeling terrible, I think.'

'I'm sorry about that.'

'You don't know what happened tonight, do you?'

'Weren't you supposed to be making a speech or something?'

'Yeah, a speech which led to an orgy which led to arrests which led to a procession which led to a riot. And I was at the centre of it all. For a while it really did feel as if I was Jesus Christ. Now I see why rock stars need to take drugs, because when they come off stage they have to match the buzz of being adored on stage. Tonight was fatal; I was guzzling icing sugar but it had a pinch of arsenic inside, slowly killing me. Do you know what I mean?

'It's great to see you but please don't start ticking me off, please don't tell me I'm a fraud. I don't think I can handle that right now. I know I'm a fraud, and I've mourned the fact, and I've mourned your loss; Christ, I've mourned your loss, but I'm just so tired. I need to sleep and I'm high and I'm low and I'm in between. All at the same time. I'm everything. I've been through everything tonight.'

The way he was finding his way around himself so precisely took her aback. His voice, its burnt-out weariness, was oddly seductive. His supernatural exhaustion leapt out, and his eyes were still, behind veils of indifference; he didn't need her, was happy to say he didn't by not saying it. He just didn't have the energy to be anxious around her. She was intrigued by this transformation and drawn to it.

'Oscar, I'm not going to give you a hard time; I've already done that.'

She finished her drink and started on her next one, using her middle finger as a stirrer.

'I wouldn't have come all this way just to sting you again. The truth is ... I actually missed you.'

'You did?'

'Yes. And in a minute I'd like to discuss it, but not before I finish this.'

He rummaged around for some cigarettes, offered her one, (she declined), and lit his. The  alcohol in his system quadrupled the appeal of nicotine and he took a succession of quick drags, inhaling deeply.

'Look, do you mind if I just get changed; this tunic feels a bit strange.'

'Be your guest.'

When he returned from the bedroom his make-up was gone, he was dressed in a shirt and jeans and the sandals had left his feet. He took up his cigarette and watched as she knocked back the final inch of her rum, at the same time giving her head a shake, as if to maximize the effect of the alcohol on her brain. She stood up with haughty aplomb, and strutted over to the stereo.

'What about some music?'

She found something she liked with tipsy decisiveness. It was a recording of *The Threepenny Opera*. An evil, guttural voice launched into "Mack the Knife."

'I love this music, it's so ... pungent,' she murmured, sitting down again, inching slightly closer to his walled-off spot on the sofa.

'Did you really miss me?' he asked.

'Yes, I did. I should say I missed your specificity. You were specifically Oscar.'

She leaned forward elastically and reached for a cigarette which she now sped through with such flair and elegance that Oscar perceived how amateur his own efforts were.

'Of course now you're specifically Oscar Babel, in inverted commas. Maybe I did feel a little bit jealous – where was I going? Nowhere fast, as they say. But the jealousy was incidental. That time in the cafe, after we saw that film, I watched your face and it was so ... full of hunger, hunger for me. I wanted you to be hungry for me, really hungry. But I didn't want to hurry things; I wanted the time to be just right, like the soufflé, remember?'

He nodded.

'When the newspapers got hold of you, when you started becoming a product, it worried me. I didn't want to go around with a man in love with himself. Not like Nicholas. Someone hidden in a performance. I wanted someone who could see himself clearly. But what chance of that was there when you were being recreated everywhere?

'When we met, at first it was perfect. Each meeting closed the gap between what we said and what we meant. I thought with you I could really say what I felt. Now it all seemed in danger of being messed up, and your real self – '

'I have no real self; I'm a series of fleeting selves, and that's why I make such a good celebrity because I'm a void and everyone can fill me with whatever nonsense they like.'

'I think that's a bit harsh, Oscar.'

'I'm not so sure.'

'When I thought about it, and I have been thinking about it, I came to certain conclusions. It bothered me that you were willing to play along with this media game, but what did some poster, some opinion about you from someone who didn't even know you, some television appearance really have to do with us, with our relationship? Was it you who'd changed or was it just your situation?

'I knew you weren't really a prophet, but I missed you. So I thought I'd invite myself back into your life. But it's only the small Oscar, the struggling Oscar I'm interested in, do you understand? Not the inflated, grand Oscar running about, making lots of noise, disturbing the blades of grass.'

She folded her arms, as if to say: 'There, I'm finished now.'

He found her remarks deeply affecting. He would have liked to have kissed her there and then – but he knew how premature (indeed presumptuous) this would have been. If Najette was magnanimous enough to let him back into her life (for he saw her being there in these terms, not the other way round) he would have to shape up. And he needed his wits about him if he wasn't to spoil this wonderful opportunity; and yet he must make light of his excitement. She really had every right to despise him. Why was she giving him another chance? Perhaps it was his very faultedness which made him interesting to her. Why did he always have to spoil everything with thinking? She was here, this was the essential thing; she wasn't a mirage.

'You know,' he began, 'you always seemed to me to be, I would say, roughly three times as alive as everyone else.'

'Oh, I'm not sure about that. I think I'm like a piece of wood which needs constant varnishing. When the painting's going well I'm shiny. But when I'm wasting time, staring into space ... yuk. I really go dry. My idea of a good day is to get up around six, go for a jog, work till noon, meet someone important – a dealer, a curator – for lunch at Valerie's, work till six, be a news junkie for an hour, reading everything I can lay my hands on, then rustle up a gargantuan meal with feta cheese and avocados and aubergines. Then get blotto with a gypsy violinist. And then to bed after poetry.'

'What poetry?'

'Emily Dickinson ... Shakespeare's sonnets.'

'I can see how that would add up to a good day. Even if you're only three times as alive as everyone some of the time I think you always manage to make life less boring. I mean if you – wait, let me show you, graphically.'

He found a piece of paper and a pen. She started to laugh.

'Right, here's a circle, or rather an oval shape. This is life. I'll shade in the part which represents excitement, adventure, fun.'

He shaded in approximately one twentieth part of the total area.

Najette's laughter subsided into a knowing smile.

'So, there we have it. Five percent of life is pleasant; the rest is boredom or work. Yes?'

'OK.'

'Now – this new circle,' – he drew it – 'this represents a life lived with Najette. I shall now shade in the part which represents adventure, excitement, fun ...'

He shaded it all in in a mad rush.

'So, as you can see, and as I have demonstrated conclusively, life is usually a piece of shit, whereas with you it is an exotic, stimulating safari.'

'Safari?'

'Yes. Can I kiss you?'

'No.'

She stood and went to the stereo; so long as there was music, music to lubricate any creaky silences, she would be varnished. She found "The Ballad of Immoral Earnings" and a waltzy, smoky pulse was taken up, leading to wistful passages from the woodwind and eventually to a duet between Polly and Mack, mingling beauty and sneering menace.

'Another drink? I'm beating you,' she asked.

'No, I think I'm all right, actually. But you go ahead.'

'I think I will. I don't want all these riches to go to waste.'

He watched her as she re-located the rum, then treated the ice bucket with disdain. Her eye peered at him from under her black hair. The sable strands reminded him of a barcode, clustered together at one end, and separated by intervals of space at the other. As she finished mixing her drink, he decided she was incapable of carrying out even the most humdrum of actions without a certain panache.

What was she like in bed? he asked himself. Images of a hypothetical union flashed through his mind. He had to stop tormenting himself like this. But her body, it was there, not five feet away, he could just reach out and touch it. No. This is ridiculous. This is not going to happen. It might in the future, when she's more comfortable around me. But not tonight. Definitely not tonight. She said no when I asked to kiss her. That's pretty unequivocal. But I shouldn't have asked. Of course not. You never ask. Stupid clumsy twit. You don't ask a woman like Najette. You beg her. No, you don't do that either. God she's beautiful. I'm going to pass out or start to cry in a minute. Or pull my hair out. Haven't I learnt anything? I've got to get a grip. I have to take the lead, I just

'What's the matter? You look like you've swallowed a maggot.' She sipped her drink lazily.

'It's nothing. I'm just tired.'

'Do you want me to go?'

'No, of course not.'

'Do you want to go to bed?'

Yes, with you.

'No, no, I'm fine. Verily, is the night not balmy? Shall we go and stand by yonder window?'

'If you like. Just, for pity's sake, don't talk like that.'

There the balmy night, like a generous host, whipped up more breezes on their behalf. They watched their reflections in the darkened glass. He thought of the women he'd met recently: the girl at the party who wanted to see exploding stars; Anna; even Cressida. Each in their way was interesting and attractive, but he knew now that when he'd spoken to them he'd been looking for Najette all the time. And here she was, two times, in the glass, and beside him.

Without turning to look at her, Oscar began, 'Did you like – '

'How long do you intend to stay holed up here?'

'I don't know; I'm making it up as I go along.'

'Don't you want to return to the real world?'

'What real world? I've never understood what people mean by that phrase. When does the world become real – when a certain level of hardship sets in, when cancer is diagnosed? Does that mean someone who's healthy and happy is living in the unreal world? Is the real world the world of corporate finance? Then does that mean engineers don't live in the real world? Is someone who lectures at university not living in the real world? Shouldn't someone pat him on the back and say, "Excuse me, you're not living in the real world."'

'God, you're so complicated.'

She traced a line along his cheek with curled fingers. Goose pimples instantly sprouted along the back of his neck.

Oh God, what does that mean? That means she is interested. Or maybe she's just being affectionate. But you wouldn't be affectionate with

'Oscar, maybe I should make tracks, as they say.'

She was just being affectionate.

'What?'

'It's getting late and – '

'OK, then, off you pop.'

'What? "Off you pop." Am I a toy gun?'

'Listen, don't go.'

'What?'

'I don't want you to go. For about two seconds back then I was trying to be – '

'I know. But don't. And now, my darling, I really –'

He planted a very wet, very bungled kiss on her lips and her eyes dilated in surprise. Then she started laughing like a maniac.

'Don't laugh at me,' he whined. 'Anything but that.'

'What was that? I felt like I'd been kissed by an octopus.'

'I'm very flattered.' He went red.

'It was ... it was so ... so wet. Wet kisses are really high up on the ladder. You don't just dive in with such a degree of moisture. Don't you know that?'

'I do now. But I was – '

'In any case, dry kisses are so much more refined.'

'I hadn't really – '

'Here – look – the monsoon season's over.'

She grabbed him and kissed him with magnificent authority and as they connected Oscar felt his body shrinking and his soul soaring. She didn't flinch – she stayed just as she was – a kisser equipped with a prodigious technique.

'There – see – dummy. Next time, choose a dry climate.'

How did she manage that? Single-handedly transmute awkwardness into comedy, friction into jollity?

'You're lovely,' he said.

'And you're a lamb ... in octopus's clothing.'

'I can't think of anything to say.'

'That's all right. Between us I think we've exhausted language.'

She turned back to her drink – and stretched out on the sofa. Oscar fell into the beechwood rocking chair.

'You're quite sure – '

'I'm never quite sure. Oscar, I think I'll need to sleep soon or I'll exceed my sell-by date.'

'If you like you could take the bed and I could take the sofa.'

She reached for a cigarette. Words and smoke wafted from her mouth.

'Ah yes, chivalry. Hardship endured for the sake of the lady. The bathtub would be more chivalric; you take the tub and I'll sink into the foam. Enamel for Oscar, air for Najette. Or is that just an implicit way of stating masculine strength? She needs her beauty sleep so she can look good for me; or he has to be alert at night so he can slay the nocturnal dragon. Don't worry. I'm not about to embark on a feminist diatribe; there's others who can do it so much better. I had a tutor like that at college. Miss Fincher. She was a fright; every day she spouted something about male oppression. She droned on and on about the evils of the male libido, about how men couldn't think straight because their brains were swimming in testosterone; castration would solve all the world's ills, she said. I think it was from her that the word "frump" entered the English language; she had these wigwam Tartan skirts with gigantic safety pins holding them tightly in check. Woolen chastity belt. She never smiled. It's not a good idea to hate men so much. It's OK to hate them a little bit, to keep your hand in. That's all right; I can live with that. I do live with that.

'I'm sorry; I don't know where this is coming from. Must be the grog loosening my tongue. Friction between men and women – what about it? We need a bit of friction. Men and women are after the same thing; they just have mutually exclusive ways of getting it. Where were we? Oh yes, the sofa – you were suggesting we be segregated. I have a better idea. When I was snooping around earlier I noticed your bed's bigger than some people's front rooms. Do you think with a bit of wriggling we might both squeeze in?'

This truly was a better idea, an infinitely better idea. And yet why did it still feel as if they hadn't pushed through that line which separates friends from whatever it was he wished them to be? Why did their connection still seem platonic? Could it be too much time had passed, that whatever urgency there was had been destroyed? In any case, she was the master now. She made up the rules, and broke them when she felt so inclined.

She stubbed her cigarette out.

'I've realized something,' she went on, taking the remaining cigarettes, passing through to the bedroom, 'I've realized what it was about that time in the Sun Well,' – she located a pair of Oscar's pyjamas with quiet efficiency, sneaking a head start on him, as it were, 'You do know I'm doing some studies of that photo you saw?' she called, sliding back behind the door and, slipping off her dress and underwear – 'Lilliana's Sun Well?' his voice asked – she got into his floral top and bottom, hurriedly buttoning herself up before he caught up with her.

'Yes, Lilliana's Sun Well.'

'No, I didn't know.'

'The reason why I think I was drawn to the smashed plant pot, why I've become obsessed with it, with the context that went with it,' (she looked at herself in a mirror and adjusted her hair, flashed a row of straight teeth at herself), 'is – is – how can I say – is because the moment when the soil fired out of the pot was a millisecond of unfettered energy, and that, for me, is the essence of creation. And ... to capture that in the stillness of paint, that would be something.'

'You look sweet in those,' he said, appearing suddenly at the door. He didn't want to talk about painting.

'Thanks. I sometimes think a painter makes it impossible for herself, because she's using this blobby, thick stuff. It's packaged in tubes, like tooth paste, for Christ's sake.

'How can you create life, even the illusion of life, how can you hook that thing and stick it in a two-dimensional frame? Van Gogh did it, Gorky kind of did it, Otto Reinhard almost did it, Modigliani didn't really – his work is dead, there's no mobility, it's exquisite but it's like an etching.

'The only way to ever do anything good is to tax the medium to bursting point. Listen to me – I sound like – like – so pompous. Isn't it liberating to talk bollocks?'

She glided through to the bathroom. Oscar tried to think of something intelligent to say but nothing came. So he got changed after switching off the stereo and closing the windows, leaving a small one ajar. He waited for her at the edge of the bed, anxious. He really hoped the night wouldn't be one of interminable, sleepless frustration. She came back and climbed into bed.

'Coming?' she asked matter of factly.

'In a second.'

He brushed his teeth, turned off the main lights, and switched on a side-lamp. So now they were to be an old married couple and he feared they had, courtesy of some maddening, perverse logic, managed to bypass all the excitement and arrive at an innocuous place drained of even the possibility of sex. He remembered the man who had come up to him in the park, zipping up his fly. Were they now going to be old friends, happening to be sharing a bed? Surely not. They had kissed, after all. But what did that really mean?

He dragged himself under the covers. She was already on her side, her face turned away so it was now completely impossible to read her thoughts.

'Are you comfortable?' he mumbled, trying desperately to postpone the moment at which the light would have to be switched off, and so finally, for once and for all, kill the idea of contact and usher in the temporary death of consciousness.

'This bed's delicious. It's nice having you next to me.'

'I'm glad. So ... can I get you anything? A glass of water? A sandwich? I could ring room service, ask for a sandwich.'

'A sandwich?'

'They'll do you any kind. Bacon, lettuce and tomato, chicken with goat's cheese; they do a really nice club sandwich actually – '

'No thanks.'

'Right.'

Silence, save for the whirr of a solitary car taking forever to get out of earshot.

'What about some hot milk? Shall I ask them to send up a glass of nice hot milk?'

'Oscar, really, I don't want anything.'

'Right you are. Oh well. Well, there you have it. Just goes to show, doesn't it?'

'What?'

'Oh ... nothing. Oh well, oh well.'

The quilt rustled as she yanked it over to her side, creating an imbalance he had no intention of adjusting.

'There you have it,' he said.

Images of the orgy in the park flashed up like a strobe.

'What about some chocolate? Do you fancy some – '

'Oscar! You're treating me as if I'm pregnant!'

More silence.

'So I suppose you'll want me to put the light out now?' he asked.

'Do you have any candles? I feel like a candle.'

'I do; that's a brilliant idea; candles, that's what we need.'

He hopped out, rubbing his hands together, dashed to a drawer, took out a little dish with a solid stump of beeswax stuck to it, lit it, turned off the side-lamp and clambered back under the covers. Shadows came to life dispassionately.

'That was a very good idea,' he said.

She said nothing.

But the idea had already exhausted all it had to offer in the way of creating delay.

He moved closer to her, peering at the nape of her neck, letting her scent wash over him. She adjusted herself, her arms curling up towards her chin, her legs bending into a more fetal position.

She wished he would shut up now; she needed some peace and quiet. It came, since he had no more escape routes. He watched the shadows rise and fall as currents disturbed the flame. Beside her, so close to her mysteries he felt a violent rush of happiness. She turned round to face him, her eyelids pressed together. Oscar could hear time's cogs turning; he felt as though he was inside a giant clock, the second hand ticking with impossible clarity. He pored over her, as if by so doing he could prevent her descent into sleep. Her eyelids were so fine he wondered if they could possibly shut out the light. She looked carnal and peaceful at the same time, her hair a slanted, wavy grille across her eyes and nose. They both settled into spaces of stillness.

Until, obeying an order seeping from exhaustion, from the trance of exhaustion, without really knowing what he was doing, he kissed her. At first her lips did not speak to his but he persisted until she pushed off the heavy rind of sleep and she kissed him back and their heads climbed and turned and succumbed to a mild fervor, pivoted at the join of their mouths. Her eyes opened, her mouth opened, her hands curled round his face, tenderly, tightly; the kiss grew like the liquid wax on top of the candle. At once, without any suggestion of dissonance, they had passed into another kind of understanding, another kind of expression. She whispered could she take this off but before he could say yes she had already reached his top button and something in him also unbuttoned and he stirred at the understatement of her touch, and pleasure coruscated through the suddenly live circuitry of their bodies. Over her head, her guiding hands cast aside her own pyjama top and in a cauterized instant he glimpsed her freckled breasts. In the candlelight, the expressionist light, the quilt slipped slowly onto the floor as upright they supported each other in a searching delicacy. She fell back into the bedsheets and taking her hair, lifting it up she brushed its length against his face, then letting herself subside the whiteness behind her as she lay back made her magical, her olive skin next to tenebrous twines the whole distilled by the yellow ochre light. He watched her, emptied of words, and leaned to kiss her and she breathed quickly and her eyes tightened and he looked for the moment at which her soul would leap from them and she stroked his neck and back, interrupted by the line which she prized her hand under and found there something which he writhed for, aching to step outside this constraint, though he wasn't sure she would like him to be naked but then she said huskily I'm hot and she broke away and she was naked suddenly and up till now her beauty had been a rehearsal a fragment of itself now it was dazzling and complete and he was greedily feasting his eyes on her completeness and saying you're beautiful you're beautiful and she was kissing him all over now brittle kisses his eyelids even he had never been kissed there and even when she stopped he was bewitched by the knowledge she would start again and when he moved away when he took a moment to pinch himself to keep up with all this pleasure it was enough merely to observe, to lose himself in the form of her and mere perception was life lived to the full and he remembered the speech in the park.

Was this what Bloch was talking about? As he ran his hand along her slender leg and came to rest at the dark mass of hair and touched her breasts with diffident fingers he asked himself how could such intensity be recreated in the absence of her flesh? And he knew now that all the ideas of the speech were just ideas, suggesting rapture could be extracted from vulnerability, when it was won only through contact with another. And the contact those in the audience had had with each other was too frenzied to allow for the rebirth he now experienced.

The contours of his lover's body, for she was his lover now, this time had told him (and yet the word, with all its grandeur surprised him) were his to blend into, to sink into, to be swept inside, as a tide sweeps over pebbles and claims them within its foam. The sweet anguish that came to him was entwined in her proximity, the appetite which increased his and satisfied it at the same time, limbs whose secrets were being surrendered. Herself nestling so near he was dissolved, her lips fastened on his neck, her hand against his, fingers slotted together like lattice, time finally rendered meaningless – a reel of film that goes on spinning, forever.

The light of the candle flickered. Outside, the odd car still insisted on advertising the power of its engine. And when the sound died away the ensuing silences were unearthly, continually signaling the day's death knell. They were in a clandestine place, lying there together, a place sealed off from the continuities of normal consciousness. For Oscar, the sweetness of these moments even exceeded what had gone before. He was engulfed in the happiness of proximity, the knowledge that he could, by willing his fingers to move, brush her hair, by willing his arm to move he could reach out to her skin and find in its golden compass the affirmation of life he'd always craved.

He retrieved the quilt from the floor and underneath its cover they held each other for a time, until she sat up and grappled for a cigarette and lit it, webs of smoke twirling, bending back on themselves, breaking up into capillaries of near transparency. She watched this languid display and thought of her studies of the scene from the Sun Well.

She smoked restfully, and passed the cigarette to him. They passed it between them, as if that cigarette was an emblem of ongoing communication, wherein they found another (tiny) place in which to further pursue intimacy.

She said (and the sound of her voice was a shock after their wordlessness), 'Did you think this would happen?'

'I think I would have been less surprised if the walls had caved in, or if a jumbo jet had landed inside the living room.'

'Well, there's nearly enough room for one.'

Then she added, after a pause, 'I think you're being a little bit dramatic nonetheless.'

'Am I? I don't know about that. It's strange to finally live out what I've dreamt about.'

'So I made your dreams come true, to invoke the cliché.'

'You did. And I have to strongly resist the impulse to get down on my knees and build a shrine to you.'

She laughed.

'I was surprised as well, you know.'

He wanted to say, 'But not sorry, I hope?' but managed to stop himself, realizing in time she would recoil from the exposed white skeleton of his insecurities.

'I've got to get some water,' she said.

She got up, her nakedness an insolent challenge to the world or perhaps to him, walking with leonine abandon. And he was transfixed by her performance, and his eye unashamedly followed the line of her legs, the dark curve of her back and buttocks, the ebony hair shivering in time with her movements, coming to a stop in the small of her back.

She appeared a moment later and in bed downed her glass in one. Then she poured the few remaining drops onto his head and whispered, 'There, I've anointed you.' Her face was everywhere cognizant of her joke, its silliness, her eyes and lips announcing her enjoyment.

'Hey ... don't do that ... it's wet,' he mumbled.

'You started it.'

'How?'

'With that octopus kiss.'

'Must we?'

'We must. You were so ridiculous earlier – asking me if I wanted hot milk and chocolate.'

'I know.'

The conversation was muted, unhurried. There was something about the exchanges which was full of grace. They sank over each other, and kissed, a different sort of kiss, a slower, thoughtful kiss. Some strands of her hair rested on his chest, parts of her he might keep.

'I wanted to ask you ... did anything come of the show at the Earl gallery?' he asked.

'No, or if it did, Nicholas didn't let on. I bumped into him in Piccadilly. He seemed to be sorry for being such an arsehole. He said he'd met a dealer who was perfect for me. I told him it was too late for that.'

'Perhaps you should give him another chance.'

'No way.'

'You gave me another chance.'

'I knew you were going to say that.'

She reached for another cigarette – there was something wonderful about the way she abandoned herself to unheeding hedonism. And it infected him, her imperturbability, the way she brushed aside life's debris and found something fresh and novel underneath it, as if being with her was like being educated all over again in the ways of living – she was a teacher whose methods were oblique and dazzling.

'You know, I have a confession to make,' she said.

'Oh?'

'I saw you that time you came to the house, a week ago.'

'Really?'

'Sure, out of the corner of my eye. You didn't exactly conceal yourself very discreetly.'

'Didn't I? Didn't you have any desire to acknowledge me?'

'No, why should I have? I was angry with you; it didn't seem very appropriate. Plus I was working.'

'I would never have known. You, unlike me, concealed yourself – or rather your reactions – impeccably.'

'I'm used to concealing my reactions. Women have to ... much more than men. I'm also used to being spied on.'

'Is that so?'

'Yes. I find it quite exciting in a way. It's a form of flattery really. In the way certain kinds of jealousy are inverted compliments. The spy as admirer.'

'Doesn't it depend on who the spy is?'

'Sometimes. Not always.'

'So who spied on you?'

'The past.'

'That's enigmatic.'

'Yes, peering at me with its beady eye.'

'No – who?'

'Oh, all sorts; men passing down the street, having to stop and imbibe, stunned by this vision in the bay window; raincoat voyeurs masturbating – '

'What?!'

'It's OK, they're just these poor bastards on the whole. What can they do? They've got nothing, no-one.'

'And you'd let them do that in front of your house?'

'I just went on working.'

'But isn't that a terrible act of abuse?'

'It is for a certain kind of woman, yes. But I can deal with it. Not because I'm strong, but because it doesn't surprise me. I mean it's only happened a couple of times.'

'You're remarkably philosophical.'

'That's not the word for it.'

And then it felt as though he knew nothing about the woman he had just made love to. But then he asked himself: why should I assume I know anything about Najette? And isn't it better to be surprised? Wouldn't it be terribly boring if I knew her so very well? He could see how compelling these revelations of hers – their effects casually disorientating – really made her.

'I'm going away ... again,' she went on.

'When and where?'

'Egham. Tomorrow. It's in the middle of nowhere. A friend asked me to house sit for a few weeks. Want to come?'

'Seriously?'

'Why not? I think you should leave this dead splendor; it's not meant for you, only for royalty, and they're mummified already. We could paint.'

'It's too late for me. I missed my chance. It's too late.'

Suddenly there were tears in his eyes; one of them escaped and began running down his cheek. She leaned over and interrupted its progress with her little finger.

'Don't cry, Oscar. It's freedom.'

'I know, freedom. Of course I'll go. How could I not? But I'm not sure how I'm going to extricate myself or what I'm going to do for money. You see, Ryan Rees has basically been subsidizing me.'

'I sold "Butterfly." I didn't tell you.'

'You did? You mean you really sold it?'

'Yes, that's why I said "I sold "Butterfly.""'

'Who to?'

'This Russian collector. A friend from Sotheby's introduced us.'

'What's his name?'

'Sergei something. Bordanov or kill-you-off. Gave me a cheque for £10,000. Just like that. Like it was fifty pence. I'm hoping it won't bounce. He told me he wants to organize an exhibition for me in Tiflis. Just a lot of hot air, I warrant. Invited me to spend the weekend with him in his Moscow mansion.'

'I wonder why.'

'Now, now, calm down. When the cheque clears I might be able to feed you. But I can't promise caviar and vodka.'

The candle, having been hovering on the brink of expiry for some time, blew itself out. Moments later, after a silence which they took to be the night's last, they fell asleep. It was as though sleep was a thought on the point of being lost, which they retrieved just in time.

*

Oscar was awakened by a signal telling him something was different. Najette wasn't there. He panicked until he found a small folded note by the pillow.

*Birds warble, Handel's Messiah shakes the pillars, etc, etc.*
*GOOD MORNING!!*
*It's a beautiful day .... I have to go for a jog, meet my dealer, be serenaded by gypsies, etc.*
*Dear Oscar,*
*No ... I haven't deserted you. Oh ye of little faith!!*
*Do you remember that time I disappeared when you came round for lunch? Here I go again. I have to pack my divine sable antelope brushes (how I love antelopes) and my studies and sea scrolls and maimeri – I love it, I keep it in jam jars, I suck it through a straw. Meet me at Waterloo at 4 this afternoon, at platform one, a nice, wholesome number. Don't tell anyone where you're going. I don't want any "gentlemen" of the press bothering us. Last night we were devils. Today let's be angels. Then we can be devils again. Etc. Etc.*
*Kisses, kisses, (wet and dry)*
*Najette*

He read the note eleven times, lingering especially over the last few sentences, savoring them. He wanted to make sure they were real, that the note wasn't a forgery of some sort. He slipped on some clothes, then walked across to stare out of the windows. It was a long drop. He noticed the small band of disciples camped outside, tiny figures stirring among blankets.

As he splashed his face with water there was a knock at the door and Ryan Rees tumbled in. He was clutching half a dozen newspapers. He started speaking very rapidly, but not so rapidly that it was a surprise in any way.

'Oscar, have you seen these? – "Babel's Crusade Leads to Orgy in the Park" – "Indecent Exposure in the Night "–"Have the English Finally Lost Repressions Due to Tibet Messiah?" Even *The Sun* loves you: "Sex Ed – Babel Style." I've printed out three hundred pages of speculation, response and approbation from the internet which just appeared overnight – let me read you some of this stuff. Some idiot posted footage of the fuck-fest on You Tube – it got 2 million views before it was removed – don't worry, we'll get it back – You Tube can shove its violated terms of service up its well-viewed, well-oiled sphincter. Never in my wildest dreams did I think we'd sell out. And let me tell you you were great, really great. Faber & Faber want you to write a book about your philosophy of life. They've already suggested a title: *The Way of Babel*. Cyril Vixen wants to take your portrait for *Rogue*. I can only assume he's dropped the lawsuit. Channel 4 want to do a documentary about you. Also: we've had an offer from Kazooi-Template, a three ad deal. For the first one they want you to pose butt naked on the back passenger seat while saying something about what makes life worth living and including in your list the experience of riding in one of their saloons. They're willing to let you write your own copy ...'

'Before you go on, I need to tell you something.'

'Yes, of course, keep talking Oscar. Oh, I knew we could do something great with you. My instincts, oh my instincts; I love those flickers of female intuition. This has all been a dress rehearsal, a little appetizer. Torrents of rhetoric, lecture circuits, next stop the United States of Hysterica. Oscar, things happen when you're around, it's just weird ... you just have this effect on people, it's ... fantastic. The only word for it, my friend.'

'Rees, I'm quitting. I'm stopping. I've had enough.'

Rees clenched his fist and stared hard at it. Then he unclenched it, dumped the newspapers on a table and pulled out a cigar. He bit the end off and lit up. Then he took a seat and smoked quietly for a few minutes. Oscar paced about, waiting for an outburst which didn't come.

'Care for a cigar, Oscar?'

'OK.'

The formalities proceeded apace, Oscar took the cigar and then a seat opposite him, grateful of the buffer of the small table between them. They smoked in silence for a few moments.

'Oscar, what did you mean just now? Did I hear you correctly?'

'Please don't get upset. The thing is ... I have to stop this. None of what I've been saying is original; it's all coming from another source. I'm not a philosopher, I'm not a guru, there's just a void here' – he stuck an index finger to his chest – 'and I've been pretending. We all know I've never been to India, we all know I know nothing about Sanskrit. All I've ever done is a little bit of projecting and life modeling. The public have a right not to be made fools of.'

'Oscar, don't you think I know you're a fraud? That's what the hell we've been doing, you and I, creating a fake, a bit of forgery, except in this case the exhibit's a man.'

'I'll offer the press a simple statement, and tell them I'm retiring.'

'But you've only just begun.'

'That's true, but I can't carry on like this.'

Rees puffed on the cigar thoughtfully, then gestured logically with it, going on evenly.

'Oscar, may I ask, do you have something against me personally?'

'No.'

'Do you see me as a cold representative of the real world, a man who does commerce with the world and fits in?'

'No.'

'Do you resent me, have contempt for me?'

'No, not exactly.'

'Are you unhappy with the life I've given to you? Are you unhappy with power, influence; are you dissatisfied with a penthouse suite in Chelsea? Would you prefer your bedshit in Elephant and Castle? Do these gold taps and this triple bed fill you with distaste?'

'No ... well, in a way.'

Suddenly, with extraordinary violence, he lurched forward and stubbed his cigar out on the palm of Oscar's hand. Oscar wailed in pain while Rees bawled viciously, 'You fuck! If you quit now I'll ruin you. I'll see to it you don't get a job as a lavatory attendant. You pathetic little shit. Is this the thanks I get for pulling you out of obscurity? I've spent thousands of pounds on this enterprise and I mean to recoup my losses. Not only that but I mean to make money, and continue making money out of you. Yes, Oscar, yesterday proved that you're a goldmine, but I can't be doing with your eccentricities. I haven't fucked about concocting lies, telling stories, wooing editors and writers to see you bow out. I haven't put you up in a luxury hotel and then glimpse success to see you quit. Oh, I see. It's unethical, Oscar; that's what's troubling you. Look around you, shitface, there are no ethics or truth anymore; grow up a little, there is no reality anymore; reality is what you choose to make up, what you choose to manufacture, or what I, Ryan Rees, choose to manufacture, to be exact. Get used to it; it's too late to cry now. You should have said something at the time. Did you think I was doing all this for you out of the charity of my heart; did you think I was trying to be a philanthropist? Did you think I was some kind of cretin?!'

He moved over and, in a single clean motion, smashed the centre of Oscar's face with his elbow as if shattering a pane of glass. Oscar toppled over, feeling excruciating pain well up in his jaw and nose. He squinted up at Rees from the floor. Rees had finally unveiled himself. And that mask-like face, those inert features – trained to register neither elation nor dismay – had changed beyond recognition. Up until that moment some part of Rees had been consistently edited, hidden from view. Now that part slotted into place and the ugliness of his soul leapt out. Oscar felt a chill creep into his bones, a chill which went deeper than physical pain.

'Oscar, you're not going anywhere. You have an all-guns-blazing press conference at 2.45 this afternoon. Every paper in town's going to be there. Waiting for me outside is my industrial strength meathead Edwin; he'll be staying and would be only too happy to pull your head off so don't even think about leaving. Remember, we're on the tenth floor. Perhaps you'd care to jump; why not? I expect you may even survive and end up a cripple; that would be good, why not; the crippled prophet – we could cart you around on a wheelchair; what a coup, a great image, the "mobile messiah." We'd get the sympathy vote – a huge market there. Let me tell you, Oscar, if you try and escape the only place you'll belong is nineteenth-century Italy in an opera house, singing as a castrato. You've got a job to do, and by God, you'll be doing it. From now on daily appearances at the Verdant Theater. Seventy quid a shot. I think you'll agree it's a nice proposition. So wipe that adolescent mug of yours, clean up and take a shower. And don't smoke anymore, Oscar, you sniveling little prick. Stick to words, you fucking ingrowing hair. *Bon voyage.*'

Taking up all the papers, he let them unfold and crash all over him. Then he gave Edwin very specific instructions not to let anyone in or out of the room.

After a long time Oscar got to his feet painfully, wiping the blood spilling from his nose. It was all over the carpet. He staggered to the bathroom. He grabbed some toilet roll and pressed it against his nose, staring at his burned palm. He plodded towards the door and peered through the spy hole. He could see the well-built, unmoving form outside. He moved away and slumped into a chair and held his nose until the bleeding had stopped. Then his eyes came to rest on the gaudy drinks cabinet in the corner. Its contents awakened in him a desire for that alcoholic membrane, the membrane that, by misting over the ugliness of reality, alchemically made it more palatable.

So he downed a double whiskey. After a few sips he felt less shaky.

I can't climb out of the windows, I'm up too high, I can't walk out of the door.

The full desperation of the situation hit hard and he gave in to panic, hyperventilating. Oh, how he wanted to be with Najette! He had another double whiskey, which calmed him down, and then another which made him feel fine, and then another which made him shout incoherent words to Edwin who didn't hear him through the sturdy door. Then, in a drunken stupor, he made a phone call.

'Hello, is that the police? I'm in trouble.'

'Yes, sir, what seems to be the problem?'

'I've drunk too much.'

'Who is this?'

'No ... no... sorry, that's not the only problem ... the main thing is ... forget what I just said ... I'm locked in ... I've been forcibly detained in my own hotel suite ... I'm calling from ... where am I calling from? ... this man ...'

There was a clear, ominous click.

He had another drink and felt buoyed up.

'This is Oscar Babel; I'm calling from the Grosvenor, and I've been forcibly detained against my will, and I have no means of getting out ... can you please come to my ass ... assis ... tance...please?'

'Who is detaining you sir, and may we speak with them?'

'A fat bear, at least a mile ... long.... a mile long....'

'Sir, have you been drinking?'

'Yes ... no ... no, of course not ... please will you come to the Grosvenor Hotel ... this is Oscar Babel and I am ... have been ... forcibly brained ...drained ...against my will ...'

'And who is detaining you sir?'

'I've already told you, a fat bear ...'

'And is it currently residing at London Zoo, sir?'

The voice laughed merrily and then added, 'Is there any coffee in the house, sir? I think that might be the best thing.'

Then – nothing.

Oscar's mind was spinning, his body was going slack, caving in on him. He began to realize he was still a prisoner, and couldn't do much about it. He couldn't shift his brain back into sobriety, paralyzed as he was by alcohol. Something in the constable's last words persisted. He tried to recall what they'd said to one another. Grosvenor Hotel ... detained ... bears. London Zoo. Then: a blank. Had I been drinking? Drinking? Coffee. That was it. Coffee. He needed coffee. He dashed to the phone, tripped up and landed painfully on his face. From where he was spread out supine on the floor, the walls and ceiling began a sickly dance.

'Room service,' he shouted. 'Room service. Coffee. Coffee.'

He lay like that for some minutes, spinning. Then he managed to drag himself up and hobble into the bathroom and drink from the taps, cold water shooting all over his face and shirt. This revived him slightly. He wondered if he should try the police again but he couldn't face it just then. He dragged himself into the shower and poured all the taps on and stood under the water which fired off in all directions, since he had not pulled the curtain across. He already noticed a dull ache creeping into his skull, the first intimations of a hangover which had arrived about eight hours ahead of schedule. He stepped out of the shower. Everything still swayed.

He slumped onto the bed and slept for about half an hour. When he woke he felt worse, shaky, feverish. He drank some more water and tried to collect his thoughts, tried to lift the fogginess from his mind. He gritted his teeth, forced his mind to engage.

He walked over to his portable cassette player and pushed a button. Bloch's voice started speaking.

*'When I was little I would stare for ages out of the window, locked in my mother's kitchen, as she busied herself with pots and pans. I would watch the rain and wonder why I had landed on this strange planet. The rain fascinated me, many hours watching it fall. But it was, as I think I've said, in this disconnected ramble, the dawn that really moved me. But what was the point of my moments of stillness? After all one lives in the world, not in a church, or in a work of art, or in lunar caves. I still have to learn to make friends with the noise, to accept it. I always had to pit my wits against the world. When you relinquish fear gifts come to you, blown in a serene wind hovering in your path. Of course I never did relinquish it; I never did accept life. And you do the same, Wormy.*

*But I want to continue staring through the windows, staring at the rain, thinking. So long as I can give the windows a friendly wipe from time to time to make sure I'm seeing clearly, or rather seeing through clarity.'*

Oscar switched off the machine. He took some more water. His head was raging. He picked up one of the papers and tried to read.

Then he had an idea. He picked up the phone again and took a few deep breaths. He practiced a few words out loud. He sounded all right. He tried to ignore his head. He summoned up the voice for a great performance.

'Hello, this is Oscar Babel in room 1008. I've just noticed my windows are absolutely filthy. It is vitally important they're cleaned as soon as possible. In order to meditate I need an environment of clarity and cleanliness.'

On the other end of the line came the eager-to-please voice of the young female receptionist: 'Of course, sir; I understand the importance of the matter. The people we usually employ could be with you this afternoon.'

'That's too late!'

'Yes, sir, but the thing is – '

'Look, do you know who I am? I am Oscar Babel and I'm holding a very important press conference later this afternoon and I have to have a clear head and a clear window.'

'Of course, sir; just a minute, sir.'

Oscar could hear some rustling and a voice raised in anger; then another voice came on the line.

'Hello, Mr. Babel, this is Felix Speace, the deputy manager. Of course I understand the situation sir. The company we usually employ can be with you in under an hour. Don't be alarmed when you see a cage outside the window. But I can't understand how the windows got so dirty. They were cleaned only last week.'

'Yes, well never mind about that, just see that they get here.'

While he waited he stuffed clothes, tapes, bottles of whiskey, and some chocolates into a suitcase, retrieved all Bloch's tape recordings and shoved them in a plastic bag. He had another glass of water, and then another. Then he urinated for such a long time that his legs ached. He peered through the spy glass. The henchman hadn't budged an inch. Wasn't he getting bored?

He waited. Two anxious hours passed. He kept up a steady stream of phone calls but they did nothing to speed up the arrival of the window cleaners. He was terrified Rees would turn up before they did. But at last, at around 2.15, a cage, about two meters by three, materialized, slowly ascending as if on its way to heaven. Inside, there were two men in overalls and cloth caps. They beamed at Oscar as they began mopping and rolling, choosing to disregard the fact of the windows' immaculate condition.

Oscar opened a large panel parallel to the faintly quivering cage. The latter was attached to a hydraulic arm connected to a truck in the middle of the King's Road. The waves of fresh air instantly revived him and he wondered why he hadn't thought to open the windows earlier.

'At last, what kept you?' Oscar asked the elder of the two, who was quite taken aback by Oscar's bruised and battered face, now clearly revealed.

'Sorry Mr. Bubble, there was more traffic than you could shake a stick at. Don't worry; the windows'll be as good as new.'

'Never mind that now,' Oscar said in irritation. 'I'm getting in.'

'What? No one's allowed in my working cage, Mr Bubble.'

'I'm Oscar *Babel* and I'm coming down.'

He placed his things, having to stretch a little, into the cage, and began climbing out.

'What are you doing?! The insurance doesn't cover this!! It's not right! What are you doing?'

As the cage hovered, out of reach, Oscar made a fatal error: he looked down. Cars were speeding back and forth, red and blue boxes. He felt a tidal wave of nausea growing and thrashing around in his stomach. He threw up all over some people who were on their way to the Chelsea Cinema. He wiped his mouth on his shirt sleeve. He tried and failed to reach the cage.

'Look, man, can't you shift that thing a little?' Oscar shouted in exasperation.

Finally the cage creaked along and Oscar slipped into it.

'Don't worry, I know what I'm doing,' said Oscar. 'Do any of you have aspirin? Christ, I need aspirin.'

The workmen stared at Oscar as though he was an alien being newly entering terrestrial society.

'Come on, then, let's go,' Oscar snapped.

One of them, emerging from his stupor, pressed a red button and with a sudden jolt the cage began a wobbly descent. Oscar peered up to see if he could still make out the hotel suite. He could. He could also see Ryan Rees, who had apparently just entered. He saw that tight set of lips moving automatically. Oscar wished the cage would hurry up. But Rees was looking away and as he now went to inspect the bedroom and bathroom the cage dipped out of sight. Oscar breathed a single monumental sigh, and all the tension in his body was gloriously dissipated. He jumped up and down, causing the cage to sway dangerously.

Upon arrival Oscar cried, 'That was fun! Here you are.'

He handed each of the men a twenty pound note, which they took in silence. (With that money they later bought too many drinks in a nearby pub and threw up all over the King's Road.)

He was a dozen yards off from the main entrance; he could make out the inevitable swarm of pressmen waiting outside the revolving doors and the camped followers nearby, still hoping to have breakfast with him (or rather lunch now.) He secreted himself into an alcove. Then, when a taxi suddenly appeared, he just managed to hail it in time, and yelled, 'Over here, gentlemen,' as he bundled inside. Some of the quicker journalists realized what was happening and started sprinting after it, but couldn't muster the superhuman levels of speed to keep up. Meanwhile, the disciples were telling each other stories about Ouija boards and so remained sweetly oblivious to the departure of their savior.

Inside the cab he was ecstatic, his sights set on Najette and Egham. He could hardly wait to see her again. As they gained speed he took in the colorful streets of Chelsea, feeling safely displaced from prying eyes and the burden of performing. He smiled quietly at the developments of the last few minutes, developments which had catapulted him into another dimension, another place, dreamy and becalmed. Then he began to compose a simple letter of farewell.

*

From *The Times*
(4 September)
## Goodbye guru
**From Professor Bart F. Walla**

SIR, The decision by Oscar Babel to retire doesn't come as a surprise, though it is regrettable. Perhaps we can assume he is going back to a more humble lifestyle, closer to the ashrams of India than the hotels of London. In other words he has probably decided to return to something like the world he moved in before. We should be grateful for the brief bursts of illumination he provided during the Imagures and his truncated speech at Kensington Gardens.

I think it was inevitable, however, that we would have to say goodbye to Mr. Babel at the height of his fame. Mr. Babel has reached the point at which he knows his teachings can only be compromised in the very fact of the expression and communication of them. He knows that true integrity lies in keeping silent, and that retreating from the spotlight is the logical terminus to any argument and speaks volumes. Mr. Babel is opting for non-negotiability. His soul remains intact even though it has had to have dealings with the sordid, so-called real world.

Yours faithfully,
Bart F. Walla,
(Professor of Theology)
University of Bangor
September 2.

## 24

Three days had elapsed since Bloch was admitted to hospital and he still wasn't eating. The osmolite drip fed into his veins. He was drinking fluids but no solid food has passed into him since he had been admitted apart from two portions of rice, a new potato, some salad, and half a boiled egg. He had aches and pains in every part of his body, though he had more energy owing to the drip and was able to resume his tape recordings.

His body continued its relentless retreat into itself, revealing the outlines of the spine, rib cage, pelvis and hip joints. As with a block of marble which is hewn down to the statue the artist sees residing somewhere within it, Bloch's old body was being hewn down to a new version of itself, chiseled by fasting. And he still rationalized his decline in terms of asceticism and purity.

When he had the energy he spoke into his microphone in an oddly tinny voice.

30 August
I'll just say this. Let the dog man leave and breed among flies. The pale yellow moon is unseen by his eyes. Dogs barking mad at the moon, running along corridors. They make the ladies swoon. Why the bloody tearing of limb from limb? Give me the dogs. I'll soon lick them ... into shape. Show them who's boss. And in the meantime all other lunatics can scrape at each other, over scraps they take for gold.

I didn't ask for this ... hammock. When the death comes to release me will it be like the anesthetic of the bow-legged woman?

Colors fading, sounds cracked.

This body must be transparency ... so pure mind will pass through it.

Soon I'll make my meals from thought, from air ...

I'm achieving luminosity, my true nature's spirit, not body.


31 August

They come, they wake me, they weigh me. They give me cups of tea; they stick things in me, temperature gauges behind my ear; they take blood. Why do they talk of sausage and mash, of scampi and chops? Why do they meddle?

Ate roll. Half of roll. Felt sick but it didn't come up.

I don't know what it would take ... to be healed ...

I keep thinking ... the times when Natty made chicken stock. Take up the carcass in those hairy arms. In the company of others I'd see a midget and cry out, "There goes Natty, she's joining the Moscow State Circus." Can you imagine? Occasionally the old spark came between the bedclothes, then all hell broke loose, she clawed at my eyebrushes. She had such sexy teeth. I liked it when she dipped her fingers in mustard, coated my face in it and licked it off. Still wasn't hot enough for mademoiselle. And green peppers.

I used to spend hours watching her floss. She took the floss with her, left nothing behind. That was always her way, to be fastidious. Natty dresser. Even when she made dinner she faxed her friends afterwards, listing the cooking time, utensils used, ingredients. God, she was Amazonian. I was the escort down river, wobbling in my little canoe. For a hairy woman she was *très* appealing. I loved it when ... Natty scribbled her appointments – always used to keep ... appointments, kept everything – on arm, hand, palm. Sometimes my kisses tasted of ink, black or blue, I forget; but you should have seen her when real, not a fiction I'm devising. But that's it. I can't tell what's real anymore. Re-inventing her so many times I forget. She brought a fucking haystack home once – said it would give the house some earthiness – we were too urban up in Islington, needed to get in touch with nature.

And those hairs on pillow case! And false eyelashes curling like tongues of flame! There, under the ground, running invisible, subterranean world ... soot and dust and hair and pus gathered in the sewer. How many years before the sink finally, in one fell swoop, would be blocked by her comings and goings? Only a real woman like Natalie could have blocked that drain properly; done it justice; shown it flesh was mightier than marble. I envied that dragon snout of hers, flames jostling from nostrils. She killed me each time with her Spanish Inquisition eyes, curling skin that to touch would mean ... third-degree burns.

I do feel better with this drip on. I wonder – does it suit me? Perhaps I'll start a new trend.

Now my lust's not even poetic, time was, I remember, I ... same lust could set a house on fire, chew through beams of wood. And drops of blood, now here, now there, found their *raison d'être* within the swollen cock, swelling after sleep. Down insolent wretch dictating like a lunatic fascist.

Now my poker's a peanut.

1 September
What nausea, the thought of ... a sickly cuddle, bodily fluids, rotting teeth, skin and dust. Yuk. I want ... to exist in a vacuum, far from human secretions. Spared all that mess ... at least let me take tea with gods. I don't ask much, my Cinderella dream – to become a vapor, drifting through space.

How could I have ever talked of the sexual ... in terms of a divine union of souls, gateway to heaven on earth? More like the gateway to stinking bodies, oozing sweat and semen. Must have been mad.

Starting to feel tired, numb. Hair's falling out in clumps – trapped.

They came with trolleys – told me "eat, you little shit" – I stuffed cod behind radiator – they snooped around later – & found it – Sister Brunhilde with strutting manner – wakey, wakey, rise and shine, fuck off sow, porky potbelly, enough flesh in your backside to fill the Grand Canyon. How much have you guzzled while little children starved?

2 September
Wish I could coat words in acid, spit out my outrage in final emission with phlegm; let me cover the world in it! All parasites, all who turn death into state opening of parliament, all disregarders of truth, beetles crawling in shrunken world. I'll get my revenge; I'll kill them all, backwards, forwards, lingering; slow death waiting in the wings. Done with charity, done with kindness. Leave it all to Wormy. So tired, and I speak the truth, truth no man, not even I, can bear. Burn photographers who film misery! Incinerate politicians who conspire with conspiracy! Holy men can get fucked; they've all along been the devil's accomplices! I ... can ... see ... everything now, don't you see with me?

4 September
Satisfied now? Do you have a life now, Wormy? Did you gain a life by taking mine?

5 September
I'll tell you something; that is, if anyone's listening: my mind's ... it's ... floating further, further away ... even the sound of my voice ... it's alien to me ... husky, dead, squeaking on and on. The bod deceives. Changes, not constant. Let's not forget smells. Armpit ... I might vomit out entrails, for want of food to vomit. See them splat like spaghetti across wall.

What about the balls hanging ... a couple of shriveled tomatoes, what from them gems! Don't let get me started on sweaty abominations, bag lady's underwear left in sun for afternoon.

Door to treasury, anus, stroke it, love it, fuck it, no matter how you do it, unimpressive morsel. Why did you make it ... all these orifices ... smell given half chance, ponging penises, arses like dead donkeys, rotting mouths, mucus breeding up our trunks.

So now you see no to bod makes sense.

No food ... to digest, no smell in mouth, no food in teeth, no flossing, no shit excrete, clear, clean colon. Load lightened.

Actually, in point of fact, my mouth feels like a cow's moved in and has been shitting in it and will go on shitting in it till the cows come home ... which they can't ... as they're all out looking for the one in my head.

My ankles have swollen into tree trunks. Calves ballooning. Why?

But do they make it easier? No, they remind me with pins, tubes, injections of vitamins, iron. The big boo-boo of force-feeding, can't do, because no longer time for force. Dr. Kennel, what does he know? Has he been married to woman who fucked Father? Has he been famous, then six-feet under?

Sometimes ... sometimes ... I feel so light, I will my arm to move and I can't feel it, I'm wafting around drawing rooms ... at the bottom of ocean, invisible, could walk into a room, no one would see me.

So light, so thin.

Running a finger along my spine, it juts out like serrated piping. Don't know how much longer can go on with speaking. Thinking.

Nut doc's back, Dr Kennel's back – the man's a numbskull; thinks I'm out to lunch (hah!) but can't give me drugs because knows it's too risky, so he's reduced to jargon and reasoning. I begin where he leaves off.

7 September
Freak show freak show

Mirror mirror on the wall who is the thinnest of them all

Made me eat salad today. Said, 'Eat, you little shit'. Said well done, said good boy, pat on your pancake back.
Maybe little soup would slip down
Not Crimbo turkey

Crisis – ripped my drip out – big hullabaloo – sectioning came up again – they put it back, couldn't find a vein, found one after much pain –

When she sat astride the toilet seat – fuck, beautiful, glorious; nothing more alluring ... than defeated beauty! Won't dwell on her bottom. But if any bottom deserved a voice hers did.

Webster here before – good person, really. Retarded but good.

If I've preached love always been safe in pulpit far from action, far from where the love is happening.

Special person came with trolley – told me "eat, shit" – I stuffed chop and spuds in drawer – under socks – he found it of course – I said, "you eat it" – he said, "it's for you" – I said "neither of us can eat it now, it's been near my socks." They tire of me.

Came later with jacket potato, hid it behind radiator, took off drip. They told me the social workers are arriving to assess me, see if I'm ripe for sectioning, then force feeding. I don't want to go, I don't want to go

8 September
Never did paint, the cretin. If only a little bit of discipline. If only could shut up, die. If only hadn't come to me. Never met him. Why didn't he ... stay in cinema, rot in dark. Like the rest of us.

9 September
Not Bloch, just assumed his form, no more Bloch than ant giraffe.

Floating through space.

Born again. Time fits in pocket. I'm a molecule. No flesh, just bone and tendon.

Done it. Don't exist anymore.

Love that burns makes clean the pus, the oily woundedness.

You the one I invoke over fire and smoke are lost.

Are lost. Are lost. Are lost. Are lost.

Night (4AM)
Floating ... weeping ... blood for tears, tears in veins.

Floating

Floating

# 25

After Rees had looked in the bathroom and the bedroom, under the bed and in the cupboard, he retrieved his stocky henchman Edwin from where he was standing outside the door, inert and monolithic, cross-examined him; learnt nothing from him, then noticed the opened window and practically fell out of it, straining to see. He spotted the hydraulically operated cage, which by then had completed its descent. Rees screamed at Edwin to go down and get Oscar, who, he bawled, had obviously just escaped seconds earlier and might still be stopped.

Ryan Rees fumed and swore; at first his cursing was functional and mundane, but then, as he found his rhythm, it became ornamental, baroque. He was like a virtuoso pianist who begins with a bald, seemingly unpromising tune and builds around it an increasingly complex set of variations.

'That syphilitic piece of cow dung.

'That piece of shit prick with shit for brains.

'I'll show that little doorstop, I'll feed him to the fucking dogs, I'll feed him to vultures peck-peck-pecking at his heart and liver.

'I'll hand him over to the cannibals then they can slice off his prick. I'll show that little idiot, pigcunt fuckpig piss-arsing around, his dick pissing in the wind, I'll get the wind to blow the wind back in his face, I'll seal his arse with dynamite that little wet fart arsing around with his gonorrhea face, I'll fuck him up the arse little sniveling gibbering cretin with mothballs for balls prick shit fuck fuck fuck.'

By the time he'd reached the end of this foul litany Edwin had returned – alone. Rees's reaction was not good: he grabbed some ashtrays and hurled them into the drinks cabinet. Smash went the brandy glasses. Then he grabbed the Viennese secession screen and jumped up and down on it until it was severely disfigured. Edwin looked on in awe and wonder. Throughout all this Rees' phones emitted a steady stream of beeps and musical medleys, these announcements of arriving text messages providing a spasmodic soundtrack to the ballet of destruction. Then Rees took one of the zinc-galvanized lamps and tossed it into the wrecked drinks cabinet. Crash went the mirror. Then he fired Edwin. Through the door and to the unemployment office went Edwin. Then Ryan Rees made some phone calls, feeling slightly calmer.

He learned that the Royal Parks Agency was planning to sue him for bringing the name of Kensington Gardens into disrepute.

*

Egham: a small and utterly inconsequential town in Surrey, near Windsor and Virginia Water. It boasted one or two Indian restaurants and very little else. Its most alluring feature was probably its train station, with its promise of passage into the outside world.

Oscar and Najette were living on a quiet street – Harvest Road – within reach of a small corner-shop, off-license and newsagent's. There was a wooded footpath nearby leading to Kingswood, one of Royal Holloway College's halls of residence (its main campus was in the vicinity), and down this Najette sometimes ambled, as it provided a pleasant walk. There was also a pub called The Happy Man, which served homemade, overcooked food. Its lasagna and chips was especially popular. The back streets were silent; so silent they could be used as pavements, which was just as well as there were no pavements.

The house sat baking in the late afternoon sun. It was small and semi-detached, with a little garden at its back and a patch of grass, bare in places like a balding head, at its front. Oscar and Najette sat inside the front room, curtains drawn, windows open, the curtains fluttering in the breeze. She was shaving his face, scraping at his cheeks and chin, a wet towel knotted around him. She was using olive oil, which she claimed facilitated the perfect shave, though he was skeptical.

His decision to go away with Najette was, he reflected, the best he'd ever made.

Surrounding both of them were canvasses propped up against the chairs and walls. He recognized the lake, the skull and face, and other works from the exhibition at the Earl Gallery. There were also paintings he'd never seen before; jagged landscapes, etiolated nudes. She'd brought them all along because she felt anxious about leaving them in London. And gathered in a corner, rolled and tied with gaffer tape were the studies for the scene from the Sun Well. She was quite excited about these; she thought she was on the verge of finding something she had always wanted – a truly resonant, truly disquieting image, whose power would unexpectedly ambush the onlooker. She wanted the smashed plant to be an emblem of fearfulness and energy. If she could invest in that one shattered certainty a greater uncertainty she would have achieved her goal. It was a lot to ask for; for the moment Najette was limbering up, stretching the tendons of her brush. She hadn't started to work with oil yet; she wanted to have all her lines and configurations mapped out in her head before she began since, in the past, too-hasty leaps into work had made the results lopsided, in her view.

She felt relieved to be away from London. She found the house – modest, tattered, dusty – provided the right environment for her work; it allowed the work to be the focus, not overwhelmed by too elaborate a setting. The front room received plenty of sunlight, which was important to her; as did the weedy, neglected back garden, where stinging nettles and a hesitant blackberry bush swayed when the wind was strong. Life was oddly idyllic there – though there were no patios or statues, bougainvillea or rhododendrons. In the afternoons, after lunch, they would sit together under the shade of the fledgling apple tree, slumped in deck chairs, reading: Emily Dickinson, Shakespeare's sonnets.

As she scraped at the recalcitrant hairs between his nose and upper lip, yanking his nose up comically, Oscar looked into her eyes, telling himself to wake up to the happiness of this sojourn, because – for once – he was going to appreciate something while it was happening. He didn't miss the hotel and the luxurious life it kept hurling at him. And here, he was anonymous again – nobody could bother him, test him, intimidate him, claim him.

He started cooking elaborate meals, spending sizable chunks of the days in the company of colanders and chopping boards. He made sausages braised in cider with apples; roast lamb with garlic; chicken with mango and sultana, all creations culled with the assistance of the owner's extensive library of cookbooks – she must have had at least twenty piled up next to the bread bin.

But he was worried about Ryan Rees, though he thought it unlikely he could track him down here. Egham was a backwater, and he was pretty sure no-one would recognize him. His fame already seemed unreal, as though only a day spent apart from the activating cogs of the media was enough to precipitate its collapse. And he liked it that way.

Every now and then it crossed his mind to ring Bloch, but he always decided against it; on a couple of occasions he even dialed his first few numbers, then stopped himself and put the handset down.

'There. Finished. Who needs foam?' said Najette, as she shook the razor vigorously in the water bowl next to her. 'This is progress – just going back to the past,' she went on. 'It's like if I started rifling through the bin I'm sure I'd find something I could market somewhere. But you know all about that – marketing. Would you care to make a statement?'

'I never want to make statements again. Just want to talk normally or shut up.'

'That sounds like a step in the right direction.'

She took the bowl and towel and olive oil through to the bath-room. From there she called, 'I think I might start soon on the mag-num opus. It's all in my head; I just have to chuck it down.'

'I think you should. You can wait too long. I'm the living proof of that. Here lies Oscar Babel who couldn't get started.'

'Hey, melancholy baby, no hysterics please. If you cry the tears have to land in the beer.'

Yes, no more hysterics; that was all over now. He was mature; he had to act his age, and if that meant placing a lid over his emotions so be it. No more self-pity, no more lies, no more excuses. If he couldn't paint he couldn't paint. Bemoaning the fact wasn't going to change it.

Najette said, 'I was talking to one of the locals in the off-license and he told me there's a small wood a few miles further out that no one knows about. You can get to it via the Kingswood footpath. Sounds enchanted. What do you think?'

'I'm game.'

She re-emerged, her sandals flopping across the floor.

'How does your face feel?'

'It feels ... it feels like it did when I was twelve ... it doesn't feel like I've just had a very good shave; it feels like you've made me hairless.'

'God, maybe I should think about waxing rich Californian heiresses.'

She started unravelling rolls of paper and, using random objects as paperweights, spread them across the floor. Oscar peered at the studies – delicate renditions of Lilliana's face, jostling with contigu-ous pencil lines, broader treatments in pencil and crayon of another face. In places, a line in ink ending in a throwaway squiggle or a wavy strand of hair in bold outline caught his eye. For him, such details were the clearest indicators of her talent. They were the kind of lines which could only be produced after years of toil, seemingly spontaneous, but the incarnation of refinement and control.

'If you've worked so hard on this thing, done so many studies, it's bound to just blaze with energy when it finally comes together,' he said.

'On the other hand all this preparation might kill it. It's dangerous to make assumptions. What do you think of this?'

She unrolled a large sheet of paper and Oscar saw a square of mingled manganese blue and silver. It made for a waxen, frictionless uniformity. Oscar thought the sky might be this color if the atmosphere could be first cleansed of pollution.

'It's terrific,' he whispered. 'It's so beautiful, eerie.'

'It's high density maimeri – it's hard to get my hands on it. I'm going to use oil and india ink as well.'

'I can't wait to see the final painting. Can you?'

'Oh sure. I'm used to being patient. it's what comes of being a slow worker. I need everything to incubate and ripen, but sometimes I'll fly by the seat of my pants, pulling something out of the hat at the last minute – and it just gives the work an extra something, makes it. But that's scary, because I have absolutely no control over that element. That blue came from a dream I had a few nights ago.'

'Tell me.'

'I was on a boat. Picasso was the skipper. He had masses of black hair. We drifted along and he took me aside and started mumbling, "You're too proud, and I'm going to tame you. I'll tolerate female artists only when they know their place." I didn't really pay him much attention. Anyway, eventually we started passing through scenery with a really unreal quality to it. Everything around us was blue – a drained, plastic kind of blue. I realized the sky and the sea were made of lace or some such fabric. We moved as if through water, but actually if I leant down to touch the water I just felt a dryness. But it was beautiful, drinking in all this color, all this blue. Then Picasso showed up again and said, "For thousands of years my name will be spoken of – now let's get down to business." He was got up like a matador and he was going to tame me. So before I know what's going on I'm making out I'm a bull, prancing around and he's flourishing this bloody great red rag. As I run up to him I can see his eyes blazing, looking at me dementedly; they looked liked they were about to pop, his face seemed to come so close. That's when I woke up. I turned to you, I wanted to wake you but you looked so sweet I didn't have the heart.'

'I wish you had; I want to be there for you, do things for you.'

'OK then. Tomorrow you can shave my legs.'

In the bed, the receptacle of birth and death, in that rectangle of imaginings and endings, under its blankets and veils, beside each other's limbs – additional canopies with which to wrap themselves – they experimented with each other's bodies. Locked padlocks loosened with one accord and the derelict caverns they guarded were transformed and new life filed into them. In the night everything was alien, alienness which blew away the dust which had gathered around sensation, so Oscar and Najette were poised always to celebrate this foreign country they had newly alighted in, which sometimes yielded a glimmer of distant familiarity.

Sometimes, in the small hours, the moon spied on them. At others the night was dead and beyond the curtains there was only a black void which threatened never to fade. Sometimes they woke together to have exchanges in the dark, whispered and hushed, as though they didn't want to disturb the imaginary person, the ghost sleeping next door.

Oscar stepped through the door, elated. He had a large box in his hand. She was at her easel.

'What's that?' she asked.

'This is a timely reminder of my past. What I have here represents the first stirrings of the cinema. It's a zoetrope.'

'What's a zoetrope?'

'I was in Windsor; they were having a car boot sale at the race course. I told this man I used to be a projectionist. I told him I'd always wanted one of these things. Unfortunately he recognized me – said, "You're Oscar Babel." I said I wasn't, but he kept banging on that I was. So I confessed; he started getting really effusive, suggested we have a drink and talk about life. I told him I had to go, but would he consider knocking a few pounds off the price? In the end he gave it to me for £30 – originally it was going for £50.'

'What's a zoetrope?'

'I'm going to tell you; or show you rather.'

He carefully pulled out of the box another box, on which a purple cylinder made of tin was mounted. Around the cylinder's circumference were a number of narrow slits.

'This is a replica of a model from 1867. You see, if you spin this drum like so and look through the slits ... can you see? There's this little man climbing some stairs ... up to the sun ... can you see?'

'Oh yes, now he's being eaten by the sun. Now he's popping out again.'

'Yeah, isn't it magical? Persistence of vision – the eyes holds onto an image for a bit after it's gone. The illusion of movement when movement is introduced. Or something.'

'I don't want to be unkind, Oscar, but I'm not sure I really share your excitement. Am I missing something?'

'But this is a piece of history. I've always wanted one of these, and never found one. Imagine.'

'I'm trying.'

That night Oscar took Najette's zen pen and started drawing. It was the first time he'd drawn anything since his sketch of Nicholas. And what he drew was a series of sketches which he hoped would facilitate the illusion of movement once tagged inside the zoetrope. At first each picture jumped too wildly towards the next; so with a pencil he tried again until he had mastered a more minute level of difference from drawing to drawing. At first he just drew matchstick men juggling. Then he drew a figure with a scythe, dressed in a hood – his version of the grim reaper. After swinging the scythe round it became locked around its head and the final sequences showed the head dropping off. These little cartoons – trifles though they were – excited him. They represented a kind of beginning, however modest. So he stayed up all night, smoking and drawing. In the next sequence a man was seated on a lavatory seat; he started sliding; his legs got upended and he was flushed down the toilet which, at the end, had expanded to twice its width. In his next series a man was cycling; the cycle tipped up at a sharp angle; it reassembled itself until it had mutated into a cycle whose handlebars consisted of the man's arms and his pinioned face stuck between them. In the final sequence a man was lying on a level surface; a woman appeared with an axe and started hacking off his limbs until by the end he was a stump in a sea of blood.

She inspected it, her hands clasped round her hair.

After a week it was already many things – the two faces were suspended in the foreground, crouched, floating free, mingling grief and the promise of consolation. She had tried to take the unreal beauty of her dream and superimpose it onto the background of her painting, tried to glean from her camel-haired brushes a crackless field of blue. With a razor, she scraped the paint down, then piled on further layers with brushes; then scraped them down again so that the brushstrokes faded. From this sea of glorious yet mute color, the two women emerged as if delivered from the past or future, inhabiting a still point, but perpetually poised on the threshold of departure. Then, with india ink and charcoal she began to sketch the central emblem of the plant. Underneath it she outlined in oil a complicated network of shadows thrown by the lines of spilled soil across a checked floor. These shadows were filled with triangles of color, bruised reflectors of light.

At night she covered the canvas up ritualistically, as though by sealing off her work she could the more easily forget about it until the morning.

Late next morning she wasn't at all happy with what she saw. She went and found Oscar who was picking blackberries in the garden and dragged him to The Happy Man. It was shut. They waited outside to see if anyone would come. Eventually the publican stepped out of a clapped-out car. Like all publicans he had a substantial beer belly, under whose spherical folds a belt struggled not to disintegrate. As he opened up the pub he eyed his customers resentfully. On stepping in to his domain he grew less hostile and once he was safely installed behind the counter his lips drew back in an aberrant smile as he croaked, 'What can I get you two?'

Oscar ordered two pints of bitter and as the barman yanked the lever with habitual wherewithal, Oscar watched for some violent, unexpected maneuver.

'Can I order some food?'

'Not till the kitchen's open.'

'And when does the kitchen open?'

'When the cook gets here.'

'So when does the cook get here?'

'Here are your pints; that'll be four fifty please.'

Oscar took the drinks over to Najette who was halfway through a cigarette. She rummaged around for some small change and slid a twenty-pence piece into the jukebox. This elicited a frown from the barman. A few seconds later a languid, jazzy voice began to sing a song called "No Ambition." It drew a smile from Najette which she valiantly kept up despite the radioactivity issuing from the bar. Oscar took some beer and her face gave in to consternation.

'What's up? You look a bit rattled; which, by the way, must be a first.'

'What do you mean?'

'I mean, I've never seen you look rattled.'

She started singing the lyrics over the lispy voice.

' "*I've no ambition, don't want to be seen in all the fancy places, don't want to sail out to sea in a boat made for me.*" I do get very rattled, constantly. I just don't always choose to show it, like you do.'

'Do I always?'

'Yes, you're congenitally incapable of disguising your feelings, so you wouldn't make a good poker player. Tell me more about what it was like when you were in inverted commas.'

'You mean when I was famous?'

' "*I've no ambition, I'm the humblest yet of a humble set, I only want to rule the world.*" '

A party of squat, fearful looking men with Alsatians piled in with much bluster. They greeted the barman heartily, who seemed greatly relieved to have real people gracing his establishment and soon all of them were clustered round the bar, regaling each other with anecdotes which had been told so often they had mutated into other anecdotes, and those who had told them originally no longer did, since others had inherited a particular story which they related as their own, wondering at the end if the detailed events had actually happened to them or not.

'When you were famous, were you – "*so please don't let them take me seriously*" – were you fawned on continually, did they give you wine and roses, did they – '

'Let's not talk about it, Najette; it's over.'

'No, go on; what did it feel like?'

'I don't know … I suppose … sometimes it was exciting … like I was traveling at the speed of light, and the earth was somewhere behind me and I could see it through the cockpit. But then I realized the safety hatch was open and I didn't have any oxygen masks.'

'The messiah as asphyxiating astronaut.'

'You could say that.'

'And then I pulled you out of the cockpit, gave you something real to mull over.'

'You could say that as well.'

'There's no "could" about it, my dear spaceman; let's get that clear.'

She smiled broadly, but her assurance had unsettled him.

'What's on your mind?' he asked. 'Are you going to – do you want to – sometimes I feel I have to be boundlessly grateful to you for allowing me to hook up with you – '

Her face turned shockingly stony, and he knew with awful certainty that what he'd rehearsed in his mind prior to utterance, having been uttered, was disastrous. He scrambled after her as she made for the door, attracting glances from the clan.

'I'm sorry ... Najette ...'

She turned to him at the door.

'Oscar, that's called over-reading – of the obnoxious, not the sensitive, sort. Can you stay out of my hair for awhile?'

He toyed with the idea of making some conciliatory gesture but knew it would just tangle things further. For Najette, the remark made it clear he was capable of thinking badly of her, pointing an accusing finger, questioning her motives. Did he think she was notching up an astronomical bill which she would later present him with? But she knew there was some truth in what he'd said – and it made her wince deep down.

The clan was watching Najette with a frightful lack of discretion. As she left she threw them such a ferocious look that they collectively cleared their throats and muttered disconnectedly.

In the company of these rustic individuals and their doted-on dogs Najette's charm and warmth impressed themselves on him at precisely the moment when she threatened to bar him access to them. How tedious people are, he thought, as he overheard starting-up scraps of conversation (the men were taking refuge in the subject of ferrets).

'Najette.'

She was already half way down the street.

Then the clan's banter fizzled out. And all at once they too sagged, borne down by life, able to find relief from its flames only in the beer mug. Their disaffection resolved into an antipathy towards Oscar, who revolted them, with his effeminate features and cultivated air. They stared at him hard as he stood there lost. The dogs began giving out regular emissions which brought the atmosphere of unrest to its apotheosis and chewed on it. He wished their masters might produce shotguns from beneath their anoraks and aim them strategically.

'Look, do you have a problem with something?' he demanded.

'That we do,' one of them said. 'We're looking at it.'

Words rose to his lips mysteriously, words he could never have dreamt up at such a loaded juncture. And yet they poured out before he could stop himself.

'Tell me; are you dog men? Do you see the pale yellow moon in the sky? Do you see anything at all? Why the tearing of limb from limb? Give me the dogs. I can lick them into shape. Show them who's master. Then all the other lunatics can scrape at each other over the scraps they take for gold.'

His adversary didn't really have a response to this and was contemplating head-butting Oscar, but Oscar, sensing the violence in the air, stepped back and slipped out of the pub, leaving the locals paddling around in a bewildered sea.

Outside he drew his breath in sharply, conscious of having had a lucky escape and looked around for Najette. Clearly she wouldn't have gone back to the house – was the best thing just to leave her alone? Obeying a random impulse he started walking down the hill towards the railway station, watchful for her slender figure, but there was no sign of it. It was a source of surprise to admit how painful the quarrel had been. He couldn't bear the idea of hurting Najette; of, even for one moment, dishonoring a woman who was perched high up on his carefully constructed pedestal.

Meanwhile, she chain-smoked petulantly, as she marched up and down the Kingsway footpath. She knew Oscar idolized her out of all proportion; she knew also that she did not want to be idolized. She did not crave such finality, such devotion. And yet when love lost its fairy-tale *élan*, when it became a working relationship and the cracks and tensions widened, she inevitably grew bored, restless. She couldn't bear the idea of love turning mundane, domesticated, sentimental. And yet it always did, which was why in the past she had had to up and go, to leave the cosy nest that one part of her wished to cultivate. The other part longed to smash it up with a witch's broom.

So she ground her shoe on her discarded cigarette and hurried back to the house. Once inside she moved quickly, gathering up her brushes and oils and paints. She found the perspex box she kept them in and, wrapping everything up in a dirty cloth, she placed the bundle inside. She carefully removed the canvas and propped it up against a chair. Then she went upstairs, taking two steps at a time, and yanked all her clothes out of the cupboard, flinging them onto the bed. It was only as she was folding them and piling them up that other issues (such as the fact that her friend was relying on her to look after the house) began to intrude. So she stopped and sat down and lit another cigarette and smoked it so completely that only its filter remained.

Why was she doing this?

The front door slammed.

'Najette!' his voice called.

She sat there; she didn't want to reply, wanted him to think she had already gone. But the presence of the easel ensured he wouldn't, though he noticed the packed perspex box, and, seized with sickening anxiety, realized she was preparing to go, so he darted in and out of all the rooms until he reached the bedroom. She was hiding behind the curtains now and he called out her name but she didn't reply and he noticed the dresses and the sight of them reinforced his fear and then he walked downstairs sadly and sat down and waited for her return.

He waited and tried to just thank God or Najette or whoever it was who'd allowed them to come together for this idyll, as though to have expected anything more was foolish. But he couldn't just sit back and look on that time as an amorous gift thrown his way, because he was tied to her; because how could he even remotely conceive of her in terms of disposability, of transience? And as she crept out from the curtains and sat down on the bed, very quietly, so quietly she hardly breathed she thought about what he'd said in the pub and tried to work out how it had led her to this point. But sometimes just one chance remark altered all, as if the world was no longer perceived in color but sepia.

He sat there, studying his watch – how long was it now since they'd quarreled?

Then he heard a voice, her voice, far off, brittle.

*"'I've no ambition, I'm the humblest yet of a humble set, I only want to rule the world.'"*

He stood up, filled with sudden joy, transported back in time to the moment before their clash, and it was as if through those quirky, accidental lyrics she was expressing regret or devotion. He followed the intangible strain, climbed the stairs, entered the bedroom, she was there, on the bed, singing.

*"'I only ... want ... to rule the world.'"*

For a moment she looked embarrassed. Her face fell and her hair flopped downwards, a fibrous shield.

'You were here all along,' he said.

'I was hiding,' she whispered.

'But why?'

'I needed to, I needed to send all that transparency packing, needed to get some mystery back. That's my fear, Oscar; that one day there'll be no mystery left between us; that one day we'll fart in front of one another, turn into two wrecks arguing about the milk.'

'Why the wistful song? Were you taking a break between packing?'

'You ask too many questions, Oscar. Too many questions; you wear me out.'

'I can't help it; I have to learn from you. I've centuries of catching up to do.'

'Stop it, Oscar! Stop making me out to be special; I'm not special. I'm just this person, I'm just trying to ... just trying to do my thing, I'm not ... I'm not remarkable ... anyway, I've stopped packing, I've stopped because ... the cases didn't need to be packed ... but you have to promise me we won't see each other through roses, won't accuse each other, because I don't want to start biting and stinging, that's the beginning of the end, because I am a romantic, see, and if it's less than perfect, then it's just a big zero. See?'

'I understand; I understand that ... that thing ... that perfection thing.'

'I'm sure.'

'I thought ... I thought I'd lost you.'

'No, I'm here; I'm here.'

She walked over to him and very quietly put her arms around him, letting her head sink into his chest. He held her very tightly.

'I'm sorry,' he said.

'No, it's I who should apologize. I'm volatile, sometimes. It's in the cell structure, the packaging.'

She tried to break away but he wouldn't let her, pinning her to him.

'What was it before,' he began in a tender, tentative voice, 'that was upsetting you; you know, before we – '

In interrupting him the tone of her voice lightened.

'Oh, it's the art. Always the art. Maybe I'm in the wrong game. Maybe I should be pointing a film camera at a motorway or be hanging around building sites retrieving bits of concrete and exhibiting them.'

'I think you're brilliantly talented,' he insisted.

'I'm old-fashioned, I'm behind the times, I should be shooting up in alleyways, then shooting the alleyways, I should be finding disused spaces on the Isle of Dogs and persuading Samaritans to talk to me about their childhoods, I should be foaming at the mouth, I should be making sculptures of hamsters, I should be doing photo realism, I should be – '

'All that stuff's ephemeral – you're trying to do something which will last.'

'Ah, the immortality angle – solid, traditional values. Give the world something deep. People don't have time for deep stuff. Maybe you were being smart all along, Oscar. Playing the game; giving people what they wanted. But as soon as you tell them "this is what you want" they're bound to say it isn't.'

He nodded but she didn't see, her eyes pressed tightly against him. He wondered how long he'd be able to hold onto her.

*

The dreaminess of the walk along the footpath made conversation pleasantly superfluous. So they just ambled down it. Brushing against a man in plus-fours they came to a locked gate. On climbing it they turned into another path running to the right, virtually swamped by wiry bushes running along either side. This suggested the way was hardly ever used, an impression confirmed by the fact that, during the walk, they didn't encounter another soul. After half a mile they came upon an open space, heralded by another gate, yawning open. Blackberry bushes sprang up as they entered the wood. Najette picked sporadically at them, her fingers soon colored by their juices. Sun found them only through triangular openings in the roof of leaves above. The light treated the ground as though it was a canvas on which to drip, dappled over violet leaves wedged to the soil and the afternoon resolved, as the rhythm of the walk settled, into a union of light and foliage. The wood grew more variegated, more expansive; it was as if each step they took further prized it open.

After half an hour the trees fell away, revealing a circle in whose core there lay a small lake exposed to the sun and so blindingly irradiated. It was as still as a sheet of glass. Occasionally a bird offered a fragment of song, which didn't seem to puncture the silence but blend with it.

Saying nothing, they both undressed and sank into the water; it rose and lapped gently against them. Najette swam away from him, her face downturned, and the still surface was hardly disturbed. He watched her float away, her ebony hair turning a darker shade at its moment of contact with the water. The trees around them formed a wall of color. Oscar stared up at them, treading water, held by their delicate symmetries. Now his nostrils detected an aroma creeping from the bank, an unidentifiable, rich perfume which gradually filled his head.

When he reached the other side Najette was nowhere to be seen. It seemed she'd consented to being sucked into uncharted territory. As he ventured into the tangle ahead the sun quickly dried him. He treaded softly, watchful of his surroundings in case he was to lose his way.

In a little while the lake had vanished and he had entered another part of the forest altogether, less busy, with little pathways running off in all directions. He found what looked like a small temple, crumbling and covered in graffiti. He slumped onto a wooden bench inside, feeling sublimely isolated, but wondering whether he should look for Najette, wondering whether he should make his way back to the lake (an option that seemed problematic as he was not sure he could find it now) and wait for her there. After ten minutes he pushed on and called out her name every now and then.

The heat was overwhelming and everything seemed to sweat because of it. Such heat did not define the moments; rather it threw them together so that time was saturated in sluggishness, and perception lost an edge of clarity. His body sagged and tired. Whereas before he had been keenly aware of sound, color, the forest's fecund store of pleasing, arresting images, he now succumbed to a numbing, stultifying sense that his mind had departed from his body and hovered somewhere, while his body ploughed on pleasurelessly, slowly being battered into submission.

The solitude increased, the heat deepened; sweat dripped from him. Thinking grew incoherent, snatches of thought repeated and circled, chiming with the rhythm of his steps and jarring with them. The trees encircled, confined him. He stared directly into the sun, until he was blind; on looking away everything was hazy, as if glimpsed through purple filters. Spots of light danced and hovered. He went on. He found a tree and placed himself against its curative bark. Sounds began to register again.

He stared into space, his eyelids frozen in their opened positions. Everything became blurred. He rubbed his eyes. And on opening them again he discerned little faces and shapes within the patterns of the ground. He tried to focus on the shapes but when he stared at them directly they vanished. When he turned away they appeared again, on the wings, peripheral phantoms, dancing as he persisted with his oblique scrutiny. He closed his eyes for a time. When he opened them the light was different. An orange, ruddy sun was falling out of the sky; clouds juggled feverishly with one another; elsewhere in the sky lines of color drifted like an oil spillage in water. The scorched afternoon was breeding apparitions.

Now the space he stared into was no longer a neutral territory to feed the mind's calm but a looking glass, an imagistic screen. He shoved his knuckles into his eyes and rubbed them. On moving his fingers away again perspective had been relinquished. The day seemed to be cracking into fragments of a mosaic as he sprinted back in the direction of the lake, overlooking Najette's fate and aware of a dull pain in his head, the pain a stone might have made if forced into his skull. Darting left and right to avoid the stems, he somehow found his way and tumbled at last onto the bank (he noticed the lake was now grey). He scrambled around for his clothes and huddled into them. Light was harsh, the trees ubiquitous; the wood had turned into a spider's web and at each step he thrashed about in it. With agonized breaths he reached the borders and found the same gateway he and Najette had entered via. He came out onto a lane and a car sheared past, dangerously close. A hot air balloon was drifting dreamily through the air at that moment.

The evening was gathering now and his walk along deserted roads advanced amid deepening shadows. The sky grew indistinct, the clouds faded and darkness cajoled the stars into appearing.

He found Najette back at the house when he returned. He stared at her and stammered, 'When did you get here?'

'A while ago. I was beginning to worry about you.'

'But ...why didn't you come back to the lake?'

'I did.'

'I didn't see you.'

'We must have missed each other. Never mind; here we are now, together.'

She kissed him. He felt his thoughts growing heavy and impenetrable. He sat down and, in a cold, impersonal voice, said, 'You have such sexy teeth.'

'Why, thank you. Unusual compliment, but it'll do.'

'I hope so. I love watching you floss. And I love it when you scribble your appointments on your arm. And I love it when you block the sink. I love your hairy arms.'

'Oscar, would you mind telling me what you're talking about? I think the sun's got to you. I don't scribble my appointments on my non-existent hairy arms. And I've never blocked the sink, at least not intentionally. What's up?'

'That's a very good question. I hope to find out soon. What indeed is up? I know what is down. I am. I have never really understood what the hell is up. Who is up? Who enjoys up?'

She stared at him in astonishment. She suspected he was sick; she touched his forehead.

'Oscar, I think you need to lie down. You're burning up. Here, take my hand; I'm putting you to bed.'

She led the way and he followed, bereft of energy and slouching as though *papier maché* rather than bones propped up his body. She gently held his hand as he languished on the bed. In a parched voice, he whispered, 'Who will water me?'

His eyes were fathomless, the dark pupils outlines of emptiness, reminders that he was a ghost poised between life and death and struggling to make sense of what lay in between.

His eyelids closed and he fell into a dank, uneasy sleep. She kissed him softly on his forehead, as if her kiss might kill the fever. Taking care not to disturb him she tiptoed out of the room.

Oscar's mind churned; he did not dream; he was not immersed in some autonomous world, he was too close to consciousness for that; he hovered between sleep and waking, and his mind was rendered shapeless. It was as though an intricate metal structure had been reduced to its original, formless state through the action of heat. Thoughts were running in a giddy chain. Bloch's words joined the stream. He roused himself into waking; the residual thoughts wouldn't disperse. He rubbed his eyes and saw Bloch's face looming. He couldn't get rid of it, it fixed itself onto the far wall as if projected there. He stared at the bloated, unreal features, the lips two yards long, the eyes as big as clocks, the sallow complexion transparent enough to discern the wallpaper beyond. It wouldn't go away.

He was sweating. He slumped back onto the bed and hid under the covers, not daring to look up again. After a scrambled, restless period in which time alternately dilated and contracted he was able to sink into sleep, a real sleep.

When he awoke the face had gone. The house was eerily quiet. He went downstairs, feeling drained. But he noticed his head was cooler. Najette was in the garden. He grabbed a bottle of whiskey and downed a couple of shots. Then, still holding the bottle and glasses he joined her outside. She was sitting reading.

'I'm fine now. I'm sorry, I don't know what happened to me.'

'It's all right. Your imagination was getting the better of you, I expect.'

'Do you want a drink?'

'Not for me.'

'I saw a hot air balloon earlier, or at least I think I did.'

'Whereabouts was that?'

'Oh, in the sky, in the sky.'

\*

During the waning evenings, the melting time, infusions of feeling spread, tempting language into trying to catch them. They sat in the garden at the table, wine and candles sitting with them, *Tristan* coming from the house, funereal continuities which erased thought, forced them to suppress movement. Above, the stars glimmered, perforating the night sky. Their bare feet slid along the cool, soothing grass. The wine was accomplishing its work of untying the knots in the day. He thought he could hear the antennae of insects shifting. She smoked a cigarette and watched him.

She ran her finger along the carved grooves of the wooden table, submitting to the repose of the barely tangible breeze, the fermented candle light, the silence. Then she began to slip, slip away from him, because at the end of happiness there came that senseless impulse to lash out. Because she had to move on, she could not live with him. Could she live with any man? She felt as though she'd glimpsed a hole from which water was pouring, into the bow of their ship. Things couldn't be the same after that.

The plant was finding its final form, its ruptured belly now unaccountably disquieting, framed by probing shadows. The background's abstraction was offset by the specificity of life and motion in the foreground.

The days were shrinking and the light slanting across the floor was of a new, elegiac cast, yellowing and dying imperceptibly.

Oscar began to wonder how long he could stay here. He would have to return to London at some point. But for the moment he cherished the sacraments they exchanged. Intervals of happiness and intrusions of perturbation vied with each other, and the house, the light, the summer's end, Najette's face, all became redolent of this mingling.

To Oscar Najette was different; her robes of cynicism, elaborately embroidered and yet at the same time almost ill- fitting, had been discarded. Wit and sophistication had accompanied all her maneuvers with others, disguising the nerves which sped through her, except perhaps in sleep. To Oscar she had always had an edge of inscrutability, unwilling to open doors except to humdrum places, places she nonetheless ended up transforming. But now she seemed loose, malleable. Hadn't her smile aligned itself more completely with her heart? Didn't she offer, rather than brilliant worldliness, admissions of ignorance, a touching vulnerability, a sincerity won after tumultuous struggles?

He spent long, hypnotized stretches of time peering into the zoetrope, as though the cylinder contained something which could unlock the secret of the universe.

He drew more sketches.

He felt a trembling, breathless urge to paint.

He started to paint.

*

'10 September. Daniel Bloch has been residing at Charing Cross now for two weeks and is still refusing to eat. He has been ripping out his drip, hiding food and generally showing an extreme rigidity of mind. Physically, his condition is deteriorating rapidly and I have noticed he always assumes a fetal position whenever I try and speak with him. I am expecting a visit from two social workers to see whether or not sectioning should go ahead. This is highly likely and I would like to think force feeding will be an option, though this matter is delicate. But if the patient will not comply. what choice do we have? His muscles are now utterly enervated and we are having difficulty in finding veins for his drip as they have all thrombosed. Occasionally he has hinted that someone else is living out his life – further evidence of psychotic ideation.'

# 26

His eyes snapped open. He turned to look at her. He was used now to the disruption of sleep which sleeping with her involved, but for every disruption there was the sweet recompense of contact between them: when she would sleepily sigh and ask him to hold her; when her arm would unconsciously slip down to his thigh and rest there awhile; when each adjustment allowed for their still being threaded through one another.

He remembered the dream.

He was swimming. He was underwater, but he had neither mask nor oxygen cylinders, drifting through deep recesses of the sea. As he floated past, silver bubbles and strands of seaweed moved alongside him at slumberous pulses and a shoal of disc-shaped butterfly fish, their golden shades catching the light, fanned out in a breathtaking arc, dissipating themselves on his behalf. They scurried off in all directions and were soon lost to furthest reaches of shadow. He was astounded by the ebb and flow of life, the squids darting about, the slow undulating arms of octopi. Looking upwards, he saw the ceiling of water shimmering with broken light whose quality was oddly serene and muted. But as he glanced down once again his nostrils and mouth were filling with water, water which was causing him to balloon and he was sinking, a deadweight capsizing to the bottom and as he fell he could see layers of dirt being dislodged and coming up to meet him in great murky clouds.

Then he knew he had to get in touch with Bloch.

His brain was rioting, overturning all vestiges of composure, as he picked up the phone, dialed, listened, on the point of hanging up, about to cross the border into relief, when he heard a sleepy voice say, 'Hello.'

'Daniel?'

'Who's that?'

'My name's Oscar. Can I speak to Daniel Bloch?'

'Oscar, hey, at last. Bloody hell. I didn't know how to get hold of you. I managed to get the name of your hotel but they told me you'd checked out.'

'Who is this?'

'Oh, sorry; it's Webster here. They told me you'd checked out.'

'I hadn't checked out; I was airlifted out, via the window.'

'What? Listen, I've got bad news; Bloch's in hospital, has been for … must be going on for a fortnight. He's in pretty bad shape. I think you should go and see him.'

In the instants before Webster formed the words Oscar was already hearing them in his head. Of course Bloch was in hospital, he said to himself. Where else would he be? Hadn't he known all along?

'What's wrong?'

'He's anorexic. I think he might be losing his marbles.'

'Don't say that – don't use that disgusting phrase.'

'Oh, sorry, so sorry. I tried to tell you that night, in Kensington Gardens, but I couldn't get to you. I've been taking him some grub but he won't eat a thing. He's on a drip. He won't take anything solid.'

'Which hospital?'

'Charing Cross. Hold up and I'll give you the details.'

Oscar heard him rummaging around.

'Hello? It's on the Fulham Palace Road. He's on the 3rd Floor. They've given him a private room. Mind you with the gunk they dole out … He said I could stay in his flat, and seeing as I was getting miffed with my van – '

'I'm very grateful to you.'

He had to ring off and sit down. All the blood had drained from his body.

This was the end.


He scribbled a note for Najette while she slept. He gently lifted up the covering around the easel and glanced at the canvas, which was now almost finished. It was good, very good. Studying its intricacies he knew he was right about her.

As he made his way down the hill he started getting nervous. Ryan Rees's minions would be beating around.


By the end of that day Najette had finished the painting. There was a deep melancholy within the female union; it had nothing to do with the smashed plant – it was simply a statement of the sadness of life, a recognition of some universal calamity. The plant itself was rendered with such rich expressivity that it seemed as potent and emotional as an atrophying face, imbued at the same time with the detached significance of a holy relic or ruined fetish. The painting was an amalgam of primitive disquiet and abstract enigma; it was two paintings spliced into one, and yet the two central tableaux managed to join. Standing back, attempting to detach herself from the work, Najette was able to celebrate the exaggerated attenuation of color, the way the painting called on the viewer to access indirect channels of communication. She signed it on the back in crayon and wrote underneath, with slapdash disinterest: "Displacement."

In the evening she polished off two bottles of red wine. The alcohol having duly rid her mind of its contents, she collapsed on the sofa and slept well into the next afternoon.

*

Oscar was standing outside his old home in Elephant and Castle, wearing dark glasses and a broad-brimmed, down-turned hat he'd stolen from a man snoring on the train. The exterior of the house looked completely different, resurrected by two coats of immaculate off-white paint.

During the agonizingly slow train ride from Egham he'd tried to establish how he felt about seeing Bloch again. On some level he certainly dreaded the meeting; but he also perceived how important a re-union would be, how necessary and vital. He wished he could put the clock back, and re-connect with the unsullied mood of their former friendship. But in the end, anxiety triumphed over anticipation and that was why he was here, in south London, apparently motivated by a sentimental hankering for the past, when he should have been in Hammersmith, at the hospital. He was trying to delay the moment at which he would have to confront him, postpone what he knew would be a painful encounter, in more ways than one.

As he stood there he craved anonymity, invisibility, insignificance. The presence of the expansive hat and glasses went some way towards reassuring him.

Then the front door opened as if Oscar's protracted, fixed gaze upon its panels had caused it to give way. And the heterogenetic figure of Mr Grindel stepped out. He was wrapped up in his old overcoat, his hands thrust deep in the pockets, the coat like an old, inseparable companion. He was so unshaven he looked ill. His shorts, his parasol, his joy – all were gone.

'Oh, it's you; what do you want?' he demanded aggressively. At once Oscar was tongue-tied, unprepared for this re-emergence of Grindel's old character.

'Mr. Grindel ... I ... was there any ... you said you'd redirect ... I just came to see if there was any mail for me.'

'You left your room in a stinking mess. I've seen cleaner pig sties.'

'Oh, but, I thought I – '

'Do you think I had time to re-direct your mail? She gave me the boot; she went back to her husband!'

'Do you mean – you didn't tell me she was married.'

'She taught me how to cook and clean, then she pissed off back to Louis. Left me with egg on my face. She mashed my heart with a wooden spoon, Babel. I'm never touching love again. She changed! Oh, she changed! She started getting crazy ideas. Said I was a capitalist pig. Said she didn't respect what I did. That, from a cleaning woman! How she changed; she never returned my calls; every time I tried to kiss her she turned green. This is it. No more. Never again. You heard it here first. Now she's with that plumber again. A plumber, for Christ's sake! How could she prefer a plumber to me! He gets to hold her hand and whisper sweet nothings in her ear. I could have whispered sweet nothings in her ear; my sweet nothings were sweeter than his. I can't bear it, oh I just can't bear it. You'd better come in.'

Oscar was genuinely overcome with pity for the pathetic lump in front of him. He felt obliged to offer some consoling words but all he could say was, 'You'll meet someone else.'

'No, I won't. No other woman gave me the time of day. I'll never meet another woman like her; she was one in a million.'

'That's not true, Mr Grindel; of course you'll meet another one; it's natural to – '

'What do you know? I've got responsibilities; I've got to make hundreds of decisions every day, people rely on me; I'm under pressure. Look, are you coming in or what?'

Stepping through, Oscar was taken aback by how luxurious the hallway now looked, with its plush carpeting and hessian wallpaper. Grindel squinted resentfully as he shut the door, as though the sight of the pristine hallway was an affront to him; as though Grindel, now sequestered in his own private hell, associated the vitality of his surroundings with the light of a heaven he'd been banished from.

Once inside his maisonette Grindel bundled into his kitchen, while Oscar noted with familiar dread the re-ignited, stifling heat of the radiators, the sealed windows. Once again, it was nearly impossible to take a breath without choking at the same time. A small television was switched on, the volume turned down. Someone was milking a cow but with each squeeze of the udder the creature grew more and more uncomfortable until it broke into a slow trot towards a place untouched by humankind. Grindel re-emerged, popping bubble gum ineptly, the meagre substitute for love he had hit upon.

'So, it looks like those builders did a good job in the end,' Oscar offered tentatively.

'Oh sure, and I ended up paying through the nose for it. The leeches. I hate the place. I hate what it's become; every lick of paint reminds me of her, seeing as she was the one who got me to hire those crooks in the first place. Just can't bear it.' The bubble gum popped loudly.

'But think of the way your property's market value will rise, Mr Grindel. And you're bound to attract a better class of tenant.'

'What better class? There is no better class; educated tenants just make more trouble for you, with their whining and griping and letters of complaint. Spongers and free-loaders trying to get a free lunch. They never pay on time, even the ones with money. They're all out to screw you.' Pop.

Oscar experienced an overwhelming desire to leave Mr Grindel's repellent views (and company) behind. He murmured in a small voice, 'Was there actually any mail ... in fact ... that you might have kept for me?'

'What?'

'Mail?'

'Are you still banging on about that? OK, OK. There's a box some-where full of all the crap which hasn't been picked up. I always keep it for a bit before I bin it. 'Cause I know my responsibilities, see.'

'You did say you'd forward – '

'Mail's lost its charm. Now it's all slush. Letters from estate agents offering to muscle in; junk mail from supermarkets; charities beg-ging for money; internet banking, internet shopping; pizza delivery, falafel delivery, noodle delivery; Jehovah's Witnesses telling us the time is upon us – I wish it was – council crap about overgrowing trees in the back yard, and it goes on. What's it all in aid of, that's what I want to know.'

'Well – '

'I'll get the box.'

His biggest bubble yet exploded and the torn skin of the gum latched onto his cheeks. He clawed at it randomly. He rummaged around the bookcase and produced a cardboard box overflowing with the kind of mail he had just savaged and handed it over.

Oscar speedily separated out those items addressed to him: a letter; a small package; seven separate communications from credit card companies; and two envelopes stamped with the words "The Earl Gallery" – he imagined these were invitations from Nicholas to private views. He opened the package first, intrigued, and found within, wrapped in transparent paper, a small music box. There was a note which came with it.

*Kentish Town*
*11 August*

*Dear Oscar,*

*Please find enclosed your belated birthday present. At last!!! I really can't imagine why it's taken so long for me to get round to sending it. I suppose I thought it would be easier to give it to you, but now that you're famous I should have known better. And now it's August, and your birthday was in May! I'm so sooorry. Originally I had a nice calathea number lined up for you but God had other plans, if you know what I mean; so I got you a music box instead.*

*I didn't know where to send this and as you never come and see me anymore ...*

*I thought I'd try your old address. I know this is a bit risky, but I don't think anyone would throw out a parcel, would they? But then again they might. I hope this gets to you anyway. I gather you're living the high life in Chelsea. It's all right for some.*

*Since last I saw you a strange man has moved in with me. This is working out surprisingly well. It's amazing what a little fire will do in one's life.*

*What's been happening to you? I'd love to hear from you. Come and see me at the usual place. Have you seen Najette? I'm afraid I'm too dull for her. It's funny how you meet people and you think they're part of your life, that your life has touched theirs in some way, and then they just seem to fade away. Do you think she's relationship material? What's her painting like?*

*I've got to go. I have to meet the strange man. He's the last person on earth I'd have expected getting together with. He's irritable, hard to pin down, but a big chunk of him is also perfect for me – perhaps because I'm not editing myself. You see, the thing is, I just feel whole when I'm around him. It's not a big romantic thing; it's just very very natural. I just feel I accept him – it's hard to put into words but before, when it came to men, I used to get upset by the slightest things they said or did, when they didn't phone, when they snored in bed – I'd think, it's not as it should be. But when he does the things which should annoy me they just don't annoy me. He's my knight in shining amour. Some day I'll tell you how we met – it's a good story, lots of love, Lilliana.*

He lifted the lid gently and the box began to play a meditative, wistful melody. As it unwound he opened the letter. He recognized the compressed outlines of Bloch's handwriting on the first sheet; the words on the second and third sheets were in the unmistakable courier type of his old Underwood.

*12 August*

*I found this*
*When I sprang cleant*
*It's piss*

*that's heaven sent*
*the last bit of that wretched fragment*

*thought you might like to see it*

*written all those pale moons ago*
*when I still resembled remotely a human*

*I LIED I LIED I LIED*

*when I said I'd written no more*

*it's the mutiny within the mutiny within the mutiny within*


Assailed by blind panic, his eye raced through the contents of what followed while Grindel launched into another aggressively stupid monologue about his old lover.

*Chapter Three : the fabrication of wisdom*

*Oscar Babel, destined for greatness, destined to be admired from afar and from near. It is true that the man ultimately acquired a status which was mythic. In the end he transmuted into a philosopher who was popular, a thinker who was entertaining. His words became honed and weighted, sacred words. People were drawn to him. He spoke to future converts, dined at plush restaurants, enjoyed the attention of certain women. He became, in effect, a spiritual teacher, a guru, and the observations he made were received with an ardor which bordered on idolatry, as he held forth and horsewhipped society for its pursuit of the vacuous. The hotel room he finally embraced became his spiritual headquarters, the shimmering, flickering lectures like no others as the lackeys of the media elected to shut their mouths for once, as they journeyed along the road to enlightenment. Oscar proved fatally effective – he spoke words which made him the blessèd one, making mincemeat of our slumberous, constipated art worlds: corpses kept barely alive with heavy-duty drugs.*

*Inevitably I noticed a certain deterioration in him, of body and personality.*

*Oh, how the shining lights of the past, the noble grand dreams of men and women have been killed by hysterical consumerism and by the noxious oil spill of the ever-expanding, ever-lobotomizing, world-wide spider's web!*

*He was borne aloft on the wings of the mass turbating media, and certain figures that must remain nameless (and were already faceless) accompanied him and facilitated the journey, lubricated it so to speak. And yet*

Past, present, future: the terms were rendered meaningless, as though he occupied a vantage point where time curved; in which earthly perspectives, having been left behind, now revealed their local, small shroudedness. He was in a different place; he could see everything, see round the corners and boundaries of sequential, linear time. If you stepped far back enough you could see everything, he thought. He was hearing a voice from the past that was the voice of the future, in the house which contained his past, now transformed. But then, wonder fled and his thoughts darkened. If all that he had become during the summer had been anticipated – had (in a sense) already occurred in Bloch's head – didn't this mean he had had no free will? Had the course of his life that summer been determined before it had actually taken place? Was he merely following a pre-laid path, as passive as a branch led by the currents of a sloping river? Was he, in fact, anyone at all; or just an adjunct to his one-time friend, a shape for a fleeting succession of masks to enfold until at last a strong wind would find him and cause him to crumble like an ash doll?

The music box stopped playing.

Grindel stopped speaking.

Oscar looked up, dazed.

What was he doing here? Why was he here? Why had he come here? He had found his destiny here, as much as it was possible for any man to. It was there, in black and white. There was nothing for him here now. He let the sheets of paper fall and walked over to the door without a word. Grindel started after him and shouted, 'Hey, where are you going? I'm talking to you! What about all I've done for you? Don't I even get a thank you then? Where are you going? I'm talking to you. Are you listening to me?'

Oscar had already reached the end of the hallway. He yanked the door open contemptuously, and turned round to face Mr Grindel. He lifted his hand to his brow, and his thumb and joined fingers pressed against it, as if trying to pluck out the thought buried within via the hand without. When he spoke his voice was expressionless.

'What ... exactly ... have ... you done for me, Mr Grindel?'

He slotted on his dark glasses and then he was gone.

The question robbed the old landlord of all his calm and for a moment he looked crushed. He groped around for something to say, some line of attack. But all he could manage was to mutter under his breath, 'Weasel.' He scrambled to the door and bawled out into the street, 'Weasel! Ingrate! No one speaks to me like that! No one!'

But Oscar didn't hear him.

He stepped back inside his detested house, shuffled off into his womb-like, hermetically sealed maisonette and didn't leave it for a week.


On the train he peered at the other commuters, searching for some assurance that he was part of their kind, linked to them in a fundamental way; but it didn't come.

From side to side the train swayed and people swayed with it. As they passed through the decrepit tunnels joy was garroted and the memory of sweet, effusive encounters, of charm and grace, of silk handkerchief intimacy, shredded. Every face wore the same blankness, apparently struck dumb by some unspeakable catastrophe.

So when Oscar finally emerged at Hammersmith station the shopping mall it was housed in seemed like an explosion of life, though ordinarily its metallic odor would have depressed him. He turned into Fulham Palace Road, at once reminded of London's stylistic incoherence, and as he finally pushed his way through the glass doors of Charing Cross Hospital he was grateful for the fact that a hospital at least was a known quantity, though the presence of the artwork on the walls caused him to re-consider even that, though he welcomed the creativity it was there to honor. Then he thought of Najette and her art and wondered how he would feel about it if it was hanging there, beside the rolling escalators and glacial lifts. He asked someone where he could find the Ely Wing and with a growing feeling of dread rode up to the third floor, listening to the sound of the synthetic voice as it intoned, 'Third Floor, doors opening,' finding in that voice the incarnation of all that was ominous about hospitals. Because hospitals tried to be like hotels but weren't. Because hospitals were where people suffered. Where people died. He was getting ready for death as he strode through the double doors and told the nurse at reception that he was there to see Daniel Bloch and the nurse showed him to his room but before she rapped gently on the door she told Oscar to prepare himself for the shock and then he stepped in.

Bloch lay on the bed except it wasn't Bloch anymore. He was a cluster of matchstick limbs, holding limply onto the bedclothes. His face was drawn and pale, his eyes sunken and cavernous, unseeing, unmoving. A thick tube had been inserted into his nostrils. He made wheezing and gagging sounds periodically and two drips rose from each of his arms like plumbing extensions. The little hair that remained was grey and lifeless. It hang damply to his skull. Lines ran from his forehead to his chin, long, etched lines. Each seemed to denote a strand of suffering. Eventually Oscar began to recognize a pattern in his features that belonged to the past. But this coinciding of images was ghostly and fragile. But what upset him was not so much the physical deterioration of the helpless child-man in front of him, his body utterly enfeebled and stripped of its purpose (a body as useless and intangible as a shadow), but rather the annihilation of Bloch's spirit, that mischievous energy he used so easily to be able to summon. And as he stepped forward – so tentatively it was as though he feared his movements might give Bloch pain – he finally felt that his heart was breaking.

Bloch tried to pierce the veil of cloudiness through which he viewed the world. At the same time Oscar's vision grew opaque, since tears flashed and burned in his eyes. And then it seemed as though Oscar was shedding tears for Bloch as well. As though Bloch, incapable of weeping, now wept through him.

There was something between them then which neither could have put into words. A bond of pain; the provenance of suffering. They were like two travelers who'd journeyed through alternate stretches of an Arctic wilderness, ravaged by the cruel beauty of the landscape, and returned, lived to tell their tales, tales which they could only relate to each other, because no one else could possibly grasp the icy desolation they had known.

'Don't cry, Oscar,' Bloch murmured at last.

The voice was scarcely audible and Oscar had to strain to hear it, and yet it filled the room.

'So ... you made it.'

Oscar crept closer and pulled up a chair noiselessly. So pathetic, it was, he thought, to clutch at these niceties in the face of extinction; so truly desperate to try and make life comfortable when life was dying in front of him. The life of this beautiful man.

'What did you think ... what did you think ... about those tapes? Trying, was trying to be ... something.'

'They were inspired. Inspired.'

'You made it then.'

'I'm here, I won't leave you.'

'You will ... you ... why's it so dark in here? ... can't we have some light ... Christ ...'

'I'll switch on the lamp, shall I?'

'No! No! ... don't go, no artificial ... no, stay, for a moment. Till I nod off.'

'All right.

'It's been so long since I ... since I ... it seems so long.'

Bloch looked ahead, wheezing. He started coughing, an agonized cough which peeled the skin off from Oscar's body. Eventually the convulsions subsided and Bloch turned and looked at his visitor, with rheumy, hollow eyes. He began to speak, slowly at first, but then with gathering force.

'They never learn, people. Always hurting each other .... never learn. You'll see that nature doesn't give a shit ... for us ants ... scurrying around, music of the spheres, where's the receipt? Where's the fucking ... the fucking ... the thing ... touch of concern sewn in the clouds? Where, where? They. They all put the knife in up to the hilt. You say you won't leave me, but you did. And she did. She did terrible things, no one should be allowed to do such ... such things. Fucked other men, she ... oh God ... I was ... I can't, I can't. Oscar, I'm scared.'

'Don't be scared, don't be scared; I'll take care of you now. I'm so sorry, I'm so sorry I've been so long, I'll look after you now.'

'Oscar, I'm scared.'

'I know, I know you're scared; but I shan't leave you, I'm here.'

'Oscar, I can't eat, I'm so far down the well, can't get out, no energy to crawl out.'

'I'll give you the energy, I promise, I promise.'

'Do you ... you mean that?'

'I promise.'

Oscar reached out his hand and took Bloch's carefully. It felt so slight and brittle. And now he noticed that Bloch's face seemed to be lit by some ineffable sweetness, some intangible delicacy, his blasted features speaking to him of unsuspected beauties in the world, or of a burnished beach where the crimson hull of the sun sat motionless, splitting the sky in two, prizing open the locked lid of consciousness. He was a good man, a noble spirit.

'I was,' Bloch whispered, 'you were ... you were my shadow, now I'm yours ... you ... we've been in a foreign land ... all around the seagulls keened ... still, I'd like to be young ... like to be light-headed, woman's scent ... to be ... oh God ... Oscar ... to feel the grass ... under my feet ... to feel ... but they all go ... all those men and women ... in the cemeteries ... they all laughed and cried ... where do they go, where do they go, I don't get it, where do they go?'

Oscar's body was taut, all his muscles and joints ached. He couldn't think of anything to say, couldn't offer Bloch even hesitant answers. If only he'd had a drink, had something which could loosen his tongue but as it was everything seemed inert, carved out of granite, unresponsive to the ebb and flow of an easy exchange.

Beyond, through the window, he could see a jagged skyline. Light had been snatched away, leaving only ashen pallor.

Slowly the room surrendered to shadow.

Rows of houses. People were probably coming home from work around now, getting ready to make supper. The indigestibility of London. The countless lives. Decay.

'Hey, Oscar,' Bloch began, 'listen to me; get this pipe out of my nose. It's so fucking awful.'

'Am I supposed to do that? Isn't it – '

'Look, get this thing out; I'm telling you, I can't breathe with this thing up my trunk.'

So Oscar leaned over him and, after a struggle, managed to remove the gastric tube. Bloch felt something of the claustrophobia the pipe had induced leaving him.

'Didn't have ... the energy ... what was I saying?'

'You were talking about – '

'It's getting darker, or is that me?'

'No, it is getting darker.'

'I've got to get out of here, Oscar. Can't you get me out of here?'

'But you're so ... so frail ... how could we – '

'I don't want to die here; I want to die in my flat.'

'You're not going to die. I won't let you speak like that.'

An iron rod sprang up and held his words. The necessity of strength sharpened him. But Bloch's tumult turned to hostility.

'Won't you? Won't you, I'm ... did you come here to spar with me? You pest – pest – come here to spar with me. Oh, I'm tired, so tired.'

Then language slumped into redundancy, having settled there in the ongoing oscillation between validity and emptiness. The drab room was home to some mystical communion, and the teachings of silence. In the empty shell Oscar sank through Bloch's memories. He saw a young woman, smiling, her hair swept by a breeze from a sea somewhere in time. A young woman who mocked with her smile, walked through a gilded drawing room and injected into it a massive influx of charisma which lingered like perfume after she had left. She mocked everyone and everything. She used humor as a merciful anesthetic, an adhesive, and as a dagger, hurling abuse at whoever hung around long enough to hear it, and self-importance, pomposity and arrogance were shredded in her orbit.

'I was in a foreign land,' Bloch mumbled. 'I was knocking on doors, no one would let me in. I was so thin, I thought perhaps people couldn't see me, I was floating. I would shout at people, shout so hard it hurt, they couldn't hear. Now I have no breath. I would touch ... touch, they wouldn't feel it. I came to a ruined church, a chapel, there was someone at the far end, I couldn't see his face. He blessed me, he blessed me. I could live again. Do you know what I mean, you: sea urchin, hedgehog, eunuch. You and I who waft through the sea, who stand a little to the sides, the fringes?'

Oscar nodded slowly. Bloch's eyelids were struggling to stay open;

Oscar knew he would sleep soon. He would stay, watch over him, protect him.

'You can leave if ... if you want to, I know the bells are ringing. Perhaps a carriage and horses await?'

'No carriage and horses await, Daniel.'

'I don't like you to see me like this, in the soup. You should go back to your carriage and horses, your powders and rouges; you need to do your toilette, howl at the moon, gnash your teeth. Need to let the wine breathe, sample the finer things in life. I'd like to too, like to too. Like the dinner gong to tell me it's time, like to dab on one or two drops, like to ... hear a bedtime story. Give me the glass slipper, the fairy tale, I want the fairy tale back, I wrote it, and you promised it to me, you owe it to me, you promised I'd be young.'

'It's true, and I meant it. I won't break my promise.'

'No, you won't ... you won't ...'

The waning voice became still. His eyelids closed heavily.

Oscar watched him sleep.

Later, when the nurse looked through the window, to check up on Bloch, she noticed that the gastric tube had been pulled out, but Oscar's eyes so moved her that she postponed the moment when she would replace the tube, and just stood and watched this tender vigil.

# 27

When he came out of the hospital there was a chill in the air, the chill of autumn, and during the moment in which he felt its cold breath all memories of summer fled. He noticed that approaching strangers were huddled up, shielding themselves against the approach of other strangers. The fallen leaves held his attention, suggesting feathers spilled from a broken pillow. In a few more weeks, he reflected, the leaves would be everywhere, as the parks and gardens of London turned golden and orange, as trees were transformed into wiry, venerable webs. Leaves piled high in playgrounds, clustered like iron filings around gutters, concealing mounds of excrement on pavements (which was both blessing and curse). He wondered whether nature's coming apart at the seams had any connection with the way couples tended to part at this time of the year.

He turned into Shepherd's Bush Road and walked through the Common where shadowy figures pursued various illegalities, and reached the roundabout, loaded as usual with cars and trucks and coaches, managing somehow to adhere to the laws of the road, making way, slowing, co-existing. He negotiated an intricate line through the wide, dangerous lanes, having to sprint at times to avoid oncoming lorries, until he reached the safety of Holland Park Avenue. He glanced at the Hilton on his way up. The plush world within seemed barred to him, which was fine by him since he no longer cared for it. As he shuffled past delicatessens and patisseries the grand girth of the avenue cloaked him. He had no idea of his destination; he just needed to walk. Outside the Gate Cinema cineastes were queuing to see a foreign film. He pushed on towards the Bayswater Road, peering at the cards posted in the phone booths, promising to cater for every sexual taste, airbrushed goddesses locked in silicon lasciviousness. A couple of beggars, crumpled in their blankets, asked him for change and he gave them as much as he could spare. When he reached Queensway he was assailed by its crass liveliness. He shared the pavement with rollerbladers, backpackers, and local residents, all paddling along the street in a cosmopolitan gyration. Inside Chinese restaurants people dipped their duck and pork into bowls of soy sauce; outside Bayswater station a party of American tourists blocked the entrance with real dedication. He walked through Whiteley's, which was full of men in suits munching sandwiches, and turned into Westbourne Grove, then into Chepstow Road, whose uniform rows of houses struck him as continentally elegant.

He emerged into almost liturgically calm backstreets, rows of antiques shops reverentially lit. At length he stopped outside a bar off Talbot Road. It was called The Lips and its gaudy exterior promised that its interior would embody the apogee of kitsch. Sure enough, after he had got past the bouncer, Oscar found the statues painted with fake verdigris, the small cocktail tables decorated with esoteric symbols (and altered to blend into consumer consciousness), the magic lanterns, the sickly music, and the gigantic illustration on the far wall of three sheep dogs wrapped in bath gowns to be as kitsch as anyone could have hoped. But despite, or perhaps because of the transcendental levels of vulgarity, he didn't leave. He was now so wretched and exhausted that all he wanted to do was to drink himself into unconsciousness. He ordered two double whiskeys at the bar. The barman obliged him with slick efficiency and soon he was sipping at his drink in a corner, where his dark melancholy immediately aroused the attention of a brunette in a party of four.

When Oscar turned a minute later, bleary-eyed and already a little drunk, to look at her table he found that more people had crammed round its small circumference, including women decked in peacocks' feathers, clicking castanets and men in cowboy boots and Stetsons.

Clearly their party depended on the best that money could buy for its life, and the women were used to champagne cocktails, designer sports cars and toxic levels of affluence. Then the group received a further injection of life as through the double doors came a statuesque, soaringly tall individual in a black cape, a vermilion scarf tossed around his neck, his appearance completed by the two dollybirds draped on either side of him. This spectacular entrance was greeted with squeals and cheers. He was the person everyone had been waiting for, the star of the evening and its catalyst. And now an endless round of greetings was kick-started. Manly handshakes were administered, kisses bestowed on outstretched hands, hectic embraces dislodged feathers, all accompanied by the rattle of the castanets. The tall man, whose mane of flowing black hair gave him an air of central European grandeur struck his arms akimbo and boomed heroically, 'I am free, my dear friends, I am free; the chains have fallen from me!!'

There was a tremendous roar and then everyone in the group was rushing for the bar, and champagne bottles and ice buckets found new homes, perched on any even surfaces which presented themselves. The energy issuing from this table was so prodigious that it allayed any possible irritation that may have laid in its wake and even those who were not part of the celebration found themselves won over by it. The tall man started to hold forth, in a deep, rasping Hungarian accent. He spoke ecstatically of the fact that he was now legally severed from his wife with whom he had had – as he put it – 'a marriage as unsuccessful as that between capitalism and communism.' Oscar watched the group with interest; he didn't think he had ever seen such an extraordinarily incongruous and yet colorful collection of people in his life.

The Hungarian instructed the two dollybirds to buy everyone in the bar Black Russians. Then he made some jibe at Russians on account of their excessive sentimentality. Oscar's drink arrived in due course and he looked over in the Hungarian's direction. For a second they seemed to make some kind of connection and then his bene-factor winked at him and looked away again. It left Oscar strangely troubled; as though in that wink there was an acknowledgement of Oscar's sadness; as though the wink seemed to say the Hungarian already knew all about him, and Oscar could conceal nothing of his inner life, no matter how hard he tried.

When he looked up again the brunette was perched opposite his chair. She had an angular, gnome-like face. Her skin was riddled with acne which she had tried concealing with foundation and her eyes were slightly alarming, owing to the green contact lenses she sported.

'Excuse me, but aren't you Oscar Babel?'

'Yes – so what?'

'Are you all right?'

'Not really.'

'What's wrong?'

'Oh, well ... this and that. That's quite a gathering you've escaped from. What do you want with me; I'm not a cowboy.'

'I thought ... I thought you looked kind of lonely.'

He studied her face. Every now and then a devout gentleness sur-faced in her eyes and for its duration he forgot about her contact lenses.

'I didn't think you drank,' she said.

'Where did you get that idea?'

'Oh, just something I read about you in the papers.'

'You shouldn't believe everything you read.'

His eyes were misting over.

'Did something bad happen to you tonight? I'm a good listener; you can open up to me.'

'I'm not sure if I can. I'm not at all sure myself what happened tonight.'

Suddenly changing tack she cried with happy enthusiasm, 'Wasn't that thing in the park wild! I wasn't there but I saw it on TV before someone pulled the plug! What happened there then? That was really bloody crazy, no?'

'Oh yeah, that – human behavior – my words; Bloch's words rather. An excuse, an excuse to sample what people have always hankered after. Like rabbits. I felt quite ashamed of all that. But I don't think I can be held responsible.'

'So how did you get to be a guru; I mean, how does anyone get to be a guru; is it just a process of – '

'Listen to me – what's your name?'

'Angelica.'

'Listen to me, Angelica. I am not, nor have ever been, nor ever will be a guru.'

'How do you mean?'

'The image the media had of me, the public had of me, was false. It was all lies. I have no claim to special knowledge, to being a spiritual teacher. It was all a big, elaborate and costly confidence trick. And people bought into it. The real master is in a hospital a few miles from here, dying.'

She tried to work out if he really meant what he said. His words were slurred, fatigue gushed from his eyes. But through the screen of drunkenness Angelica thought she could detect the ring of sincerity.

'You mean that ... you mean then that you're just this ordinary, random – '

'Before I became famous, I was a complete nobody; I was a projectionist in Camden. That's all. A man, Ryan Rees, you've got to hand it to him. His publicity machine should have won some kind of ultimate Bullshit Prize. In the end that bastard locked me up in my own hotel suite; do you believe that? After smashing up my face and stubbing out his cigar on my hand.'

He held out his palm, where a faded, pinkish scar remained.

'I could expose you. I could tell the world that Oscar Babel is a fake.'

'Be my guest. I doubt if anyone would be interested. I've had my spell in the limelight. Some new bit of gossip, some new scandal, some new next big thing is already being cooked up somewhere, courtesy of … of whoever. You see, Angelica – pretty name that – you see, people like someone who wears the robes of authority, who looks important. But those bigwigs – most of the time, they're just facades. Well, that's all I was. A cartoon. The really important people, the people who count, they're behind the scenes, off-stage. And all those people who write about you, they're all under the illusion that they know you, know what's going on in your head. But they haven't a clue. How could they? There's so much they don't know about how I came to get to where I got. They wouldn't believe it if I told them. No one would.'

'I'd love to hear the story.'

'It's too long, far too long. I don't want to talk about that now; I want – '

'Oh, tell me what happened. Just tell me how it started.'

'It … it started with a cat.'

'A cat?'

'Yes. Let me finish. You have to understand. People aren't interested in what someone's actually saying; that's why so much of what's said gets distorted. They're just interested in the game, all the noise and hype. If someone comes along, if someone comes along who makes a big enough noise, it attracts more big noise. The quality, the substance, it just … falls by the wayside. If you're blessed with good looks, if you can string a sentence together and if you have powerful connections, bingo! Eureka! Just get yourself noticed, be seen at all the right places, it's incredible; suddenly, somehow, you're being talked about like you're actually important. And the media – it's crazy because it creates this thing and in the same breath it's crucifying its creation. It's like the media exists in this state of schizophrenia – it's so big it doesn't know what its other half is doing, so what's getting trashed somewhere is being appraised somewhere else as gold dust. And the only thing you can do to stay sane is to get out of it.

So I did. I got out but now I've nowhere left to go.'

'What do you mean?' she asked, undoubtedly fascinated by the savage revelations and insights pouring out of him.

'A few miles from here, in a hospital room a man is dying.'

'Is that the master you mentioned? Is he a friend of yours?'

'He was a friend. And now he's dying. And I think ... I think it's because of me.'

'I don't understand.'

She studied him earnestly, vaguely aware of having stumbled on something so outside her realm of experience that it turned all her pre-conceptions about the world on their head. As if she had had some terrifying brush with a powerful animal, after which she could no longer feel quite safe and secure again. And yet, despite this palpable sense of danger, she felt strongly drawn to Oscar and his damaged luminosity had already gone a long way towards bewitching her. She was baffled by him; by his outspokenness; by his heavy-duty seriousness; by his exquisite aura of suffering; by his being unlike any other man she had ever met in her life. Baffled and held.

'Listen, Oscar, you see that guy over there; that's Béla. He's an Hungarian millionaire; he's just got divorced and he's decided to throw a wee party. We're all going over to his place in a bit. Why don't you come along?'

'That's terribly kind of you, but I'm in no fit state, so if it's all the same to you – '

'Oh, go on; I'm really enjoying talking to you.'

'No, listen, I'm, I don't want to go to another party. I never know what to say at parties; everybody's always so happy at parties.'

'Look, you can be unhappy with me; you won't have to talk to anyone else but me. Now, how does that sound?'

She smiled sweetly. And in that instant something floated up and settled into the air between them and he recognized a familiar feeling of dread and excitement filling his stomach. She watched him with such attentive kindness that he did find himself tempted to do as she asked. But he didn't know if he could sustain a conversation with her, despite her flattering interest in him.

'I can't, really; please understand. I'm sorry.'

'All right then. Well, I tried. Can I at least have your telephone number?'

He scribbled a made-up number, just to be rid of her, and at length she walked off. He watched her go, with an expressionless face.

But a few seconds later Béla himself had taken Angelica's place.

'Mr Babel, tonight I find you under the weather, as the English say. The English language is so crazy. Full of meaningless expressions. He wants to have his cake and to eat it also. A slice of cake. To sell like hot cakes. My favorite: shut your cake-hole. Why this obsession with cakes? Why lust after pleasure and do nothing about it? Why the muffling of meaning? Is it because the English cannot face reality, find it too hard, and so disappear into apologies, stiff upper lips and chins that are up, the firm handshake? But I can see you want to be left alone. But isn't it logical to assume you'd feel better at my party? I will invite you. And it would be impolite to turn me down. But first, before you decide, may I tell you a story?'

Oscar was so taken by the unexpected acuity of his observations, his self-confidence, and his beauty and charisma that he nodded slowly. Clearly he was in the presence of an incomparable host and raconteur. He was intrigued, despite himself.

'A woman has reached middle-age and still not managed to marry. So she goes to see the wisest woman in the village for the answer to her problems. She tells her that the problem is not with her face, for it is beautiful; nor her body, for it is slender; nor her character as it is good. The problem is that she must learn to cook. If she can cook she will ensnare a man. So the woman goes away and within a week turns herself into a marvelous chef; she makes men's mouths water, she ravishes them with her secret recipes. But always after the dishes are piled away the man makes his excuses and leaves. So the spinster goes back to the wisest woman of the village. She tells her the problem is that she needs to play a musical instrument, to catch her man. The harp is the instrument for her. So the spinster takes lessons with the best teacher, paying him handsomely. And she plays beautiful melodies for the men and they listen, but always afterwards they make their excuses and leave. Weary now the spinster goes for a third time to see the wise woman. The problem is she has to learn to gamble, that gambling is something a man understands and responds to. So she learns to play poker, and to bluff. And the men are impressed with her, there is no doubt about it. And they make their excuses and leave. Finally the spinster, exhausted and miserable, goes to see the woman and says, "I have done everything you told me to do. I can cook, play the harp and gamble but I still can't catch a man."

'The woman says, "In all the time you have been coming to see me, did you not notice something important about me?"

'The spinster asks, "What do you mean?"

'"Something about my life?"

'The spinster shakes her head.

'"I am alone. I, too, lack a husband. If I knew the answer to your problem, would it be so? And if I knew the answer, I would not be able to tell you since I would be far away, in a dream."'

Béla folded his arms and produced a cigarette and lit it triumphantly, grinning at his companion.

Oscar was strongly attracted by the story, though he was not sure of its real meaning.

'Wasn't it cruel of the woman to offer those suggestions then?' he asked.

'Of course not – that's very naive of you. She thinks her suggestions have a real chance of helping her, and, after all, now the spinster is a more accomplished person. Now, you've heard my story; will you come with me, Oscar Babel?'

Oscar said that he would.

They all piled into a couple of waiting Mercedes; inside people experienced an irresistible urge to stretch out onto someone else and stay there. He tried to detach himself from this spread-eagling but couldn't quite manage it and the women shoved against him provocatively, their untethered breasts bouncing in his face. He muttered small talk about the weather, which they completely ignored. But at last they arrived at a sumptuous house somewhere and as they all bundled out there was much laughter and horseplay. One or two of the cowboys decided to drop their trousers. Judging from people's reactions this seemed to represent the height of comic invention. The company was ushered into the front room by a butler, and soon drugs, smoke and drink were circulating round it. Oscar was by now quite drunk and decided to try and find an anonymous corner to retreat into, where he might snatch some sleep. But Angelica, who was thrilled to find him there, latched onto him and continually asked him questions about his fame. When Oscar's answers shrank to monosyllables she eventually gave up, leaving him snoring on some steps.

Béla told endless stories and parables. He danced the tango with a Spanish woman, the gathered audience behaving even more adoringly towards him after his masterful display. He sliced a colossal watermelon in two with a sword, and everyone fed from its spilt red domes like dogs gathered around a couple of dish bowls. Afterwards people migrated into the kitchen to make gazpacho laced with marijuana. Shrill, unending, lunatic laughter ensued. Then an albino made an egg vanish; a Scot played the bagpipes badly (though most people thought that even when played well the bagpipes didn't exactly produce an agreeable sound); a heavily pregnant woman juggled with nine large candle sticks. Afterwards these were lit and Béla proceeded to hypnotize a young man with an earnest face. He turned into a neighing, snorting donkey, wandering around on all fours, smiling stupidly whenever his master fed him non-existent berries from the palm of his hand. Then, when prompted the donkey confessed to its fondness for dressing up in women's underwear. The episode went down very well, but on recovering his senses, the young man locked himself in the toilet and wasn't heard from again. By now most people were mind-numbingly drunk. At around four in the morning a man blessed with sobriety and garish red hair presided over a seance and petrified everyone with his ventriloquistic sleights of hand, revealing finally that the unearthly wailing of the soul trapped in hell was coming from his own vocal cords.

Throughout Oscar slept fitfully, feverishly.


He was awakened at around five-thirty by Angelica. He looked and felt terrible.

'Come on,' she whispered. 'We're going.'

'What? Where?' he stammered.

'Béla's hired a hot air balloon; we're going to take a sky-ride. Come with me, Oscar Babel.'

She very quietly took his hand and kissed it.


Béla saw in the balloon trip a happy emblem of liberation from his wife. He saw the act of rising above the earth to be a final – and necessary – way of symbolizing his release from her clutches. That was why he had organized the trip, to round off the evening's revelry. They had to drive to Tower Bridge where hot air balloons flying over London took off from a small, deserted field nearby.

It was seven in the morning when they finally got there. The sky was relatively clear and the sun glared coldly. No sound punctured the crepuscular silence. The bridge, its intricate design standing out above the Thames, looked sombre and impressive. In the distance the city was beginning to come alive as brokers made their first phone calls. The outline of St. Paul's Cathedral was visible from between the cluster of grid-like buildings and cranes and office blocks, an arc of elegance in the messy rectangles of concrete.

A group of men in green overalls were busily assembling the balloon. Most of those who had decided to come along for the outing were currently having second thoughts. In the end only three people felt well enough to go up, despite Béla's outraged remonstrations. He insisted they were all missing a wonderful opportunity; that the view would cure them of their hangovers in one fell swoop; that up there they would be princes taking tea with the gods. But even his baroque rhetoric failed to change anyone's mind. So the only passengers apart from Béla were Giselle, a quiet, shy woman clutching a shriveled teddy bear protectively (her mascot), Angelica (who had replaced her green contact lenses with red ones and now looked rather frightening) and Oscar, who was finally waking up.

He watched as the nylon canvas of the envelope was inflated slowly, a wicker basket, large enough to contain a dozen people, at its end. The expended heat was stupendous and he felt it pass through him even from a dozen yards off. He was surprised to find how big the thing in front of him was growing by the second, assuming a swollen hemispherical shape. Finally it reached its full length of a hundred feet. It hovered there, bobbing imperceptibly in the wind. A cloud passed sluggishly, blocking out the sun. He studied the horizon of buildings and geometric patterns in the distance: London, still sleeping, a million embryos in a concrete womb. Ravens flew past in a flock, then vanished into the secret places only they knew how to reach.

Then it was time to get inside. The pilot hoisted himself in first. Once installed he helped the others. Inside, the heat was greater than ever.

The ballast was removed by the men in overalls, piece by piece. Oscar glanced over to the bridge: a last appraisal before they became airborne. The bridge was deserted, but when he looked again a second later he could make out two men making their way across it. They seemed to be in a fantastic hurry, presenting a picture of hysterical mobility, arms and legs virtually shooting off their bodies. In a moment of horror Oscar recognized Ryan Rees, earphones plugged into his ears, his face disfigured by fury. They were dashing across the field now. Oscar noticed that he was gripping the sides of the basket, not out of a desire to feel secure, but with panic and fear.

'Stop the balloon!'

Rees ripped the earphones out of his ears. Bits of wax were jettisoned.

'Stop that balloon!' he bawled, slightly ridiculously.

'Who the hell is that? What does the big oaf want?' Béla demanded.

'He wants me, my blood,' said Oscar.

'Well, he shan't have it,' Béla growled magisterially. Oscar found this reassuring.

Rees' voice, shouting incoherently, was drowning in the wind. His companion stumbled and tripped onto the grass. Rees tripped over the inert body. From his prostrate position Rees' arms stretched and reached, the fingers splayed out. He picked himself up and advanced unsteadily, cutting an absurd figure.

But he was too late. The balloon had started to rise.

As Rees watched, the triumphs of the summer raced through his mind but brought him nothing but pain. A frightful pain he could not fathom. Then he was back at school, again, but long before his reign had started, back to a virtually buried, erased time. He was a sickly, flimsy seven-year-old, having the sand kicked in his face, bawling and screaming. He tried to resurrect his famed impassivity. But it was no good and as he looked on, impotence spilled out of his every pore.

As the balloon climbed, Béla, his body swaying with anarchic joy, boomed, 'I'm a free man! Free! Free! Free! Free! Free!'

He stretched his mighty arms out to heaven and addressed the sky.

'God is big, I am free of the pestilence. The plague! *La peste!*'

Oscar glanced down; Ryan Rees had already started shrinking.

The sensation of soaring Oscar had expected didn't materialize. The balloon felt strangely passive; it was merely a chamber passing through space, unmarked by any sense of discernible power.

At first it felt as though he was standing on top of an impossibly tall building somehow unanchored to any foundation; furthermore, this building was not even connected to the planet which now seemed to be left behind in a serene whirl. Because the balloon was drifting with the wind it was impossible to discern any sense of its having independence from it; rather, the wind was part of the vessel, as integral as the burner causing the canvas to shudder and flutter sporadically. Oscar looked down again, feeling a certain indefinable unease and anxiety, and made out Rees' arms, waving frantically. Oscar knew that the man below was angry but the anger seemed strangely abstract, as though it was the anger of someone in Beijing.

But in another moment all his feelings of dread had vanished. And then the journey started to grow magical.

After that no one, not even Béla, said anything. They were beguiled, wrapped up in the same voiceless wonder. Giselle clutched her teddy bear, wearing a serene smile; Béla's ebony locks fluttered in the wind; a cigarette dangled between Angelica's lips, but she was too surprised to light it. The pilot was occupied with the burner, which gasped and choked like some antediluvian monster, pushing the rate of ascent. Oscar's eyes told him they were moving – he didn't feel it – as they climbed higher. Below buildings and bridges continued to grow smaller and more unreal, turning into the appearance of cardboard models. From this perspective everything gained new meanings and shed the old ones. Oscar found it hard to equate the matchbox patterns with real people with worries and hopes and dreams. Row upon row of houses, miniaturized, packed delicately together. This was society, uniform, full of lines: horizontal and vertical tokens of order, but stripped of any suggestion of idiosyncrasy, rendered small, crushable. From up there civilization was no longer able to mask the fatal hint of futility which underlined it. But there was clarity, catharsis in this realization, and Oscar was filled with spectacular benevolence, and waves of beauty passed through him. He felt as though he had been granted entry into the clouds and the stained glass colors of the sky, placed side by side with nature, allowed to ride in tandem with it. Mental malleability was matched by the plasticity of this new universe. The freedom to think great things was created by the freedom of space.

Najette's face flashed through his mind, her glittering eyes portals into dreams. He slipped through them, to the other side ...

He looked past the cluster of intestinal pipes and tubes fitted to the burner and into the envelope above, a majestic, circular dome.

Still they climbed, higher and higher, until the balloon had reached its greatest altitude and from their vantage point, moving as somnolently as a cloud, London acquired its final pitch of insignificance. Suddenly everything was very clear. After all the hectic, supine clawing at beauty one thing awaited.

He could make out the Telecom Tower, a small candle. Underneath them, the Thames was a blurred, dull line. It must have been stirring with life, but it was impossible to discern any of it. He glanced up at the partially obscured sun, whose light was growing warmer and more golden. As if to oblige it, the clouds pulled back and rays spilled unbroken across the basket. As his eyes grew accustomed to the brilliance it seemed that up there the light was different; it was closer to him, almost tangible. He put out his hand and allowed it to revolve in the luminescence. Very slowly, when he was sure the others were looking away, he eased himself onto the edge of the basket. He waited there for a moment. Or centuries.

He slipped into the nothingness below, and instantly became a speck, turning and spinning in the void.

He was moving quickly. In the burning, coalescing space patterns could not be retained. They came and flashed and were lost; thoughts and impressions conjured up by them vanished.

The footpath was narrow but his feet were wedged to the pedals and his hands glued to the handlebars so he had control, so he was gliding, a flash of moving light in the forest, caught in the fast dropping sun. The cycle reached a steep decline and sped down it.

And now he was in an opening. He spied the trees around him until he was satisfied he was alone. A silver lake. He crept in, naked, unobserved; the light dimmed, the clouds raced. He felt the water pour over him, until immersion in it was perfectly right. The water's sound was melodious; it reverberated in the deep, where no life stirred but silhouettes stretched like spindly fingers. He turned and saw a woman standing in the water – she must have been there all along, and yet he hadn't noticed her. The edges of her hair skimmed against the water. He couldn't see the face. He motioned towards her. Distance collapsed.

And then, with a shivering sweep, the lake began to tremble; its transparency turned black, it became a watery bruise. The pleasure which had glowed in him in his watery grave of awakening died. Then she was gone.

He opened his eyes.

He wished he could re-enter the dream, find again the nameless woman within it. He felt so light, bathed in sweat. When he moved them he could not feel his limbs. He wanted so badly to be saved by a deep sleep, a real sleep, awaking to find he was truly rested.

He yearned to get up, out of bed, but he couldn't energize his wasted limbs. He pictured the inside of his body, its contents spilling out in a dark line, forming a tunnel of indistinct, palpitating curves, and within the tunnel another tunnel formed, his intestines unravelling, and there at the end, his stomach, dripping with fluid, and then his heart, his spleen, his kidneys, floating in the starry desolation of space. Then he imagined holding a brush to each organ, wiping each of them with one serene movement. They tumbled back into his body, which had miraculously opened and closed itself, leaving no visible traces or scars. And in his skull his brain had been dusted over also, doused in pure oxygen. For so long it had felt like that skull had been stuffed with cotton wool.

He stared at the tubes feeding into him. He peered around with sightless eyes.

What was he doing here?

And where was the rain?

Light.

Starting slowly – a suggestion, brittle in the bowels of his brain, buried as if by folds of dead skin, folds reaching back, stretching out to the earth, buried beneath his feet, in the bowels of the earth; he was falling fast, as if through an elevator shaft, a weight in the earth, the light persisted, would not give up now and he had gone some way towards

the light world.

And – again, once more, more distinctly, the voice cried: how had he got here?

The antiseptic curtains, a cold plastic landscape sealing him from the world. The ward with its bays, the smell of bleach, of disinfectant, the hospital with its ailing life. He was making a trap, had devised a labyrinthine trap for himself, had written himself into this perfect nightmare, had drowned, had died, was already a ghost, a memory. He asked: was that what the afterlife was? Memory? Were dreams the afterlife, or windows into it, or were they merely the afterimages of the day? Or was that what the afterlife was – afterimages of life, still persisting and the memory of those who were missing brought them back, made them real, as in the terrestrial mind, which could also be a maze so he needed to step out of his mind, that menagerie, this trap he'd devised; what did he think he was doing and he needed to turn towards

the light finally.

Because he was sick to death of this; he was sick to death of being so enamored of death, of this skeletal morbidity, of being a living corpse; what did he think he was playing at? Because now canopies of gelatinized tears turned into angels; they soared and held a sheet aloft at each of its corners, beckoning to him, preparing to wrap him, dry him, a child after bathing. So he wanted an apple; he wanted an apple with a glistening hide, wanted to take a bite out of it, its juice spitting half way across the room or he wanted a plum, an egg – anything to rescue the poor steel barrel from its vacuum.

This trembling inside him. He struggled to name it; he'd forgotten it since it had been absent for so long: an ancient friend who'd moved away, how dare he? And he didn't have him in his phonebook anymore but he'd heard the friend was back now, so ... this trembling.

And light, save me, hold me, till my tears are spent.

I want bottled light I want time I want to taste the sweetness of life, to be marinated in it because I can recognize beauty and it's all around me and it's there when I'm not looking, I want to be wheeled out of here, and beauty hides in ambush and strikes me down with infusion of color, it's everywhere, in the glassy film of eyes, in tentative smiles, I used to walk across fields of wheat, wipe my mouth across my sleeve, get muddy, a schoolboy in the sweaty field. I see configurations of clouds but I don't want to swim through them anymore thank you, I'd rather watch from my gravity-weighted seat, and when the voice rises like flames I can slip into a smoking jacket or go for a run, re-admit my body, run through warm waves on the beach or make sand castles; I never did that, I have to make up for lost time, I have to find my smile, there's so much to do, I'd better hurry up, catch the sun's corona ablaze in the sky, or the smell of onion soup, I'm going to have to find her, win her back all over, God I'll have my work cut out, the great big ladle (I love ladles) and the smell of cut grass, or toast the way I like it, to share it with someone, or the first taste of wine, the light of the moon, a voice rising and becoming tendrils, fingers, ribbons of flame.

**Baret Magarian** is of Armenian extraction, from London, and lives in Florence. In London he was a freelance journalist and contributed articles to *The Times, The Guardian, The Independent* and *The Daily Telegraph*. He has interviewed such diverse figures as Peter Ustinov, the brilliant actor-director and raconteur, John Calder, iconoclastic publisher of eighteeen Nobel prize winners, and Salman Rushdie, the celebrated novelist. He has worked as a lecturer, translator, fringe theatre director, actor and nude model. He is also a composer of piano music that is in the vein of Jarrett and Alkan and draws on the tonalities of Armenian music. His fiction has appeared in *World Literature Today, Journal of Italian Translation, White Fly Press, The Sandspout,* and *Sagarana*. His most cherished dream is that his writing might be a conductor and transmitter of light. Please contact him here: baretbmagarian@hotmail.com

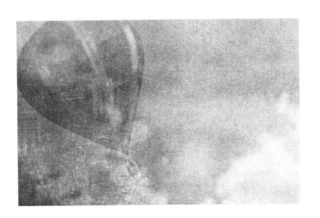

*The Fabrications* is published by Pleasure Boat Studio: A Literary Press. This press was founded in 1996 by Jack Estes and William Slaughter and has only recently been moved to Seattle, Washington, under the new guidance of Lauren Grosskopf. In addition to literary works published under the Pleasure Boat Studio name, the press also includes mysteries under the imprint of Caravel Books, non-fiction under the imprint of Aequitas Books, and poetry under a separate division called Empty Bowl Press. Please take a look at our website at **www.pleasureboatstudio.com**.